The Many Shades
of Midnight

C M Debell

Dear Miranda,
Thank you so much for taking
part in the hour. I hope you
enjoy the book.
Lotte

CONTENTS

PART ONE

BRIVAR

It was the first day of spring when they met the woodsman a week out from Orleas. For Brivar, apprentice surgeon and cousin of the king's envoy to the erstwhile Duke of Agrathon, it was the day blue star-violet flowered, and he longed to abandon his diplomatic duty and pick some, because there is no more potent painkiller in all the land than the dried blossom of blue star-violet harvested on the first day of spring. More importantly, it was also the day he met the Duke of Agrathon. That was the day his life changed forever.

Of course, Brivar didn't know that then. At the time, the directions the woodsman gave them meant only that they were saved from one more night of sleeping under the stars, though with the pace his cousin set, Brivar would have preferred another night on hard ground to the harsh ache in his thighs from so many hours in the saddle. And he quickly came to regret the lost opportunity to collect blue star-violet blossom on the first day of spring, because he would soon need it rather badly.

Perhaps that's what the woodsman was looking for, out here in the wilds so far from any settlement. Certainly, as he stood a little off the path, watching them with his hood drawn up, his stance was less easy than it should have been. Apprenticed to the guild of surgeons at the age of ten, Brivar was trained in observation. He knew how to read people, how they held themselves, how they moved and spoke, how to look for the truth beyond what words could convey—or conceal. His teacher, the Varistan Alondo, had a bad hip. Brivar always knew when it pained him by the way he walked, the stiffness when he sat, and those first few limping steps when he stood. Of course, he never complained or asked for help. Some people were too stubborn for their own good.

The woodsman looked like one of them. His attention reluctantly drawn from the temptation of blue star-violet, Brivar watched the forester spar with his cousin, observing the tension in his shoulders, the way he held his left arm close. An old wound, most likely, that had healed badly. Brivar observed other things about him, too. The half-hidden worn leather sheathes for paired blades. Only professional soldiers and duellists used such weapons. Since you were unlikely to find a duellist wandering the wilderness, he had probably once served in a kingdom army, which made sense since he knew where the Duke of Agrathon was holed up. Once King Raffa-Herun Geled's most trusted commander and confidant and now a renegade military captain whose fame had made him friends, and enemies, across half the continent.

And this one wasn't giving him up easily.

Brivar's cousin, the rather pompous Lord Sul-Barin Feron, had exhausted his meagre supply of patience. Brivar couldn't understand why the king had chosen him for such a delicate mission. As far as he could see, his cousin was without an ounce of either subtlety or tact, as demonstrated by the way he lost his temper and his dignity arguing with a woodsman in front of the entire royal embassy.

It had started badly when Corado, the half-Flaeresian captain of their guard, had rudely hailed the man walking the track ahead of them, asking him where they could find the Duke of Agrathon. He had followed this with a flick of his whip when his question got no response, an insult the man had sidestepped easily enough but which had done their cause no favours.

Ignoring Corado's glare, the man's shadowed gaze skimmed their party and fixed on the ostentatious figure of Lord Sul. "I don't know a duke."

This was not well received. "Everyone knows the Duke of Agrathon. He is in these mountains somewhere. Tell me where he is and you can go on your way."

It wasn't a threat, though it could be taken as one when considered alongside the guard captain's attempted assault. But Brivar had the distinct impression the man was amused rather than afraid.

"Who's looking for him?"

"The King," Lord Sul informed him with an arrogant tilt of his chin.

The man laughed. "Which one?"

"Which one? His king, man!"

There was a dangerous silence, which was almost certainly lost on Lord Sul. Then the man said, "The captain doesn't have a king. Best remember that when you see him, or you won't get far."

"I'll thank you to not give me advice," Lord Sul snapped. "Just tell me where to find him."

The woodsman gave a one-shouldered shrug. Definitely an old wound there, Brivar decided. He let his attention wander back to the carpet of blue star-violets as the man told his cousin what he wanted to know, and he wondered whether he would have time to pick some of the precious blossoms when they stopped for the night.

The woodsman's parting words put paid to that hope. "You'll have to hurry if you want to reach him before night falls. You'd be better off turning around and starting out again early tomorrow. You don't want to be out after dark in these mountains."

"I am well protected," Lord Sul answered haughtily, hauling on his reins to wheel his stamping horse around.

Again, that awkward shrug, but there was a different tension to the man now. A kind of watchful stillness Brivar had observed in many old soldiers. For the first time since their journey began, he felt a touch of fear.

His cousin, of course, was oblivious to such things, and was not a man to take advice in any case. He was already waving his escort on, snapping at them to pick up their pace. He did not bother to look at their guide as he rode past. He certainly didn't thank him.

Trailing at the back of the column, Brivar reined in as he passed. Careful that his cousin should not see or hear, he said quietly, "Blue star-violet, dried in the sun and crushed into a paste with spring water, is an excellent pain reliever."

He sensed the man's surprise and kicked his heels into his horse. He hadn't gone more than a few paces when he heard him say, "I meant it about nightfall. It's not safe."

Brivar looked back, but the woodsman was already disappearing into the trees and his cousin was shouting at him to hurry.

※

They were spared the perils of the mountains at night, but only just. Emerging from the forests of the lower slopes onto the mountain track, the woodsman's directions took them quickly away from the main path into the depths of a canyon. The temperature dropped, the sting of cold edging Brivar's fingers and misting his breath, and the fading light brought with it the wraiths of his imagination, crawling out of the rocks and from behind trees until all around him he felt the presence of their midnight threat.

There was a flicker of movement ahead and they were no longer alone on the track. The lead horses shied and Brivar started so hard he nearly toppled from his saddle. But the figures emerging from the twilight were merely human in shape, though they were armed, and their spears were pointed with definite intent at his cousin's escort.

A woman stepped forward from the deep shadows lining the canyon walls. She pulled down the hood of her fur-lined coat to reveal a face that was as hard as it was young. "You've missed your way," she told them, an uncompromising note in her voice. "Road to Orleas is two miles back."

Lord Sul looked down at her with disdain. "We're not looking for

Orleas. We're here to see the Duke of Agrathon."

The woman raised an eyebrow. "Agrathon is two hundred miles to the west."

His cousin, Brivar saw, had had enough. Ignoring the threat of the spears, Lord Sul stalked his horse up to the woman. "He's not in Agrathon. He's in these mountains. I demand that you take us to him this instant, in the name of King Raffa-Herun Geled."

The woman gave Lord Sul a level stare. "That name means nothing here."

Brivar heard a hiss of outrage from the guardsman to his right as his captain surged forward, sword in hand. There was an answering movement in the shadows and they were surrounded by drawn bows as well as ready spears. Brivar clutched the pendant of Yholis in his left hand and his voice shook through a muttered prayer.

"Hold!" The woman raised her hand and the archers stepped back, bows dropping but arrows still nocked. "Not here."

She made a gesture and one of the spearmen turned and disappeared through a cleft in the canyon wall. Brivar's stomach churned in an unpleasant manner. He thought he might be sick but he was too afraid to move.

Lord Sul snapped, "I demand –"

The woman put a hand on his bridle, her touch calming the nervous horse. "I wouldn't," she advised.

A tall man, his dark hair peppered with grey, emerged from the cleft. He was dressed in a black leather brigandine that fell to his knees, quite different from the short scale coats worn by their Avarel escort, and was pulling thick gloves onto his hands as he walked. He checked in surprise when he saw them, frowning at the royal standard that hung limp in the still evening.

Lord Sul nudged his horse forward. "Are you the Duke of Agrathon?"

The man gave a derisive snort. "No." And started back the way he had come.

Not to be deterred, his cousin kicked his horse after him. "We are here to see the duke on behalf of King Raffa-Herun Geled."

The man turned. His gaze raked over Lord Sul and his escort, resting a moment on Brivar's pale blue temple surcoat. "You're wasting your time. He's not here."

He turned to leave again and this time it was not Lord Sul who stopped him, but the woman. "At night, Esar?"

So, this was Esar Cantrell, foster brother to the man they had come to find. Brivar studied him as a whole welter of unspoken communication passed between him and the woman with the spear. Varisten Elenia said it was just as important to understand a patient's state of mind as their physical state, that it was often critical to their treatment and sometimes to their survival. You could read more than just pain in how a person moved and spoke, and watching Cantrell, Brivar saw a man who was tense, angry, and worried. And not at all happy to see them.

"Fine," he said, turning away. "But they leave in the morning."

Lord Sul, who was rapidly confirming all Brivar's fears about his diplomatic skills, announced, "We will not leave until we have seen the duke."

"You will," Cantrell said without stopping. "Or you can spend the night out here."

On cue, an eerie call echoed through the canyon. Not the howl of a wolf, which Brivar knew well, but a long, high wail that was picked up and answered by more voices until it was no longer possible to discern where it was coming from or how many there were. He found himself recalling all the lurid tales he had heard of the savage Lathai tribe who inhabited these mountains. From the tense faces all around him, he knew he was not the only one.

Lord Sul's mouth snapped shut on further protest. His horse stamped nervously.

"Your choice," the woman said.

He nodded, pale in the light of the rising moon.

Her face relaxed. "All of you, dismount. You need to lead your horses."

※

They did not have to go far, but the path through the cliff was narrow and dark. At several points the overhanging rock would not have permitted a mounted man to pass, and the horses were skittish and hard to handle. The wailing cries followed them through the crevice, nipping at Brivar's heels till his nerves were strung so tight and his breath so shallow he feared he might faint.

Then they were through and the glow of firelight and the cheerful sound of laughter dispelled the terror. It was dark now, the light of the fires burning away Brivar's night vision so he could see little of the camp itself. Cantrell had disappeared, but a red-haired woman led his cousin towards one of the deeper shadows that Brivar saw was the mouth of cave. It smelt of horses and other creatures, but it was big enough for them and their mounts, and it was dry and safe, and at that moment, that was all he cared about.

More women entered, spears and bows strapped to their backs, and lit Isyrium bulbs so they had enough light to care for their horses. Brivar was a little shocked at such extravagance. When he tried to thank the woman who positioned a bulb for him, she merely shrugged as though it was nothing to adorn a cave in the mountains with luxuries that cost a silver mark apiece in Avarel.

The king's embassy, more accustomed to luxury, did not seem to notice this oddity as they grumbled their way towards sleep. Brivar had hoped for a moment of privacy to rub cannavery liniment on his saddle sores, but his cousin summoned him with a curt gesture and Brivar spent his last hour before sleep—and the last of his preciously hoarded liniment—attending to Lord Sul's comfort. He tried not to resent him for it too much. It was, after all, partly why he was here.

Apprentice surgeons were rarely called on to travel, and almost never outside Avarel. By requesting his presence in this embassy, Lord Sul had given Brivar an opportunity he would not have otherwise had, but the ache in his muscles went to the bone and it was a struggle to feel suitably grateful. Once he exchanged his pale blue surcoat for a surgeon's green, he would either be appointed to a wealthy household as a personal physician or he would remain at the temple, tending to all who came in need of care. He already knew which he would choose. If all wealthy men were like his cousin Sul-Barin, he would rather spend the rest of his days treating the city's street sleepers and mine workers.

Finally dismissed to find his rest, Brivar was too tired to do more than collapse into his bedroll, fully clothed. The night was cold and the stone floor was hard, but he fell asleep almost at once, only to be jolted awake some hours later by running footsteps and muffled voices. He grasped the thin blanket tighter around himself, ears pricked for inhuman sounds, his fear magnified by the fey light of the Isyrium bulbs that cast their eerie blue glow across the cave.

Then Cantrell's voice rose above the rest. "…what in Ithol's name did you think you were doing?"

A voice, rough with weariness, answered, "Testing a theory."

"Testing my bloody nerves more like," Cantrell growled. "You could have been killed."

The footsteps stopped. "Are they here?"

Silence, then Cantrell's curse. "So that's how they found us. What do you want us to do with them?"

Whoever he was talking to said something too quiet for Brivar to hear. Cantrell, exasperated concern clear in his voice, said, "You're wrecked. Go to sleep. Let me handle the morning."

The response was muffled as they moved away, but before he dropped back to sleep, Brivar clearly heard Cantrell say, "Now, Alyas? Why?"

D awn came early in the mountains. Sunlight poured through the gap in the curtain that hung across the cave entrance, burning bright against Brivar's heavy eyelids. He rolled over, every muscle protesting, and felt the sharp edge of stone between his shoulder blades.

"Ithol's bollocks," a gruff voice complained from somewhere behind him. "I've spent more comfortable nights in a Qidan prison cell."

"You've never been in a Qidan prison cell," someone else said. "Stop talking shit."

"But if I had…"

Then Corado's harsh voice snapped at them to shut up and Brivar buried his head under his cloak. Their escort captain was vicious and unpredictable. Brivar didn't doubt he knew what he was about, but he had a scathing contempt for his betters—Sul-Barin Feron excepted, for some reason—and an equal disdain for those beneath him. He was half-Flaeresian and a bastard, and no doubt that was the problem. It meant he had only one name in a society that based merit and honour on how many names a person could list after their birth name, though even the highest in Avarel were restricted to the formal use of just three (after the current king's grandfather, furious at the hours it took to announce his nobles at court, decreed that no man or woman in the kingdom could use more than names than the king and promptly shortened his own to three). Brivar thought he would be forever grateful that he had surrendered all names but his birth name upon entering the temple, and thereafter never had to worry about such things as whether the man he was talking to could count back twenty named generations or merely nineteen to determine who had precedence in any situation.

Brivar waited until Corado had left the cave before he unrolled his cloak and stood. The camp that had been wreathed in darkness the night before was revealed by the new day in all its organised chaos. Eyes like saucers, Brivar watched in fascination as men and women emerged from other caves on both sides of a wide, deep canyon like the one they had travelled through the night before. This one could be reached only via the narrow passage at one end, where they had entered, and a winding defile that led up and out onto the clifftops at the other.

Hide canopies shaded the cave entrances, which were hung with thick curtains. Canvas tents were dotted throughout the main clearing, some with their doors tied back to reveal neat bedrolls or stacks of crates. Even to Brivar's unpractised assessment, it was clearly a camp of some permanence.

"Impressed, are you?" Corado snarled by his ear. "Don't let it fool you. These are nothing but scum, and their captain is a charlatan. You'll see."

Brivar watched him walk away, hostility in every line of his body. If last night Cantrell had been tense and worried, Corado was a vibrating well of anger and aggression waiting to explode.

Brivar crept out to join his cousin, making sure he put several bodies between himself and Corado. They ate a cold breakfast alone, the residents of the camp keeping a wide berth. They had been given pails of icy water to wash with and a fire had been laid at the entrance to their cave, but they were otherwise left alone. No one spoke to them beyond what was necessary. It was clear they were not welcome.

They saw Cantrell once from a distance as he emerged from a tent, a lean, black-haired man by his side. Brivar watched them speak together before disappearing into the largest of the caves. Lord Sul was arguing with Corado loudly enough that his voice could be heard throughout the camp. Brivar saw several looks cast their way, and one or two frowns, and he studied their owners curiously as he chewed on his stale bread.

This was his first journey of any length outside Avarel, and his first outside the borders of Lankara, although that last point was disputed and rather fluid. King Raffa-Herun Geled and his father and grandfather before him claimed these mountains as part of their realm, as did the neighbouring king of Flaeres, and the territory passed between them on a regular basis, with little regard for the wishes of the Lathai tribe that called the mountains home. That endless feuding had something to do with the exile and disgrace of the former Duke of Agrathon, whose camp this was, but Brivar was too young to remember the details of a scandal fifteen years in the past and so far removed from his life. He had not been interested enough to find out, even after he had been assigned to this embassy. He regretted that now.

But though he might not be well-travelled, Avarel was a powerful trade city, and he was a surgeon. Many travellers came to the Temple of Yholis seeking solace and healing. He recognised Janath from far-off Qido, their pale hair braided and coiled above slanting cheekbones and sea-blue eyes, scattered among the more familiar sallow complexions of the central Ellasian nations, Lankara, Hantara and nearby Flaeres, indistinguishable except for their accents. There were even a few dusky brown faces from the southern steppelands. None of them returned his stares with friendliness, though there was no open hostility. They were, he thought, as curious as he was to see what would happen.

"We will not leave," Brivar heard his cousin insist. Under the sun and after a night's sleep—*his* sleep cushioned by the bed of furs loaded onto his spare horse along with all the other luxuries of his rank— Lord Sul had recovered the nerve the evening before had stolen from him. "If he is not here, we will wait until he returns. I have a duty from the king, and I will see it through."

Brivar recalled Cantrell's lack of welcome and thought it unlikely such obstinacy would be rewarded, but his cousin in this mood would not be dissuaded.

"Which one of you is Sul-Barin?"

Brivar started, dropping his bread, and turned to see the dark-haired man standing behind him. Cantrell was a few paces back, arms crossed and brows drawn together in a frown. They both wore the distinctive long, flared brigandine, daylight showing the scuffs and small damage of long use. The speaker was smaller and lighter than Cantrell, all sharp angles against Cantrell's burly strength, and his manner thrummed with impatience.

There was an awkward pause. Brivar eyed his cousin warily as he retrieved his breakfast, noting the flushed face that boded ill. Newly come into his title, Lord Sul guarded the privileges of his rank like a jealous lover, and he was already smarting from their rough treatment. Now, with deliberate insult, he turned his back on the two men and continued eating.

Brivar's gaze slid back to the man who had spoken as an expectant hush fell over the camp. An alarming suspicion began to form.

The newcomer surveyed the back of Lord Sul's head with narrowed eyes. "I was told you had a message from Raffa and were most insistent."

Even Lord Sul could eventually recognise the obvious if it slapped him in the face hard enough. He surged to his feet, scattering crumbs from his lap. "Your Gra –"

He was speaking to the man's back as he walked away. "There are no titles here," the Duke of Agrathon called over his shoulder. "Come with me."

❧

Lord Sul had planned this audience for weeks, down to the clothes he would wear and who would be with him. Brivar knew, because he had been forced to participate in endless rehearsals, his role—even his words—drummed into him over the course of their journey. None of those preparations included the king's envoy scurrying after the retreating figure of the former duke in the clothes he had slept in, having first offered him a grave insult, under the watchful stares of his mildly terrifying company.

Hurrying along at his heels, his heart thumping with nerves, Brivar wished he were back at the temple. He missed his masters and his fellow apprentices. He missed his patients, even the difficult ones. But most of all he missed problems he understood and knew how to deal with. It had seemed a great adventure when he had been assigned to this mission, carrying an appeal for help that surely no reasonable man could refuse. Their need was urgent and terrifying— he knew that better than most—but his innocent certainties had begun to fray the moment they arrived. There were currents swirling beneath the surface of this place that spoke of worse troubles and deep resentments.

The duke's quick steps led them into a stone basin, shaped like the amphitheatres of the ancients, with smooth, sloping sides rather than ranks of stepped seats. The morning sun crept across the land from the east, cutting across the floor of the basin, casting one half into shadow and making the other a pool of light, where Lord Sul now stood, blinking against the brightness, exposed and unprepared.

Brivar edged to the side, out of the glare of the mountain sun. It was his testimony that mattered here, not his person, and his cousin was too focused on the grim pair facing him to object.

"So," the duke said. "Raffa remembers me. Should I be flattered? You seem to think so."

Brivar saw his cousin bridle at this casual use of the king's birth name, but he managed to curb his objection. "Your Gra –"

"I have warned you," the duke said, "not to use that title here."

Lord Sul seemed to be suffering from a rare moment of uncertainty. He floundered about for an acceptable form of address. "My lord –"

The duke's eyes narrowed. Behind him, Cantrell coughed, turning his head away.

Brivar felt a twinge of sympathy. By the king's order, exile had stripped both title and name from this man, and his cousin would never think to use one he had assumed for himself because Lord Sul was Lankaran nobility, and to him names were everything. Besides, he had come here—he had been sent here—to find the former Duke of Agrathon and rescind his exile. In exchange for his service, of course, but they were coming to that.

Corado, his eyes alive with hatred, leant forward and whispered in Lord Sul's ear, who, looking relieved, tried again with, "Captain." Then ruined it with a bow barely less formal than for titled royalty.

The answering silence was long and awkward. The duke sighed. "Yholis have mercy, just get on with it."

Lord Sul took a deep breath, his hesitation falling away as he prepared to deliver the speech he had practised for weeks on end.

"Spare me the pretty phrases," the duke said with vicious timing. "Just tell me what he wants."

Lord Sul deflated like a pricked bladder. Brivar felt a spark of anger. His cousin was a pompous fool, but that had been cruel and deliberate. Greatly daring, Brivar said, "Your help, Captain."

The man's eyes snapped to him in surprise and in that moment Brivar knew him. The clothes and voice were different, but there was no doubt this was the woodsman they had met yesterday—the same man, he realised now, he had heard arrive deep in the night. If his cousin guessed, he gave no sign of it, and since Lord Sul had all the subtlety of an uroc in heat, he could not have concealed his recognition. But to Brivar's eye, the stiffness of the left shoulder was unmistakable. They were one and the same, and now he could see the man's face, he liked less and less what he saw.

The duke's skin was so pale it was almost translucent, the lines of his face pared down to sharp angles and his eyes smudged in shadow. Brivar's gaze dropped to his hands, the only other part of the man he could see. His skin was stretched tight over prominent bones and had the blueish tint he usually only saw in starving street children. Whatever else he was—and he was certainly angry—he was also gravely ill, or Brivar had wasted the last thirteen years of his studies.

He raised his eyes and saw the duke watching him, an odd expression on his face. Cantrell, too, was staring at him, and his expression was much easier to interpret. Brivar had seen it too often in those who brought their loved ones to the temple.

"My help," the duke mused, his gaze still on Brivar. "With what could he possibly need my help?"

"Lankara is threatened, my lord," Lord Sul said, anxious to regain the initiative but forgetting his carefully planned speech. "A mysterious enemy, a horde of *things*. It has already devastated parts of Hantara and the Donea and the king fears Lankara will be next. Already we are seeing incursions along our borders. And…" he hesitated, his face paling. "It is not human, or no longer human. It spreads a poison wherever it goes, a sickness."

His voice faltered, the words falling flat against the duke's silence.

"A sickness?" Cantrell demanded. "What kind of sickness?" He did not look at his foster brother, but Brivar felt the sharp rise in tension between them.

Lord Sul focused on him with pathetic gratitude. "A terrible one, my lord. The enemy carries it with them. It transforms men and beasts into more of itself, if it does not kill them. Many have died, and many more have been consumed. It has already reached the borders of Lankara." He looked at Brivar, gesturing him forward. "The Temple of Yholis can tell you more, my lord. They have treated many with the sickness. They have even cured some. My cousin Brivar…"

Brivar took an obliging step forward, aware of the weight of Cantrell's stare, waiting for the question he knew was coming. The identifying signs of the duke's illness were plain to see now he knew what he was looking for. The wound that bothered him was not an old one that had healed badly. If Brivar was right, it hadn't healed at all.

The duke stirred, silencing Cantrell before he could speak. "What does he expect me to do about it?" he asked Lord Sul. "And why? He was quite clear about how he felt fifteen years ago when he took everything from me. I cannot believe he has changed his mind. Why now does he ask for my help?"

It had seemed so simple back in Avarel, Brivar thought, watching his cousin's nervous face. They would find the former Duke of Agrathon and present to him the king's offer: a full pardon and restoration of all his lands and titles in exchange for bringing his elite military company to the defence of the realm. If he had given any thought to how that offer might be received, it was to assume it would be welcome. Now, as his cousin hesitated to even voice it, he knew it was dangerous at best.

Once again, Lord Sul took a deep breath. Brivar could not, at this moment, fault his courage. "King Raffa-Herun Geled wishes to convey that he bitterly regrets your quarrel —"

"Our quarrel," the duke echoed in a hollow voice.

"— and, further, that he desires to make restitution through the return of your family's names, lands and honours, and begs you to retake your place at his side in this time of Lankara's need."

"Restitution," the duke said flatly. "Returning to me what is mine is hardly restitution."

"Your Grace..." Lord Sul stuttered, then faltered, realising his mistake.

But the acid didn't come. "Just go," the duke said. He ignored Cantrell's concerned glance, Lord Sul's gaping surprise, and turned on his heel and walked out.

L ord Sul took refuge in anger, as Brivar knew he would. Thoroughly rattled, his composure in tatters and his pride in no better state, his cousin stalked away, his shoulders set in silent fury.

Brivar's move to follow was arrested by Cantrell. "You, stay," he growled, a sharp look ensuring his command would be obeyed.

Brivar hovered, uncertain. His cousin gestured impatiently, sweeping out with his guards at his back. Cantrell was by his side, talking urgently, his words too low to hear. Whatever his message, Brivar didn't think his cousin would be receptive. He wasn't surprised to see the king's envoy wave the man rudely away.

Cantrell turned back, his expression a curious mix of emotions.

Hesitant, Brivar said, "My lord…?"

Cantrell's eyes brushed his. He indicated with his head that Brivar should follow.

They walked in uncomfortable silence for a minute, until Brivar asked, "You have need of my services, my lord?"

"I'm no lord, boy." Cantrell glanced at him, taking in his youth, the blue of his apprentice surcoat. "He was telling the truth? About the sickness?"

"Yes, my lord."

"Then you'll see soon enough."

They crossed the camp, passing the cave where Brivar had spent such an uncomfortable night, and stopped outside another with its heavy curtain drawn shut. Brivar felt his cousin's eyes on him as they passed and dropped his head to avoid his gaze. Cantrell pushed the curtain aside, gesturing for Brivar to precede him.

He found himself in another cave, its walls lined with more precious Isyrium bulbs that illuminated the desk at its centre and a sleeping platform on one side, padded with furs. The duke stood with his back to them, apparently unaware of their arrival. Brivar looked at Cantrell, but the older man made a quelling gesture.

His back still turned, the duke said, "He offers me my title, Esar. My title in exchange for my aid. As if he could give me back something that has always been mine to compel my help. And that he should do this now…"

Cantrell cleared his throat. "Alyas."

The duke turned. At first Brivar thought he was looking at a different man. Gone was the weary woodsman, gone the impatient military commander. Before him stood what both those facades had been hiding—someone altogether harder and more brittle. And very, very tired.

His eyes settled on Brivar then returned to Cantrell, one eyebrow quirked in polite query. "You brought the boy?"

"The healer," Cantrell replied. "The healer who has knowledge of this sickness."

"I see," his captain replied, clearly amused. To Brivar, he said, "You are an apprentice of Yholis?"

Brivar nodded.

"Fourth level?" the duke guessed.

"Fifth, Your Grace." Fifth level, and only two years from achieving a surgeon's green.

"Not you too," the duke sighed, but it lacked the cruel bite he had used with Lord Sul. "Tell me, Brivar—that is your name?—am I to understand that you have treated men with this sickness?"

"I have, Your Gr… I have."

The duke studied him, ignoring Cantrell's simmering impatience. Eventually he said, "Your cousin says it transforms men. Into what?"

Brivar felt the words twist out of his grasp under the weight of that gaze, as they always did when he was nervous. If the duke wanted details of the threat they faced, he should not have dismissed Lord Sul, who, for all his faults, had memorised every scrap of information they had about this terrifying new threat—but he wasn't going to say *that*. He was only an apprentice surgeon and he did not understand such things. He focused on the man instead, on the paleness of his skin, the tightness around his eyes. It steadied him. That he understood.

"I have not seen them, my lord. It is… too quick. Only the sick are brought to the temple."

"And you have cured them?" Cantrell demanded.

Brivar looked between them, reading Cantrell's stubborn hope and the duke's resignation. "Some," he hedged. Many years of dealing with relatives' impossible hope did not make it any easier. "If they were in good health and we were quick enough."

He saw the quick look that passed between them. Cantrell leant his fists on the desk. "Alyas…"

The duke waved him to silence. To Brivar, he said, "How many in Lankara? How far advanced is this… invasion?"

Brivar looked at his feet and said with quiet reproach, "You will have to ask my cousin, my lord."

There was a silence, then the duke said, "Very well, I suppose I deserved that."

Brivar cleared his throat. "Will you let me see the wound?" In all those he had treated for this illness, the infection had come through an injury. If he was right, and he was sure he was, it meant these men had already encountered the enemy.

The duke cocked his head to one side. "How did you know?"

"I know when someone is in pain." He turned to Cantrell. "My apologies, my lord, but your reaction when my cousin spoke of the sickness…"

Cantrell frowned, arms crossed. "Don't blame me," he told his captain. "You couldn't keep it a secret forever."

Brivar thought the duke would refuse, that he would argue it was already too late, but Cantrell's silent hope bore down on him, and he nodded.

The duke unbuckled the brigandine one-handed and allowed Brivar to open the shirt beneath. He felt his heartbeat steady as he went through the familiar motions. His youth was forgotten as his training kicked in, the shyness that tied his tongue and stopped his words vanished. Varistan Alondo said that all men, no matter how rich or powerful, are made equal under a surgeon's care. "You are the lord of all of them when they are your patients, Brivar, and they will respond to your calm and your confidence because they need you, and they are afraid."

This man was not afraid. Brivar didn't know what he was, but fear was not a word he would use. Brivar looked at what the shirt had concealed and met the duke's eyes. "Are you eating?"

There was silence for a beat, then Cantrell ground out, "No, he is not."

The object of their mutual attention shrugged. "I try, but I have no appetite."

Ignoring the tension, aware that the soldier beneath his hands knew as well as he did that the situation was dire, Brivar turned his attention to the wound, unwinding a soiled bandage as gently as he could. It was a ragged six-inch gash close to the left shoulder that had been neatly stitched at least twice. Those fine stitches had pulled loose at the top of the cut, and recently.

"How long ago?" he asked. The stitching was not new, but the wound itself could have happened a day ago or a month. It showed no sign of closing.

Cantrell said, "Three weeks. On the north border of Flaeres."

Three weeks. Brivar looked at the wound again, measuring this new information. It was not the cut itself that was worrisome. On its own, it would heal with barely any impact on the movement of the shoulder joint. It was the illness it had induced that would kill him. Aware of the fragile exhaustion of his patient, he completed his examination quickly and efficiently.

"Well?" Cantrell's gruff voice intruded on his thoughts.

Brivar met the duke's eyes and understood there was no need to soften the blow. "You are dying, Your Grace. You don't need me to tell you that."

He heard a growl of frustration behind him. "You told us you have cured this!"

"We have," Brivar agreed. "There is a cure, but it is dangerous. Almost as dangerous as the illness."

"But there is a chance?"

Brivar kept his eyes on the duke as he answered Cantrell. "There is a chance, but you must understand, both of you—this poison has been allowed to run its course for three weeks. We have never attempted a cure after so long. No one has lived so long to allow it."

The duke shrugged his arm back into his shirt, covering his shoulder. A tremor ran through his muscles that Brivar was certain had nothing to do with fear. "I understand."

"No," said Brivar. "You don't." He looked around the cave, cataloguing what he would need. He turned back to the duke. "Did you pick any blue star-violet?" What was coming would be agony. If nothing else, he could make dying hurt less.

The duke shot a quick look at Cantrell. "I meant to. I had more urgent priorities."

Brivar sighed. His own stock lacked the potency of the spring blossoms, but it was too late to regret that now. "First, you need food, and some wine." He gave the duke a pointed look. "And you will eat it. Then we need a place where we can be private."

"No one will disturb us here," Cantrell told him. "I will see to it."

Brivar shook his head. "I don't doubt that, but we may disturb them. And you will need restraints."

"Restraints?" The duke's head jerked up, something dark flashing in his eyes. "I don't –"

"You will," Brivar cut him off. "With all respect, Your Grace. You will."

An appalled look crossed Cantrell's face. "What exactly is this cure?"

Brivar sighed. "Na'quia."

They had found out by accident. The Temple of Yholis could take no credit. An infected farmer, terrified that he faced the transformation, had stolen some of the infamous poison from the herbalist's stocks, prepared to suffer the agonies of a na'quia death rather than the horror of transformation.

But he had not died. Instead, for a full night, Brivar sat by his side as he screamed in agony, fingers tearing at his face, his eyes, his mind lost to insanity as the poison ran its course. Then, in the final hours, when na'quia victims fall silent as the drug does its most deadly work, Brivar had watched with growing astonishment as the farmer's breathing had evened, not into the slow decline of death, but steady and deep. Come morning, the man had opened his eyes, weak as kitten, mind scoured to despair by the horrors of the drug's hallucinations, but alive. Over several more days he had recovered, one poison driving out the other. They still did not know how or why.

The farmer had been young and strong. While the duke could not be much more than forty, he had suffered the ravages of this illness for three weeks. He was exhausted and weak, no matter how well he tried to hide it.

Cantrell's hand clenched around his knife. "You will kill him!"

Brivar eyed him warily but did not back away. It was not the first time he had been threatened for delivering bad news. He had never yet been attacked. "He will die anyway."

"You don't know that!"

"Esar..."

"I do. And so does he."

"Esar," the duke repeated. "Look at me."

"Alyas, please. Don't do this," Cantrell pleaded. "Na'quia is deadly."

"Look at me, Esar," the duke said again, and Cantrell couldn't. "This wound will kill me. If I'm a dead man anyway, what does it matter when?"

"It matters to me!"

Just because he had been here so many times before did not mean Brivar was immune to the grief and denial that followed such a diagnosis. Nor had he forgotten why he was here. The king seemed to believe his former commander—the man who had broken the siege of Druine and had, so legend said, rescued the Emperor of Qido's daughter from an assassination (or was that his father?)—could save Lankara from the unknown evil that threatened it. Brivar had no way of knowing whether that was true, and it was beyond his skill to measure that chance. He was more than capable of assessing this one, and both men deserved the truth.

To Cantrell, he said, "It is possible the na'quia will kill him and it is possible it will not. But it gives him a chance he would not otherwise have." And to the duke, who had listened with a twisted smile, he said, "The greatest torment of na'quia is not the physical agony but the horrors it visits on the mind. It is possible to survive the poison and still be destroyed by it. It is your choice to make, and you should not make it lightly."

"But quickly, yes?" The duke looked past Brivar to Cantrell. "You brought him here. This is the choice. What would you have me do?"

※

Brivar withdrew. He did not leave the room, but he had learned how to make himself an unobtrusive presence. It was an essential skill of his profession.

Cantrell argued that they should wait until Avarel. He said Brivar was only an apprentice. They should consult the masters of the temple. And that was how Brivar first learned they were going back. He realised then that the complete disinterest the duke had shown in Lord Sul's broken, partial warning had masked a decision already made. Given the wound he carried, it was clear they already knew of the threat.

Cantrell only gave in when the duke said bluntly, "Avarel is two weeks away. I will be dead before we get there." Then, very gently, "I am not my father. I would not do that to you."

Brivar averted his eyes from Cantrell's face. Some things never got easier.

After that, it was just a matter of practicalities. Cantrell was sent to make peace with Lord Sul and inform him that his petition had been successful, leaving Brivar alone with his patient. As the curtain swung closed behind his foster brother, one more layer of deception fell away, and Brivar saw the depths of the man's exhaustion stripped bare.

He made a quick decision. Time might be running out, but to try such a harsh cure in this state was almost certainly a death sentence. Excusing himself, he returned to the cave where the king's delegation had been housed, where he had left his things, giving thanks to Yholis that his cousin was currently occupied with Cantrell and could not interrogate him about where he had been. He regretted again the lost opportunity to collect blue star-violet blossoms, but it was not pain relief he needed to administer at this moment, it was sleep.

The duke was surprising pliant. Brivar was not surprised. If he had walked alone from where they had met him yesterday, through the dangers of the mountain night, it was no wonder. And the emotional toll of the morning had hit like hammer blow. He took what Brivar offered him and was asleep within minutes. With any luck, he would sleep through to evening. After that, it was in Yholis's hands.

Cantrell returned and Brivar left to find a few hours of sleep himself. He would need it. Lord Sul was waiting for him, the suspicious face of his guard captain at his shoulder.

"Well, cousin, what have you to say for yourself?"

Brivar looked at his feet and mumbled an apology.

"I don't want your apologies," his cousin snapped. "I want an explanation. What business could they have with you?"

"What business but his business?" Corado sneered. "I told you, my lord, the man's ill, weak. He's no use to us. We're wasting our time here."

Brivar risked a glance through his lashes, surprised at both the perception and the venom. But then, Corado was a soldier. He would recognise the signs.

Lord Sul flapped a hand for silence. "Well, is he? Cousin, it is your duty to divulge what you know for the good of Lankara."

It was not only the code of the temple that drew the lie from Brivar's lips; it was also respect for the man he had left, in spite of his hard edges and the minor cruelties he had inflicted that morning. That and the certainty the duke would not want knowledge of his condition to fall into such hands. "There are wounded here. I have been tending them."

After a searching look, his cousin nodded. This was a military camp. There almost certainly were injuries that needed attention. He made a mental note to seek those out when he had leisure.

"May I sleep, my lord?" he asked, eyes downcast. "I'm afraid the effort has wearied me. I am not used to such hard travel."

Lord Sul nodded his assent. Corado gave him a hard look.

"I know you're lying," he murmured as he brushed past in Lord Sul's wake, and Brivar knew it was a threat. He just didn't know why.

He let out a breath and sat. He *was* tired. And he was dreading what was coming. He was a surgeon of the Temple of Yholis, near enough. It was his life's work to ease suffering, not to cause it. It was on that bitter thought that he rolled himself up in his cloak and closed his eyes. Sleep came almost as quickly as it had for the duke.

B rivar was shaken awake by one of their escort several hours later.

"Someone in need of your services," the man told him as Brivar rolled over and blinked blearily at the blue glow of the Isyrium bulbs, lit once more with the approach of evening.

It was the woman who had challenged them the night before, without her spear this time. She smiled at him as he emerged from the cave, her expression much friendlier than it had been, and loped away across the camp, leaving Brivar to follow at a run, clutching his bag to his chest.

"What's happened?" he asked, a little breathless, when he finally drew level with her. In the daylight he could see that she was no more than a handful of years older than him, if that, and almost as pale as a Qidan, her face a blend of Janath severity and the softer features common in central Ellasia.

She stopped and gave him a smile that made her eyes dance and his stomach do strange things. Brivar tripped, dropping his bag. He heard a tinkling laugh and a female voice called out a comment that made Brivar blush to the roots of his hair as he quickly gathered his scattered equipment, fingers curling around the undamaged vial of na'quia with a sigh of relief.

He met the eyes of the laughing woman as he stood, a halo of black curls framing a brown face and large liquid eyes that were straight off the steppes. She was dressed like the spearwoman—her own spear resting against the rock she was sitting on—and she was visibly pregnant. He thought, in a moment of panic, that she was the reason he had been summoned, but an instant's evaluation told him there was no birth imminent. The woman laughed again at his obvious discomfort, one hand pressed to her swelling belly and the other to her back.

He looked around and saw other female faces watching him. His flush deepened. He knew at once he was in the women's camp, and he could not work out why until Cantrell emerged from a cave on his left. He saw Brivar and beckoned to him.

The woman beside him brushed her hand across his arm. "Come and find me when you're done," she murmured in his ear. "Ask for Della."

Brivar blinked. "What? Why?"

The sound of laughter followed him as he hurried after Cantrell and into the merciful escape of the cave.

They were waiting for him there, both of them, and the atmosphere was fraught with the weight of unspoken things. A table held the remains of a half-eaten meal and after a glance at the duke's face Brivar decided against insisting he finish it. It would do him no good if it came back up again. At least he looked fractionally less exhausted, though his lips were set in a tight line and a muscle twitched in his jaw.

Brivar placed his bag on the table and looked around as the red-haired woman from the night before removed the tray of food. It was smaller than the cave in which he had spent the night, and much more comfortable. Several sleeping pallets lined niches in the walls, which were adorned with yet more Isyrium bulbs. A rack of spears and bows stood near the entrance, and a handful of blades hung from hooks driven into the stone wall. Brivar saw the double sheaths of the duke's weapons among them.

Then, because he could put it off no longer, he turned from his scrutiny of the cave to the men within. They were both watching him, the duke with a tense half-smile and Cantrell with a glower that would have terrified Brivar if he had not known it was not directed at him.

"I am in your hands," the duke told him, his voice not quite steady. He had not been scared by dying but he was frightened by this, and who could blame him? Tales of na'quia poisoning were lurid and horrific, and unfortunately, mostly true.

Brivar wished Varistan Alondo were here. His master would not find his tongue so twisted in knots that he could barely speak. He took a deep breath, then another, and reminded himself that this was what he had trained for—that if he did not do this, this man would certainly die—and tried to ignore the treacherous voice that insisted he was just giving him a worse death.

It steadied him, sort of, and while Cantrell fretted, Brivar poured a cup of wine and emptied a whole packet of blue star-violet into it. It might not have been picked on the first day of spring, but it would still deaden pain. Then he carefully added three drops of na'quia. The farmer who had stolen it in desperation had swallowed near twice as much. They had experimented with much smaller doses in the patients who followed. Too little, and all the torment of na'quia would be for nothing. Much more, and many would not survive, so Brivar measured three drops, no less and no more.

His own hand shook as he held out the cup. The duke's eyes met his as he took it.

"If this doesn't work," he said matter of factly, "no one here will blame you. I swear it."

Brivar blanched. Until that moment, he had never considered the immediate implications of the duke's death at his hands, in his own camp. Or worse, the reaction of the Lankaran embassy. "My cousin…"

The duke saw his fear and frowned. His voice was hard as he said, "They will not touch you either. My people will protect you. Esar?"

"My word," Cantrell growled. "But if you die, I swear I will kill you myself."

The duke choked on a laugh and drained the cup. Brivar replaced it on the table.

"Lie down," he said, his confidence returning now there was no turning back. "You will soon be dizzy." There was enough blue star-violet in that wine to fell an uroc.

The duke quirked an amused eyebrow at his tone and sat on one of the pallets, but he did not lie down. Instead, he watched as Brivar carefully unpacked his things. When his eyes fell on the length of silk cord, he said, his voice hoarse, "Not yet, please."

Brivar looked at his face and nodded. "Not yet."

The duke closed his eyes and tilted his head back. His skin looked drained of colour in the blue-tinted Isyrium glow and Brivar could see the rapid beat of the pulse in his throat. Brivar waited silently, and when the duke started to slip sideways, he caught him and eased him down as the massive dose of blue star-violet took effect. The na'quia would come later.

⁂

They waited without speaking through the first hour, until the early signs of the na'quia twitched through the duke's limbs, his face creasing in pain. Brivar tried to send Cantrell away when the drug began to work in earnest. He refused to go. Later, he did, when his captain and brother could no longer silence his screams, when the tethers that bound his mind to the present began to fray and the raving started. Grey-faced, shaken to his core, he did not resist when Brivar propelled him from the cave. No one should have to listen to that.

His ears stuffed with soft balls of rolled cotton, Brivar caught the duke's thin wrists when he tried to rip out his eyes and tied them down with trembling fingers. He focused his attention on the physical agony and tried to block out everything else, but cotton could only do so much. No man should have his private demons exposed in such a manner.

There were moments when the duke was aware, when he looked at Brivar and knew him, and tried to stifle the words that spilled from him; there were others when Brivar was sure he would lose him, when it seemed that the damage already inflicted by the illness was too great for his body to endure. It surprised him how much that hurt. It was always painful to lose a patient, when all his skills were not enough to heal what was broken, but it was an impersonal pain. It had to be. The na'quia forced him to share in this man's private torment; it laid him bare. He could not listen to that and not be moved to something more than the detached compassion he felt for all those under his care.

Then, finally, a few hours past midnight, silence fell. Brivar sat up, aware of a tension that had nothing to do with hours of uncomfortable vigil. He listened for the sound of breath, of life, and heard nothing. He pushed himself to his feet and approached the sleeping platform. Blood marked the furs where the duke's struggles had caused the restraints to cut into his wrists, and fresh blood spotted the bandage on his shoulder. His face was pale, almost white, and completely still. Brivar blinked, fatigue and the hot sting of tears blurring his vision. He thought of what he had heard—memories and hallucinations dragged from deep inside, of terrible grief and horrific acts he could not understand—of Cantrell's grey, shocked face, and wondered whether perhaps this was better.

The twitch of movement was so slight he almost missed it. Then the man on the bed took a shuddering breath, his ribs leaping up under Brivar's gentle fingers. He coughed once, his breath gasping, then subsided, his chest rising and falling in a shallow rhythm.

Brivar took his own deep breath, suddenly unsteady, and stumbled to the curtain that hung across the cave entrance. He found Cantrell outside, hunched under a cloak in the swaddling darkness, another shape bundled up by his side.

He looked up when Brivar appeared, his expression lost to shadow. "Is he —"

"Alive," Brivar croaked, trembling with exhaustion. "For now."

"Yholis's mercy," Cantrell muttered, disentangling himself from the woman curled against him. Brivar caught a flash of red hair as Cantrell eased himself to his feet, almost as creaky as Brivar felt. "Can I...?"

Brivar stepped to one side as Cantrell pushed past and pulled the curtain closed behind them. His legs sagged but he dared not sit; sleep would claim him instantly. And he could not leave the duke's side. The worst was over, one way or another, but it would hours before they knew whether this stillness was forever.

Cantrell tracked his restless steps, his own eyes red with fatigue. Eventually, he said, "You haven't asked how it happened."

Brivar turned to him, surprised. "It is not for me to ask. It is not our way. The temple cannot refuse healing to anyone who comes seeking it, but we are still bound by the king's laws."

"And if you don't know that the man bleeding out in your temple was injured committing a crime, you can't be expected to turn him in? I didn't realise the goddess's disciples were so pragmatic."

Brivar shrugged. "When we need to be." Politics and religion had always been uneasy bedfellows, and rulers could be jealous. He thought of the secret stocks of Isyrium hidden beneath the temple, so essential to their work, their possession of even as much as they admitted to a point of almost continuous contention with the king, his council, and his nobles.

"We were in Flaeres," Cantrell said, surprising him again. "Chasing rumours. Did you know Ado has been cut off?"

Brivar shook his head. Ado was far to the northeast, hugging the edges of the vast Qido Empire. It was small, poor, and of little consequence to the rulers of Ellasia since its wealth in Isyrium had dried up a century ago. What it had to do with Flaeres he did not know, and he was quite sure from Cantrell's tone that he did not want to.

Cantrell stared through him. He was talking, Brivar suspected, for much the same reason as Brivar was pacing. "Qido has closed its borders with Ado. Nothing gets in or out. No one knows why, or if they do, no one will say." He blinked, pressing his knuckles to his eyes. "They came out of nowhere. I have never seen their like. Blue from their heads to their feet, naked. The colour of midnight. There were beasts with them, and it was almost impossible to tell one from the other—who was human and who was not." He lapsed into silence, his gaze drifting. Then he said, "They went straight for him. I don't know why. We barely got him out of there. I still have nightmares about it."

Blue from their heads to their feet. The colour of midnight. Brivar shivered. He had heard similar tales from others who had come to the temple. Not human, some said. Or no longer human. No one had ever heard them speak, or they had not lived to tell of it. "What happened?"

Cantrell was staring at his hands. "It was bad at first, then he seemed fine. We went to Sarenza to report to the king and came back here. But then…"

Brivar could imagine the rest. Then the poison had started to work, or the duke had no longer been able to conceal its effects. The deterioration would have been rapid and frightening for someone not used to physical weakness, but he had proved remarkably resilient for all that. Brivar had only seen one person last longer than a week, and that was a young woman with a new baby. She clung defiantly to life until her husband was found and took the baby from her. Then she died.

The surgeon in him wanted to press Cantrell for details, to understand the course of the illness, but he stayed silent as the other man sat lost in his dark thoughts. If they could not halt this threat before it swamped Lankara, he would have too many chances to study the strange sickness; he did not need to plunder painful memories.

A yawn overtook him, and he turned to pace back across the cave. His gaze snagged on the paired blades hanging on the wall, the elegant hilts the unmistakable cool blue of Isyr steel. Unable to help himself, Brivar ran his fingers over the cold metal, feeling the legendary silkiness of the steel that never lost its edge. They were weapons fit for a king—rare, priceless treasures. Irreplaceable. It had been impossible to mine pure Isyrium for decades. The rough ore that was mined these days was sufficient, after processing, to power Ellasia's burgeoning new industries and the work of its temples, but the purity required for Isyr steel was lost to the past. Wars had been fought over it. Even now, possession of it dictated relations between nations.

Cantrell, looking up, said bitterly, "Beautiful, aren't they? Worth as much as the whole of Lankara. They were his father's, a gift from the emperor of Qido. Much good they did him."

Brivar dredged the details from his memory. The old duke's death had been almost as dramatic as the scandal that exiled his son. "His father... He died in the New Year Games? Killed in a duel?"

The death had led to calls to ban real weapons from the games. Brivar had been a child at the time, but he remembered his father arguing with his uncle about it.

Cantrell gave him a hard look. "He wasn't killed. He killed himself, before all the high and bloody mighty of the court. In front of his son."

Brivar frowned. "I thought he was drunk, that he slipped..." Something in Cantrell's eyes made his voice trail away.

"He had been drinking all day, but I swear by Ithol's blood, he was stone cold sober in every way that counted when he impaled himself on his best friend's blade. Tyonn knew it, too. Man drank himself to death a few years later. Never got over it. What kind of a man uses a friend like that?"

Brivar let his fingers drop from the sword, his gaze drawn to the sleeping man. *I am not my father.* "A desperate one?"

"That man was never right. He never could shake the shadow. Just like..."

"Just like?"

Cantrell didn't answer. Whatever had prompted the confidence had dried up. But he had said enough. Enough that Brivar could make sense of some of the ravings he had heard. He tried hard not to think about things he had no right to know.

He turned back to the Isyr blades. It was almost painful to look away. The Temple of Yholis in Avarel had a few items of pure Isyr steel, but they were kept secret and hidden. Rulers had been known to plunder temples for Isyr, such was its allure. "Why didn't the king take them?" Why settle for confiscating a man's lands and leave him a wealth greater than an entire nation?

Cantrell snorted. "Raffa's a bastard but he's not stupid. He took what he could and left what he couldn't."

They lapsed into silence. Cantrell rested his head against the wall and was soon asleep, the tension in his shoulders finally unravelling. Brivar watched him jealously, fatigue pressing on him like a physical weight, but he could not sleep yet. Positioning the brightest bulb by the bed, he washed and bathed the duke's raw wrists, wrapping them in soft linen, and restitched the wound on his shoulder. The man didn't even twitch, the unnerving stillness unbroken by the pull of needle through damaged flesh.

After that there was nothing to do but wait. Too tired to pace, Brivar found a place on the floor from where he could watch both men and set himself to reciting the one hundred principles of the surgeon's code, and after that the three hundred and six uses of Isyrium. He was only halfway through when he fell asleep, head pillowed on his arms, and when he woke hours later it was to see the duke's eyes open and staring at something over his shoulder.

Brivar raised his head cautiously, careful to make no sudden movement. He had seen too many na'quia awakenings in recent months to do otherwise, and a distant quality in that stare told him its owner was not quite awake or aware.

When the duke didn't stir, Brivar eased himself to his knees and turned his head to see what had captured such intense scrutiny. The Isyr blades hung from their place on the wall, the blue tint to their steel glowing faintly in the reflected light of the scattered bulbs. He frowned, looking closer. The bulbs were darker now, their power fading, and the steel had not glowed before…

"I thought it would be different," a rough voice whispered.

Brivar looked round. The duke's gaze shifted from the blades to his face as Brivar reached for the cup of watered wine he had kept ready to ease a raw throat. "I thought I would be free." He avoided the cup Brivar held to his lips, looking away from him to the other wall, hiding his face.

Brivar frowned, conducting a quick visual examination as he grappled with how to respond. Na'quia hallucinations were vivid and terrifying; many upon waking were still in their grip. He did not want to reinforce those terrors with an unguarded word, but it seemed to him that the duke was lucid enough. "Free from what?"

Fingers curled fretfully into a fist, discovering the pain of abused wrists. There was a hitched breath. "Everything."

Brivar held his breath, hearing the despair. Was that also the na'quia or something deeper? *I am not my father.*

"I can still hear them," the duke murmured. "I can still feel them. They are quieter, but they are not gone."

Brivar felt a cold shiver, at the words and the tone. He tried again to coax the duke to drink. The wine was drugged with the same sleeping draught he had used the day before, and it would give dreamless rest, free from ghosts or visions, or whatever this was.

"Alyas."

Cantrell was awake and looking down at the bed with a conflicted expression.

The duke turned his head and his eyes lost some of their unsettling distance. His gaze brushed Brivar, and this time it was clear that he knew him, before resting on his foster brother. "Esar."

The word was a harsh scrape followed by a cough that left him gasping. Brivar seized his chance and this time he was successful. The drugged wine took effect almost instantly.

When the duke was safely asleep once more, Brivar rocked back on his heels, unutterably weary. Cantrell stood unmoving by the bed, his gaze still rivetted on the sleeping man.

"Is it over?" he asked. The words were toneless, dull.

Brivar nodded. It would be two days at least before the duke would be strong enough to rise, and many more before he shook off the effects of the na'quia poisoning. But if all Brivar's experience to this point held true, the other poison was no longer killing him, burned away by the na'quia. It might take time, but like the others who made it this far, he would recover.

Looking at Cantrell, Brivar wondered whether the same would be true for him. The man had been deeply shaken, like someone who had seen the foundations of their world ripped away.

Unwilling to interfere, aware that he needed to rest, Brivar quietly packed away his things.

"What did he mean?"

Brivar looked from Cantrell to the bed. He did not realise those waking words had been overheard. "I was going to ask you."

Cantrell shook his head bleakly. "I have no idea. But I know where I have heard its like before."

"Where?"

"From his father, right before he killed himself."

B rivar did not precisely recall leaving the duke the morning he survived the passage of na'quia poisoning. He remembered pulling aside the curtain to find the woman, Della, waiting outside. He had been dead on his feet with exhaustion, weighed down by an inexplicable sadness, and he let her lead him away. He remembered nothing more after that. But when he woke, a full ten hours later, he was not in his bedroll in the cave with his cousin and his escort, but curled up against a warm body, with soft furs beneath him and the smell of pine forests filling his senses.

He froze, confused, and the woman shifted in his arms. Della's face peered into his.

"You're awake."

He sat up so fast that dizziness almost sent him back down again. "How… where…?"

She smiled. "Relax. You were exhausted and it was cold. It was not wise to send you back to your own in such a state."

No, indeed. Brivar could see that. But he had been snuggled up around her—a woman he didn't even know!—and he could feel the heat rising in his face.

He looked towards the silent cave, seeking refuge. "Is he –?"

She followed his gaze. "He's sleeping. They both are. Esar told us what you did."

"Were you here? Last night?" The curtain was heavy, but it would not have blocked out all sound. If the rest of the camp had remained in ignorance, the women would not have been so lucky.

She nodded. "We were here. But no one else. We made sure of that." She saw him wince, and added, with emphasis, "We heard nothing."

They had guarded their captain's privacy and would continue to guard it. He was glad.

He started to untangle himself from the cloak and felt her hand close over his. He looked up, his face so hot he thought he might melt.

She smiled, shyly this time. "Now that you're awake..."

And he found himself quite unable to resist as she pushed him back down.

❧

For three days the duke did little more than sleep and the camp hovered in tense limbo. Cantrell rebuffed all Lord Sul's requests for an audience with the simple lie that the duke was elsewhere, and Brivar watched with growing unease as Corado and his men became more and more suspicious and their temper frayed to a dangerous edge. But he did not have much time to spend on such thoughts. Between checking on his patient and calming Cantrell's worry, he was kept busy from dawn till dusk. And after dark, Della kept him occupied in creative and revelatory ways.

Nothing was said to him directly, but by a myriad small acts Brivar was given to understand that the company knew what he had done for their captain, and that they were grateful. The women took it upon themselves to adopt him, inviting him to share their fire in the evenings, and though he refused—good sense and protocol dictating that he take his proper place with his cousin—he always found his way to the women's camp, and Della, at nightfall.

The pregnant woman, a fierce steppelander called Keie, allowed him to examine her, and when he announced that the baby was healthy, she kissed him and gave him a bracelet of wooden beads she had carved with a blessing in her native tongue. Della told him it was a love charm and laughed at him when he blushed scarlet.

The men poked gentle fun at his temple innocence and offered to teach him to fight. He declined, but not before he demonstrated his own skills with a knife in a delicate operation to reset a splinter of bone in a man's wrist that had healed badly after a break.

He treated minor injuries and dispensed remedies for everything from embarrassingly private rashes to sleeplessness. Handing over this last to Cantrell, Brivar frowned at the black circles under the man's eyes and tried once more to reassure. He knew it was not the prolonged sleep that worried Cantrell—Yholis knew, the duke *needed* the sleep—but the unnerving words he had spoken on waking. And Brivar had no remedy for that.

On the morning of the fourth day, he found his patient not only awake but alert and impatient. The duke endured Brivar's examination with poor grace. He snapped irritably when told to eat before he tried to get up, but he was forced to accept the wisdom of the suggestion when the faintness of so long with no more sustenance than occasional spoonful of bone broth made it impossible to stand unaided. Of what had passed, he said not a word.

Brivar sighed and retreated, leaving the duke to the women's tender mercies, who ignored his snappish temper as though their captain was no more than a bad-tempered child. He spent that day with the Lankarans, obeying an instinct that warned of trouble on the horizon and not wanting to push either his cousin or Corado too far, and it was from the Lankarans that he first heard the rumours of Lathai on the slopes around the camp. It was Corado who brought the news to Lord Sul, along with a suggestion that he take out a patrol to "show those savages Lankarans are not all cowards".

Brivar watched his cousin through downcast eyes. When the king had chosen Lord Sul for this mission, he had been so puffed up with pride that he had been all but unbearable. The duke's reputation was such that it had grown to overshadow even his disgrace and exile.

But Corado had been dripping poison in his ear since they arrived, and that humiliating initial audience still rankled. Brivar knew Lord Sul interpreted the duke's refusal to see him since then as a deliberate insult, but he dared not reveal the truth, not with Corado and his sharks circling. They already sensed weakness. If they knew the object of their hatred was barely able to stand, he did not like to think what they might do.

Whatever Lord Sul might have decided, however, Corado's ambitions were dashed by Cantrell, who refused to hear of sorties against the Lathai. In fact, he threatened quite graphic harm to anyone who left the camp without his authorisation, worse for anyone who provoked the tribe. He was still tired, but the haunted look had left his eyes, and as he faced down Corado's simmering fury he looked like he would enjoy nothing better than the chance to make good on his threat.

Brivar spent that night with Della, frightened by the latent violence of the Lankarans, but he did not sleep well, his senses straining after every sound that might mean someone was testing Cantrell's decree. But all was quiet. In the morning as he was returning to the Lankaran side of the camp, he was hailed by Agazi, the man's whose wrist he had reset.

Agazi was a steppelander like Keie and Brivar strongly suspected he was the father of her baby, though she had never said as much. The pair of them were often together.

Thinking perhaps his wrist was paining him, Brivar changed course towards the fire around which several of the men were eating breakfast.

Agazi held out a flatbread, hot and fresh, and waved Brivar to a seat beside him. Brivar took the flatbread and yelped, blowing on singed fingers. It smelt wonderful, warm and savoury with a tang of garlic.

Agazi grinned at his pleasure. "Storn made them. He found wild garlic yesterday. Aren't they good?"

Brivar agreed they were delicious, smiling at the blond-haired Qidan crouched by the fire cooking the flatbreads on a hot stone.

"The Lathai make them best," Agazi continued as Brivar choked on a mouthful. "They put all kinds of spices in them, don't they, Storn?"

"Lathai?" Brivar squeaked.

Agazi laughed. "You Lankarans. You're too easy. Don't tell me you believe the tales about them drinking the blood of their enemies and worshipping devils?"

Brivar frowned, aware he was being teased, but also aware it was not malicious. "Aren't the Lathai our enemy?"

"You're their enemy more like," the Qidan murmured, flipping a flatbread to toast the other side. "Hard to see what they've done to you. They never leave these mountains."

Brivar set down his half-eaten flatbread and it was promptly snagged by the man next to him. "I thought we were at war with the Lathai. Isn't that why the duke was exiled? Because he lost an army fighting them?"

"I made peace, or tried to," a sardonic voice informed him.

Brivar, a flush creeping up his cheeks, looked up into the sharp-featured face of Alyas-Raine Sera, the recently unexiled but not quite formally reinstated Duke of Agrathon, finally upright. His skin had lost the translucent look of dire illness, though his eyes were still smudged from exhaustion and the fingers that held an apple were far too thin.

The duke dispersed the men at the fire with a quick gesture then stood looking down at Brivar.

"I'm sorry –"

"Why? It's what he wanted everyone to believe. The truth is that my efforts were not appreciated by my royal cousin, who accused me of treason, stripped me of my names and title, married my wife, and sent me into exile where I spent years fighting the same people for money that I refused to fight for my king's honour." He took a bite of the apple. "Ironic, isn't it?"

Brivar recoiled from the brittle mockery and everything it was hiding, recalling the unguarded despair of those first moments of na'quia awakening. He could see Cantrell watching them through narrowed eyes from across the camp.

He looked up at the duke. "If he did that, why are you going back?"

Something flashed in those dark eyes. "Because he asked me to," the duke said, his head turning to where Esar stood glowering at his back. "And I think that's enough questions for today, don't you? Get your things. You're coming with me."

"I am?" Brivar shoved to his feet and hurried after the duke's retreating back. "Where?"

"You'll see," was the infuriating reply.

Cantrell stepped out to block their way as they walked towards the far end of the camp. "Alyas…"

The duke side-stepped him and kept walking. Della and one of Brivar's breakfast companions, a man named Aubron, were waiting up ahead. She winked at Brivar as they approached, and he felt his face flush with heat.

"It's not far," the duke told Cantrell. "And they would not have come here, now, if it were not urgent." He stopped, glancing at Brivar, still empty-handed. "Get your things," he repeated. "I suspect you'll need them. Quickly."

The last command sent Brivar scurrying to obey. When he returned, his bag clutched to his chest, he found four horses saddled and ready. Della took his bag and strapped it to one of the horses as the duke mounted another. The movement was easy enough, but he couldn't hide a flash of pain or the rapid pulse in his throat. Only yesterday he had been unable to walk more than a handful of steps.

No less observant, Cantrell grabbed the bridle and made one last plea. "If you must go, at least let me go with you."

The duke shook his head. "I need you here. There's likely to be trouble."

There was? Brivar looked over his shoulder in alarm, remembering the simmering anger among his cousin's escort at news of Lathai sightings.

"All the more reason not to go," Cantrell protested. "I can only stall them for so long."

Brivar was inclined to agree. His own instincts aside—which strongly disapproved of unnecessary exertion so soon—this seemed like a bad time for the duke to leave the camp. Given why they were here, the presence of Lathai was bound to stoke old resentments among men who had been raised to believe the king's charge of treason and had made it clear they saw the Duke of Agrathon's reinstatement as a grave insult.

"It's precisely why I must go," the duke replied, tugging his bridle free and nudging the horse into motion. "We will be back by nightfall."

Cantrell stood aside. He caught Brivar's eye and Brivar could read his thoughts as clearly as if he had shouted them. He said something to Della as she passed and she nodded, then spurred her horse alongside Brivar, her thigh pressing into his. "He says you're to do your best," she murmured with a grin, relaying Cantrell's instruction, then she was past him, spurring ahead with Aubron.

Brivar trailed at the rear, his muscles reacquainting themselves with time spent in the saddle, and wished someone had the courtesy to tell him where they were going and why. His absence would only add more fuel on the fire of his cousin's resentment. That anxiety was quickly succeeded by another, however, as their way took them along a narrow, rocky path that wound upwards into the mountains, hemmed in by tall pines on either side. The going was difficult enough that ensuring his horse picked a safe path consumed Brivar's entire attention until he realised that his mount was finding its way without any intervention from him. It was then he realised they weren't alone. Shadows flitted through the trees on either side, keeping pace with the horses, so dark they rippled through the trees like wraiths.

He hauled his horse to a stop, crying out in alarm. The duke twisted round with a frown. Then his gaze followed Brivar's and he relaxed. "Lathai. They've been with us since we left the camp."

"Lathai? What do they want?"

"To talk."

He looked grey, the shadows on his face more pronounced. *You're to do your best,* Cantrell had said. Easier said than done, Brivar thought bitterly, as the duke turned away from his scrutiny before he could say anything. Brivar hoped he had been truthful when he said they were not going far, because he did not look like he would last much longer and what Brivar was to do then, he did not know. Della and Aubron were out of sight somewhere ahead and there were Lathai—*Lathai!*—all around them.

Two hours later, Brivar decided that their definitions of 'not far' diverged significantly, and he was starting to feel the beginnings of panic when he saw Della and Aubron waiting for them on the track ahead. They had dismounted and were sitting on a boulder, their horses held by two of the most outlandish figures Brivar had ever seen. Dressed in fur cloaks and plain tunics that left their arms and lower legs bare, every inch of their bared skin was painted in whorls of dark green and brown, even their faces and shaved heads. Lathai.

The duke reined in and leant forward on his saddle. "Eldruin." He was perfectly calm, despite finding two of his people prisoners of a tribe renowned for their savagery. Except Della and Aubron didn't look like prisoners, and everyone here clearly knew each other, as unlikely as that seemed.

One of the men inclined his head. His facial whorls were more elaborate than his companion's, and Brivar could see the glint of a ring in one ear. "Captain, thank you for coming." He had a curious accent, skipping lightly over the hard edges of the Lankaran words. It made Brivar think of a breeze through the leaves of a tree. His tone was polite, respectful. Not quite friendly, but certainly not hostile.

The duke looked down at him, and said in much the same tone,

"Is your father well?"

"He is waiting to greet you. Come."

Two more figures flitted out of the trees, a man and a woman who took hold of their horses as they dismounted. Brivar didn't miss the way the duke wavered as his feet hit the ground. No matter what he wanted to pretend, no one recovered so quickly from na'quia poisoning. Brivar hoped he didn't collapse before they finished whatever they had come here to do, because he didn't understand anything that was happening.

They followed Eldruin through the trees to a large clearing filled with wooden lodges of various sizes, raised above the ground on thick stilts. Moving between them, and sitting on their broad steps, were more tattooed Lathai. Lathai children chased each other shrieking with laughter through the forest of stilts, while their parents watched Brivar and his companions with cautious curiosity.

An old man waited on the steps of the largest lodge. Around his neck was a carved pendant of Iysr steel, most likely a family heirloom. He smiled at Eldruin as they approached, and the younger man dropped back.

The duke stopped. "Ailuin."

"Alyas." The old man stepped forward and kissed his forehead, then held him by his shoulders and looked long at his face. "I apologise. I have made you travel when you are ill and need to rest. Come, sit, and let me tell you what is so urgent it could not wait."

He walked up the steps, the duke following. Without any instruction otherwise, Brivar started after them and found Eldruin's outstretched arm blocking his way.

The duke turned. "He comes with me."

Ailuin nodded at his son. To Brivar he said, "We do not hold with temple ways. If you do not invoke your goddess, you are welcome here."

Brivar blinked. He had never heard of a people who did not revere Yholis in one form or another, goddess of spring, of healing, and new life. Everything else was her brother Ithol's domain, and though Ithol touched almost every aspect of people's day-to-day lives, it was Yholis who was beloved. Even in the steppes, where they knew her as Ola, Yholis held sway over people's hearts. Except here. It was so shocking that Brivar could not at first find the words to respond, but he could feel the duke's eyes on him and managed to convey his understanding.

Ailuin smiled. "Then be welcome. We may not love your goddess, but we respect the skill and learning of her followers. And your coming here is most fortuitous."

Brivar caught the duke's eye. His face was grim but not surprised. He had guessed the reason for this summons. There were sick people here.

Inside, the lodge was furnished with low chairs covered with bright cushions, positioned around a central brazier with an iron chimney that rose all the way to the roof. Ailuin took his seat on the grandest of the chairs, and only once he was settled did the duke sit. Brivar followed his lead and did the same. He looked around for Della, but neither she nor Aubron had entered the lodge with them.

"Your companions are in no danger," Ailuin said with a smile as he set the chair gently rocking. "They are known here, and they also are welcome." He leant forward and scattered water on the hot coals, sending a cloud of fragrant steam into the air.

The duke waited until the steam dispersed, then said, "Ailuin, you called, and I have come. Will you tell me why?"

The old man looked from Brivar to the duke and said, "I think perhaps you have guessed."

"Your messenger was distressed. I have seldom seen a Lathai in such a state."

Ailuin nodded, the rocking of the chair making the motion long and deep. "Then you too have encountered the midnight children?"

"The midnight children?"

"That is what we call the lost ones and the sickness they bring."

"We have," the duke said grimly. "In Flaeres."

Ailuin bowed his head. "They have infected the mountain lions and many others of the small animals. We have lost two of the tribe to their number." His voice shook, and Brivar saw the fear and disgust beneath the calm mask. "They forgot themselves and us and became as the midnight ones. Others have succumbed to a vile sickness, that saps life and strength. Our healers can do nothing to stop it. Three have already died. Do you know of this too?"

"I do."

Ailuin's head came up and his eyes sharpened on the duke's face. "This is what ails you?" he asked. "The midnight sickness?"

The duke shook his head. "Not anymore. There is a cure."

Ailuin was silent for a moment, but when he reached out to sprinkle more water on the coals, Brivar saw his hand tremble. "A cure." It was almost a whisper, full of hope and trepidation. The smoke curled, its sweet, smoky aroma suddenly cloying. Then he sighed, and said, "Forgive me, Alyas, if I say that you do not look well."

There was a pause, then the duke said, "The cure is... not easy." His voice was steady, almost too steady, and Brivar could not look at him. "What you see is merely the lingering effects of the treatment, not the illness."

Ailuin rocked gently. To Brivar he said, "You brought this cure? Will you share it with us?"

Brivar hesitated, recalling Cantrell's horrified reaction, fearing what this man's would be. His eyes slid to the duke, who nodded. "Na'quia."

"Na'quia." Ailuin's hand went to the Isyr pendant and his lips mouthed words Brivar did not understand. "How?"

"We do not know," Brivar admitted, and he told Ailuin how the cure had been discovered. "We do not understand it, but it reverses the illness in those who do not face transformation—if they are not already too weak to withstand its effects."

Ailuin listened. He was very still. "And those who do face

transformation. What does na'quia do to them?"

Brivar shook his head. "None have come to the temple in time."

"I see," said Ailuin, and lapsed into a silence that lasted a long time. The glow of the coals dimmed, their warmth dying away, and still he did not speak. A cramp threatened in Brivar's leg, but such was the quality of the silence that he feared to move and break the spell.

At last, Ailuin moved, his hand flicking out to stoke the coals. He met Brivar's startled eyes and said, "What you have done… it is very dangerous. The Lathai know na'quia. Its use is part of our way, but we have learned its uses and its danger. We respect it."

Brivar wasn't sure he had heard that right. "You *use* na'quia?" he echoed, astonished.

Ailuin rocked. "For many hundreds of years. To see into the ways of the soul, to understand our destiny and our past. But we teach its use from a young age, and only to those with the strength to bear its price. And no one," he said, looking at Alyas, "walks the na'quia path alone, as you have done."

Aware of the stiff silence beside him, Brivar asked, "The price?"

Ailuin did not answer him directly. "Will you go with our healers? Tell them what you know of this sickness and its cure, and see those who are afflicted?"

Again, Brivar looked at the duke for permission. Again, he nodded his assent.

"However I can help, I will do so gladly."

"And we thank you," Ailuin said gravely. To the duke he said, "We must speak of what you saw in the na'quia."

Brivar had not thought it possible for the man to look any paler, but Ailuin's words drained all the colour from his face. "I would rather not."

"It will not be pleasant," the old man agreed. "But it is necessary. There is a terrible truth in na'quia, but there are also dangerous lies. You must be able to know one from the other."

When Alyas did not answer, Ailuin said gently, "Even for the young among us who have never known tragedy, na'quia is a hard road to walk." He looked past Brivar and said, "Eldruin."

Brivar turned, surprised to find Ailuin's son at his shoulder. He had not known he was there.

Ailuin smiled and rocked. "Will you take the temple's healer to Caira and explain what he has told us?"

Eldruin touched Brivar's arm. "Come," he said.

He had no choice, he had already promised, but he knew they were being deliberately separated, and he knew why. "Your Grace...?"

The duke looked up. His face was set in a determined grimace, but his eyes were staring at something far away. "Go," he said hoarsely.

Brivar thought of the things he had heard and did not want to leave, but he did not want to stay either, so he allowed Eldruin to lead him from the lodge. The last thing he heard as they descended the steps was Ailuin saying, "You will rest here tonight and return in the morning. I will send a messenger to Esar before moonrise. How will it look to the Lankarans if you return from the Lathai unable to sit straight?"

For all the obvious differences between Lathai and Lankaran, healer and surgeon, Brivar found much that was familiar in Caira with her brisk, no-nonsense manner, and was immediately at home in her presence. More at home, in some ways, than he had felt since leaving Avarel and the temple. She reminded him of Varisten Elenia, though she was not so old as the temple's venerable matriarch and had a twinkle of humour in her eyes that the Varisten was usually at pains to suppress around the apprentices.

Her lodge was small and chaotic, filled with the heady scent of drying herbs. Most Brivar recognised—the subtle fragrance of blue star-violet, the astringent tang of cannavery, and the almost over-powering pungency of wild garlic—but there were others he could not identify. At any other time he would have spent hours exploring her concoctions and peppering her with questions. But he was acutely aware of why he was here.

Eldruin introduced him in a flurry of words in a language that must be Lathai. He heard Ailuin's name, and Yholis. Caira answered him in the same language, looking Brivar up and down with a critical eye, directing a stream of quick questions at Ailuin's son, who answered them briefly then withdrew, leaving the two healers facing each other in silence. Brivar was at a loss to know what to do. He spoke not a word of Lathai.

Caira solved that for him by saying in fluent Lankaran, "Ailuin says you mean well but you do not understand what you are doing."

"You speak Lankaran?" He should not have been so surprised.

She clicked her tongue and returned to the stems of cannavery she had been tying in careful bunches ready for drying. "Lankaran and Flaeresian. We trade with both of you, and fight you too, sometimes. Though less often now since Alyas guaranteed our independence."

"He did what?" Brivar felt his head spin as yet another revelation upended his view of the world. It was turning into a day for it. "With whom? The king claims these mountains as part of Lankara."

She laughed. "Well, he might think that, but when was the last time you saw a kingdom soldier here, eh? Or Flaeresian? Now, tell me what could possibly have possessed you to give that man na'quia?"

There was a stool behind him, covered with an untidy stack of silk pouches. Brivar carefully moved them to the work bench and sat down. It seemed a wise precaution if the conversation progressed in the manner in which it had begun. "He had the midnight sickness," he said, using the name Ailuin had given the mysterious illness. "He was dying. We have discovered that na'quia reverses it."

"That is what Eldruin said," she agreed. "If you knew him better, you never would have done it."

"Then he would have died," Brivar protested.

Caira didn't reply. Instead, she placed a stoppered clay flask on the workbench. As she leant over, a pendant swung free of her tunic, Isyr glowing in the light from the window, and he was surprised again at how freely these people displayed their treasures. These days, Lankarans were more likely to lock their Isyr jewellery in vaults and hope people forgot they owned it. Here they wore it as if it were of no more importance than any other metal. "Ailuin told you that we use na'quia in our rituals?"

He nodded.

"It surprised you," she observed. "But na'quia has many uses. Your temple knows some of them, I think. The petals, if mixed with hafta bark, can strengthen the function of the heart, for example."

He nodded again, no longer surprised by her knowledge. It was one of the contradictions of na'quia, that one part of it could be protective to the same organ another part attacked. "But the petals do not contain the poison."

"What is a poison?" she asked him. "Surely, it is merely something that is used incorrectly or by the wrong person?"

That echoed the teachings of the temple, and in most cases it was true. "And you use it correctly?"

She smiled. "We use it *carefully*. Come." And she picked up the clay flask.

He followed her out of the hut. "Where?"

"To see our sick," she said, leading him towards another lodge.

Brivar had been surprised not to find them with the healer, but the lodge was too small to accommodate patients. They stayed with their families, she told him. When their need was dire enough, she stayed with them.

In the first lodge they found a young man with his wife and child. He was not bedridden, but Brivar didn't need to examine him to know that was not far off. Like the duke, he was painfully thin and obviously in distress, but he still had the strength to hold his daughter and sit with the family for meals. Around his neck hung a pendant of Isyr.

At Caira's request, he showed Brivar an ugly bite on his calf as his wife watched with worried eyes from the other side of the brazier, their little girl asleep on her lap, her small hand tangled in a necklace hung with copper. The bite looked recent, but Caira said it had happened almost a month ago, and when Brivar met the man's eyes he saw the same acceptance he had seen in the duke's. He knew he was dying.

He waited patiently as Caira explained the na'quia cure. She spoke in Lathai so he did not know what she said, but he saw the man's eyes widen as he looked from her to Brivar. His wife said something, sharp and desperate, and the man shared a long look with her before he finally nodded.

Caira handed the flask to Brivar who measured three careful drops into a cup the wife fetched for him. Caira added blue star-violet, as Brivar had done, and then they left.

He stopped on the steps of the lodge. "Just like that? You leave them alone?" He could not believe it, knowing what was coming. "You said you use it carefully."

She turned. "They are not alone. Their families will care for them. And all of them have taken na'quia before."

"But..." He looked back at the lodge, memories of too many na'quia poisonings rising in a wave that made his stomach roil.

"We have many more to see," Caira told him, gently but firmly. "I cannot stay with them all and some are closer to death than Tandu. You must trust me when I tell you that we understand na'quia."

He swallowed, realising what she was saying. If they treated one sick member of the tribe at a time, some would die before they had a chance to risk the cure. He wondered how many there were.

After the third, he realised that his presence hadn't been necessary at all. There was nothing he could do for any of them that she could not do herself. He saw Ailuin's lodge from a distance as they walked from one patient to another and knew he was here simply so he was not there—and hoped he had done the right thing.

But he did learn something. With little to do as Caira spoke to each afflicted Lathai in turn, Brivar was free to observe, and when they were finally done—all seven patients provided with the means to perhaps save themselves—he asked her, "The necklaces you wear? Is there a reason why some are copper and others Isyr?" He kept thinking about the duke's Isyr blades, glowing gently in the blue light of the fading bulbs.

"Not the reason you think."

He suppressed a flash of irritation. He *had* brought them the means to save the sick members of their tribe. The least she could do was answer his question. "Then why?"

They were back in her lodge. The na'quia had been returned to its shelf and she was turned away from him. Her back was very stiff.

"Caira?"

She took a deep breath and faced him. He saw then that she was not so sanguine as she appeared about what they had set in motion. She touched the pendant round her neck. "It is… a personal thing. We are given them as children, each child according to their individual aspects. Some are copper, some are Isyr. Others are silver, or bronze."

"All those who are sick wear Isyr."

She hesitated, then said, "Not all of them. Three have already died of the sickness."

Their eyes locked. Brivar felt a flicker of apprehension coil through him. "What were their necklaces made of?"

"One was silver. The other copper."

It might mean nothing, pure coincidence, but Brivar was temple trained. He worried at the detail. "Ailuin said not everyone uses na'quia, only those who are strong enough. How do you determine who those are?"

Her hand reached up to encircle the bright Isyr necklace. "It is decided as children—when we receive these."

※

When Brivar returned to Ailuin's lodge, night was falling and the old man was alone in near darkness, puffing on a pipe. He saw no sign of the duke.

"Your captain is quite safe," Ailuin told him, gesturing to a chair. "He was tired and now he sleeps. He will not wake before morning. You may ask me what you want to know."

Brivar sat cautiously, his eyes on the old face in the shadows and the curl of smoke from his pipe and wondered about the nature of that invitation. At last, he asked, "What is the connection between Isyrium and na'quia?"

Ailuin took a long draw on the pipe. The cloud of smoke filled Brivar's lungs and made his eyes sting. "Why do you ask?"

He offered the pipe to Brivar, who shook his head. It contained some kind of narcotic. Even the smoke was making his head light. If these people took na'quia as part of their rituals, he would be wise to treat any of their herbal concoctions with caution.

"All your sick wear Isyr on their person. Your healer told me that those who have already died did not..."

Ailuin nodded. "Isyr is one of many metals from which we make our amulets. It is one of the uses of na'quia, to determine each child's amulet when they reach their third year."

"... and the duke carries Isyr blades."

Ailuin smiled through the smoke. "He does. He also has a name."

Brivar looked down, flustered. Strict Lankaran tradition was too ingrained, even now. Friends and family might use birth names with each other, but no temple acolyte or social inferior would dream of using anything less than the full formal title for one of the ruling class, and the Duke of Agrathon was inferior only to the king. Brivar was far too timid to navigate the treacherous waters of a man whose names had been taken from him, and who was not yet formally reinstated. "I know. I can't…"

"You must," the old man told him gently. "Names are important. He is not and never has been just a title, though the loss of it has defined him. He must be reminded who he is, and his friends must remember too."

That did not make sense. Brivar thought he had never met a man who knew more clearly who and what he was, but the heavy, narcotic smoke was tangling his thoughts.

Ailuin took pity on him, taking a final puff on the pipe then setting it aside. "Do you know what na'quia is?"

Brivar nodded, relieved to be back on safer ground. "It comes from a plant. The poison is in the leaves. It grows only in certain places."

"What places?"

"On rocky soil, near old quarries…" The words trailed away. He met Ailuin's sharp eyes. "Near old mines."

Ailuin rocked, his eyes never leaving Brivar's face. "What kind of mines?"

"Isyrium mines."

Brivar was suddenly aware of the thud of his heart and the flow of blood through his veins. He dropped his head into his hands, unable to bear its weight as his thoughts spiralled away and his vision was splintered by flashes of light reflected off a succession of Isyr pendants.

A rush of sweet, cool air hit his skin, and distant voices drifted in on the breeze. Ailuin was standing above him, looking down with a frown. "My apologies. I forget that others are not accustomed to our ways."

Brivar took the cup Ailuin offered him and thought about his assertion that the duke would not wake until morning. He felt like he could sleep for a day with that smoke in his lungs, even as its effects tried to untether his thoughts. He was quite sure its use had been deliberate but was too tired to care. "What did he say to you?" he asked Ailuin.

The old man resumed his place in his chair, rocking it gently. "Enough." He eyed Brivar. "Do you know what he saw?"

Brivar looked away. "I know only what I heard." Much of which he could not interpret and most he did not want to. He would not share it, but he found there was something he did want to know, quite badly. "Did he... did speak of his father?"

Ailuin studied him. "That is what Esar fears, isn't it? That they are too alike. But that is not the question you must ask."

"Then what is?"

Ailuin smiled sadly. "Why are they so alike? That is the question you must answer."

B rivar's dreams that night were vivid and strange, filled with the painted whorls of the Lathai and their strange amulets, punctuated by roaring lions, midnight blue, surging through the forests, and after them an indistinct horde of human and animal, sweeping over everything.

He woke sweating with a cry on his lips and found Della crouched by his side. "Are you well? I've been trying to wake you."

He lay back, an arm draped across his eyes, and tried to calm the beat of his heart.

"Brivar?" She sounded worried. "We're leaving soon. Can you get up?"

"I'm fine," he said, sitting. The lodge was empty except for the two of them and daylight was streaming through the windows. His stomach chose that moment to remind him he hadn't eaten since the morning before.

Della grinned. "Come on. If you hurry you might find some breakfast left. Taste some real Lathai flatbreads."

His stomach rumbled again as he caught the smell of cooking on the breeze. He followed Della out of the lodge and found the duke and Aubron sitting round a fire with Eldruin and a gaggle of children. The duke was talking quietly to Ailuin's son, picking absently at a flatbread, feeding most of it to a child sitting cross-legged by his feet. He gave Brivar a brief nod, and Brivar resisted the impulse to scold him to eat. It was not the time.

One of the older children handed Brivar a flatbread straight from the fire with a shy smile. The smell was so good it made his mouth water. He barely waited for it to cool before he ate it and accepted another. He ate this one more slowly, savouring the flavour, trying to guess which herbs had been used in its preparation. When the duke stood to leave, he stuffed a third flatbread into the pouch at his waist as he hurried after him.

As they reached the edge of the Lathai's clearing, he glimpsed Caira in the distance, her face pale with fatigue. He started towards her, to ask what had happened, but the duke stopped him. "They will tell you what they want you to know."

Ailuin was waiting by the horses. He embraced Alyas as he had on their arrival, eyes studying his face, and murmured something to him that Brivar did not hear.

The duke nodded, his jaw clenched, and turned away.

To Brivar's surprise, he also received an embrace. "You look like you slept well," Ailuin said with a twinkle. "On behalf of the Lathai, we thank you. I have spoken with Caira. Five of our number will return to us."

Two had died. Brivar bowed his head. He did not ask who. It was not his place.

"We will mourn them," Ailuin said. "But we will also celebrate five lives that have been spared. The friendship of the Lathai is yours, always." He set a hand to the Isyr amulet and his eye's sharpened on Brivar. "Trust your instincts."

They led the horses back to the track. The children ran alongside, waving farewell clustered on the rock where Della and Aubron had been waiting the day before. Then began the arduous trek back to the camp, and Brivar winced as the aches of the day before returned with a vengeance.

They rode back into the camp at mid-morning, at some point along the way exchanging their silent Lathai escort for the duke's men. Cantrell was waiting for them on the outskirts, no doubt alerted by his scouts. Even from a distance Brivar could see he was not happy.

The duke dismounted, the movement easier than it had been even a day before. Cantrell watched him with narrowed eyes. "Any trouble?"

The duke shook his head. "Nothing we did not expect. You?"

Cantrell's mouth thinned. "The same."

"So all is well."

"Alyas…"

"Later." He turned to Brivar. "Thank you. You did well."

Brivar nodded and hid his flush of pleasure at the praise by busying himself unbuckling his bag from the horse. Cantrell caught his elbow as he started towards the Lankarans' quarters. "Watch yourself. There's an ugly mood."

He wasn't exaggerating. Corado was sitting in the middle of a knot of Lankarans, talking together in low voices. They fell silent as he approached and he dropped his gaze before their hostile stares. It was not wise to provoke a dangerous animal by making eye contact.

Corado tracked his steps as he crouched by his bedroll, tucking his surgeon's pouch safely back into its folds. He tried to keep his movements slow and calm, but the eyes boring into his back made his palms sweat and his heart race.

"Brivar!"

He jumped, almost falling backwards, and looked up into Lord Sul's furious face.

"Where have you been?"

What should he say? Bad enough that he had been with the duke, when Lord Sul-Barin, the king's envoy, had not been permitted to see him. But to admit that he had been with the Lathai, Lankara's enemies, was to invite not only his cousin's rage, but potentially charges of treason—for all of them.

"Are you laughing?" his cousin demanded, incredulous.

Appalled, Brivar wiped the nervous smile from his face. "No, cousin."

Lord Sul advanced on him as Corado loomed up to fill the cave entrance. "I'll ask again, shall I? Where were you? Tending to more minor injuries?" The words were a sneer.

Brivar seized the lifeline with both hands. "Yes."

"He's lying," Corado snarled. "We saw you leave the camp, boy. You and the traitor."

How quickly things changed. They had arrived six days ago to beg the duke for help, offering him every honour that had been stripped from him. Now he was a traitor again. It made no sense. Brivar sighed. "Then why ask me?"

He regretted the words almost at once. Corado's hand struck him across the face, knocking him down, and a spurt of hot blood filled his mouth. The shock was almost worse than the pain. No one had ever struck him. Before he could move out of reach, the captain had a fistful of his surcoat and was dragging him across the cave.

"You think you're clever, boy?" he hissed, sending him sprawling on the hard ground outside in the centre of a ring of Lankaran guardsmen.

Brivar skittered backwards. He could see his cousin standing by the half-drawn curtain as though he did not know whether to cheer Corado or stop him. Surely, he would stop him? They had never been close, but their fathers were brothers, they had played together as children...

Corado's fist slammed into the side of his head, catching him above the ear. For several breaths there was nothing but pain, his vision hazy and dark, then thought returned and with it a kick to his ribs that made him cry out. His body curled instinctively around the pain, eyes squeezed shut. A fist grabbed his surcoat, hauling him to his feet, and Corado's harsh, angry breath washed over his face. He stank of wine. The Lankaran guardsmen were cheering their captain. Brivar felt sick. He had treated some of these men; they knew him.

"You consort with a traitor, and you'll share his fate," Corado snarled in his ear, and let him go with a shove.

This time, when he fell, he put out his hands and felt something in his wrist go as he landed badly. He rolled onto his side and saw Della's face in the distance behind the circle of Lankarans. He did not know whether to be ashamed that she had seen his humiliation or glad because she might stop it. Then Corado's foot came down on his bad wrist and he screamed, losing sight of Della as his vision exploded. When he could see again she was gone.

He curled in on himself, arms around his head, as the blows rained down. He did not try to get up, didn't try to run. He was sure Corado would kill him if he did.

Then the blows stopped. Brivar became aware of the sound of his own ragged breathing in the sudden silence. He opened his eyes. Someone stood between him and Corado's fists

"Lay a hand on my surgeon again," the duke said, "and I'll cut it off." His voice was ice over simmering rage.

"Your surgeon, Your Grace? He's not yours." Corado sneered. Brivar couldn't see his face, but his contempt dripped from every word.

"My surgeon," the duke repeated. "The king has seen fit to return my rank and all its privileges, one of which is a personal surgeon. He is mine."

Corado laughed. "He's not yours, Raine Sera," he slurred in blunt insult. If using someone's birth name was reserved for family and close friends, only intense dislike would prompt someone to use only house names. "You think you've got your names back and you can do what you like, but you're still a traitor and a coward. The king might have forgotten, but I haven't."

The silence that followed was full of threat. Brivar could feel the promise of violence in it and tried to sit. They could not fight. The guard captain was fit and strong, the duke only just back on his feet, and they were surrounded by Corado's men.

"He's an apprentice. You can't take an apprentice."

"Who's going to stop me?" the duke asked. "You, Corado?"

His hand moved, and for the first time Brivar saw the blades that hung from his hip and remembered his reputation. Corado must have remembered it too because he backed off a step.

"I haven't forgotten," he said again. "And I'm watching."

Brivar watched through the duke's legs as his tormentor retreated. He flopped back onto the hard ground, his head spinning.

The duke's face appeared in his vision, white lines of anger round his mouth as he took in the damage. "Can you walk?"

Brivar nodded, though he did not know if he could, and let the duke help him to his feet. An arm steadied him as he wobbled, the rush of blood to his head darkening his vision. His entire body throbbed.

"Good. Now walk. You can collapse later."

The Lankarans were drifting after Corado, but Brivar felt their hostile eyes on his back. Then Della was there, Cantrell beside her, and she slipped an arm under his shoulder as he heard Cantrell say, "What was that about?"

"What do you think?" the duke said bitterly, surrendering Brivar to Della.

She shored up his sagging weight. The fact that she was there—that she did not think him weak—gave him the strength to stay upright until they reached the women's section of the camp. Everything was rather blurry after that. He was aware of sitting—falling, really—and Cantrell catching him and propping him up. A flurry of female voices washed over him and something cool and wet on his face, then nothing…

…he came back to himself to see Della's anxious face inches from his. He blinked, trying to focus. Something was holding one eye shut and he lifted a hand to explore his face. She slapped it away. "Leave it. It's a poultice to take the swelling down. Your eye looks like a blackberry pie, but I don't think it's damaged. How are your ribs?"

"My ribs?" His hand slipped to his chest and he tried to straighten…

…he swam back to consciousness to the sound of distant voices.

"…with me?"

"Mmph," he managed, and heard someone laugh.

"He's fine," a man's voice said. "Give him some space. You lot are going to suffocate him."

That sounded like Cantrell.

He opened his good eye. The fight. Corado. His cousin's anger.

What seemed like most of the women in the company were crowded around him. He shut his eye again, his face flushing, which caused a ripple of laughter that only made him blush more. Then he heard Della angrily shooing the others away.

He cracked a cautious eye. They were alone again.

"Don't mind them," she said. "And try not to move. You scared me."

But he had to move. His cousin was already angry. The longer he stayed here, the worse it would be.

He must have spoken the thought aloud because Della frowned. "No, you don't. You're ours now. Alyas won't let anyone touch you."

"Ours?"

"His household. Didn't you hear him? Or were you more out of it than you looked?"

"No, I mean yes... But I thought..."

"That it was just for show? Fool," she said fondly. "He likes you."

"He does?" said Brivar, greatly taken aback.

Della smiled. It transformed the severe lines of her face. Made her beautiful. "Yes, can't you tell?"

"Not really," he muttered, making a show of testing the bandages on his wrist to hide his confusion. She had done a good job, the binding neat and professional—firm but not too tight. The wrist itself was a throbbing mass of pain, but he could move all his fingers. Sprained but not broken.

She saw his approval and laughed. "Not bad for an amateur? We have some practise with wounds, you know. Alyas makes sure we know what to do. What is it?"

He looked away, flustered, nausea rolling. "Nothing, it just sounds strange when you call him that." *Names are important*, Ailuin had said, and he saw now that Della's simple use of his name bestowed a humanity on the man that the theft of his other names had tried to take from him.

Della's forehead kinked in a way he might have found adorable if he hadn't been concentrating on not being sick. "Alyas? It's his name."

"I know, I... I can't even think of him like that."

To Brivar, who had grown up in the strictly formal environment of Avarel society and then the temple, her casual use of the duke's birth name was almost as jarring as the way the duke referred to the king simply as Raffa.

She grinned. "He's not always so spiky. The last few weeks..." Her smiled slipped and she gave a small shrug. "And your cousin's presence is like constant pressure on a sore spot. He'll get over it."

Brivar wasn't so sure that was true, but he wasn't going to argue with her, mostly because his eyes were drifting closed again and he had no energy left.

※

Next time he woke, Della was gone and Cantrell was sitting opposite him, a tankard by his elbow. It was getting dark.

Brivar's raised his head from his chest, feeling the ache in his neck. He cautiously shifted his position to straighten his back, well-warned about the consequence of sudden movements. Even so he had several bad moments.

"We don't think they're broken," Cantrell said, a supportive hand on Brivar's elbow as he settled himself into a more comfortable position. "But you'll know best."

Brivar decided that determination could wait. Broken or merely bruised, his ribs were like a spear-thrust of agony in his chest. Cantrell sat back down, watching him with a faint smile.

The expression made him uncomfortable. "What are you doing?"

Speaking was an effort, each breath a new wound.

"Making sure you don't die in your sleep," Cantrell said cheerfully. "Here." He passed him the tankard.

Brivar took a tentative sniff, expecting wine and instead breathing in the nose-searing fumes of strong spirits. He thrust it back towards Cantrell. "Why?"

Cantrell held up his hands. "You saved his life. Do you think we would have less care for yours? Drink. It will take the edge off."

"Only until tomorrow," Brivar muttered, taking an experimental swallow and immediately choking. His ribs flared, the pain excruciating for a long second, his vision fading to black.

Cantrell had rescued the sloshing tankard and was back by his elbow, watching him with a sympathetic grimace. "Tomorrow can take care of itself. You don't have anything to do."

Which reminded him of the duke's extraordinary intervention and Della's assertion that he was now part of his household. "I am only an apprentice." Corado might be a vicious, half-Flaeresian bastard, but he wasn't wrong about that.

Cantrell shrugged, unconcerned. "What of it? I doubt Alondo will make any objection once he knows the facts. Besides, you can finish your apprenticeship—as long as you're there when we need you."

Brivar found the tankard back in his hand and took a long drink to hide his confusion. He didn't know whether to be grateful or offended that they should commandeer him so high-handedly.

It was getting chilly and the alcohol burned a warm trail to his belly. He passed the tankard to Cantrell, but it soon found its way back to him. And he had to admit, the warm buzz was taking the edge off his bruises.

Cantrell sat with him in companionable silence, occasionally taking a drink, but more often passing the tankard to Brivar untouched while he worked on a broken belt strap. At some point Brivar stopped noticing that he was the only one drinking. When it got too dark, the man lit an Isyrium bulb and continued his mending.

Brivar watched him, the pleasant glow of strong spirits melting his reserve. It loosened his tongue, too, made him bold. "Esar." He rolled the name on his tongue, shocked by his own daring.

Cantrell snorted. "That's it. You can do it."

"Esar," he said again. Then, "Did the king really marry the duke's wife?"

Cantrell's hand stilled. He looked up, his brow creased in a frown. "Did he say that?"

Brivar nodded. "Did he mean the queen? Was the duke married to the queen?" Even in his drowsy, drunken haze that didn't sound right.

"No," Cantrell said firmly, "he was not."

"Not the queen? Does the king have another wife? I mean, did he?"

Cantrell sighed heavily. He plucked the tankard from Brivar's hand and placed it out of his reach. "No. The king has just the one wife. Queen Mari-Geled. She has just the one husband, and if I were you, I would not speak of this again."

"But –"

"To anyone." He rose, taking the tankard with him. "Get some sleep."

ESAR CANTRELL

Esar Cantrell had cursed the name of Raffa-Herun Geled many times over the years. Fifteen years ago, he had even done so to his face. He was lucky to have survived that. But Alyas had dragged him out of there, white and shaking, before he could do worse than curse, Mari watching them, eyes wide with shock. He had never forgotten that. The look on her face.

He had cursed the king many times in the years that followed, as they travelled from place to place, as he risked his life in increasingly reckless endeavours beside a man who had no interest in living most days and sometimes was more alive than any person he had ever met. But they hadn't died. Instead they had prospered, the success of those first, rash escapades securing a reputation that had kept them in much more sober, less lethal work for more than a decade. He had cursed Raffa less in those years.

But he was cursing him again now, with a vengeance. It had been years since he had had to worry what might happen if he was not there. Until Flaeres, things had been good. The wound of names lost had scarred over, even the loss of Lankara had become a distant pain. All the rest of Ellasia was open to them, and they had replaced lost family with a new one, fiercely loyal, who did not care about scandals and disgrace that had happened so long ago and for whom a name was merely the thing you called yourself and not the embodiment of your worth.

Now they were headed back to that vipers' pit Avarel and everything they had put behind them was once more spreading its poison through their lives. It didn't matter that the reason was something they could not avoid—that they could not walk away from this—he would still blame Raffa, and curse him, because if he had never stabbed his best friend in the back, none of this would have happened.

He looked down at Alyas, sitting propped up in the corner of his sleeping platform. His eyes were closed and he looked exhausted, but he wasn't asleep.

"Raffa married your wife? Really?"

Alyas opened one eye. "How would you characterise it?"

"Not like that!" Esar exploded. "Ithol's balls, man, do you want to —"

He stopped, the words fading into an awkward silence.

Alyas was watching him with a troubled frown. "Is that what you think of me? Still?"

Esar ground his teeth, refusing to think about the na'quia and all the things he had thought were done that had reared their ugly heads again. "What am I supposed to think if you say things like that? We're going back to Avarel, man. She's been the queen for fifteen years."

Alyas sighed. He leant back, eyes slipping closed. "I'm not interested in Mari."

"No, you just want to needle Raffa, and I swear, Alyas, if you don't see sense, I'll beat it into you myself, if Corado doesn't do it first."

"You think he could?"

"Right now? I know he could. And then I'll have to kill him, and what kind of a mess would we be in then?"

Alyas's lips twitched. "Fine. But don't tell me you're not itching to kill him anyway."

Esar snorted. "That man always was an animal. He's not improved with age. Are you going to tell me what Ailuin wanted?"

The mood instantly darkened. "As we thought. It must be coming over the mountains from the north. They lost two to transformation. Three more died." His jaw tightened. "They had several sick. Brivar told them the cure. We came home."

Esar watched him steadily. "What else?"

"Nothing."

"You know I know when you're lying."

Only silence answered him, and Esar sighed. He looked at the sheathed blades lying on the bed. "Brivar—do you think he guessed?" The Lathai would not have hidden their Isyr. They refused to. "It is part of our way," Ailuin would reply whenever Alyas suggested it. That was a large part of why they were here. Why they allowed no one else to get close enough to the tribe to realise what they had. Greed wasn't just ugly. When Isyr was involved, it was also bloody.

"Possibly. Probably." Alyas sat forward, one arm massaging an aching neck. "He's sharp enough, but he was distracted."

Esar thought about that, and about Corado's corrosive hatred of the Lathai. If the Lankarans or anyone else ever discovered the tribe's secret, it would be more than they could do to protect them. If Brivar had realised… "I see why you had to take him, but that's a dangerous piece of knowledge to burden anyone with. And a problem we don't need."

"Brivar's with us now. If Corado goes near him again, I'll kill him. He knows it."

"And when Brivar goes back to the temple? What if he talks to Alondo?"

"I think he'll come to us before then, and if he doesn't… well, we have time to think about it. It's two weeks to Avarel. Besides, it's not Alondo we need to worry about."

Esar raised an eyebrow. "Not the temples? Are you feeling all right? They burn through Isyrium faster than anyone, even the bloody king."

"I know," Alyas sighed, looking away. "Do you ever wonder… I always thought it was about Mari, but what if he knew? What if that's what all this was about?"

"You think Raffa knew about the Lathai and Isyr? No." Esar shook his head. "You think he would have stopped there? That he would have let you protect them all these years? If he—if *any*one knew— these mountains would have been overrun with kingdom troops years ago." Or worse.

But they would have been—if Alyas had obeyed the king's orders. When Raffa had sent them to deal with the Lathai, only six months after Alyas's father had killed himself so publicly, it felt like a mission dreamt up to get him out of Avarel and give him something else to do, something else to think about. And it had been. They had only been wrong about why.

These mountains had changed hands between Lankara and Flaeres a dozen times in the last hundred years. They meant little to either kingdom except pride. They were wild, dangerous, and home to a tribe that resisted all attempts at assimilation. But when tensions between the two rival nations soured, they would clash across the border, let off steam by killing a few hundred of each other and the Lathai, then make peace and go back to sniping from afar. So, when Raffa sent Alyas out specifically to subdue to Lathai, they had assumed it was the king's attempt to shake him out of the grief that followed his father's death.

Seeing little point in making war on a people who had no interest in fighting them just so his friends were not forced to watch his downward spiral, Alyas had done the opposite of what he had been ordered and not a life had been lost. But when he had presented the peace treaty to the king, Raffa's rage had been beyond anything, and he was a man given to passionate rages. On the spot, he had stripped Alyas of everything he had—the man who had been his closest friend—and banished him from Lankara.

It hadn't made sense until later, when they heard the king had taken for himself the Agrathon estates and everything that went with them, including Mari-Geled, the woman to whom Alyas had been betrothed since the age of ten, who had grown up with them after her parents died, who was as close to them as a sister. Well, it had made sense to Esar. Alyas was mostly drunk in those days, or trying to get himself killed, and what he thought about it was anyone's guess.

Could it have been about Isyr after all? Kings had done much worse for less, and that was the greatest prize of them all. The Lathai's wealth in Isyr steel—that pure, priceless, lost form of Isyrium—made Alyas's blade seem like trinkets. And Raffa had always coveted those.

"No," Esar said again. "That makes no sense."

Alyas had his head in his hands. He looked up at Esar through splayed fingers. "But what happened to the army? If it was for Mari… why did he need to do that?"

If it had been for Mari, Esar reflected bitterly and not for the first time, he could have just asked. The breaking of an engagement of such long standing would have been a scandal, but nothing that hadn't happened before, and the king rarely cared about scandal. There was great fondness between Alyas and Mari, but it did not go deeper. He would not have stood in their way if that was what they both wanted. But the army…

"I don't know," Esar said carefully. That was dangerous territory, even now, fifteen years later. Four hundred men had gone into the mountains with them. Four hundred men had trusted them, and had vanished from the barracks outside Avarel and were never heard from again. The rumour had reached them nearly a year later. The lie. That Alyas had taken that army into battle against the Lathai and lost them to a man. That the king, in his grief for those loyal men, had exiled the Duke of Agrathon and struck his names from the scrolls as a punishment.

That had been a bad day, Esar remembered, and it had been followed by a lot of bad days. It was the root of Lankaran hatred of the Lathai, whom they had previously regarded with curiosity. It had also, ultimately, led them back to where it had all started, where they were now, and to the secret they had spent the last ten years protecting.

"Four hundred men," Alyas said. "Why?"

"Stop it," Esar snapped. "They're gone. It's done. There are others relying on you now. Think about how you're going to protect them, because Corado is not alone. There will be thousands like him back in Avarel, who think like him and hate like him, and our people will be a target."

Alyas's mouth thinned. "Do you really think I would put them at risk? Until we know what Raffa wants—until we know we can trust him—they stay here."

"They do, do they?" Esar demanded, arms crossed. "Then who's going to protect *you*?"

Alyas flashed him a smile that didn't quite reach his eyes. "You are."

Esar threw up his hands. "Yholis preserve me, why do I stay?"

rivar's injuries delayed their departure by another three days, a decision that enraged the king's envoy and his guard captain. Alyas dealt with their furious objections much as he had dealt with their arrival, only this time he did it publicly. It was a sight Esar would have enjoyed a lot more if he hadn't known Alyas was deliberately provoking Corado, and doing it when he was still in no fit state to deal with the consequences if he succeeded in pushing him over the edge. And that was coming. It was only a matter of time.

Privately, Esar thought Brivar probably could have ridden after two days if they didn't push too hard, but the delay wasn't only about giving him time to heal. Alyas was making it clear to anyone who didn't already realise it exactly who was in charge, because once they left they couldn't afford any misunderstandings. Part of the company would be with them part of the way, but Alyas would take them no closer to Avarel than Orleas. The ghosts of the four hundred would not permit it. And after Orleas, they would have only the Lankarans' fear of him—and the much less certain promise of Raffa's favour—to protect them. The prospect was not filling Esar with joy.

"Did you never think we might need allies?" Esar asked Alyas after he had sent Sul-Barin away raw and bleeding for the second time.

"I've thought about it," Alyas agreed. "And we don't need a man who would stand by and let Corado loose on his own kin."

Which was a fair point, but not *the* point. "You didn't have to make him an enemy."

"At least we know he *is* an enemy. That's more than we can say of anyone else in Avarel. Make sure Brivar stays with our people. I don't want him anywhere near his cousin or Corado."

A more cynical person than Esar—and there must be some; Ellasia was a big continent—might have assumed that by keeping Brivar close, Alyas was protecting the knowledge he may or may not have gained from the Lathai. But Esar had seen his fury after Corado's savage attack; he saw it every time Alyas pushed the man one step closer to violence. He liked the boy, and Yholis knew, he owed him. If he guarded Brivar now, it was not only to protect the Lathai.

Still, that too sent a message, and Alyas's novel brand of peacekeeping held the balance until their departure and throughout the first four days of their journey. It wasn't until they were clear of the mountains and onto the plains that it all broke apart.

It was Della who brought word of the massacre. She appeared on the road in front of them, alone, quite still except for her eyes. Alyas dismounted and approached her, waving the others back. Esar had to restrain Brivar from going after him. A surgeon's trained observation was more than capable of reading her shock. Whatever it was, it was bad.

They spoke for a few minutes. Esar saw the muscles in Alyas's shoulders tighten, and turned to give quiet orders to Agazi, who nodded and spurred back down the line. Their people were good; they knew what to do.

When Alyas signalled, two groups were already moving forward. He sent them on, each circling round from a different direction to find and reinforce the scouts already out there. When Della moved to join them, he shook his head, leading her back to where Brivar was bouncing anxiously on his horse. She had a wild look about her, one that Esar recognised from their frantic retreat in Flaeres when they had encountered creatures out of a nightmare.

"What is it?" He had a horrible feeling he already knew.

"Mining outpost," Alyas said grimly, as Della mounted his horse. "Wiped out. They're still in there." Alyas looked up at Brivar's frightened face. "Stay here with Della. We'll send for you when it's safe."

Della, her colour returning, took the reins from Brivar's slack hands and led the horses off the road. Alyas was already moving away, giving orders, and Esar signed a question to Della. She nodded and he swore. *They're still in there.*

He caught up with Alyas, crouched in the middle of a knot of his officers, sketching his instructions into the dust of the track, Corado looming over them. Esar ignored his glare and concentrated on what Alyas was saying. The scouts had come across a handful of survivors fleeing south. They had gone to investigate, cautiously, and confirmed the wild tale. Much as he wished otherwise, Esar knew they could not skirt safely around this. They had to go in. They could not allow what was in the town to get out, to spread its poison further. Preventing that was why Raffa had finally rescinded Alyas's exile. Not that they were doing it for him.

As Alyas relayed Della's intelligence, he gave his orders, and Esar was relieved. He was playing it safe. Still, the faces of their people reflected the reality—they knew what they were up against.

"We've done this before," Alyas reminded them. "We know what they can do. We take no chances. They're still there, we burn them out. Do not engage directly unless you have to. Do not let them touch you, and let nothing out. Do you understand?"

They nodded. They understood, Esar thought grimly. They remembered Flaeres and what had come after.

Alyas stood and came face to face with Corado's hostile sneer, planted firmly in his path.

"Corado –"

"They probably drank too much moonshine and ran from their own shadows. We're a hundred miles inside the border. There's no monsters here."

"Take your men round to the south," Alyas told him. "Block the road. Nothing gets out."

The man dug in his heels and crossed his arms. "So your girl saw something that spooked her. That doesn't mean shit. This is a Lankaran mine—a syndicate mine. We're not torching a syndicate mine because a girl got scared."

"Get your men into position," Alyas snarled. "Do it now."

Corado spat. "Make me."

There was a moment of silence. Then Alyas said, "Shoot him."

Esar heard the creak of the bow as Lord Sul kicked his horse forward. "You can't!"

Alyas turned to face him. "Why not?"

"Because he is a Lankaran officer, commissioned by the king, and I will not permit it!"

Corado's mouth twisted into a triumphant sneer. Alyas shook his head. "Shoot him," he said again, turning away.

Corado lunged. Alyas had been expecting it. His elbow caught the guard captain in the side of the head, dropping him in the dirt. His foot came down on the wrist of Corado's knife hand, grinding with his heel until his fingers released their grip. He kicked the weapon away. Esar stooped to pick it up, meeting Alyas's eyes as he did so. There was no need for his warning.

Alyas stepped back and Corado rolled over onto his knees, his wrist cradled against his chest and loathing in his eyes.

Alyas looked up into Lord Sul's shocked face. "If he's a kingdom officer, ensure he behaves like one. That means obeying orders. My orders." To Corado, as he staggered to his feet, he snapped, "Your men, Captain. In position, now."

Corado bared his teeth in a snarl. "Next time, Raine Sera."

Alyas showed his own teeth. "Next time you won't get a warning."

Esar held out the knife and Corado snatched it from his hands. At least six bows were trained on him. "You too, Cantrell."

"Any time, Corado."

"Your men," Alyas said. "Now."

Eyes burning with hatred, Corado gave the order, and his men stirred from their shock. Esar noted the looks that were thrown Alyas's way as they moved to obey, a mix of hostility and veiled approval. Not all the Lankarans were firmly behind Corado, but there were plenty who needed watching.

He said to Alyas, faintly accusing, "You enjoyed that."

"That man wants me dead."

"You threatened to kill him first," Esar pointed out.

"No, I threatened to execute him. Next time, I will."

"The sooner the better. The man's a canker. Alyas, Flaeres –"

Alyas stopped. "You don't… I remember."

"Do you?" Esar asked. His own memories were muddled enough, and he hadn't been semi-conscious and bleeding all over the place. But he would never forget the single-minded nature of that attack. How the creatures kept coming, relentless in their efforts to reach Alyas. In the end, they had set the fire that had saved them and given them time to withdraw. They were lucky it had not been later in the season, when the grasslands of northern Flaeres were tinder-dry and the fires could rage out of control for days. King Diago might not have been quite so grateful if they had devastated an entire region.

"Stay behind," he said now. "There's no need to come." They did not know why he had been a target. What was the sense in risking it a second time?

"Yes, there is," Alyas retorted, his eyes on Corado's retreating back.

"Fuck him," Esar said with feeling. "He makes trouble, I'll kill him."

Alyas swung round. "You won't touch him! We don't know what Raffa's game is. I won't risk putting you at his mercy. When Corado dies, it'll be by my hand or at my orders. If he didn't execute me for four hundred deaths, one more won't make a difference."

It was an argument Esar would not win. "Fine. Just be careful."

❧

They found two of their scouts with a frightened huddle of survivors, the mining foreman and a family from the town. Alyas listened patiently to their jumbled account, then ordered the scouts to take the family back to where Brivar and Della were waiting with the horses. The children were mute with terror, their bare legs scratched raw by their flight. Esar prayed to Yholis that none of the bleeding cuts had been caused during the attack. You couldn't subject a child na'quia.

The foreman hugged his arms to his chest and watched them leave, but he nodded when Alyas asked him to accompany them to the town. They needed someone who knew the layout.

They spread out around the outskirts of the settlement, unimaginatively named after the huge outcrop of grey rock in whose shadow it was built. *They're still in there.* And there they had to stay. This corruption, this sickness—whatever it was—it spread too fast, too easily. They had to stop it here; they had to burn it out. And if it had spread... If it had spread, oh mercy, he did not want to think about what they might have to do then. He never wanted to think about it.

The town, when they reached it, was like something from a nightmare. It was Flaeres all over again. Esar looked at the remains of what had once been a prosperous mining outpost and could see how it had happened as if he had been there—the wave coming at them, again and again, driving them back, taking a few more each time, herding them together, cutting them off, before finally breaking over them. And what it had left in its wake... Somewhere behind him the foreman was being messily sick.

He glanced at Alyas, saw the lines around his mouth, the tightly clenched jaw. Esar didn't know how much he remembered of that bloody, desperate fight in Flaeres. They had left the bodies of too many of their own behind that day, protecting him, bodies that had been mauled and mutilated as these had been. They had seen some bad things in their time. They had been the cause of some of them. But nothing like this.

There would be no sick here for Brivar to treat, no injuries to mend. If anyone was still alive in this mess, they would burn with the bodies, because there was no way they were sending anyone in there to find out.

Dark shapes moved among the dead. *There are no monsters here*, Corado had said. Well, there were. He was looking at them.

"Yholis, that's Gregan," the foreman sobbed. "That's my brother."

Esar shot him an appalled look. 'Gregan' was on all fours in the carnage, his skin mottling from white to blue to black like the corruption of a wound gone bad, spreading its poison through him, changing him. He had once had a name; now he wouldn't even recognise it. All around him were other changed things, men, women, children—Yholis have mercy, there were children here—and weaving between them the smaller forms of dogs, rats, and wild creatures from the plains. And everywhere they went, whatever they touched, they left it starting to sicken and die, changing like they had changed.

"Alyas," he urged. They needed to torch this place and be done. They had seen all they needed to see.

There was no answer.

A creature raised its head. It sniffed the air, head swinging from side to side like it was trying to track a scent.

"Alyas," Esar warned, fingers clenched around his hilt.

The head whipped round to stare directly at where they were hidden.

Movement beside him. "Burn it."

A dozen arrows soaked in Isyrium and burning with blue flame plunged into the ravaged town. Clay jars followed, smashing where they hit and spilling their volatile contents into the Isyrium-set fire. More arrows, from the south this time. Corado's men. Flames were rising at the eastern side of the settlement where Agazi's men had been stationed, pockets of cleansing fire amid this violation.

As one, the creatures recoiled. Monsters they might be, but they were alive and so they feared fire. A convulsion rippled through their hordes and a cry went up that froze Esar to his bones.

Every head turned to where they stood. He felt the fear yawn deep and ugly, the urge to run an instinct so primal it almost won, right there.

Then the flames roared, the scattering of smaller fires leaping up into one huge conflagration, blue-white and furious.

Alyas hefted a clay jar and hurled it with careful precision into the centre of that tower of flame. The Isyrium inside it ignited with a soundless thunderclap and a flash that left its imprint on Esar's vision. He followed it with another, and another after that, until the flames were thirty feet high and in danger of engulfing more than just the town.

They were lucky it was spring and the ground was wet and the air still. The fire devoured its Isyrium fuel, burning up in white-hot fury and down to ashes within the hour, controlled and deadly. They waited as it burned itself out, and any charred thing that managed to crawl out of its edges they dispatched without mercy, no matter what it had been before. And when everything was black and grey and smouldering, they walked through the scorched town, the burn of hot ash under their boots, and made sure that every living thing was now dead.

Esar saw Corado standing at the end of what had once been the main street before they had torched it. For the first time since their paths had crossed again, his face did not carry its customary sneer. Smudged in ash, he looked as shocked as any of them. Then his wandering gaze fastened on Alyas and the hate flooded back into his eyes. There would be so many more like him in Avarel. Each of those four hundred had left family and friends behind.

As Corado stalked to where Alyas was talking to the shaken foreman, Esar changed course to do the same.

Alyas lifted his head at Esar's approach, and after a look at his face turned in time to meet Corado's blistering anger head on. Only this time it was not directed at him, but at the foreman.

"What did you do?" Corado shouted, lunging for the man, and

only Alyas's hand on his chest prevented him from trying to throttle an answer out of him.

Esar quickened his pace, a sharp signal bringing several of their people in his wake.

"Out of my way, Raine Sera," Corado snarled, hand on his sword.

Alyas shook his head. "Back off, Corado." The words were hard, but they lacked the provocative edge Esar was used to hearing, as though he recognised that even Corado was allowed to be a little unhinged by this.

It was more understanding than Esar would have offered him and as he inserted himself between them, he let Corado see it. The man glared at him, his eyes as hot as the fire that had devoured the town. He pointed at the foreman. "He did this!"

The man in question was sobbing, his face a mess of tear-tracked ash. *That's my brother.*

"We don't know what happened here," Alyas told Corado in a steady voice. "We'll find out, I promise you."

"I don't need the promises of a traitor," Corado growled, but the manic edge had receded, replaced by something Esar liked even less. "Kill him, now. He's tainted. We can't risk it."

Alyas heard it too. His eyes narrowed. "No one's killing him. He's a witness. Do you understand?"

There was a moment when Esar thought Corado would take matters into his own hands, and he tensed to stop him, then the guard captain backed off a step and spat a gob of blackened saliva into the ash. "A witness," he agreed. And by Ithol's blood, Esar did not like the look on his face.

He stayed planted between them as Alyas turned back to the foreman. "You said they came from the east of the town. Will you show me?"

The man gave a barely coherent nod, his eyes straying from Alyas to Corado, but he didn't move. His features had a slackness that suggested deep shock, and Esar couldn't blame him.

Alyas put a hand on the man's shoulder, said in a calm voice, "It's over. They're gone. But we need to understand how this happened. Then we'll take you away from here."

The man nodded again, arms hugging himself as if his life depended on it. He turned and started stumbling down the road towards the mine.

Alyas took a step after him and stopped. Corado blocked his path.

"Where you go, I go, Raine Sera. If he's a witness, so am I."

"Like hell you are," Esar retorted. "You're staying right here where I can see you."

"What's wrong, Cantrell?" Corado sneered, getting up into his face. "Worried he can't take care of himself?"

"Esar," Alyas said.

"Esar, Esar," Corado taunted, his name an obscene caress. "I'm a kingdom officer, which is more than he is. I go, or no one goes. The king needs a witness, and it's not going to be him."

"He's right," a shaky voice informed them, and Esar saw Lord Sul picking his way towards them, his face bleached of colour. "I speak for the king. Corado goes. As my witness."

"Then so do I," Esar said, staring his own challenge into Corado's mad eyes.

"Esar…"

"Fuck it, Alyas. If he's going, so am I."

Alyas nodded towards where their guide had veered off course and was now weaving his way as fast as he could towards the southern road, his desperation to escape the town winning out over his resolve. Esar swore and whistled, and two of Agazi's squad moved to intercept him.

Alyas turned back to Corado. "You and one other," he said. "Two of us, and two of you."

Corado gave a mocking salute and called one of his men over. He was far too pleased with himself.

"He'll make his move soon," Esar muttered as he fell into step beside Alyas.

Alyas didn't look at him. "I know."

They retrieved their guide from Agazi's men and calmed him down, but the nervous looks he shot Corado were testament to the fact that he maintained his faculties despite his shock. He was quite sensibly terrified of the man.

Alyas placed himself between the foreman and Corado, and a constant stream of questions kept the man's attention away from the guard captain. Esar looked at the ominous black mouth of the mine as they passed, overturned carts spilling their precious cargo amid a tangle of bodies, and tried not to imagine the horror of that first attack. He turned away. They would come back with fire and burn this too before they were done.

But this horror had not come out of the mine, the foreman told them, and they were a mile past the entrance when Esar became aware that something was *not right*.

Alyas had stopped talking and Esar could see the tension building as his back stiffened. When the foreman stopped, pointing ahead and gibbering incoherently about Isyrium ore and some kind of accident, Alyas barely seemed to notice. It was left to Esar to calm the man and untangle his confused explanations. Not that it made much sense to him. He was not a miner, and all he knew about Isyrium ore in the days since its purity had degraded was that it had to be refined by some alchemical process before it was usable. What the foreman was trying to tell them now was that the waste products of that process were usually transported elsewhere for disposal, but the mine had been too productive and whatever arrangement had been made was insufficient to take it all. Rather than slow their mining operation when they had such demand to meet, they had buried it instead. Up ahead.

"How long?" Alyas asked, his voice a harsh scrape. His face was very pale. "How long have you been burying it?"

The man shook his head, his eyes wild, pushed beyond the ability for sensible communication. Esar gave up, more concerned about whatever was bothering Alyas, and he missed the moment the man made his bid for freedom. He grabbed for him as he darted away, but the foreman twisted like an eel and evaded his grasp.

Alyas snapped out of his daze to shout, "No!" as Corado's knife took the foreman in the back, dropping him midstride.

Alyas whirled on him, breathing hard, anger and something else in his eyes. Then he winced, rolling his left shoulder, and inexplicably *let it go*. Esar was so surprised he almost killed Corado on reflex.

Alyas turned away from Corado's triumphant smirk. "We look, we leave. Understood?"

"Understood," Corado sneered, pushing ahead, the Lankaran guardsman hurrying in his wake.

Esar studied Alyas, worried now. "What is it?"

He shook his head. "We look, we leave," he repeated, following after Corado.

They didn't have to go far. The track took them to the edge of the old quarry where the miners had been burying the Isyrium waste, but even before they reached it, Esar knew what they would find. Tendrils of blue-black corruption snaked across the path under his feet, growing denser and darker the closer they came, whole patches of undergrowth blackened and dead. And when they reached the quarry itself...

"Yholis have mercy," he breathed, horrified. "What happened here?"

If the town had been sickened, this place was dead. Worse than dead. The corruption leaking into the ground they had walked had its heart here, in this abomination. Standing on the rim of the pit, Esar felt he was teetering on the edge of hell itself. The earth and everything that had grown on it wasn't just dead, it was desecrated, deformed, corrupted by the poison spewing from the makeshift waste pits. Around the lip of one he could see the remains of lead sheeting, evidence that the miners had at least tried to contain the filth that had polluted this place and turned its inhabitants into monsters, but whether they had been careless, or the stuff itself had eaten through the lead as it had eaten through everything else, he could not guess. He did not want to try.

No one answered him, the awful silence punctuated only by Alyas's harsh, shallow breathing. It sounded wrong. Esar turned in time to throw his arm out as the other man staggered back, his face grey and his hand pressed to his chest.

He looked at Esar, panic in his eyes. "I can't…"

That look… he had never once seen Alyas panic.

Something slammed into him from behind and he lost his grip on Alyas as he fell to the ground, pain exploding across his back. He had taken his eyes off Corado! The world faded out of focus as his face hit dirt and the breath slammed out of him. For several seconds his chest was an airless agony, then his body took a great heaving gasp and he was rolling over and up, looking desperately for Alyas.

Corado had him by the throat. His lips were blue.

Esar lurched to his feet. His sword came free with a metallic scrape. Corado heard it and dropped Alyas, who collapsed to the ground like all his strings had been cut. He wasn't moving, and suddenly Esar was pure rage. He threw himself at Corado, sending them both sprawling to the ground, his sword forgotten in the blue dust as he used his fists to take out his fury.

Sense returned. His fists were screaming and raw. Corado's shattered face leered up at him, broken nose running with blood, blood in his mouth, a fleck of tooth on his chin. He choked, his breath wheezing through his ruined teeth, and Esar realised with horror that he was *laughing*. Disgusted, sick to his stomach, he shoved himself off the man's chest, staggering away.

For the second time that day he took his eyes off Corado when he really shouldn't have. The tackle took him at the knees, bringing him down hard, and then it was his back against the ground and Corado on top of him, and *he* hadn't forgotten *his* weapon. But as Corado drew back his dagger, he jerked, and Esar barely managed to throw his head to one side to avoid the knife as the captain's body collapsed on top of him.

Warm blood soaked his chest. Revolted, suffocating, he heaved the body to the side and crawled out from under it, breathing in hard, sharp gasps. The hilt of Alyas's Isyr dagger stood out between Corado's shoulder blades.

A shaky voice invoked Yholis's mercy.

"Not for him," Esar growled, looking up at the Lankaran guardsman. "She's got better things to do."

The Lankaran made the sign of the temple, though whether that was for Corado's benefit or his own, Esar couldn't guess. Little more than a boy, his face was slack-jawed with shock, one hand frozen on the hilt of his sword. Just as well. If he had helped his captain, there could have been a very different outcome. If Esar hadn't been distracted, if Alyas hadn't... He twisted, searching for his brother. He was on his knees where Corado had dropped him, listing to one side, the hand that had thrown the dagger braced against the ground.

"You're a witness," Esar said savagely to the stunned Lankaran. He staggered over to Alyas and lifted him unprotesting from his knees. "He attacked us, unprovoked."

The boy nodded, eyes rivetted on Corado's corpse. Esar bent down and pulled Alyas's blade from his back. The blood slid off the Isyr steel like oil on water and he slid it carefully into its sheathe at its owner's hip before adjusting Alyas's arm over his shoulder.

The Lankaran called after him. "Are we... are we leaving him?"

"He can rot here for all I care. You want him, you can bring him. I'm not touching him again."

And he wasn't waiting around for the man to make up his mind, too aware of the silent presence hanging by his side, too frightened by what he had seen and didn't understand.

It was hard going for the first fifty paces, Alyas almost a dead weight against him, his breathing too rapid, his legs barely participating in the effort to walk. But the further they went, the steadier his steps became and the less weight Esar had to shoulder, until after a couple of minutes he pushed himself free and staggered to a stop, hands resting on his knees.

Esar looked him over, from the whiteness round his eyes to the red marks at this throat and the braced hands that ran with tremors. "What happened? What was that?"

Alyas eyes met his. The raw panic was gone, but a shadow of it remained. "That place. I couldn't breathe. It was like…"

"Like what?"

He shook his head, turning away. They stood like that for a few moments, neither speaking. Then the Lankaran appeared at a stumbling run on the track behind them, Corado's body abandoned, and Alyas said, a little desperately, "I need…"

"What?" Esar asked, beyond worried now. "What do you need?"

"To go." And he did.

"How do you feel now?" Brivar asked.

They had been back with the main company for hours but only now did they have a measure of privacy. With the day drawing to a close, Alyas had wanted the company camped as far from the mine as possible, and the ugly confrontation with the Lankarans on their return had been a delay they did not need. Esar had posted guards outside the tent, and it wasn't just their privacy he wanted to protect. The mood was dangerous.

Brivar, his face still patterned with fading bruises, had listened to Esar's account of what had happened, and now he was studying Alyas with an expression Esar did not like.

"Fine. Like it never happened. Tired."

He did seem fine, Esar conceded, apart from the red mottling around his throat that was starting to darken. By the time they had returned to the town he had regained his composure and had overseen the withdrawal of their company to where they were now camped. He had even stood down the fury of the Lankarans at the death of their captain, and endured Lord Sul's tirade on the retrieval of Corado's body with something approximating patience. Whatever it was that had affected him at the quarry, it had passed almost as quickly as it had come on, but it had been *something*. Brivar was here now because even Alyas couldn't dismiss it.

There was a pause. Then Brivar said, "What aren't you telling me?"

The silence that answered him was hardly a surprise. Esar crossed his arms and glared down at Alyas, which had as much effect as it usually did. His face was closed tight. Brivar was right. There was something else.

Never a particularly patient man, Esar could feel his temper fraying. Brivar, with more forbearance, said, "I can't help you if you won't talk to me."

Alyas sighed, his head in his hands. "I can't explain it."

"Try," Esar growled.

"I don't think you want me to," Alyas retorted, looking up. "Do you want me to say that I felt like I could hear them—their voices, their presence? *In me.* You don't want to hear that, Esar."

Esar felt cold. He didn't. Not again.

I can still hear them, Alyas had said on waking from na'quia, only half aware. *I can still feel them. They are quieter, but they are not gone.*

And so much worse, *I thought I would be free.*

He remembered his foster father, the old duke, standing in the arming room as Esar helped him buckle on the blades that Alyas now wore. *They won't leave me alone*, he had said, staring at nothing. *Why won't they leave me alone?* Then he had gone out into the arena without another word, and he was dead before Esar had even taken his seat in the stands. Old memories. Bad memories. Suddenly too close.

Brivar, his face rather pale, crouched beside the cot on which Alyas was perched. "You said there was pain. Where? In the wound? Lower down?" His hand touched his chest, above his heart.

Alyas flinched, pulling away. "I… I don't remember."

"Why?" Esar demanded, lurching from one crisis to the next. "What are you getting at?"

"I don't know." Brivar looked frustrated and worried. "There can be side effects of na'quia. We don't know enough about it yet. Before this, no one survived poisoning with na'quia, so when it does… damage… we don't know whether it is permanent or just a short-lived impairment."

Esar stared at him. "Damage? What kind of damage?"

Brivar spared him a distracted glance. He was concentrating on Alyas, who was watching him with *that* look on his face, the one Esar really hated, that shut out everyone and everything. "We know na'quia targets the heart and lungs; that's how it kills. But it also affects the brain—the hallucinations. So, it's possible…" His voice trailed away unhappily in the uncomfortable silence.

Esar drew a hand over his face, hiding behind it for a precious moment.

"But it's also possible… Would you go back, tomorrow? To where this happened?"

Esar dropped his hand. "What for?"

"To see if it happens again."

"Why?" he demanded after a glance at Alyas's blank face. "Why would it happen again?"

"It seems certain there is some connection between this sickness and Isyrium," Brivar said, his eyes still on Alyas. That was an understatement, Esar thought, given what they had seen today—what they were all avoiding because it was too big, too hard, to confront. "But there is also a connection between Isyrium and na'quia. Maybe it can explain this. When you were in Flaeres, were you by a mine or a processing centre?"

Alyas shook his head. "I don't think so."

But that wasn't quite true, Esar realised. There were no active Isyrium mines in that region of Flaeres, but there had been once. "Yes, we were. Orsena used to be a mining town."

Brivar was nodding, a spark of excitement in his eyes. "Na'quia only grows near Isyrium mines, and you and all the Lathai who were ill—you all wear Isyr steel. We do not yet understand why some people transform and others sicken and die, nor why the illness takes some more quickly than others. It might be chance. The same disease that kills one person can leave another only mildly unwell. But it might not be chance. Perhaps Isyr is the key."

Esar shrugged. "Or it could be coincidence." Half the Lathai wore

Isyr. In the mountains, possession of it was not the rarity it was in Avarel and elsewhere.

Alyas said quietly, "It's not. It draws them in—the Isyr. It attracts them."

Esar's eyes narrowed. "How do you know?"

"Because when I was without it, they did not come straight for me."

They both stared at him. Esar pinched the bridge of his nose in despair. "I know I'm going to regret asking this, but what are you talking about?"

Alyas looked at Brivar. "The day we met. You told me to pick blue star-violet. I meant to, but…"

I had more urgent priorities, Alyas had said. They had suspected the infection was spreading across the mountains from Flaeres. Ailuin had confirmed it, but it seemed likely now that Alyas had already known. And Esar could have throttled him—for going out there in the first place, for nearly giving Esar a heart attack when he had found out, and for not bloody talking to him.

Brivar frowned at the memory. "You had the blades with you—I saw them."

Alyas shook his head. "I had plain steel on me that day."

"Why?"

The hesitation was longer this time, deeper. And Esar did not miss the way Alyas avoided his eyes when he finally said, "Because some days I cannot bear to wear them, and since… since it happened, it is worse."

The tent suddenly felt very crowded, the old duke's unquiet ghost filling the space between them, and Esar wished the bloody man was still alive so he could kill him himself. He wished Raffa had taken the Isyr weapons along with everything else. But Alyas would have murdered him if he tried, and everyone in that room had known it. So when he had stopped wearing them every day, when he occasionally put them aside, Esar had thought it a good thing, and he had not dared question it in case he upset whatever delicate peace had been achieved.

Brivar, who had no such history to stop his tongue and the peculiar ability to ask the awkward questions, said, "Why? Why can't you wear them?"

Fifteen years, Esar thought in frustration. It had been fifteen bloody years and they had never talked about this. Oh, he had tried a few times in the early months, and later, whenever Alyas was drunk enough to drop his guard, but mention his father or those wretched blades and he closed up tighter than a clam. After all this time, Esar didn't think he was capable of talking about it, but it turned out he had just been asking the wrong questions.

As though he could feel his thoughts, Alyas looked up, rueful apology in his eyes. "Because they make me feel things, things I don't understand, and I don't know how to explain it."

Brivar was still crouched by the cot, a position that must be hell on his bruised ribs. "Like what you felt today?"

Alyas nodded. "Like that, but the blades don't cause me pain. And since Flaeres, until you came—until the na'quia—it was unbearable. Like there were voices in me, but I couldn't understand them. And they were *screaming*. But the na'quia—it quietened them."

Esar felt sick, listening to that. The na'quia had been bad enough, but he had managed to convince himself that was hallucinations caused by the poison. This—he didn't want to deal with this. He didn't know *how*. Which, of course, was why Alyas had never told him. And now, after all those years of not talking, Esar just wanted him to *stop*.

"At first, I thought it was my memories. They were all I had left... of him. I tried to ignore it, to drown it out, but it was always back again when I woke up. Then I thought it was me..." He stopped, drawing his hands over his face. "I think my father heard them too. I think that's why he killed himself. I thought..."

"That whatever was wrong with him, was wrong with you too?"

Brivar asked when Alyas couldn't finish. Then, in a tone that was at odds with the confession he had just heard, "But that's the wrong question. Not whether you are like your father, but why you are like him. And now we know. It's not you. It's this." He tapped his finger against the blade of the rapier, lying innocuously next to its paired dagger. "It's Isyr."

❦

They went back, the three of them, in the morning before the camp was fully awake. It was obvious Alyas did not want to, but Brivar was adamant that they needed to be sure. They took the horses, and it was a good thing they did. Whatever it was, it came on quicker this time. They had barely got past the mine before Alyas was clearly in pain. They never even made it to the quarry. It didn't fade as fast either. Brivar, worried and apologetic, forced him to drink something when they got back to the camp and made him lie down. He also took the blades. More shockingly, Alyas let him.

Esar looked at the Isyr weapons with revulsion. "Throw the bloody things away."

Alyas shook his head helplessly and Brivar said, "No."

"No?" He had expected Alyas to refuse, but Brivar? "You heard him—you saw him. They did that to him."

"We don't actually know that," Brivar said. "All we know for certain is that something in the quarry caused the reaction we saw today, and yesterday. We do not yet know what that has to do with the effects of Isyr. If we get rid of them now, we never will."

There was logic in that, Esar had to admit, but Brivar hadn't watched the man he had called his father for most of his life kill himself because of those blades. He would not understand the deep-rooted fear Alyas's confession had stoked. Never understanding why they did what they did seemed a small price to pay for *making it stop*. But he knew that argument would go nowhere so he tried another.

"If you're right, and these things are attracted to Iysr, then we're walking around with a bloody beacon. It's going to lure them straight to us. You can't take them into Avarel." Not if the blades would draw these creatures. There were tens of thousands of people in Avarel.

"Avarel is full of Isyr," Brivar pointed out. "All the cities are—all Ellasia is. We cannot get rid of it all, and we need to understand why this is happening if we want it to stop."

Esar glared at him. He had forgotten what the temples were like. They wanted to know everything. If there was something they didn't know or couldn't explain, they could be relentless in pursuit of it—or they suppressed it. But Brivar wasn't just a temple surgeon, he reminded himself. Alyas had made him part of his household, and he had already shown they could trust him.

"Then why take them now?"

Brivar looked down at the weapons in his hands. "Because…"

Because for all that you don't want them anywhere near him either. It was a compromise he would have to live with. "Fine. Keep them." And Brivar scurried out before he could change his mind.

Alyas, one arm draped over his eyes, appeared to be asleep. But as Esar followed Brivar, he said, "What are they doing with the rest?"

What indeed? The disaster they had stumbled on here had happened because one mining operation had been greedy and sloppy and had buried its waste on its own doorstep. But where should it have gone, and what happened to it when it got there? And what about all the other thousands of Isyrium mines in Ellasia?

Esar couldn't stop thinking about that as he took a party out to the quarry. He couldn't stop thinking about it as they soaked the place in Isyrium and set flames to it. The question worried its way through his thoughts as they did the same to the mine, using the last of their fuel to turn the bodies to ash and burn out the corruption that had infected the town.

It was still bothering him when he returned to the scorched settlement and found Alyas, awake and alert, directing the construction of firebreaks along the southern edge of the town. There were still smouldering pockets of heat in the blackened ruins. If they reignited and the wind picked up, the fire could spread south across the plains towards the larger towns.

The Lankarans were standing in a moody group around Lord Sul-Barin, watching the company work. The furious aftermath of Corado's death had died to a sullen simmer. No one had liked him, but he had been their captain and his death drove the wedge deeper between the two groups. They were lucky the surviving guardsman had been too shocked to dissemble. Where his comrades would never have taken Alyas's word for what happened, even with the marks of Corado's attack clearly visible, they had appeared to accept the guardsman's shaken account. But Esar dared not hope that would be the end of it. Raffa's lies had gone deep. Too much anger and resentment lay between them.

He eyed the Lankarans warily as he joined Alyas. "Any trouble?"

"Not yet. They don't know whether to be outraged or relieved. Give them a chance and they'll realise they're better off without him."

His voice was still raspy from Corado's assault, but he otherwise appeared recovered. Esar, his eyes grainy and sore from lack of sleep and smoke irritation, regarded this cheerful energy with disfavour. "Where's Brivar?"

"Doing some hard thinking."

"Why?"

"He asked me why the Lathai are not affected by Iysr."

"Ah."

"Yes."

"And?"

"And that's a very good question."

Esar's eyes were drawn to the empty place at his hips. "Where are they?" He had come to hate those bloody weapons, but he liked even less Alyas going around unarmed when the Lankarans hadn't decided how to react to Corado's death.

"Still with Brivar. As I said, he's doing some hard thinking."

Esar rubbed sore eyes and scowled. He didn't ask whether Brivar was protected while he did his thinking, because he was certain he would be. "Why aren't you worried about this?"

Alyas turned to him. "Which bit, precisely, do you think I'm not worried about?"

"The Lathai. Ten years, Alyas. Ten years we've been keeping that close—keeping the bloody peace!—and you go and leave responsibility for it in the hands of a boy who is too clever for his own good, and a *temple acolyte*."

"Ah, that."

"Yes, *that*."

Alyas didn't answer at once, his gaze drifting back towards the mountains. "Maybe we shouldn't have. Kept it close."

"What does that mean?"

"I don't know. But I'm hoping Brivar might be able to tell us."

I f Brivar reached any conclusion, he didn't share it with them. He
returned the blades to Alyas that evening without saying a word,
and Alyas took them in the same manner. There was something
faintly accusing in the look Brivar gave him, and the reproachful
silence with which he treated them over the next few days told Esar he
had at least guessed at the truth of the Lathai's relationship with Isyr.
And that wasn't something that Brivar, as a temple acolyte, would
want to know. Not when his loyalty to the temple *should* compel him
to reveal it. And they all knew what would happen then. The temples
were second only to the syndicates in their hunger for Isyrium.

To Esar's frustration, Alyas did not attempt to explain and left
Brivar to brood, more concerned, for the moment, with getting them
safely across the plains to Orleas.

The plains that were rich in Isyrium ore and pitted with mines.

Each one of those mines was a potential danger. Alyas kept the
company well clear and sent scouts to observe the operations from
a distance. He also had Esar send some further afield. Those they
would not hear from for weeks. Yet even when the scouts returned
from the nearby mines and reported no sign of the corruption, that
didn't stop Esar from wanting to shut them all down. But not only
did they not have the manpower, they didn't have the authority.

Ellasia ran on Isyrium. It was its wealth, its fuel, its culture. From
the rulers who taxed its production to amass vast wealth and the noble
families who had built their fortunes on it—and whose vaults hid
uncounted Isyr treasures—to the temples that used it to power their

rituals, Isyrium was both money and power. And so reliant had they become on its myriad everyday uses—domestic, military, religious, medical, artistic—that without it, the continent would simply grind to a halt. And the mining syndicates would never permit it.

Money *was* power, and while in the plains you could still find a few small, independent operations, the big syndicates controlled most of the mines across central and southern Ellasia. And you did not cross them. Only in Qido, where the emperor personally owned all the mines, and in the steppes, where the individual tribes were at constant war over territory and the mines within it, was the power of the syndicates curbed. If they made any move against the mines, they would have the syndicates on them before they could blink. And not even Alyas, with the full weight of his newly restored title behind him, could stand against that. Though Esar suspected he dearly wanted to try.

The first evening after they burned the Grey Rock mining settlement, Alyas summoned Sul-Barin and asked him for everything he knew about the threat that had brought him to them. Lord Sul, his eyes on the now-livid bruising around Alyas's throat, swallowed his outrage over Corado's death and told him. It did not amount to much when set against what they thought they had learned, but it did tell them something important. Until now, almost all incursions of the creatures and their sickness had come along Lankara's southern border, as had the larger wave that had devastated parts of neighbouring Hantara before it had been contained. The assumption had been that it had come out of the wild southlands—it wouldn't be the first time a virulent contagion that spread across Ellasia had started in the south—but now they knew it was also in Flaeres, coming from the north.

"They're dumping it outside Lankara," Esar said grimly after Lord Sul had left. It made sense. The mining company that had first discovered how to purify Isyrium ore had been Lankaran, and the big syndicates' operations were largely concentrated in the countries of central Ellasia, whose rulers had greedily embraced the wealth they offered and given them a degree of freedom in their operations that the more autocratic north or the chaotic south would never allow. Why pollute their own countries when they could make it someone else's problem?

Alyas looked through him. "We need to know where."

"They won't tell you. Even if they know it's causing this—especially if they know."

Alyas's gaze came back into focus. "If they have even the smallest suspicion, I'm going to break them, and everyone who helped them."

"And if that includes Raffa?" Alyas's feelings about Raffa were complicated. Esar's were not.

"Then I'll break him too."

Esar sighed. Raffa wasn't stupid. He knew Alyas would never forgive him. He would permit a degree of defiance in return for getting what he wanted, whatever that was. The syndicates were arguably far more powerful than the king, and they dealt harshly with interference. "If they don't break you first."

"They are welcome to try," Alyas retorted, and sent Esar to round up their best scouts.

As he sent them off with their instructions, Esar reflected that he had not given this nearly enough thought in the last ten years, despite the efforts they had expended to keep the mining syndicates out of the Lathai mountains. He hadn't been thinking about how far the syndicates' control of the continent's economy extended. It had been enough to know where the hunger for Isyr would lead. The ink was barely dry on the histories of the last century when the pure Isyrium deposits had become rarer and rarer until they had disappeared altogether. The wars that followed had only ended when a mining company had discovered a way to extract traces from the ore of other metals and given birth to what would become the first mining syndicate.

Of course, they hadn't known then that even purified, the ore would not produce Isyr steel. It had taken years more of experimentation to establish, finally, that they had lost the ability to make the most precious commodity in Ellasia.

Isyr. Stronger, brighter, and more beautiful than other metals. A weapon made from Isyr would always be sharp, no Isyr ornament would ever tarnish, no jewellery lost its lustre, no detail ever faded.

In those days rich women wore their Isyr jewellery openly, Isyr plate was displayed proudly in homes, kings and queens wore crowns of Isyr. Now those same treasures were locked away, its value making it too dangerous to own. Today, only kings and the Lathai wore Isyr.

And Alyas, and he had had to kill to defend it more than once. There was a lot of blood on those blades, one way or another.

Isyr had been the most desirable thing in Ellasia. Now it was priceless. And into the vacuum left by its absence, the mining syndicates had spawned like ants, taking everything that was left and establishing their stranglehold on the new Isyrium economy. And perhaps doing much worse than that.

So Esar slept badly and studied the mines they passed with suspicion and disgust. He was not alone. They had not told the king's envoy what they had found at the quarry. Esar had taken his own people to burn it, and Alyas had carefully focused the confused testimony of the Lankaran guardsman—and the attention of Sul-Barin—on Corado's death. But though they didn't speak of it, Esar could see its shadows in the eyes of the men and women he had taken to the quarry. He could see it in Alyas's tired face, and Brivar's distant frown. They had stumbled on something huge and profoundly wrong, and they were still grappling to grasp the shape of it. Until they did, until they knew who they could trust, they would keep it close, as they had kept the Lathai's secret.

Maybe we shouldn't have.

He had no idea what Alyas meant by that. He had been close-lipped about the whole thing since they left the devastated outpost. That was not a surprise, even if it was frustrating. Where Esar liked to worry problems out loud, Alyas would chew them over in silence, and he rarely shared his thinking until he had decided what to do. But this time—this time, Esar was determined not to let that silence stretch on too long. He was too wary now of what it might be hiding.

Della interrupted it first, appearing beside them as they approached Orleas, the city sprawling out ahead of them nestled in its valley. "What did you do?" she asked Alyas.

He blinked, pulling his thoughts from wherever they had been. "You'll have to be more specific."

"To Brivar. He's barely spoken in two days."

Alyas glanced behind to where Brivar was riding a little apart from the main body of the company. "He has a lot on his mind."

"He saved your life," she hissed.

"I am aware, Della. I promise I have done nothing."

"But you're not helping either, are you?"

He sighed. "What do you want me to do?"

"Talk to him," she said, her tone making it clear she should not have to tell him that. "It's not fair, what you're doing."

Esar wholeheartedly agreed, but he had already tried and failed to make the same argument. Alyas was adamant that he wanted Brivar to come to them, though he had not explained why, but the closer they came to Avarel, the more nervous Esar became. Everything else they had learned aside, the truth of the Lathai's relationship with Isyr was knowledge that could start a war—that *would* start a war—and Della was right. It wasn't fair to put that burden on Brivar's shoulders. There was a temple of Yholis in Orleas. If Alyas was wrong—if Brivar chose to take what he had almost certainly guessed to the temple instead—the consequences would be catastrophic, and Alyas would only have himself to blame.

"It's not fair," she repeated, when he didn't reply.

Esar thought he would refuse, but instead he gave a distracted nod. "Very well. I'll talk to him."

"When?"

"Della!"

She shrugged, unapologetic. "I know you, Alyas. You're quite capable of twisting promises to suit your own purpose."

Alyas gave a frustrated sigh and Esar was struck by how tired he looked. No one had been sleeping well these last few days. "Soon," he promised. "Let me deal with Orleas first, and then I will speak with Brivar."

She nodded, satisfied, and dropped back. Esar said, "You're expecting trouble in Orleas?"

Alyas's mouth was set in a tight line. "I'm expecting to find out how genuine Raffa's offer really is."

The Dukes of Agrathon had owned several estates in and around Orleas. Estates the crown had appropriated after Alyas had been stripped of that title and the family name struck from Lankara's record. What would happen to those estates now? They did not know whether Raffa had kept them or distributed them among his lords and advisors. Getting them back could be a legal nightmare, even with the king's decree to support them. Esar realised with a sinking feeling that Alyas meant to force the issue.

"We could camp outside the city and find out how the land lies before you do anything," he pointed out.

"We could," Alyas agreed.

"But you're going to ride up to the gates and kick the door in?"

The newly reinstated Duke of Agrathon grinned. "Of course."

That's what they did. And Esar thought he observed a certain amount of disappointment when those doors opened for them without a squeal of protest. Not only did the doors open for them, but a full staff was waiting behind them, the hallway lined with men and women wearing the badge of Agrathon. Alyas regarded them with an expressionless face, but Esar could see the tension in his jaw and knew he was angry, and not just, he suspected, because his fun had been ruined.

A middle-aged man in the formal uniform of a house steward stood at the head of the line. He stepped forward and gave a correct bow. "Your Grace, welcome to Orleas. We have been expecting you."

"I can see that," Alyas observed dryly. He said nothing else.

The man didn't miss a beat despite the coldness of his reception. He gestured to the doors at the end of the hall. "If you will proceed to the salon, everything will be explained."

Alyas gave him a long look. To Esar he said, "I want everyone standing ready."

Esar nodded and passed the order back to the company in the courtyard.

The steward said, "I assure you, Your Grace, that is unnecessary."

Alyas ignored him. With Esar beside him, he walked past the waiting servants without a glance and pushed open the doors to the salon.

Someone was there already. Tall, thin, her iron-grey hair pinned up in a severe style several decades out of fashion, the woman stood with her back to them, leaning on a cane. As the door swung shut, she said, "Don't stand there gawping, Alyas dear. You really don't have time."

Alyas gave a choked laugh; there was no amusement in it. "Aunt. I don't know why I'm surprised."

"I don't know either," that formidable woman replied, turning to face them. "You are not the only one who can be obnoxiously high-handed. I've liberated your estates from Raffa's clutches. You can thank me later. I know you'll find it hard just now."

Esar took step to the side to avoid the sparks as the two of them glared at each other.

"Aunt Hailene," he murmured, giving her a more diplomatic peck on the cheek.

She held him out by his shoulders and looked him up and down like a school mistress inspecting a miscreant, which was largely how she had always regarded them. "Esar. I must say, you have done very well, but you should have known better than to let him come back. It's not too late to take Gerrin's name. It would be some protection."

Esar shook his head. His foster father had offered him his house names when he had reached his majority, but Esar had refused him then, and every year since until the old duke had died. He had nothing left of his own father but his name, and he had no interest in adding the third name that would shift his life forever into a constant dance for precedence—a dance in which he would always come last, whether he shared Alyas's name or not.

"Well, it's your choice," Hailene replied. "And I suppose I can understand why you have made it. But it will keep you apart, which I know you will not like."

"I won't let that happen," Alyas said stiffly.

She inspected him much as she had inspected Esar. "You don't make your own rules anymore, Alyas. You chose to come back, and now you have to play the game. When did you last sleep?"

He ignored that. "What do you want, Hailene? You hated my

father. I'm surprised you didn't cheer when Raffa struck out his name."

"Such drama, Alyas," she sighed. "I've always been very fond of you. And much as I would love to stand here trading insults and getting reacquainted, we do have some urgent business to discuss. Will you unbend enough to listen?"

Esar kept his eyes averted from Alyas's face. He had often thought Alyas got all the most difficult aspects of his character from his mother's family. He and Hailene were simply too alike to tolerate each other's company for long. Apparently, fifteen years had not changed that.

Taking his silence for agreement, Hailene said, "Raffa would have recalled you months ago if he had his way. That he didn't is as much a problem for you as anything else. However, I am not without influence at court. Knowing his intention, I persuaded him to hand over your estates into my care in readiness for your return. Both Camling and Headdon are prepared for you."

"Are they?" Alyas said with a bite. "I'm touched by your concern, Aunt, and that you would put your busy spies to work on my behalf."

"You should be," she told him tartly. "Raffa's lies were effective. There are not many left who disbelieve his version of events, not where anyone can hear them, anyway. No one else is going to look out for your interests."

"I don't need them to," Alyas retorted. "I can take care of my own interests."

Hailene snorted. "You have no idea what you're walking into."

"Oh, I think I have *some* idea."

"My dear, if that were true you would not have let him lure you back. There is nothing for you in Avarel except trouble."

Alyas showed his teeth. "That is certainly my intention."

"No doubt, but this is trouble even you haven't encountered before. And if you insist on marching headlong into it, you had better be prepared."

"And I suppose that's why you're here?"

"Yes, that's why I'm here," she agreed, quite unmoved by his hostility. "Because despite what you may believe, you are my sister's son, and I have had quite enough of Raffa's attempts to destroy this family and everything else he touches. So, listen to me carefully. The moment you walk back into Avarel, you will be in the middle of a tug of war between the king and the syndicates. Raffa wants someone to stand up to them who's not him. He knows you will because you never did know when to back down. And he knows you already hate him, so he doesn't have to sacrifice a friend with his proxy defiance. He has precious few of those left."

"And I thought he was overcome with remorse and wanted to renew our friendship."

"Don't take that tone with me, Alyas. It will do you no good at all. Learn to accept help. It's not too late."

Esar covered his smile and said smoothly into the furious silence, "You suggested time is a factor."

Hailene nodded, tapping her cane on the tiled floor. "It is indeed, if you want to stay ahead of them, and you took your time coming here. I have been waiting two weeks already."

He grimaced, thinking of all the unavoidable delays. "It could not be helped."

"What do they want?" Alyas asked, finding his voice again. "The syndicates?"

"Broadly, money, power, and an end to restrictions on their operations. Precisely, in this case, other than protection for their mines from whatever this is, I don't know. But they don't want *you*, and for that I will endure all your prickly barbs, my dear. Though I warn you, they will do you no good against their court representative, who will no doubt appear any moment."

That was all they needed, thought Esar. The syndicates poking around in their activities, particularly their most recent activities. "How long before he gets here?"

"*She* is already in Orleas," his aunt told him with obvious relish. Hailene-Sera Ahn had always been vocal in her disgust that women were mostly excluded from positions of power in Lankaran society. She might hate the syndicates, but she likely took great satisfaction in their more egalitarian attitudes. "In fact, I am surprised we have been given so long before she simply 'drops by'. And you will need your wits about you. She is nobody's fool, and the syndicates are already out for your blood."

Alyas frowned. "Raffa called me back to help protect Lankara. Presumably that includes their mines."

"Oh Alyas, you really are not ready for this. You have stood in the way of their ambitions for too long. They have been pushing to expand into Lathai territory for years. It's the one thing Raffa has stood firm on, and they know perfectly well it's because you were there." She studied his face. "Make of that what you will. But be prepared to deal with attacks overt and subtle. They will use any weapon they can so do try not to hand them any."

There was a knock at the door and the voice of the steward announced the arrival of Ovisia Galea, king's advisor and syndicate liaison.

"Ah," said Hailene. "Here she is."

Ovisia Galea was Flaeresian, and she swept into their midst with that country's flair for the flamboyant, wafting trails of scent and dripping in Isyrium. She was not young, though Esar would have been hard pressed to guess her age. Her hair was still black and her forehead smooth, but the lines around her eyes and her mouth were etched deep by a disposition much given to expression. Her dress was dyed the deep blue only Isyrium dye could achieve, while faceted Isyrium chips set in silver glinted at her wrists and throat. And in her ears… Esar controlled his surprise with an effort. Her earrings were old Isyr. There was no imitating that cool blue. A statement, indeed.

He did not look at Alyas. There was no chance he had not noticed. And she made sure of it a moment later.

"Your Grace," she said, giving him a precise bow. No deferential curtsey for her, Esar noted. "I see I have found a fellow lover of Isyr. Such a shame, don't you think, that such beautiful things should be hidden away? I would love to see the day Isyr is brought back out of the shadows. Wouldn't you agree?"

As a first blow, that was a direct strike, and Esar found himself wholeheartedly agreeing with Hailene. They should never have come back.

Alyas's smile was polite but stiff. "I have not thought about it, Sayora Galea."

"Call me Ovisia, please," she responded with a smile. "Everyone else does. Isn't that right, Lady Hailene?"

"I'm sure I don't know what *everyone* calls you, Ovisia dear," Hailene replied, ignoring the outrageous familiarity. Flaeresians did not share the Lankaran's naming traditions or reverence for formality, but as the syndicate representative to the Lankaran court, Ovisia Galea certainly understood their significance. Trying to force the conversation onto first name terms was another roundabout attack. But this one missed its mark. Alyas had spent too long without his names to take offence, and Hailene certainly did not. She made that clear when she said, "I'm sure you can call my nephew whatever you like. He is, after all, unaccustomed to Lankaran formality, and I've never held with it."

Beaten back, Ovisia turned her devastating smile on Esar. "Esar Cantrell. I have heard so much about you. Is it true you put down the Evarius rebellion and held the Silent Keep with only twenty men?"

He smiled with genuine amusement. That one would go nowhere either. Esar could stand there and claim sole credit for everything they had done together in the last fifteen years, and Alyas wouldn't care. He never had. But it served to underscore Hailene's warning. The syndicates would probe for every weakness, for every fracture to exploit, and Alyas would already be isolated when he returned to Avarel.

"In a manner of speaking," he replied, glancing at Alyas, expecting to see the same awareness in his eyes, but Alyas's face was tight and strained.

Hailene tapped the tiled floor sharply with her cane, the sound loud in the small silence. "How very surprising to see you, Ovisia dear. Alyas has been here less than an hour."

The Flaeresian woman smiled. Her teeth were very white against her tanned skin. "Then I am lucky to catch you, Your Grace. I am only in Orleas a short while on business. The city has several of our ore processing centres. There is one close by, in fact, where I have been today, so it made sense to stop by on my way home to see if you had arrived."

Alyas said, "Is that so?" as though it was the most uninteresting thing in the world rather than one of the most terrifying things Esar had ever heard, and suddenly he knew what the problem was.

He swore silently. If she had been to a processing centre, she was probably covered in traces of alchemical waste. It was nothing like the quarry, but it was clearly affecting him. For a horrible moment, Esar wondered whether it was deliberate—whether this was another attack. But that wasn't possible. *No one* knew about its effect on Alyas except Brivar, and he would not have shared that with anyone, regardless of his current feelings towards them.

Alyas's tone did not go unnoticed. Ovisia's dark eyes studied him. Then she said, "I apologise for arriving unannounced. You have had a long journey and you will be tired. But it is of your journey that I wish to speak. We have lost contact with one of our mines on the plains. Their Isyrium shipments have not arrived at our warehouse here in Orleas for over a week. Did you by chance pass through? We would appreciate any information you could give us. We will, of course, send our own investigators."

I bet you will, Esar thought bitterly as Alyas said, "Yes. I'm afraid your mine is no longer operational."

Esar winced at the blunt words. Ovisia's smile remained in place, but it no longer reached her eyes. "No longer operational?"

"We don't know what happened," Alyas told her. "It was already over by the time we arrived. The contagion that threatens Lankara—it seems it had reached your mine. Perhaps brought by a trader." He gave a regretful, one-shouldered shrug. "There was no one left alive. We burned the town and the mine as a precaution."

There was no point denying it. There were too many witnesses, and the syndicate's investigators would see it for themselves. Even so, it was a dangerous admission, and the fire had burned away the evidence of the corruption that would provide the justification for his actions. If the syndicate chose to make an issue of it, they could make Alyas's life very difficult. Esar could see the thought mirrored on Hailene's face. Despite her warning, Alyas had just handed them a weapon to use against him.

The stark confession had also silenced the syndicate representative. She had probably never heard anyone claim so calmly, and to her face, that they had destroyed a syndicate mine. In Lankara, the king had long ago given the syndicates the power to punish as they saw fit those who robbed, sabotaged, or otherwise interfered with their mines. If they were looking for a way to take down the Duke of Agrathon, the destruction of a mine was the perfect excuse, which was why Alyas had stolen the initiative from her.

"The contagion?" Ovisia said at last, her tone carefully neutral. "If that is true and it had indeed reached the mine, we owe you a debt, Your Grace. I will inform our investigators what to look for."

"I hope they won't find anything," Alyas said. "We did our best to destroy all traces. It seemed safest. Better perhaps for your investigators to focus their attention on how it got there in the first place. The king will want to know." His eyes drifted away from her, as though the topic barely warranted his attention. "Will you be staying long, Sayora? We have, as you see, only just arrived, and there is much I need to see to. Perhaps we could continue this conversation another time? You can make an appointment with my steward."

Esar winced. This was a woman who didn't need an appointment to see the king. Alyas must be desperate to be rid of her, and as to the rest… if she was as clever as she seemed, she would not miss the warning. It had not been subtle.

A sliver of shocked surprise escaped Ovisia's control, but she recovered quickly, bowing to Alyas's blunt assertion of precedence. She didn't have a lot of choice. "Of course, Your Grace." She flashed her teeth again, and this time the smile lacked all warmth. "But I think we can defer our discussion to Avarel. I wouldn't like you to have to repeat yourself to my colleagues there."

"Indeed, that would be a waste of time," Alyas said in a bored tone. "Especially when I will be so busy carrying out Raffa's orders."

Esar suppressed a sigh. The battle lines had been well and truly drawn.

He wasn't the only one to find that frustrating. "As satisfying as that was, it was also bloody stupid," Hailene snapped when the door closed behind the syndicate's representative and her cool parting words. "You could have waited until your second meeting to make an enemy of her."

"Aunt," Alyas said firmly, cutting her off. "I have just arrived and I do have much to do. I thank you for your efforts and your warning, but I really must defer this discussion as well. My company is tired."

Her sharp old eyes studied his face. "I daresay they are," she said at last. "Was it true? About the mine?"

"Unfortunately," Esar told her, attempting to usher her to the door.

She whacked his leg with her cane. "I'm going, boy. No need to herd me." To Alyas, she said, "Let me help. You can't take them on single-handed. Don't try, do you hear me?"

He didn't reply, his face unreadable.

"I know you heard me, Esar," Hailene sniffed as she left them. "Make him listen."

As soon as the door closed behind her, Alyas walked to a window and flung it open. He took a deep breath, then another, the mask slipping. Esar watched him, not saying a word. He didn't have to. This was going to be a problem.

"Keep her away from me, Esar."

Esar snorted. "Which one?"

That drew a shaky laugh. "Not even you can stop Hailene."

"She's right, you know."

Alyas turned from the window. "No, she's not. If we don't, who will?"

Esar sighed. "Let me keep the company. Raffa asked for them. You need them. I'll keep them safe. They'll come anyway," he added when Alyas did not respond. "You know they will. They're safer under your protection than without it."

"I wouldn't be too sure of that," Alyas replied. "But you're right. We *are* going to need them."

Della was hovering outside the door to the salon. Esar shook his head. "No, Della, it's not a good time." Alyas was angry and exhausted. His patience would be non-existent.

"No, Esar, *now*."

Her tone stopped him short. "Why?"

"There are syndies here. They're questioning everyone about the Lathai and the mine. Our people know what not to say, but the Lankarans don't. Brivar doesn't. And Alyas hasn't exactly given him a reason to keep quiet."

Esar swore. He started towards the courtyard. He should have known the syndicates would be crawling all over the company the moment they arrived, but Ovisia's arrival had distracted them. As she had intended.

Della hurried to keep up. "He needs to understand he's not just protecting Alyas's private enterprise. He needs to know this isn't about money."

"Is that what he thinks?" Esar was genuinely startled. That interpretation had never occurred to him.

"I don't know," Della said in frustration. "He won't talk to me about it. He's protecting your secret. Let him know he's doing it for the right reasons. You know what syndies are like. They get a whiff of anything and they'll never let it go."

Esar stopped, torn. There was nothing he could do to stop the Lankarans talking—and anyway they knew nothing more than Alyas had already told Galea—but the wrong word from Brivar, even unintentional, and they would be in real trouble. And not just them. "Fine," he said. "But fair warning—he's not at his diplomatic best."

Della grinned. "Is he ever?"

He stepped out into the courtyard as an argument was about to tip over into violence. The company was as he had left them, more or less, but their order had fractured around a knot of syndicate reps who were arguing with Agazi. He recognised Frey's red curls beside the steppelander and picked up his pace. She had been with him when they burned the quarry, and Alyas had sent her to one of the more distant mines on the plains. There was no way syndies were getting her intelligence before he did. If they so much as touched her, he might do something he would regret.

Agazi saw him coming and took a step back to let him through.

Esar nodded to him. "You can stand the company down. Find everyone somewhere to sleep. You too, Frey. There's a steward in there who will help you." The man would be appalled at the thought of accommodating soldiers in the main house, but he would have to get over it. There was plenty of room.

The man with whom Agazi was arguing, said, "Your people will stay where they are. We have not finished our investigation."

"What investigation?" Esar asked. To Agazi, he said, "You have your orders. Go."

"And I have mine. From the king's advisor," the syndicate rep insisted. "You will stay," he told Agazi and Frey. "As will you, Esar Cantrell. I have questions for you, too."

Esar made a show of looking around. "I don't see any advisor. And you haven't shown me an order. So you can save your questions until after my people have eaten and rested, and after you have produced a writ that entitles you to question them. This company is in the employ of the Duke of Agrathon and any *investigation* should go through him." And good luck with that.

The man treated him to a condescending smile that Esar very much wanted to wipe from his face, preferably with his fists. "Even the Duke is subject to the king's laws, which give us full rights to investigate crimes against our property. And the Duke himself admitted that he destroyed one of our mines. Therefore, since he is the subject of this investigation, I must insist…"

"You can insist all you like," Esar snarled. Ithol's blood, he hated the syndicates. He didn't have the patience for this, and he was too tired to pretend. "But you don't get to talk to my people before I do. And since there are more of us than you, I suggest you accept that gracefully and go and complain to Sayora Galea. She can take it up with the Duke." *If* she could get in to see him.

The man opened his mouth to insist anyway when unexpected help came from Sul-Barin Feron. In his travelled-stain riding clothes and three-day stubble, the Lankaran was a far cry from the pompous lordling who had ridden into their camp three weeks ago. He directed his scornful gaze at the syndicate representative. "As the king's witness to the events you are investigating, I have already provided full testimony. There is no need for you to keep these men and women from their rest. If the king's advisor takes exception to that, I am more than happy to discuss it with her myself—tomorrow."

The syndicate rep hesitated, trying to decide whether he had the authority to stand firm.

"Even the syndicates are subject to the king's laws," Sul-Barin said silkily. "And as the king's representative, I speak with his voice. You are done here."

Had Ovisia Galea herself been present, it might have gone differently, but in her absence and without a writ, her representative had no choice but to bow to the precedence Sul-Barin had asserted.

"Very well." He snapped his fingers, then waved his colleagues towards the gate. He offered Sul-Barin a shallow bow. "Until tomorrow." It was a threat and it moved no one.

Esar watched them go, then he turned to Sul-Barin. "Thank you."

"The syndicates forget their place. It is my duty to remind them. I didn't do it for you."

Esar smiled, amused. "All the same, thank you."

Sul-Barin eyed him with only fractionally less dislike than he had regarded the syndicate representative. "The king will have my full testimony about everything that has happened. Including the death of one of his officers and the abduction of my cousin."

"As he will have ours. But I would leave Brivar out of it, unless you want him to tell the king how you allowed an apprentice to the Temple of Yholis to be assaulted by that same officer. The temple wouldn't like it much either."

A flush crept up the younger man's face. "I never ordered that."

Esar said nothing. He might not have ordered it, but he hadn't stopped it either.

Sul-Barin looked away. "This isn't over. They'll be back." He hesitated, then added, "The syndicate would never have destroyed that mine. The king owes you for that. I will make sure he knows it."

Esar nodded his thanks and the king's envoy made his escape.

"Alyas's diplomacy is rubbing off on you, I see," Frey said with a grin as the company began to disperse. "Where is he? It isn't like him to miss a chance to savage a syndie."

Esar looked at her and felt a wave of relief that she was back by his side. There was a drag of fatigue beneath her smile. She must have ridden hard to catch up with them so quickly, but her manner told him there was no immediate cause for alarm. "He's already done his share of that today. Can it wait, Frey? Or do you need to see him now?" He could see Della approaching with Brivar in tow, his once pristine blue surcoat showing the wear and tear of several difficult weeks. After the confrontation Sul-Barin had temporarily averted, Esar shared Della's urgency to resolve that problem. They really didn't need another one on top of it.

Frey shrugged. "Depends. It's not another Grey Rock. But I think I have a lead on where they're sending their waste."

Esar held up a hand to stall Della. "Tell me."

૨૯

A train of covered wagons heading east had passed through the mine Frey had been sent to, and she had watched them load two of the wagons with crates carried out of the processing centre attached to the mine.

"How do you know it wasn't Isyrium?"

"Because that went with a different convoy. And you should have seen the way they handled these crates. They never touched them— they lifted them with poles and dropped them into the wagons as though they were afraid of them."

As well they should be, Esar thought, recalling the blackened devastation of the quarry. Frey yawned, her eyelids drooping, and he remembered how far she had ridden.

"Get some sleep. I'll pass your news onto Alyas. You can talk to him in the morning."

She yawned again and nodded. Then said, "Is he all right?"

He froze. "Why?"

"You're gatekeeping again. You only do that when he's not fit for company. And, well, he doesn't *look* all right."

"It takes time, Frey. You know that. He'll be fine."

"And what about you?" She wouldn't do anything as obvious as touch him in full view of any syndicate watchers, even though their relationship was no secret, but he could feel the warmth of her concern. "You look bloody awful too, you know. Is no one round here getting any sleep?" She smiled up at him. "I could help with that."

"Don't tempt me, woman." He tilted his head to where Della and Brivar were waiting. "Something I need to see to first."

Frey glanced where he did and sighed. "He's still not sorted that? Make him be kind, Esar. Brivar's a sensitive soul."

"He's tougher than you think." He squeezed her arm. "I'll see you later."

"Not too much later," she called over her shoulder as she walked away. "I'm for my bed."

Esar watched her for a second, wishing he could go with her, then he turned and beckoned to Brivar. The boy approached warily. "Are we in trouble? With the syndicates?"

"Not yet." He looked at Brivar's anxious face as they walked and tried to ease the frown from his own. "We owe you an explanation. It's time you got it."

"Because of the syndicates?"

"That too," Esar sighed, pushing open the doors to the salon. It was empty.

"He's not here."

Esar turned to see Hailene standing in the doorway. "I can see that. Where is he?"

She walked into the room, her cane tapping on the tiles. "I have no idea. He did not tell me. He was too busy climbing out of the window. I saw him from up there." She pointed her cane at the ceiling. Her rooms must be directly overhead.

"Out of the window?" Brivar squeaked.

The estate sloped down towards the river. The back of the house where the salon was located was two floors above ground level.

Hailene treated Brivar to a head-to-toe inspection as Esar walked to the open window and looked down.

"An apprentice of Yholis. What's your name, boy, and what are you doing here?"

"He came with the king's envoy," Esar told her before Brivar could answer, hoping he would take the hint. There were ornamental flower beds planted around the edge of the house. They were reassuringly undisturbed. Alyas had clearly made it safely to the ground, but that wasn't what Esar was principally worried about.

"Really, Esar," Hailene said with exasperation. "I meant what is he doing here *now*?"

"Reporting on the health of the company," Esar replied, looking out across the grounds to where the city of Orleas butted up against the walls of the estate. A city that was not only a hub of syndicate activity but also, right now, full of syndicate investigators intent on bringing Alyas down. "He's the house surgeon."

"He's an apprentice."

"So?" He had no intention of discussing Brivar with Hailene, now or at any time in the future. He turned back to the room. "Why didn't you stop him?"

Hailene said dryly, "I wasn't aware I could or should stop Alyas doing whatever he liked. You never have, and he listens to you. Though why he thought it was a good idea to go out into the city unarmed with the syndicates after him, I don't know."

"Unarmed?" Then he saw the blades, discarded on the floor by the chair on which Alyas had been sitting. He swore. Of the number of things that could mean, he liked none of them. He saw the same thought on Brivar's face.

"Wretched things," Hailene agreed. "With all the trouble they've caused, you would think he'd have the sense not to leave them lying around."

Esar agreed, though walking round syndicate controlled Orleas wearing a king's ransom in Isyr was equally foolhardy. So there was that. At least Alyas wasn't wearing anything that would identify him. His brigandine was draped over the back of the chair, another thing that would have marked him out, if not specifically, then as belonging to a military company, and it was unlikely there was more than one in Orleas. Esar didn't know whether to be reassured or alarmed that Alyas had taken pains to ensure he would not be recognised.

Hailene regarded his tight-lipped silence with suspicion. "What is he playing at, Esar? The last thing he needs is open war with the syndicates."

"If I knew, I'd tell you," he lied.

"I doubt that very much. I'm not his enemy. Don't treat me like one."

He felt a pang of guilt. "Aunt Hailene —"

"Don't," she snapped. She gave Brivar one last look, then tapped her cane to the door. "Well, I shall leave you to worry. You do it so well. I am returning to Avarel tomorrow. When Alyas is ready to accept my help, he knows where to find me."

As the door closed, Brivar said, "Was that…?"

"Hailene-Sera Ahn. Aunt on his mother's side."

Brivar's mouth formed an 'o'. "She's a legend. You don't trust her?"

Esar pinched the bridge of his nose. Frey was right. He *was* tired. And despite what Hailene thought, he wasn't about to sit up all night. If Alyas had wanted his help, he would have asked for it.

"Right now," he said, with patience he didn't feel, "we can't afford to trust anyone in Lankara. It's been too long. We don't know anyone, or their motivations—even Hailene."

"But you trusted me," Brivar said with more than a little heat. "And you didn't even ask."

Esar cursed Alyas. He should not be the one having to explain this.

"It's all right," Brivar said. "I know what you were doing. I think I know why. The Lathai have pure Isyrium. That's how they make Isyr. It's also where all your Isyrium comes from, isn't it? Probably for years. I wondered how you could have so much. You were protecting them from the syndicates."

Esar watched him cautiously. "You're not angry?"

"I was," Brivar admitted. "But I think I understand that too, in a way. And I do have some theories."

His voice held a note that Esar did not like. "Do I want to hear them?"

Brivar glanced at the discarded Isyr blades as they both contemplated their absent owner. "Probably not right now, no."

Esar growled. He hooked the blades off the floor, scooped up the brigandine, and walked to the door.

"Where are you going?"

"To bed—and so should you."

Brivar looked helplessly at the open window. "But –"

Esar felt his patience snap. "What else can I do? I have no idea where he's gone. If I send out search parties, they won't find him, and all we'll do is let the syndicates know something is amiss. You can be sure they are watching this place." Which was why Alyas had gone out through the window when all eyes would have been on the confrontation in the courtyard. "He'll come back when he's ready, and if he doesn't, then I'll worry about it."

It sounded good. He almost believed it himself. "Get some sleep in a real bed while you can. It might be the last chance you get before Avarel." And Yholis help them when they got *there*.

E sar gazed up at the once-familiar ceiling of the room he had slept in many times in his youth, his memory filling in the details it was too dark to make out. Frey's head rested on his shoulder, her fingers trailing patterns on his chest. It was late and he was, distressingly, still not asleep, despite the best efforts of the woman in his arms.

"Stop it, Esar," she murmured. "You're worrying."

He tilted his head so he could see her face. "I'm not."

She jabbed him in the chest. "Liar. I know, you've been doing it for fifteen years. It's a habit. But you've got to break it sometime."

He sighed. "I don't think now is the time."

"You said it yourself. You can't go after him. He'll be back by morning, you'll see. You're keeping us both awake fretting about it now."

He pulled her back down against him. "Sorry."

"I mean it, Esar," she murmured, her voice muffled against his chest. "I love him too, but sometimes I wish it was just the two of us."

The hand that had been stroking her hair froze. She kept her head turned away so he couldn't see her face. He said quietly, "He's my brother, Frey." Not by blood, but in every way that mattered since Esar had become the old duke's ward at the age of four. Alyas had been two and his mother had recently died. Gerrin had been absent in many ways for years after that, and his heir had been largely left in Esar's care, a child not much older. Frey was right, it was a habit, learned early and set in stone later, first by Gerrin's death and then

Raffa's betrayal and everything that had come after. They had been through too much together for him not to worry, especially now, though Yholis knew, Alyas was capable of looking after himself. He always had been. Except then Flaeres had happened, and he still wasn't right.

"I'm not asking you to abandon him. Just to think about yourself sometimes."

"He'd do the same for me. He has done." Esar really didn't like where this conversation was going.

She sighed, propping herself up on her elbows. "I never said you weren't as bad as each other. I just… I don't want this to be my whole life, Esar. I love it, but not forever, you know?"

There was too much in that for him to untangle now. He was too tired, and their immediate prospects too uncertain. But this was Frey. She wouldn't say something like that if she didn't mean it, and he couldn't simply dismiss it if he wanted to keep her, which he did, very much.

He reached out and caught a curl in his fingers. "I know. But this is important." And if they didn't deal with it, he wasn't sure there would be a future for any of them.

She smiled sadly. "Afterwards, then."

"Afterwards," he promised, and hoped the gods wouldn't conspire to make a liar of him.

❧

A pounding on the door startled him awake a couple of hours later. Frey rolled off him and out of the bed, pulling on her leggings as Esar collapsed back against the pillows, his hands pressed against his face.

"Esar!" Agazi.

"Fuck." He sat up, reaching for his clothes. "What is it?"

"Trouble. We need you."

"Of course it is," he growled, his eyes meeting Frey's. He dressed quickly, hopping to the door as he pulled on his boots, and dragged it open.

Agazi shoved his way into the room and flung open the shutters. "Look."

He did look. Then he swore. Orleas was lit up by the light of a huge fire, blue flames rising high into the night sky.

"Fuck," he said again.

"Syndies are here. They want to see Alyas."

Esar took a deep breath. He didn't ask whether Alyas was back. Agazi would have gone to him first. "Where?"

"Salon."

He reached for his sword. It made him feel better. "Make sure they stay there. I'll be right down."

Agazi nodded and left. Esar could hear him clattering down the stairs. He turned to Frey. She was watching him with a curious mixture of compassion and exasperation. "Stay here. They still want to question you."

She nodded and he looked away from her too-sharp gaze.

"Esar…"

"What?" He hadn't meant to snap, but neither did he have any intention of revisiting their last conversation.

She stood on tiptoe and kissed his cheek. "Be careful."

He pressed his lips onto the top of her head, breathing in the scent of her, steadying himself. "I'll be fine."

The Orleas syndicate was there in force. When he strode into the salon, he counted six of them, not including Ovisia Galea herself, who this time made no pretence of her suspicion.

"I demand to see the Duke," she told him. "Now."

"He's asleep," Esar said, crossing his arms. "As I was. What's this about?"

Her eyes narrowed. "You know perfectly well what this is about. Wake him—if he's even here."

Esar's retort was lost as the doors swung inwards and Alyas walked into the room. "Where else would I be, Sayora Galea? Will you please explain why *you* are here at this hour."

He was barefoot and half-dressed, and buckling on the blades with clumsy fingers. His hair was in convincing disarray and his face shadowed with exhaustion, like someone just pulled from a deep sleep. Or someone who hadn't been to sleep at all. It didn't stop him treating the king's advisor to his most infuriating look. "This is not what I meant by making an appointment."

"Your Grace," Ovisia said, the honorific dragged from between clenched teeth. "We apologise for waking you. Someone has set fire to one of our processing centres."

Alyas walked to the window and inched open the shutter so he could see the blaze. "So I see. That fails to explain why you are *here*. Unless you are accusing me?"

"You burned our mine," one of the syndicate representatives snarled.

Alyas raised an eyebrow. He looked at Ovisia, whose tight-lipped anger promised unpleasant consequences for her colleague. "I have explained the circumstances and I dislike having to repeat myself. If you don't believe me, you can ask the king's envoy. He was also there. Now, if you would please leave, I would like to go back to sleep."

Ovisia studied him with an intensity Esar found disturbing. Then she smiled. "Very well, we will leave you to your sleep. But I am making my appointment now, Your Grace. We will see you in the morning."

"If you must," Alyas replied, gesturing to Agazi, who held open the doors.

Ovisia accepted this pointed dismissal with no further cracks in her dignity. "Until tomorrow." And she swept out of the room with her escort in tow. Agazi followed them. He would make sure they left the grounds. Even so, Esar waited until the sounds of their departure had faded before turning to Alyas.

"Before you say anything, I didn't intend that to happen."

Esar regarded him with barely controlled anger. "Didn't intend what? To put everyone here in danger? To paint a target on your back for every syndicate in Ellasia to aim at? What exactly did you intend?"

The lack of a stinging retort was telling. He really hadn't intended it. "What happened?" Esar asked, calmer. Alyas didn't make mistakes like that. "How do you accidentally set fire to an entire factory?"

"When that factory is full of highly flammable material, quite easily as it turns out."

Esar reminded himself to breathe. That as satisfying as it might be, in this moment, to beat some sense out of him, he would regret it in the morning.

Alyas abruptly sat. "I went to look around. Soon every syndicate rep in Lankara will know my face. I'm as anonymous now as I will ever be." He paused. It didn't approach an explanation, and he seemed to realise that, as he added, "I couldn't stop thinking about what Corado said back at Grey Rock. The way he went for the foreman. The way he blamed him. Why would he do that? There's no reason—unless he knew what caused it. And if Corado knew…"

If Corado knew, then the syndicates certainly did. Esar would not throw Raffa's name into this, but he was sure Alyas was thinking it. Worse, if Corado knew, then he had probably been working for the syndicates all along. Yholis, what a mess. What a gods-damned fucking disaster, and here they were in the middle of it. Because if the syndicates knew their activities were the cause of this plague, they would see Alyas's actions in burning the mine—let alone the bloody processing centre tonight—as evidence that he also knew it. And since they had shown no sign of trying to deal with the problem they had created, or even pausing their operations, it meant they were going to cover it up. And that meant silencing everyone who could point the finger at them. Unless Alyas could convince them otherwise. Thinking of Galea's face tonight, Esar didn't like his chances. It was entirely possible they had already tried to kill him, that Corado's attack at the quarry had not been driven by hate but was meant to eliminate all witnesses to what had happened.

"I thought I might be able to find out where they are sending the mining waste," Alyas said, mistaking his silence for anger. "I got too close, and…"

In other words, he had been overwhelmed as he had been at the quarry. He had probably been seen and found himself out of options. But he wasn't going to admit that and on the whole Esar preferred not to think about it.

"If you'd waited, you could have asked Frey," he told Alyas, without sympathy. He should have known not to go near a processing centre.

"She's back? Where is she?"

"Upstairs, safe. They wanted to question her when she arrived. They still do." He didn't bother to point out how much more determined they would be after tonight.

Alyas pressed the heels of his hands to his eyes. "Esar. I'm sorry." Then, "What did she find out?"

Esar took pity on him and dropped into the chair opposite. "She saw a wagon train from Orleas collect the waste from a mine and head east. She didn't follow it because she thought you would want to know. She can do." It would get her out of the way of the Orleas syndicate, although it wasn't without risk.

Alyas looked up. "I can send someone else."

Esar shook his head. He had already considered that. "She's better off kept out of this for a while. I don't want syndies anywhere near her. But you can make sure she doesn't go alone."

Alyas nodded, listing to one side, and caught himself on the arm of the chair.

Esar sighed. "Yholis's infinite mercy, Alyas. Go to sleep. They'll be back in a few hours. She'll walk all over you in this state." And there was more than his life and freedom at stake. The whole company was at risk, but it would have been cruelty itself to point that out now.

He stood. Alyas put his head back and closed his eyes. "I'll sleep here."

Esar stood looking down at him. He thought about what Frey had said and nearly left him to it, then decided that the chance of Ovisia Galea walking in on him asleep in a chair at the first crack of dawn warranted intervention.

"No, you won't," he said, hauling Alyas to his feet and manhandling him up the stairs to his room. He was asleep even before they got there, and Esar, returning to Frey's sleepy embrace, was aware of nothing further after his head hit the pillow.

BRIVAR

Brivar was awakened at dawn by the Duke of Agrathon marching without ceremony into the room he shared with Della and throwing open the shutters.

Della rolled over with a groan, pulling a pillow over her eyes and swearing at her captain, who showed not a shred of remorse and ordered Brivar to get up.

"Why?" Brivar asked, half asleep, as he sat up and groped for his clothes. The room wasn't big, a servant's lodgings in the attic, and the bed was tiny, but it was a real bed, and he had been cosy and warm pressed against Della, sleeping deeply for the first time in weeks. He looked blearily up the duke, standing with his back to the window and the sun spilling in behind him, and had to shade his eyes from the glare.

"Because I need you and I don't have a lot of time."

Brivar sighed and kept his uncharitable thoughts to himself. He found his temple surcoat—badly in need of a wash—and pulled it over his head as he followed the duke from the room. They had been lucky, or Della had been particularly resourceful. Even the Duke of Agrathon's estate didn't have enough rooms for two hundred tired soldiers, and most of the company were sleeping on floors—comfortable floors, to be sure—or piled on top of each other on old mattresses dragged into the bigger bedrooms. Descending from the attic into the hallway of the second floor, Brivar had to pick his way over sleeping bodies as he hurried after Alyas. It was the same one floor down. As they passed the closed door to Cantrell's room, Brivar could hear the quiet murmur of conversation.

Descending the grand staircase, the duke led him not to the salon, scene of last night's excitement—Brivar had watched the fire and the syndicate's arrival from the attic's tiny window—but to a smaller room off to one side that had once been used as a study and had somehow avoided colonisation by those looking for somewhere to sleep.

The duke perched on the desk and crossed his arms. "Esar and Della think I owe you an apology."

"But you don't?" Brivar asked, more curious than offended. The whole company knew what had happened last night. The commotion of the fire had woken all but the deepest sleepers, and most of them had been hanging out of windows in time to see Agazi throw the syndicates out of the house. It wasn't a stretch to work out why they had come—nor to make an educated guess about whether they were right.

He studied the duke in morning light. He didn't look like a man who had been running around a city setting fire to things half the night. Tired yes, but Brivar had never seen him look well-rested, something he would have to address at some point. He was neatly dressed and more alert than he had any right to be, but Brivar remembered the man they had met in the woods what seemed a lifetime ago and knew that appearances counted for nothing.

"An explanation, yes," Alyas replied. "But I'm pushed for time so let me just say I had my reasons for not telling you about the Lathai, some better than others. I take it you spoke with Ailuin?"

Brivar nodded. It had taken him longer than he wanted to admit to realise what he had been told during that brief, surreal interview with the Lathai chieftain, and even now he wasn't sure what it *meant*. But after the disastrous experiment at the quarry, when he had sat with Alyas's Isyr weapons in his hands for half a day, he had started to line the pieces up. They didn't fit together yet, and he was sure he didn't have all of them, but he suspected that the main reason for Alyas's refusal to explain about the Lathai and Isyr had been to give him the unbiased space to do just that.

He *had* been angry when he realised the knowledge he had been entrusted with, without warning or explanation, and the burden it placed on him—he knew what would happen if the syndicates discovered the existence of pure Isyrium in the Lathai's mountains. But he was increasingly convinced there was more to it than that. *I had my reasons. Some better than others.*

He met Alyas's eyes and asked, "How do the Lathai make Isyr?" And when he saw him flinch, he knew he had been right. "Their Isyrium isn't pure, is it? They just refine it differently."

It had bothered him, when he realised it, why none of the Lathai seemed affected by Isyr as Alyas was, as his father had been. He did not believe it was something peculiar about them, except that they were among the only people other than the Lathai who were in close, daily contact with the metal. Its value and scarcity meant most other Isyr treasures were locked away in vaults. Whether that Isyr would have this effect on its owners were that not the case was impossible to know. It hadn't in the past, but that was no reliable guide. There hadn't been an Isyrium-driven plague then. The king had a crown of pure Isyr, but Brivar did not know whether he actually wore it. It was unlikely, even for a king. Therefore, he had decided it must be a difference in the Isyr itself.

The silence that answered him was not denial or refusal, it was the silence of a man who had had his fears confirmed. Eventually, the duke said, "When we discovered what they could do, we kept it a secret. We've spent most of the last ten years keeping the syndicates out of the mountains. There were rumours, but as long as that was all they were, we thought we could keep the Lathai safe. Now I count that decision among the worst mistakes of my life."

All these years, the Lathai had been safely purifying Isyrium into Isyr—the prize the syndicates coveted above all others—and the company had concealed it. They had thought they were protecting a secret that could start a war. What if, instead, they had hidden knowledge that could have prevented something much worse? But how could they have known? That it was the way the syndicates mined and processed Isyrium ore that was the cause of this contagion had not become apparent until Grey Rock. Even if they had allowed the Lathai's secret to leak out years earlier, there was no telling what the syndicates would have done with it. Nothing good, Brivar was sure.

But now—now it mattered.

"I have sent messengers to Ailuin, explaining what we've discovered. Asking for his help. He did not share their method with me. I did not ask. I didn't think I needed to know."

It was, Brivar guessed, a rare confession of error. It reminded him, for an uncomfortable moment, of the na'quia ravings, something else he would need to deal with at some point.

The duke looked away, towards the window, and said, "Ovisia Galea, head of the Orleas syndicate, will be here any minute. I suspect she will try to arrest me, and there is something else we need to discuss first."

Brivar blinked, shocked. "Surely you're not going to let her?"

"I shall endeavour not to, but for that I need..." He hesitated, clearly reluctant to ask for help. "Yesterday, she had come from a processing centre. Even just her presence... and last night... I cannot afford to be incapacitated every time I'm in the presence of this poison from their mines. I need to know if there is anything I can do."

Somehow this admission was more surprising than the one that preceded it, and unfortunately Brivar didn't have an answer for either. He had spent a lot of time thinking about it, and none of his theories were terribly reassuring, which was why he hadn't shared them with Cantrell last night, who seemed to have reached his limit of things to worry about. And none of them would achieve what Alyas needed.

He shook his head apologetically. "Until a few months ago, we had never encountered this sickness. Until a few days ago, no one knew that what you experienced at the quarry was possible. As for a solution… My best guess is that somehow either the illness or the na'quia has sensitised you to the by-product of the refinement process, but it is a guess. It tells us nothing about how to counter it."

The duke's face didn't change, but Brivar sensed his disappointment. More than disappointment.

He said, "When we return to Avarel, will you allow my master…?"

"No, only you."

Brivar sighed, though he had expected no other answer. He studied Alyas, seeing the small signs of strain in his pinched face and shadowed eyes. "It would help if you…" What should he say? He could hardly tell him to go to bed for a week and actually give himself time to recover. Not only was that simply not possible, but Brivar knew it would be counterproductive. You had to tailor the treatment to your patients. Some people were happy to do nothing and rest, others found such inactivity stressful, and he had known this man long enough to know he did not stay still for long.

"It would help if I what?"

He opted for, "Didn't push so hard. And you should also stop wearing those." He nodded at the Isyr blades. Just because they could not get rid of them, as Esar wanted, didn't mean he had to suffer them. "I don't know if the two things are connected, but they cannot help."

Alyas's hand strayed to the rapier's hilt. "I can't. Everyone associates the Duke of Agrathon with these weapons. If I set them aside now, I may as well shout from the rooftops that I know what the syndicates are hiding."

Brivar suspected he had already done that, and much louder, but he chose not to comment. If Alyas wanted to convince himself that was the reason, Brivar wasn't going to change his mind at the first try.

There was a knock at the door, and Alyas broke his gaze to say, "Come."

The steward entered the room. "Sayora Galea, Your Grace. She is waiting for you in the salon."

"Tell her I will join her shortly and see that no one disturbs us. No one. *Especially* my aunt."

The steward nodded. "Of course, Your Grace."

Brivar watched the door close and said, "I should go."

Alyas stood. "No, stay. I need a witness, and Esar has more important things to do this morning."

֍

Brivar had not yet met Ovisia Galea, advisor to the king, and according to the duke, the head of the powerful Orleas syndicate, who was reclining in a leather chair in the salon. He rather wished he didn't have to, and from the moment her wolfish eyes fell on him, he was convinced of it.

"Your Grace," she said with an insincere smile when Alyas entered. "Forgive our intrusion last night. It was unseemly."

The duke shrugged. "Of course." He was standing as far away from her as he could without making it obvious.

Her smile became sharper. "You are generous."

"Not really," he replied. "I'm busy. If I argue with you about it, you'll just be here longer."

Ovisia's eyes flickered to Brivar before returning to the duke. "It's interesting that you think I'm leaving."

"Are you not?" he asked in mock surprise. "I would offer you accommodation, but as you can see, we are rather full."

"I apologise," Ovisia replied. Her smile had vanished. "I should have clarified—I meant, without you."

Brivar felt a ripple of shock. He had not believed Alyas's assertion that the syndicate would try to arrest him, but it was clear that this woman thought she could do just that. Beyond the closed doors he could hear the sounds of the house coming to life—the clattering of armed men and women moving around—and he wanted to run outside and call for help, but he couldn't leave. The duke had asked for a witness.

Alyas himself was quite unmoved by this threat. "I'm afraid I require clarification of your clarification, Sayora."

"No, you don't. Who is this?" She gestured at Brivar.

"He is here as a representative of the Temple of Yholis, as an independent witness. I am entitled to that, surely?"

"Then you do know why I'm here."

The duke examined a speck of something on his sleeve. "I know why you think you're here. I'm also quite sure you're mistaken."

Ovisia stood. Alyas didn't actually back up a step, but Brivar saw him flinch as she closed the space between them.

"We know you were responsible for the unprovoked attack on our processing centre last night," she told him. "And the unwarranted destruction of our Grey Rock mine."

"On the contrary, you can't possibly."

"And why is that?"

"Because it wasn't unwarranted." Brivar noted he made no denial of the fire, but at this point it would have made no difference.

"So *you* say, Your Grace."

Abruptly, Alyas turned away and walked to where Brivar stood. There were faint lines of pain on his face.

Without looking at him, Alyas asked, "How many survivors did we find at Grey Rock?"

Surprised, Brivar said, "Six."

"What did they say attacked them?"

Ovisia turned her predatory gaze on him. "Yes, what did they say, these survivors?"

Brivar licked dry lips, his heart thumping with nerves. "Their own people." It came out as a whisper. "Driven mad and transformed by the contagion."

"And did you see these *transformed* miners?"

He hesitated, then shook his head. Because he hadn't. The duke had made him stay back with Della while they dealt with the mine. He had arrived only later, after the fire had done its work.

Ovisia turned back to Alyas. "Not a very good witness, is he? Either you lied to him, or he's lying to protect you."

"He's a surgeon of the Temple of Yholis," Alyas pointed out. "He can't lie."

"He's an apprentice. He hasn't yet taken his vows. His testimony is meaningless. Will you stop this now, Your Grace, and walk outside with me?"

Brivar felt a shock of fear. He had heard of other people 'walked outside' by the syndicates. It was not as benign as it sounded; they were rarely heard from again. So he fully expected Alyas to refuse or put up a fight. If he went with her, if he let them take him to a syndicate facility, Brivar was quite sure he would die there. But he didn't refuse. Instead, shoulders slumping, he just gave up. "Very well."

Ovisia's triumphant look made Brivar feel sick. He cast a panicked look at the duke, who refused to meet his eyes.

"Please," he said in desperation. "You can't –"

"I assure you I can. Shall we go, Your Grace?"

Brivar watched them, stunned into inaction, but as Alyas followed Ovisia through the door, he could not let him go alone. Outside, the steward and the house staff were standing in a line along the hallway, as they had been on their arrival. Hailene-Sera Ahn stood with them, her face set in an expression that reminded Brivar very much of her nephew. There was a shocked quality to the silence that stood in direct contrast to the brevity of the duke's occupation of the house.

Brivar looked wildly around for Cantrell, for Agazi, for Della—for anyone who could stop this—but there was no sign of them. Then they passed through the main doors and out into the courtyard and he saw why.

Ovisia stopped on the threshold. "What is this?"

"My company."

And it was. Drawn up in the courtyard, the entirety of the company that had accompanied them to Orleas, mounted and ready to ride. The six syndicate representatives who had come with Ovisia stood alone in circle of empty space to the right of the steps. There were no weapons on them. They were not threatened in any way. They were also hopelessly outnumbered.

Triumph fading to anger, Ovisia turned on him. "What are they doing?"

"Waiting for me. We have an appointment with the king in Avarel."

Brivar felt a laugh bubbling up and clamped down on it hard.

Ovisia snarled. "You said –"

"That I would walk outside with you," Alyas said, jogging down the steps to Esar, who handed him the reins to his horse. "Which I have. And now I must take my leave. Brivar."

Brivar dragged his eyes from Ovisia's furious face to see Della approaching with his horse. He hurried to meet her, looking back to see the king's advisor frozen in impotent rage. She knew she was beaten. But it was not over.

He mounted his horse, dragging the beast around to give Ovisia a clear path as she descended the steps after him and gathered up her escort. Alyas gave them a cheery wave as they turned away and Brivar was not the only one who felt profound relief as the small party stalked away. As soon as they passed through the outer gates, the company erupted in cheers.

Over the noise, Brivar heard Esar say, "Whatever happened to stalling her as long as possible?"

"She insisted on getting straight to the point," Alyas replied. "Did you get Frey safely away?"

"An hour ago. And you're still here, so things could have gone worse."

Alyas smiled grimly. "That was just round one. Let's see what they have in store for us in Avarel."

PART TWO

BRIVAR

The journey to Avarel was, if not restful, then at least unexciting. Scouts drifted in and out, some to and from nearby mines and the road ahead, others catching up from assignments further afield. Brivar wasn't privy to their reports, though Della, coming in from one of her scouting trips, told him, yawning, that everything was quiet enough. Then she pulled him down onto the bedroll and he had forgotten what they were talking about.

Perhaps the most surprising thing about that week, other than the absence of catastrophe, was Alyas coming to him, unprompted, on the evening of the first day and handing over the Isyr blades.

"Only until Avarel."

Brivar looked at the weapons and nodded. He wanted to ask what had changed his mind, but he didn't think he would get an answer. That last interview with Ovisia Galea, perhaps. It didn't matter, as long as he gave them up, even for a short time.

They didn't speak about it again, and Brivar carefully wrapped the blades in two blankets and strapped them to the bottom of his pack. He had no intention of experiencing their effects first hand; they were at least partly to blame for some of what he had heard during the na'quia and had driven at least one man to suicide. So he put them away and tried not to think about them, which was not as hard as he had thought it would be, because the closer they came to Avarel, the stronger the strange feeling in the pit of his stomach became.

He had missed the temple so much it hurt at the start of this journey. Arriving in the midst of the duke's company and confronted with a crisis, he had missed it even more. He had missed his teachers' counsel, the familiarity of duties carried out every day for thirteen years, of feeling like he understood his place and purpose in the world. Now they were going back, and suddenly he wasn't sure he wanted to.

It wasn't only the prospect of leaving Della. He could still see her. There was no requirement for celibacy among the devotees of Yholis as there was for her brother Ithol. It wasn't just the feeling that he was needed here. He had a right and a duty, as the appointed house surgeon—the small matter of his continuing apprenticeship aside—to attend Alyas or any of this company at any time he was required. It was, he decided, all those things and more. He had seen a life outside the temple now. He had friends outside the temple. And he was part of something. It was big and frightening, but it was also important and he knew he could help. Spending all his days at the temple, his opportunities to do that would be severely curtailed. His only consolation was the temple library—one of the most extensive in Ellasia—that promised at least the possibility of solving some of the mysteries with which they were faced.

They camped for the last time half a day outside Avarel, the great walls of the city visible in the distance clinging to the edges of the hill on which it was built, the fields around waiting for planting and the roads clogged with trains of wagons, each hitched to the next and pulled by teams of huge, placid urocs. That night Brivar returned the blades to Alyas. Esar was with him, scowling as Alyas took the weapons back. He seemed reluctant to reclaim them, and Brivar briefly regretted not trying to keep them longer. He looked better for it, though that might equally have been the result of a week with nothing more stressful to endure than one mile following another in endless succession. Even so, Brivar resolved to enforce breaks when he could.

When he had buckled the blades on, Alyas looked up at him. "Do you need me to come with you to the temple tomorrow?" He was offering to explain his actions in essentially kidnapping Brivar from his cousin's party and adopting him into his own household, without the knowledge or consent of the temple. It was not how things were usually done.

Brivar shook his head. "I'm sure Varistan Alondo will request an explanation if he feels one is required."

He saw a flicker of amusement cross the duke's face, but it was oddly subdued. Esar, too, seemed on edge, his eyes straying frequently to the vast edifice of the city in the distance. Brivar felt a flush of guilt. He had been so wrapped up in his own confused response to their return that he had not thought about how much this moment meant for these two men who had been banished from their home fifteen years ago, never expecting to see it again, and were returning now on the brink of a crisis with more enemies than friends waiting for them.

He left them alone. He was an intruder in that homecoming. Della, seeing the look on his face, said, "Keie had pains today." And laughed at him when he hurried to get his things, grateful for the distraction. "She's fine," Della assured him, tagging along. "But she thinks the birth is close."

"It can't be," he said firmly. "She must have another two months."

"Says you," Keie retorted, hand on her belly. "My baby. I know."

He shook his head. "It's too soon."

"Tell him to wait," Keie said with a flash of her white teeth. "I'm sure he'll listen to you."

"He?"

Agazi laughed. He was reclining against his saddle by Keie's side. "That's what she says. I'm not going to argue with her."

Brivar looked at Keie for permission before placing his hands on her belly, feeling for the baby. After a minute or so, he sat back on his heels. "*He's* not in position yet. His head's still here, see."

He placed her hand over a slight bulge that could be felt on her right side. "He's not coming today."

"Did I say today?" she said. "Soon."

He stood. "Well, if soon means in a few weeks, I'll be much happier. You will send for me, won't you?" He would be back at the temple tomorrow. No longer right here, ready to help. "You can, you know. You're part of his household. It's your right."

Keie laughed. "Silly boy. Who else would I want?"

He grinned at her, overcome with warmth for all of them. More his family in a few short weeks than his cousin had been in twenty-three years.

"I'll get you," Agazi assured him. "Alyas already promised you."

He had, had he? Somehow that made Brivar feel better about their impending separation.

"Come on," Della said, tugging at his sleeve with a significant look at the two steppelanders. "Let's leave these two alone."

He flushed, seeing the way Agazi's arm was curled around Keie, and let Della lead him back to their tent, where they made the most of their last night together. He found himself hoping that Keie's baby did come soon—not too soon, obviously—so he could find his way back to this company for a while. Because he missed them already.

※

A protest accompanied the Duke of Agrathon's return to Avarel. Entering through the grand main gate to find their way blocked by shouting crowds wearing masks and holding placards, Brivar thought for a horrible moment that they were there to protest against Alyas. Then he saw the slogans on their placards and realised it had nothing to do with him.

"They're the Nameless," he shouted over the din. The protestors were surging around them with no regard for their safety and appeared not to realise the real danger that they might be trampled by the horses.

"The who?" Alyas called back.

"The Nameless. They believe the traditional naming conventions are too elitist and concentrate power and wealth in the hands of the few." He was quite proud of that summary, having read several of their pamphlets over the last year. It was hard not to. They were everywhere. "They have given up their own names in protest."

Alyas shot him an incredulous look as he was jostled from both sides by protestors screaming their outrage. "They're about to give up a lot more than that." He turned to Cantrell. "Clear a path. We'll go by the side streets. These idiots are going to get themselves killed if we try to go through them."

Only the head of their column had made it through the gate. The rest of the company was strung out down the road leading up the hill to the city, unable to move forward with the mass of protestors in their way. Brivar's horse stamped and snorted, frightened by the crowds, not as well-trained as the horses the soldiers rode. Alyas grabbed his bridle and dragged him back into the relative shelter of the gate arch.

Esar, three on each side, was slowly forcing the crowds back to give the company space to come through the gate, using the bulk of the horses to create a corridor from the gate to a narrow street on their right. The protestors shouted and rushed at the line of horses. One tried to duck between the forest of legs and Esar leant down and grabbed him by the hair, shoving him roughly backwards where he fell and took down several more in a tangle of limbs.

Alyas swatted Brivar's horse on its rear. "Quickly."

He needed no further urging, nudging his nervous horse forward and into the shadowed quiet of the alley, the company following. He looked back.

"Go on," Aubron called, and he realised he was blocking their way.

After a hundred yards, the alley opened onto a wider street. Aubron drew alongside. "Which way?"

Brivar looked at him blankly, then realised he was the only one who knew Avarel. The duke and Cantrell were still back at the gate, funnelling the company through, and his cousin and his escort were at the back of the line.

He looked around. The temple was on the far side of the avenue they had just left, cut off for now, and anyway he could not take them there. He knew Alyas must own property in Avarel, theoretically at least, but he had no idea where it might be, and the duke had not told him where he intended to take the company.

"Where are we going?" he asked Aubron.

The man grinned. "You know Alyas. Where do you think?"

The palace, of course. Straight into the lion's den. Where else? And it looked like Brivar was going with them.

He oriented himself on the palace and led the company through the cobbled streets, hoping Alyas or Esar would catch up before they got there. It occurred to him that he was currently leading an armed company through the streets of Lankara's capital. He was not, under any circumstances, leading them onto the palace grounds. The very thought made him a puddle of nervous sweat. He was amazed they had been allowed to make it this far unchallenged, and guessed they had the protestors to thank for that.

Fortunately, that responsibility was taken from him. A fast clatter of hooves announced the arrival of Alyas, Esar beside him. They were both angry.

"Bloody fools," Esar swore when Brivar asked what had happened. One of the protestors had stuffed a bundle of their pamphlets in his horse's girth and he reached down to drag them free. Alyas plucked one of the pamphlets from his grasp before he could hurl them away. He scanned the badly printed text without comment, then folded it and tucked it into the top of his boot.

Esar shook his head. "You're not going to read that?"

Alyas shrugged. To Brivar he said, "I'm sorry, but I can't get you to the temple today. The garrison has cordoned off the Carpera and the streets around it. The protestors will be between us and the temple."

The Carpera was where the rich built their mansions. It was also where the temples of Yholis and Ithol were located. And up ahead, Brivar could see the familiar scale cuirasses and red sashes of the Avarel garrison forming a barricade across the street. They had seen the approaching horses and their frantic activity had a distinctly aggressive flavour. He grasped his temple amulet and gave his heartfelt thanks to Yholis that Alyas had turned up when he had.

Alyas signalled the company to halt and rode ahead with Esar. A tall man with a gold sash came to meet them, hand on his hilt and one of his men on either side. Alyas dismounted. He handed his reins to Cantrell and walked forward. Brivar was too far away to hear what they said, too far to glean much from the men's body language, and he couldn't suppress his flinch as the man in the gold sash suddenly made a grab for Alyas. He wasn't the only one. The company at his back flinched with him, and only Esar's raised hand prevented their instinctive response.

The garrison commander enveloped the duke in an embrace. Then he held him out by shoulders, laughing, before releasing him and walking to Esar, who reached down and grasped his arm.

"Well, that was unexpected," Aubron murmured, easing his hand from his sword. He looked as surprised as Brivar felt, and relieved. As well he might. There were too many armed soldiers in one street for anyone's comfort.

Esar waved them forward, and as Brivar and Aubron drew level, he said, "This is Nicor-Heryd Zand, commander of the king's guard. He will escort us to the palace."

Up close, Brivar recognised the man from his visits to the palace with Varistan Alondo, who was the queen's personal surgeon. Nicor-Heryd was a big man in his early fifties, tall and broad, his hair turning grey, and he had an old wound to his thigh that still bothered him. He had come to the temple a few years ago, not long after he had taken it, and Brivar had listened as his master berated him for not caring for it properly.

He was smiling now, still shaking his head. "Alyas-Raine and Esar Cantrell. We heard you were on your way. I still can't believe you came back. Some of the boys had a wager going. A few of them will be drinking their winnings tonight. Those are mostly the ones who want to stick a knife in you, mind, so watch yourselves."

"There are some who don't?" Alyas asked, his voice light. "What about you, Nicor? Where did you put your money?"

"I thought you'd have more sense. Why, man? You had something good. We've all heard the stories."

Alyas shrugged. He was smiling but his eyes were guarded. "Most of them are no more than that."

Nicor-Heryd laughed. "I know that. I expect the king knows it too, deep down. Still gets to him, though. He's not the same. He hasn't been, not since you left."

Alyas stared straight ahead. Cantrell scowled. "We didn't just *leave.*"

Nicor-Heryd winced and dropped his gaze. "I know. I was there, remember? I know what happened, even if no one else does. I'm just saying…"

"What? What are you saying?" Cantrell demanded.

Alyas said, "Esar."

Brivar hadn't known one word could say so many things.

Nicor-Heryd glanced sideways and a flush crept up his face. "Whatever you're expecting, you're going to be wrong. Take that as a warning from one of the few friends you have in Avarel. It's good to see you, Alyas. But as a friend, I wish you hadn't come."

Well, thought Brivar, that was reassuring. Esar evidently thought so too, his frown so deep the lines on his forehead could have been carved in stone.

Alyas shrugged. "Well, we're here. Shall we get it over with?"

He collected his reins and would have remounted. Nicor-Heryd stopped him. "Can't take a mounted company into the palace grounds. You know that. You, yes, not the rest." He looked up at

Cantrell. "Take my advice, Esar, and don't go with him. I doubt the king has forgotten you threatened to kill him. Best not to remind him in front of the court."

The duke and Cantrell shared a look. Alyas said, "Can you spare some men, Nicor? Esar will take them to Camling, but you've locked down the Carpera. Send someone with him to let him through."

Esar didn't look happy, but he didn't argue. They had anticipated this, if not the protests that had shut the city down. The garrison commander nodded, satisfied, and passed the order to his men. "Anyone going with you?" he asked Alyas.

The duke indicated Brivar, who started in alarm and surprise. Nicor-Heryd noticed him for the first time. "An apprentice of Yholis? That's a suspiciously non-confrontational choice." His eyes narrowed, then he smiled. "I know you, don't I? You helped me with this." He patted his thigh. "Very well, let's go."

As he moved back to his men to clear a way through the barricade, Brivar asked, "Why me?"

Alyas said innocently, "Why not?"

rivar had been to the palace before. The queen's household was extensive, and as Varistan Alondo's apprentice, it often fell to him to treat the ailments of its less important members. He recognised many of the palace officials and even some of the king's advisors and state ministers, but he had never been inside the royal audience chamber, nor attended court, and he had never expected to. Certainly not in such circumstances.

As he followed Nicor-Heryd Zand and Alyas-Raine Sera through the corridors of Avarel's royal palace, it felt like he was seeing it for the first time. As an apprentice of Yholis, he was virtually anonymous. No one paid him much mind, and no one stopped and stared as he passed. The Duke of Agrathon's return to the court of King Raffa-Herun Geled was a sensation that brought the entire palace to a stunned halt. Eyes followed them every step of that interminable walk. People stopped what they were doing to watch, or whisper, and rumour ran ahead of them so that the further they went, the more crowded the corridors became. And the bolder the watchers. By the time they reached the doors of the audience chamber, more than one insult and accusation had been hurled at the duke, who ignored them all and looked neither left nor right, though Brivar could see by the set of his jaw that he was far from oblivious.

The footmen at the doors were well warned and better trained. Their faces showed no expression as they ushered him into the antechamber where the king's herald waited. He bowed to Alyas. "If you're ready, Your Grace?"

Alyas gave him a tight nod and the great doors opened to the sound of the herald proclaiming, "His Grace, the Duke of Agrathon, Alyas-Raine Sera."

The herald did not bother to announce Brivar, who was neither surprised nor offended and scuttled quickly to one side and tried to blend into the crowd—which was almost larger than the chamber could hold.

If Alyas had hoped for a relatively private first audience with the king, that hope was dashed as soon as the doors opened. Anyone who could claim the status to be present was crammed into the room, some of them still red in the face and adjusting their elaborate court clothes as though they had run here from whatever they had been doing as soon as they heard he was back. Which they probably had.

The heat and their curiosity were stifling, and Brivar could feel the sweat collect around the high neck of his undertunic. Alyas, dressed as he usually was in close, leather armour, looked small and strange amid the puff and pageantry of current court fashion. And they watched him with expressions that veered from outright hostility to naked disdain.

But that wasn't the worst thing. Not by a long way. Worse than their contempt was the woman who sat to the left of the king's empty throne, her blue-dyed court dress studded with Isyrium and her dark hair piled high on her head. Ovisia Galea, king's advisor and head of the Orleas syndicate, and a most vengeful looking enemy.

"Sayora," Alyas greeted her as if they were merely continuing their last conversation and he did not have the full assembly of Avarel's court glaring at his back. "How delightful. Are you going to try to arrest me again?"

"I've a good mind to let her," a deep voice said. When Alyas turned towards it, Brivar saw him visibly start at his first sight of the king.

Brivar had never known King Raffa-Herun as a young man. At forty-five, he was far from old, and only two years older than Alyas, but he looked much older. He had once been known for his physical prowess—in his youth, he had participated with distinction in every New Year Games, the celebration of Ithol that closed the old year and opened the new—but he had given that up years ago and would be hard-pressed to fit into his armour these days, even if he had been inclined to. He was tall—a half head taller than Alyas and twice as broad, the breadth of his shoulders matched by his girth—but his skin had the unhealthy tinge of a man who drank too much, slept too little, and rarely moved more than he had to, and Brivar happened to know that was indeed the case.

Of his queen, of whom Alondo frequently made the same complaints, there was no sign.

"Is this how you repay my generosity in inviting you back to court? By burning syndicate property, my property?"

Alyas, his face bleached white, said, "I wasn't aware I owed you anything, Raffa. The opposite in fact." And if he heard the shocked gasp that ran around the room, he gave no sign of it. They may as well have not been there for all the attention he gave them.

As the two men glared at each other, Ovisia leaned forward and said with satisfaction, "He does not deny it, sire."

"Well," Raffa grated. "Alyas-Raine, do you deny it?"

"Which bit?" Alyas asked testily, "Sayora Galea's accusations are as confused as she is."

"The bit," said Ovisia, rising from her seat, "where you deliberately destroyed a syndicate mine, and then one of our processing centres in Orleas. Which you continue to deny."

"I have never denied burning the mine," Alyas pointed out. "In fact, I told you I had done so when we first met, and I told you why."

"Ah yes, the contagion. And I see you have brought along your witness who didn't see anything." Brivar shrank further back into the crowd as heads turned in his direction. "But the flaw in your tale, Your Grace, is not only the absence of any evidence, but the location of the mine. This contagion is spreading out of the south—how could it have reached Grey Rock, bypassing everywhere in between?

And you can't possibly claim it had reached Orleas."

"It is not only in the south," another voice said, and Brivar turned with the rest of the court to see a man in bright Flaeresian dress emerge from the crowd to stand beside Alyas. "As I have already told you, sire"—he bowed deeply to Raffa-Herun—"Flaeres has also been touched by this contagion and the creatures it creates, across our northern border, and we have the Duke of Agrathon to thank that it has not spread further." To Alyas he said, "King Diago remains in your debt."

Alyas acknowledged that with a nod, while Brivar and everyone else waited to see how the king would respond. But he merely looked at Ovisia Galea as if to say *your move*. She shot a narrow-eyed glare at the man who must be the Flaeresian ambassador and said savagely, "Or so he told you, Lord Gaemo. What proof do you have that Flaeres is threatened?"

"Are you suggesting some kind of conspiracy, Sayora?" the ambassador asked. "Because that seems most unwise. The syndicates would be better served by not obstructing our investigations or making false accusations against those who are attempting to defend us from this menace."

It was a threat and one that came directly from her king, even if the crown in Flaeres was almost as deeply entangled with the syndicates as Lankara was.

Alyas chose that moment to add, "Raffa, your envoy Sul-Barin Feron can confirm my account. He was at Grey Rock."

"I was there," a voice agreed from the back of the room, and Brivar turned to see his cousin. He looked flustered and out of breath. He *had* been sulking at the very back of the column. They had not spoken since the incident with Corado. As far as Brivar knew, his cousin had made no effort to approach him, though he was not unaware of the company's subtle protection. So he had no idea, at this moment, what he would say next. Corado was dead and his death was a potential weapon.

The king latched onto his envoy's presence with evident gratitude. "Lord Sul-Barin, please share your testimony."

Brivar watched as his cousin made his way between the ranks of spectators to the side of the Flaeresian ambassador and prayed to Yholis that his version of the truth would support the duke and not the syndicates. Alyas was watching him too and his face was impossible to read.

Sul-Barin glanced at Alyas once before he said to the king, "Grey Rock had been consumed by the contagion before our arrival. It could not be saved. The Duke of Agrathon merely did what was necessary to protect your realm when he burned the mine. I have no knowledge of Orleas. I cannot speak to events there."

The king, looking as relieved as Brivar felt, said, "Well, Sayora, are you satisfied there was cause to burn the mine?"

From the set fury on her face it was obvious she did not, but equally obvious that she had no choice but to retreat. For now. "I am prepared to accept the possibility, sire," she snapped. "For Grey Rock. Orleas remains unanswered for."

Irritation flashed in the king's eyes. He was bored with this now and annoyed with all of them. "Well, Alyas, what do you have to say about the processing centre?"

Alyas shifted his gaze from Ovisia to the king. "What if I told you I burned it because I felt like it?"

Brivar groaned and felt for his amulet. The king's brow darkened in anger as Ovisia's expression morphed to predatory glee.

"Are you telling me that?" the king demanded, and it was clear to Brivar that he did not want to be put in the position of dealing with the fallout of that confession. He might very well choose to abandon Alyas to the syndicates.

Alyas shrugged. "Merely curious, Raffa, to see what you would do."

The moment hung between them, fraught with dangerous tension, as the entire audience stilled in anticipation of the king's reaction, and Brivar seriously considered that Alyas had brought him here just so he could carry word of his execution back to Esar. Then the king threw back his head and laughed, and a ripple of relief fanned out through the room. The crowd wanted blood, but not right here, right now. "You haven't changed. Gods, I've missed you. Welcome back, brother." And he hooked Alyas round the shoulders, pulling him into an entirely one-sided embrace.

The king seemed not to notice the lack of enthusiasm in response to this gesture of affection. To the court, he said, "You may leave us now to speak in private." A pointed look at Ovisia Galea included her in his command. As the disappointed crowd moved slowly to obey, carrying Brivar with them, he heard the king say, "Sayari Gaemo. Please attend us. I would hear Flaeres's account of this contagion one more time."

Brivar, jostled by the departing spectators, desperately sought to catch the duke's eye. He had no idea why he was here or whether he should stay—he could not honestly say that he wanted to—and was relieved when Alyas turned and tilted his head towards the door in dismissal. He was less reassured by the expression on his face, or rather the lack of one, which he had come to associate with nothing good, but there wasn't anything he could do, so he left.

A familiar figure was waiting in the courtyard, watched by nervous guardsmen who probably found his battle-scarred armour and numerous weapons rather threatening.

"You don't look like you just witnessed a murder, so I'll take that as a good sign," Esar said when Brivar reached him. "How did it go?"

Unsure how to answer that, Brivar said, "Sayora Galea was there."

Esar cast a dark look at the palace. "Was she?" He didn't sound surprised.

"The Flaeresian ambassador was also there."

Esar raised an eyebrow, his expression thoughtful. "Melar Gaemo? That's a dangerous man if ever there was one. And he owes us a favour."

"I think he just repaid it," Brivar said, recalling the timely intervention that had deflected the syndicate attack. "They're not going to give up, are they?"

"The syndicates? No, they're not."

"What are you going to do?"

Esar didn't answer him. Instead, with a last look at the palace, he said, "There's no point waiting around. I'll take you to the temple and make Alyas's apologies to Alondo. He might not think we need allies, but I'd rather not anger the temples if we don't have to. Tell me about it on the way."

MARI-GELED HERUN

The day Alyas-Raine Sera returned to Avarel, Queen Mari-Geled took to her room and would not be disturbed. She spoke briefly with her husband before retiring, reminding him of everything they had discussed—everything he had promised—then she shut the door with her ladies on the other side, and waited.

It was not guilt that took her there. And certainly not because she was overcome by the return of a former lover. She could hardly call him *that*. No, it was because she knew she wouldn't be able to keep from giggling when that awful syndicate woman tried to take Alyas down in front of the court and he savaged her for it. She didn't doubt that he would. The rumours of Ovisia Galea's thwarted attempt to arrest him in Orleas had already reached them, and much as she wanted to watch round two, neither her dignity nor her husband's would withstand the sight of the queen dissolving into helpless giggles at the humiliation of their syndicate advisor.

And, if she was being quite honest, she did not want to be there for their reunion either. If it was as angry and hurtful and shocking as the last time they had seen each other, she had no wish to spectate. Bad enough that it had to happen in front of everyone, but sometimes the court was beyond even Raffa to command, and she had come to accept that Alyas must make his entrance as publicly as possible or his return would forever be dogged by rumours of what he had said and done.

Besides, she would see him afterwards. Raffa had promised.

A good while afterwards, as it turned out. Long enough for boredom to replace amusing speculation, and for the slightest hint of concern to pierce her confidence. Raffa had *promised*. And he needed Alyas badly. He needed his prickly, unbending defiance and especially his private army. Badly enough for him to set aside years of jealousy and hurt and admit that, if not in the wrong, he had at least acted hastily and too harshly. That he had misjudged, and it was time to recognise that. And, gods, it had taken her years to get him to that point.

Yet when the door snicked open and light footsteps entered the room, she had not expected to be so overwhelmed by the way the years disappeared and so many things she had not thought about for so long were suddenly vivid and sharp in her memory. She would never regret not marrying him. The circumstances, yes. That could have gone better. And she had never missed the life she was supposed to have. She was even prepared to believe that he felt the same, but this was *Alyas*. She had grown up with him, her and Esar, Gerrin's pair of strays, and he had been as close to her as a brother. They both had. She had loved him dearly, and she had been so cross with Raffa when he had made such a mess of things.

Alyas said, "Mari?" It was half question, half greeting, as uncertain as she had ever heard him sound.

Fifteen years on the throne next to Raffa had taught her how to hide her feelings. She emerged from her bed chamber into her salon and said brightly to cover her sudden urge to weep, "Alyas, darling. I'm so sorry about Ovisia. She insisted. Did Raffa put her in her place? He did promise." In a manner of speaking anyway, but who knows who had spoken to him after she did. He was not very resolute like that.

Alyas hesitated, a half-step into the room. He was looking at her as if he were experiencing that same rolling back of the years, to a different time, a happy time—before Gerrin had ruined it all. She studied him in turn. His sharp-angled face was a little sharper, a little older, and his dark hair had more grey in it than she had expected, his face too, but he was seven years older than her and had lived a different life. A harder life. Though that did not account for the shadows in his eyes. In them and beneath them.

"Not directly, no. Was he supposed to?" His tone was guarded.

Infuriating man. She wasn't quite sure which of them she meant. "He promised," she said, with a shrug that acknowledged all Raffa's shortcomings. Then, because it was suddenly achingly true, "It's good to see you, Alyas. I've missed you."

His face relaxed a fraction. "It's good to see you too, Mari. I confess, I did not expect Raffa to allow me to see you. When you weren't with him…"

He had assumed it meant something else. She laughed. "I can't stand that woman. I knew I wouldn't be able control myself if you went for her."

He quirked an eyebrow. "Why should I do that?"

"You know perfectly well why. Don't be annoying. How's Esar?"

"Looking forward to seeing you. Will you come and see him?"

She pouted. "Just give him your name, Alyas, and he can come to me." She hated going out into the city. It was hot and dirty and so much effort. She had never understood why Esar had refused both Gerrin's and Alyas's offer to formally bring him into their house. It would have given him a place at court that not even Raffa's dislike could gainsay. As it was, if she wanted to see him, she would have to go to Camling. Raffa was never going to invite him to the palace.

"He won't take it, you know that. And I can hardly blame him. So go to him, Mari. He's missed you." He hesitated. "We both have. We worried…"

She bit her lip. It had all gone so wrong, her plan to marry Raffa, and she had had no time to talk to Alyas before he had been banished. The last time he had seen her she had been shocked and frightened, watching him wrestle Esar out of the room and away from the king he had just threatened to kill. They would only have heard about the wedding later and they might well have worried whether she was willing, whether she was happy.

"I'm quite well," she told him. "Well, my knees ache, but I am reliably informed that if I lose weight they would be much improved." She had never been slim, and frankly she had no time for anything energetic. Time and too many court banquets had their inevitable effect. She did not care. Men still desired her, even if her husband's attention was mostly elsewhere. But when this attempt to lighten the mood failed to raise more than a smile that did not reach his eyes, she frowned. Once she had been able to chase away the shadows with just a laugh. Now they looked harder to shake loose. "But you—you don't look well, Alyas."

"People keep telling me that."

"And do you think you should listen?"

"What makes you think that I don't?"

"Because I know you. Let me send you my surgeon. It's Alondo. You know him."

He shook his head. "There is no need. And anyway, I have my own."

She raised an eyebrow, both at the lie and the admission. "The apprentice? I heard that rumour, and the one about the Varisten throwing a fit when she heard what you'd done. He's a nice boy, but he's still an apprentice."

"You know him?" he asked, surprised and perhaps a little discomfited.

"He's Alondo's apprentice. Of course I know him. Who do you think told me to lose weight to help my knees?" She laughed at the memory. "Alondo wouldn't dare. The poor boy was mortified. And that, darling, is how I know you're lying, because if he would say that to his queen, he has certainly had words with you."

Alyas finally smiled. She would have been more reassured if it hadn't been intended as a deflection. "I've missed you, Mari. Are you happy here, with Raffa? I can forgive a lot, but not if he's made you miserable."

"Oh, I'm happy enough," she replied, permitting the change of subject because she didn't have a choice, even letting pass the outrageous lie. "Happier than we would have been, darling. You would always have been thirsting for adventure and I, as you see"— she gestured ruefully at her ample figure—"am far too lazy for adventure. Can you see me following you on your campaigns?"

"Had we married, I hope I wouldn't have gone on any." He was half serious.

"Oh, Alyas," she laughed. "You could not have sat quietly at home, no more than I would have enjoyed sitting quietly at home waiting for you. You know it's true. So perhaps this suited us both very well."

He stiffened, his face closing off. "It was for the best?"

She realised what she had said and cursed the thoughtless words. He would not have forgiven Raffa, whatever he claimed. He never would. She knew him well enough to know that. "I didn't know what he was going to do, Alyas, I swear it. He was supposed to talk to you, to ask you. We agreed…"

"You agreed? Why didn't you tell me how you felt, Mari? Did you think I wouldn't listen? That I would refuse you?"

"Gods, Alyas," she exploded. "Do you have any idea what you were like then? You weren't talking to anyone. You drove Esar half out of his mind with worry. Raffa thought he could send you off for a bit and shake you out of it. Then when you got back, he was going to ask for me. But the syndicates were at him constantly the whole time you were away, going on about those wretched mountains, and he hoped you would solve that for him too, and then you walked back in with that bloody peace treaty, and he just lost it. He's regretted it ever since…" She caught sight of his face, and the words died in her throat. "Alyas?"

He had backed off a step, his face frozen. "You make it sound so reasonable, Mari. Like he did nothing more than lose his temper. As if he didn't take everything I had –"

"Alyas…"

"As if he didn't take my name and make a ruin of it. As if he didn't lie and steal and murder four hundred of his own men to cover it up. As if I brought it on myself."

Silence hung between them. The kind of silence there had never been, even after their worst arguments. She could not ask him now about Orleas as she had promised, though she had never really intended to. A distance yawned between them that not even shared memories could close, and she hated it.

"I didn't mean that," she said in a small voice. "You know I didn't."

"Do I?" he asked, and it was like he was talking to a stranger. Then something in his face changed, and suddenly he just looked tired. "Am I being unfair, Mari? He is your husband and this is your life. What should I expect? Can I tell Esar you will come? We are at Camling."

He was leaving. She did not try to stop him. It would have been awkward and painful, and it would not have worked. Instead, she plastered a smile on her face and pretended that inside she wasn't weeping.

At the door, he turned back. "Do you have any Isyr jewellery, Mari?"

The question startled her, caused a flutter of panic. Words tumbled out. "Of course, but I never wore it, even before Raffa locked it away. It doesn't suit me. Too cold. I don't have that Janath colouring. I prefer warmer metals." She showed him the rose gold earrings she wore.

"Raffa doesn't wear his crown."

"Ugly thing," she said, keeping her eyes on his face and away from the bright blades at his hips. "It was too tight. It gave him headaches. I made him lock it away with all the rest."

"*You* made him, Mari?"

"Yes." It had done worse than give him headaches. By the time she had taken the crown from him, Raffa's nightmares were so bad he would sit up half the night, desperately trying not to sleep. It had taken a while for them to fade even after the dreadful thing was hidden away. Now she understood the shadows that marked Alyas's eyes and his face. "Why?"

Alyas shrugged. "He always loved Isyr."

His meaning this time was plain. She shook her head. "That was not the reason, Alyas. I promise you."

"If you say so, Mari," he replied, and then he did leave.

※

The door closed and suddenly her knees ached and her legs felt weak. She sat, staring at the place he had been, wishing they could start again. Trying hard not to regret what she had never regretted and had promised herself she never would, because didn't she have everything she ever wanted?

It had not always been that way. For many years, Mari-Geled had been quite content with her life as Gerrin Raine-Sera's ward and her allotted fate. The Duchess of Agrathon would have as comfortable a life as it was possible to have. But then Raffa-Herun Caen, as he had been in those days, had started to look at her differently, and she had come to realise there was a higher target to aim for. She didn't have to be just a duchess; she could be a queen. It didn't matter that she had no more romantic feelings for the young king than she had for her betrothed. She was a young Lankaran woman of noble birth and in such circumstances one did not expect to actually care for one's husband. But she was woman enough to want her husband to want her, and not to approach the matter dutifully as Alyas would have done.

And they had been happy enough, her and Raffa, the small hiccup of Alyas and Esar's exile notwithstanding. The only fly in her ointment was the lack of an heir, but Raffa had what seemed to be hundreds of nephews and she had never really cared for children, so when he finally accepted that the throne would pass not to his son but to one of his brothers' children, it had been a great relief to both of them.

Lately, however, other problems had intruded, and their happy equilibrium had been tested. More than tested. The syndicates had become unbearably uppity, and Raffa seemed not to know at all how to handle them. To the point where he was quite in their power, and was even able to admit it to himself, so she had done what she had not thought she would do, and she had begun trying to persuade him to bring Alyas home. Because if ever there was a man who would put the syndicates in their place and enjoy doing it, it was Alyas-Raine Sera. The danger had always been what else he might do.

She was still sitting where she had dropped when her husband entered, and she eyed him with annoyance. He must have been hovering nearby to be here so soon, waiting for the sound of the door.

"Well?" Raffa demanded, and she caught herself comparing his dissipated appearance with the neat, lean man who had just left. Then she decided she was in no position to make such complaints and put that thought firmly aside.

Ovisia Galea followed him through the door and Mari felt irritation overwhelm her. It wasn't just that the woman had been Raffa's lover—Ithol knew, he had had plenty of those—but it didn't help. And right now she had no patience for the syndicates and their incessant scheming. "Well, what?" she snapped. "What is *she* doing here?"

They both ignored her, which enraged her all the more. "What did he say?" Raffa asked. "Did he admit to Orleas?"

"Of course not. He's not an idiot. He trusts me about as much as he trusts you. What is she doing here, Raffa? You know how I feel about you flaunting your conquests in front of me."

"She's here because I requested it," Raffa said peevishly, flushing. Mari knew that was a lie. It was Ovisia who did the *requesting* in that relationship, and she merely stared coolly at the queen, secure in her power. It was infuriating. "Did you actually ask him, Mari?"

She could lie, too. "I asked him. He denied it. I believe him." She could handle Raffa perfectly well when they were alone, but he was hopeless where the syndicates were concerned, which he proved a moment later when he said, "Sayora Galea says she has proof that he set the fire."

"Then why doesn't she use it?" she asked, ignoring the fact that Ovisia was standing right next to him. "Or have you found your balls and remembered that you *need* Alyas. The syndicates have failed to contain this. You can't spare the men and they can't move fast enough. Someone has to protect Avarel, and it's not you and it's not her."

Anger marked white lines around Raffa's eyes and mouth. "Only if he doesn't know what's causing this. Ovisia says he does."

"And whose fault is that?" she retorted. This whole mess was the syndicates' fault. When she had finally persuaded Raffa to bring Alyas back, they had been furious, and they had gone straight for him. They hadn't even waited to see what he would do. And so of course he was suspicious, which ruined all her careful plans. They needed Alyas and the trained forced he commanded to contain this threat while the syndicates worked on solving the problem. Ovisia and the other syndicate heads had assured Raffa it was possible, they just needed time, and since neither she nor the king wished to give up their luxuries, and certainly had no desire to upend the economic and social stability of not only Lankara but the whole of Ellasia, they had agreed to give them time. But it had been too long. This plague was spreading too fast, and it was worse, far worse, than they had been told. They could not afford to alienate Alyas any further.

"We do not need him," Ovisia said now. "Sire, his men are in Avarel. They are yours if you wish to take them. Remove the duke and put one of your own in charge."

Mari laughed. "You stupid woman. You have no idea how this works, do you? You are loyal to nothing except money. *They will not serve under anyone else*. Try to take him from them and you will find out what that means."

She should already know, if the rumours about Orleas were true, but the syndicates had been allowed their own way for far too long. They only knew one way to deal with defiance, and they had already tried and failed to take Alyas that way.

"If the king himself orders it –"

"He is not such a fool," Mari scoffed.

Even Raffa was shaking his head. "No, Ovisia, it will not work. You must find another way."

She snapped. "Ithol's bollocks, Raffa, you *need* him. Stop looking for a way to get rid of him. Use him. So what if he has guessed the cause? The outbreaks are getting worse, and they are getting closer. Send him to deal with them and he will be too busy to do anything else. And in the meantime," she said to Ovisia, "you and your colleagues will *find a way to stop this*. As you swore you would."

Ovisia ignored her as if she had not spoken. "Sire, using this man would be a disaster. If you will not remove him from his position, we must find a more permanent way of dealing with him."

Kill him, in other words. Black rage filled her, both at the suggestion and the insult Ovisia had just offered her. Even Raffa was looking a little pale. Whatever had passed between them fifteen years ago, whatever he had felt about Alyas in the years since, once they had been friends. But he was so malleable these days, so easily led in whatever direction the syndicates wanted, and Mari dared not let that suggestion take root.

"Get out," she hissed at Ovisia, and Raffa finally seemed to realise he had made a mistake in bringing her here.

"Sayora," he said coldly. "You may leave."

The syndicate woman bowed, shooting Mari a vicious look, and backed out of the room, leaving husband and wife to stare at each other in anger and wonder how it had come to this.

Except it wasn't really a mystery. They had been fine, happy even, when things had been fine. When all their problems were minor or easily solved, they had worked together well. But when things got difficult, really difficult, when syndicate pressure and a string of bad decisions had made a mess of everything, instead of pulling together they had pulled apart, until every conversation was fraught with unspoken resentment and every comment taken as criticism.

She no longer knew how to fix it; she no longer cared to. What mattered now was not how much or how little she and Raffa despised each other, but that they could resolve the syndicates' disastrous error and things could go back to the way they had been, when she had nothing more stressful to consider than which dress she would wear and whether it would still fit.

"That woman is poison," she told her husband, when she could speak without her voice shaking with rage. "You will not touch him, Raffa."

He looked at her sulkily, as at a loss as she was at the yawning chasm that now lay between them. "Why, Mari? Are you regretting choosing me over him?"

She walked to her bedchamber. "I have never once regretted that in all these years. Don't make me start now." Then she slammed the door in his face.

ESAR CANTRELL

Esar was still smarting from Varisten Elenia's tongue-lashing when he was told Melar Gaemo had arrived at Camling. Apparently the Varisten did not think Brivar was suited to the life of a military company and that Alyas had overstepped his rights in attaching an apprentice to his household. Esar had refrained from saying he thought the boy was perfectly suited to handle both the company and its captain. She was scared, and she wanted to protect Brivar from what she quite reasonably saw as a dangerous position. Yholis knew, Alyas *was* dangerous company at the best of times, and there was nothing safe about what was coming. So he kept his thoughts to himself and promised her Alyas would explain himself at the earliest opportunity, and he was wondering uncomfortably about how differently both parties would interpret that when Gaemo walked in.

"We must talk," the Flaeresian ambassador announced.

"He's still at the palace, Melar."

Gaemo unhooked his Flaeresian cape and sat down in an armchair. "I know. I will wait. And while I wait, you will tell me what really happened at Grey Rock and Orleas."

Esar said nothing. Gaemo might owe them, but he was a subtle man with his own agenda whose his first and last loyalty was to his king. And Diago's gratitude was as reliable as any ruler's. He had dealt with them fairly in the past, but that meant nothing with the stakes so high.

Gaemo tapped his gloves on his knee and treated Esar to an impatient look. "I am not here to trick you, nor do I have any intention of handing Alyas over to the syndicates. If I wanted to do that, I would have stayed silent today. My king gave me specific instructions should I see you both here, and I must know the truth. Though I admit, when I last saw him at Sarenza, I did not expect to see Alyas again. Would you mind telling me how he survived what none of our people have?"

"Go to the Temple of Yholis and ask them," Esar told him. "They found a cure."

Gaemo looked thoughtful. "Well, that does change things."

"It does not," Esar said with feeling. "You will realise why when they tell you. What were your king's instructions?"

"To put myself and my intelligence at your disposal. The syndicates have closed their facilities in Flaeres to our investigators and obstruct us at every turn. Unsurprisingly, my king suspects they are hiding something, and you and Alyas are the only people who have openly defied the syndicates and survived to tell of it—so far, at least. If Sayora Galea is right about Orleas—and, knowing your brother, I think she is—then you must also suspect their involvement in this contagion that threatens us all. We should work together."

It was tempting, and Gaemo had done them a good turn today, but he had not waited for Alyas to return to make this offer, which meant he was either desperate or thought Alyas would refuse.

The ambassador saw his indecision. "You have no other allies here, Esar. You must know that. I was at court today. I saw how they looked at him. They will fight him at every turn. You need influence from outside if you are to achieve anything."

The door cracked open. "Are you offering Diago's support or your own, Melar?" Alyas asked as he entered. He was unbuckling his armour as he walked and had clearly come straight here as soon as he arrived. "Thank you for your intervention. I confess I allowed my anger to get the better of me."

Esar was surprised by the admission, even though Brivar had faithfully related the meeting before the throne so he knew it was true. He would almost certainly have done the same, which was the only reason he had allowed Alyas to go alone. Brivar had been the best choice to go with him: unobtrusive, observant, and beyond reproach—should such a quality be required.

Alyas did not seem angry now, however, which Esar found deeply suspicious. His manner was brisk, his face unreadable, but they were not alone, and it was likely as much for Gaemo's benefit as his own.

"I didn't notice," Gaemo said with a thin smile as he stood. "And in answer to your question, both, Your Grace."

"Do not make me take that back," Alyas retorted. "We have known each other too long for such formalities."

"My apologies," the ambassador murmured. "I thought you wanted your title back."

"So did I," replied Alyas. He threw the brigandine over a chair and slumped into it. To Esar he said, "I saw Mari. She promised to visit."

Esar nodded. There would be more to it than that, but he could wait for the details. He was not prepared for Gaemo to say, "Be careful of the queen. I am aware of your family history, but that does not mean you can trust her."

"Leave Mari out of this," Esar growled, stirred to instinctive anger. To him, Mari would always be the lost little girl Gerrin had brought home after her parents died. The little girl who had tagged along behind them on their childhood adventures, getting underfoot and into trouble. She had been twenty-one last time he had seen her and fifteen years was a long time. He could not pretend to know her now. But she was *family*.

Gaemo gave a small shrug. "I would love to be able to."

Alyas did not meet Esar's eyes, nor did he immediately spring to Mari's defence. He was studying Gaemo with an intensity that would have discomfited a less confident man. "Let us concern ourselves with our sister. If you have truly come to help, tell me what Diago really knows about what is happening. Not just what he will admit to."

"Did you burn the centre in Orleas?" Gaemo countered.

It was, astonishingly, Alyas who broke eye contact first. "Why?"

Gaemo smiled. It did not reach his eyes. "Because I have a feeling we need someone who is prepared to burn it all down. And I want to know if that is you."

It would be folly to admit to what happened at Orleas to anyone. Esar knew that. So did Alyas. As long as he continued to deny it, even if no one believed him, it gave him some protection against the syndicates' schemes. Gaemo might be on their side now, but in the shifting sea of diplomatic relations, Lankara and Flaeres were frequently opposed and sometimes at war. So Esar could have strangled Alyas when he said, "Yes."

Gaemo sat back with a sigh. "You have surprised me. Not about the processing centre. I was fairly sure you were responsible for that. But admitting it to me…"

Esar felt a knot of tension. Were they about to hear the terms of Gaemo's latest blackmail? It was the unexpected consequences of one of those schemes from which they had recently untangled him and gained the favour he had repaid today.

Alyas, unconcerned, gave a small shrug. "You were right. We need allies and we don't have any here. Besides, I hope to give the syndicates far more cause to destroy me than that, for which I need your help. And Diago's. So, Melar, tell me how high this goes."

꒰꒱

"He's using you," Esar said as the door closed behind Gaemo.

"He's trying to," Alyas agreed. He rested his head back, eyes half-lidded. "But we're going to use him too."

"Oh well that's fine then," Esar said with deep sarcasm. "I was worried for a minute you were going to trust him. What happened up there?" He had been gone for hours.

There was a long silence. Esar kicked the chair.

Alyas opened his eyes and glared at him. "I was not asleep."

He might not have been, but he looked like he wasn't too far from it. Esar did not like this tiredness that would not go away. At first, he had assumed it was the lingering effects of the illness, then the na'quia, with almost no time to recover before this nightmare began, but the lack of improvement was starting to bother him. Worry made him snap. "I heard you couldn't resist provoking Raffa. What were you thinking?"

"Exactly what you would have been thinking," Alyas shot back, sitting up. He *was* tired. Esar could hear it in his voice.

"That's fair," he conceded, making allowances. "What happened after Brivar left?"

Alyas rubbed his forehead. "Raffa tried very hard to pretend he was pleased to see me. Gaemo relayed his news from Flaeres. A much-edited version of what he told us tonight. And we discussed how to respond in the very vaguest of terms." He hesitated. "Then I saw Mari."

"Alone?" Esar asked, eyebrows climbing into his hair.

Alyas sighed. "I know. It surprised me too. She was not with him at court. I asked why and he told me to ask her. He is… he is much changed, Esar. So is she. But she wanted this life, she told me that much. When he left me alone with her, I expected her to ask me about Orleas."

They had expected Raffa to keep them apart not to throw them together. He had always been a jealous man, and it didn't matter that Alyas and Mari had never been lovers. The broken betrothal would be enough. If Raffa had willingly left them alone together, Esar could understand why Alyas had been suspicious. They had been gone a long time and people did change, but surely not Mari. She had never had any time for court scheming. It took far too much effort.

"Did she?"

Alyas shook his head. "She didn't have a chance."

Esar looked sharply at him. "What did you do?"

"She tried to explain. I was tired. I may not have taken it well." He slouched back, looking up at Esar from shadowed eyes. "If she comes here, you talk to her, but we may be gone before that happens."

"Why?" Alyas wasn't the only one who was tired. They had not rushed the final leg of their journey, but they had been on the road for more than two weeks, and they had been several weeks in Flaeres before that. The whole company needed time to recover, especially if there were more Grey Rocks in their future.

"There's not a lot we can do sitting around in Avarel, and the syndicates will be all over us," Alyas replied. His eyes were closed again. "We need to get out there and see what's happening. Raffa did not tell me much. Either he doesn't know, or he's hiding what he does know. We will have to find out for ourselves."

Esar thought about that for a minute. "Brivar will be delighted. He didn't seem overjoyed to be back at the temple."

"Well, he's staying there, for now at least. We've kept him away from his studies too long."

That was not at all what Esar wanted to hear, for any number of reasons. "You can explain it to him then. And while you're there, you can also apologise to the Varisten, who is most unhappy with you." And maybe, while he was there, he might ask for help. "What are you going to do about Melar?" Silence. Esar kicked the chair. Nothing. He contemplated kicking it again, harder, to take out his growing frustration, but it would just hurt his foot, so instead he left Alyas where he was and tried not to think about how much he missed Frey.

❦

When the alarm came a few hours after midnight, Esar reflected that he really should be used to this by now, then decided he was just getting too old. At least this time he wasn't pulled from Frey's warm embrace, although that only made him miss her more. They had spent more time apart than they had together in the last few weeks and he could not help but worry.

Alyas was already up when he made it downstairs, although that was mainly because he had never made it to his bed and therefore it didn't count.

"What now?" Esar asked, yawning. His head was still spinning from being back in Camling—*Camling*, where he had grown up and had never thought to see again—and now it looked like they were leaving, almost as abruptly as they had left last time, and without even a few hours rest let alone a few days.

Alyas shot him a sympathetic look. He was still in yesterday's clothes and looked about as happy to be awake as Esar felt. "Riders came in from Cadria. They lost contact with a string of villages. A handful of villagers apparently ran into a patrol from the city. They went to investigate." He handed Esar the message from Nicor.

"Fuck," said Esar, reading it.

"Yes, quite."

"Where are you going?" Alyas had shrugged into his discarded brigandine and was buckling it as he headed to the door.

"To the garrison to talk to Nicor. Get everyone up and ready to ride at first light. It's three days to Cadria and we need to move fast."

"Not alone," Esar objected. "Take the watch with you. We're getting up now anyway. *Yes,* Alyas," he insisted, seeing the objection coming. "Have you forgotten Corado? And you told Gaemo about Orleas. You are not leaving this place without a guard."

Alyas waved a hand as he walked out. "Fine. I'll take them. Be ready. I'll be back soon."

The door shut. "Fuck," Esar muttered again, left alone in the empty room. He looked down at the message in his hand, then he screwed it up and hurled it into the fireplace. "Why can no one wait until morning?"

Alyas was back two hours later accompanied by Nicor and a detachment of his guards. Esar had rousted the company and they were assembling in the courtyard, grumbling and complaining. Della treated him to a black look when he told her Brivar wasn't coming with them.

"They won't be happy, Esar. They liked him. Made them feel better having him around."

It had made him feel better too, but even if Alyas was amenable, they did not have time to get him, and Esar had no desire to test the Varisten's anger by taking Brivar back mere hours after returning him.

"We'll be back in a week, Della." At least, he hoped so. "You can see him then."

"I will look after him for you," Keie told her with a wink. She was too far along to come with them.

Della stuck her tongue out at the steppelander. "It's not me I'm worried about, Esar." She was looking at Alyas where he stood talking to Agazi and his other officers. So, he wasn't the only one who had noticed.

"We'll be back in a week," he said again, more firmly. And when they got back he would march Alyas down to the temple himself.

Three days hard riding brought them to Cadria, Lankara's easternmost city and one that had made its wealth through the cloth trade rather than mining. That alone was enough to make Esar nervous—of all places, this part of Lankara was an unlikely region to be affected—and they doubled their scouts all the way there. Alyas sent them out in all directions, looking for signs of how the plague had reached this remote region.

In Cadria, Nicor's authority got them an interview with the garrison commander and an escort to the affected villages. The man had been wary at first, his gruff exterior hiding a shock that Esar could empathise with, but after he learned what they had seen at Grey Rock, some of his caution disappeared. He was no longer afraid they would think him mad.

"Lucky that patrol was out there," he said for the third time. "Wouldn't normally have been. What is it? What happened to those people?"

Alyas patiently explained, again, what little facts the official version contained. The garrison commander shook his grizzled head. "Makes no sense."

"This makes no sense," Alyas agreed as he stood in the centre of the devastated village a day later, the ash of its funeral pyre marking streaks up his boots and on his clothes, flecks of it settling in his hair.

That was an understatement. Nothing was right about this. Close to a hundred people had lived in this village. It was the largest of the three that had been destroyed by the contagion and its creatures—

Esar could not bring himself to think of them as the villagers—and it was as far from any mining operations as the others had been. There was nothing to connect them except proximity. They were not even linked by the corruption of the land.

The company knew what they were looking for now, and Alyas had their people scouting all around this place, looking for signs of where it had come from and how it had spread. They had found nothing. It was as if it had sprung out of nowhere in each village and that didn't just not make sense. It wasn't possible, not if everything they knew so far was right. And as uncomfortable as those facts were, this would be worse.

"They could be dumping the waste somewhere nearby," Esar suggested. It was the only explanation that might fit, but they had been looking for that too, and unless 'somewhere close' was under the villagers' beds, he couldn't see how that could be it either.

Alyas gave a non-committal shrug. "Everything suggests they are disposing of it outside Lankara, probably outside Hantara and Flaeres as well, if we can believe Gaemo. And about this I think we can. He has good spies. No, there is something wrong here."

He moved towards the centre of the village, where reports from the terrified survivors suggested the disaster had begun. There was nothing there except blackened earth and the charred remains of the little wooden shrine. Soldiers from nearby Cadria had set the fire days ago, before the company had arrived. Esar had led their cautious sortie into the burned village, armed with Isyrium and lit torches, but nothing remained, here or in the other villages, of the plague that had destroyed them. If not for the confused, panicked accounts of the survivors, he might not have believed it had been the contagion at all.

Esar dug through the ruins of the shrine with his sword. He wasn't expecting to find anything. Isyrium burned hot and little was left of the village. His sword point snagged a snarled lump of dull grey metal, warped and melted, and he flipped it over.

There was a sharp intake of breath behind him. He turned. Alyas's hand was curled tight around the hilt of his rapier and his face had paled. Esar crouched beside his find, drawing his dagger and poking at it. Its form had been lost in the fire, but he knew what it was. He looked at the scratches he had made on its surface with his dagger. Lead. Perhaps the remains of a lead casket. Memory showed him again the edges of lead sheeting around the pits in the quarry at Grey Rock. And Frey had said the crates of waste loaded on the wagon train had been lined with lead. She had watched the miners closing and sealing them.

He stood. Alyas had moved back, away from what Esar had found. His face was tight, pained. Esar swore. "They planted it."

Hard on the heels of that realisation came anger. The syndicates had deliberately seeded the contagion in these villages, far from any mining operations, to draw suspicion away from its real cause. The brazenness of it was staggering. The incalculable risk was unforgivable. Bad enough that through carelessness or greed or sheer stupidity they had created this crisis in the first place, but to unleash a deadly plague on these innocent, unsuspecting villagers, and in a remote region where help would be slow to arrive—where help might arrive *too late* to contain it—was sheer evil.

"Take it. We need it. If there are others…"

Esar focused on Alyas through the red haze. Evidence, this was evidence. Except it wasn't—not to anyone but them. He looked again at the lump of melted lead. It was pure chance they had found it, and only even unluckier chance that Alyas could sense the traces of what it had held, and that was not something they could risk revealing to the syndicates. They could hardly present it to Raffa and expect him to act on it, but if it was part of a pattern…

"Esar."

He looked up. Three of the Cadrian garrison troops who had led them here from the city had appeared at the far end of the village. They were watching them.

"Walk away," Alyas said. "We'll come back for it." He was already moving towards another burnt-out building.

Esar kicked ashes over the ball of lead and followed, forcing himself to walk casually. Alyas was picking aimlessly through the ruins of the building before moving to the next. The troopers watched them. Esar was glad they were too far away to see his expression.

It had been reckless even for the syndicates to risk an uncontrolled outbreak of the contagion by loosing it here, where it could have spread for days before anyone discovered it. But help had come, and quickly enough to contain it. Help that had known to burn it out. The survivors had run into a patrol from Cadria who *just happened* to be in the area. A peaceful, remote area, far from the border, an area there had been no reason to patrol. The report they had seen suggested the patrol had been sent out because the city had lost contact with the villages, but that seemed unlikely. The villages were far enough from Cadria to make frequent travel between the two difficult, and poor enough that they would have been of little significance to a city like Cadria. If a few farmers missed the market, it would hardly raise an alarm so soon.

"Esar," Alyas said again, a warning in his voice, and he realised he was glaring at the Cadrians.

Alyas turned to leave. "Let's go."

Esar caught up with him. The colour had come back into his face now they had left the lump of lead behind. "What if they take it?"

Alyas shrugged. "If we're right, we'll find more."

At the other villages. Anger stirred again. This couldn't have been done for their benefit. There hadn't been time. It was purely a precaution to stop anyone making the connection between Isyrium mining and the contagion. He still could not believe they would risk it.

He glanced back. The Cadrians had entered the village. They were walking slowly and without apparent purpose, but they were heading to the remains of the shrine. He suddenly did not doubt that they knew what they were looking for.

"If they think we suspect…"

"That would not be ideal," Alyas agreed. His jaw was clenched tight, a sure sign he was furious.

Elsewhere in the village, other members of the company were searching for anything that had survived. Alyas waved them over, sending them back to where the rest were waiting with the horses. Then he called to the Cadrians that they were leaving. He didn't wait for them.

"Where to?" Agazi asked when they reached them. He looked again at their faces. "What's wrong?"

"It's a set up," Esar growled. "The syndicates did this."

Alyas shot him a sharp, warning look. "Don't look back," he told Agazi as he mounted.

"They're in on it?" Agazi asked, his eyes narrowing in anger as he turned his back on the Cadrians.

Esar cast a covert look at the village as he fiddled with his horse's girth strap. Two of the men were watching them as the third dug through the ashes. When the company started to move out, one of the others nudged the crouching man, probably telling him to hurry, and Esar had to look away. He thought he might kill them otherwise. He was certain he wouldn't regret it.

❧

The Cadrians caught up with them before they reached the second village. Alyas made no comment as they rejoined the company. Esar rode on ahead. He didn't have the same self-control.

Nicor was waiting for them at the edge of the village. He walked over as they approached, hand reaching for Alyas's bridle. "We've combed through every inch of this place," he said. "There's nothing here. You?"

"Nothing," Alyas agreed, dismounting. "Nicor, we're going to stay out here another couple of days, look around. Will you take your men back to Cadria and thank their commander for their service? We've kept them from their duties long enough."

As the king's guard commander, Nicor-Heryd Zand had authority for all kingdom garrisons. The Cadrians were technically his men; if he ordered them back to the city, they had to go. He glanced from Alyas to where they were waiting, then took him by the arm and walked him a short distance away. "Are you trying to get rid of me?"

"Not you, but you should go back to Avarel. We'll see you there in a few days."

"Mind telling me why?"

"I will," Alyas promised. "But not yet."

Nicor-Heryd frowned. "I'm not sure that's good enough."

"And I have nothing to tell you yet that is not suspicion. When I do, you will hear it."

Nicor dropped his hand, his face darkening. "And you suspect these men, king's men, of something? Why?"

"I have reasons," Alyas told him. "I want to see if they are justified, and I can't do that with you here."

"Why not?"

"Because the people who might move against us won't dare interfere with you."

Esar saw the struggle on Nicor's face as a memory of friendship warred with fifteen years of absence, unknown motivations, and the strained relationship between Alyas and the king. The king Nicor-Heryd Zand was sworn to protect. "Tell me one thing," he said at length. "Is there any risk to the king in what you intend to do here?"

"Not from us," Alyas said.

Nicor studied him. Finally, he nodded. "I'll go back to Avarel. Don't make me regret it."

As Nicor gathered up the Avarel detachment and the Cadrians, Esar said, "That will cost you." It would confirm the Cadrians' suspicions and alert the syndicates. "You want them to come at us?"

Alyas watched the troops ride out. "They have taken a huge risk here. I want to know why. Are they bold because they are confident in Raffa's backing, or worse, because they control him? Or have they just made a mistake we can use against them?"

Esar thought about that. "If they have Raffa's backing, Nicor's presence would hardly deter them."

"I know. I don't want to put him at risk."

"He would be the best witness we could ask for," Esar pointed out. And their best protection against syndicate accusations.

"Not if he's dead," Alyas said bluntly.

"You really think it would come to that?"

"I think it already has."

Corado. But how much of that attempted killing had been Corado's own loathing of Alyas and how much syndicate orders? He looked at Alyas's tense face. "What is it?"

Alyas sighed. There were shadows under his eyes as dark as his hair. "Why did Raffa call us back, Esar? Does he really want us to dig him out of his hole with the syndicates, or was it not about him at all?"

"What do you mean?" He just knew he wasn't going to like the answer.

"I am starting to become concerned," Alyas replied, turning back to where the company waited, "that we have not yet heard from the messengers we sent to the Lathai."

Free from the watching Cadrians, they searched all three villages again. The lump of misshapen lead Esar had found was retrieved without incident. It was still there among the charred remains of the shrine when they returned. Either the Cadrians hadn't found it, or they hadn't known what to look for after all. Esar showed it to the search parties, and they scoured the last two villages, bringing any lumps of metal to Alyas. It wasn't the method Esar would have chosen, but it was what they had. Alyas handled each one in turn. One he dropped as soon as he touched it. That was enough for Esar. Another he held for several minutes, his expression undecided. Eventually, he shrugged. "Maybe."

So, they had two. That could not be coincidence, but whether it was enough to convince anyone else, Esar did not know. He wasn't yet sure what they would do if they could convince Raffa that the syndicates had done this, or what would come next. The consequences were too enormous. If Alyas had a plan, he hadn't shared it. Perhaps that was what was keeping him awake at night, because he certainly didn't look like he was sleeping.

Alyas gave the pieces of lead to Aubron and sent him back to Avarel with a small escort and instructions to take what he carried to Brivar at the temple.

"The syndicates have agents in Cadria," he said in answer to Esar's raised eyebrow. "We can't risk taking it there. No one will look for it at a temple of Yholis."

Esar wasn't sure why they should risk returning to Cadria at all, but nothing was happening out here. They had ridden aimlessly around for three days, pitching camp each night in places he would not have liked to defend against an enemy that knew what it was doing, but as tempting a target as they made of themselves, they were left unmolested. Cadria was an altogether different kind of danger, and he saw no reason to walk right into it—except that Alyas was right. If they didn't force the syndicates into the open, they didn't have a hope of convincing Raffa to move against them, and only the rulers of Ellasia had any chance of curbing syndicate power. At least, he hoped they did.

Esar half expected Nicor to be waiting for them when they arrived back at the city, despite his promise to return to Avarel, but the king's commander was nowhere in sight when they rode back into the garrison. Alyas didn't own any property in Cadria. They had to quarter the company in an unused section of the garrison barracks, itself a remnant of the Isyrium Wars when the city had been a strategic outpost in Lankara's long-running conflict with Hantara.

Cadria's guard captain stuck his head out of his office as they rode in and called Alyas over.

He handed off his reins to Esar. "Get everyone settled." Then, seeing Esar's frown, he added, "I'll be right there, where you can see me."

But when Esar emerged from the barracks to look for him a half hour later, he wasn't there, and he wasn't inside with the company either.

He marched to the captain's office. The man started when he entered, the point of his quill pen scratching a long line across the list he was writing.

"The duke received a message from the king's commander in Avarel," he said in answer to Esar's question, staring at the ruin of his careful writing. "He left with the messenger."

Esar swore. He would kill Alyas when he found him. "From Nicor-Heryd Zand? What was the message?"

The captain shrugged. "It was a verbal message. I didn't hear it."

It was a small office, with barely enough room for the two of them. It would be almost impossible not to overhear.

The captain was watching him, a nervous tic in one eyelid. He was frightened. They were in trouble. Already.

Instead of taking the guard captain by the throat and shaking the truth out of him, Esar merely said, "When he gets back, tell him I need to speak to him." And concealed the rage he felt at the relief on the man's face.

Back with the company, he sought out Della and Agazi. "They've taken Alyas. It's likely we're going to be attacked." There were distressingly few other possibilities. The syndicates couldn't just take Alyas out. They had to know what the response would be. This was aimed at all of them. He couldn't quite believe they would go so far, so soon. They were either desperate or extremely confident, and he liked neither option.

Della didn't even blink. "When?"

"That's what we need to find out." He moved to the window so he could see the comings and goings in the courtyard. Now he knew to look for them, he could see the strategically placed watchers. "They have eyes on us. We don't want to do anything to provoke them until we're ready."

She nodded. Agazi said, "And Alyas?"

"He'll have to look after himself for now." Alyas would have quickly realised what was happening and he could be exceedingly obstructive when he put his mind to it. Esar had to trust him to keep himself alive for the moment because he had to see to the company before he could do anything else.

Della and Agazi didn't argue. They knew how this worked.

Esar took stock of their situation. It was tempting to try to take the company out of the city before this went any further, but they would be no help to Alyas out there, and he suspected that any attempt to leave would trigger whatever trap had been prepared for them. So, if they couldn't leave, they must defend what they had.

The garrison compound was built around a courtyard. Only one of the three accommodation wings was occupied, the garrison being far smaller these days than it had been at the height of the Isyrium Wars. The fourth side housed the stables and offices. The section of the barracks where the company had been housed was in part of an empty wing that adjoined the guards' quarters on its western side; on its other side was an empty block. Each of the blocks had its own entrance but at one time it must have been possible to move between them on the inside. He sent Della to find and secure all the exits.

With Agazi, he found the wall that adjoined the empty section of their wing and they stood there with their ears against it for several minutes, straining to hear what might be on the other side. Nothing. Esar put his hands against the wooden boards and tested them. The main structure of the building was solid stone, but the large original rooms had been sub-divided over the years with wooden partitions to create more private quarters. It so happened that the wall between their section and the next was wood. And not terribly solid.

"You think we can get through?" Agazi asked.

"I think it would help if we could." He used his dagger to prise loose the edge of board and peered into the darkened room beyond. It was empty. "Get some men up here with axes. We may need to get through in a hurry."

"Fire?"

He nodded. The syndicates were anything but subtle and now they had started this, they had to see it through. "It's their most obvious course if they want to finish us quickly." A few flasks of Isyrium fuel through the windows would make a bonfire of this place in no time. The Cadrian garrison was no bigger than the company, possibly smaller, which made confronting them directly a poor idea, and the syndicates would know it. If they were pinned down in a burning building, they were an easy target. But a fire was risky. It could easily spread out of control and engulf the entire compound.

Unless that's what the syndicates wanted. Easier to explain away as a tragic accident. Either way, they would have to come out, so they had to hold the exits, but he had no particular desire to wait around for the attack to come to them. If they could get through here, they could start moving the company into the empty wing on their eastern side. It was also closer to the stables, and they would need their horses.

Esar wiggled his dagger, easing the board loose across its length, and they pulled it free. The light from their window illuminated an empty storeroom. It was dusty, but not the kind of dusty that suggested it had been disused for a long period. The door was closed, but if this section was arranged like the one they were in, it would open onto a main corridor that led to the stairs down to the lower floor.

"What about Alyas?"

He was trying not to think about that. If the syndicates didn't simply kill him, the biggest danger was that they would use a threat to him to force the company's surrender, and then they would be in serious trouble. If Esar couldn't get him back—and he had no idea where to start looking—they had to assume they would soon be faced with that choice, and they needed to know now how they would respond.

"Get this wall down as quickly and quietly as you can. Find a way into the next wing, I don't care how. Start moving the company from here to there, but make sure they don't see you, because if you have to surrender, we're all dead. So don't, whatever happens. And I mean that. If you can get a party into the stables without being seen, even better. And when you come out, forget that these are Lankarans, do you understand? You get our people out—whatever it takes."

Agazi nodded. His face was hard. "Where will you be?"

The company was as prepared as he could make them. Agazi knew what he was doing, they all did. Time to take away the syndicates' leverage. "I'm going after Alyas."

❧

To find Alyas, Esar took the practical view that everyone in the Cadrian garrison was an enemy. So he grabbed the first man he saw, dragged him into an empty room, and threatened to put an end to his ability to procreate unless he got he wanted. He was fortunate on two counts. The man was not only fervent in his desire for children, but he had also seen Alyas leaving the garrison in the company of several men dressed in Nicor's colours.

"Which way did they go?" Esar demanded, the point of his sword still pressed uncomfortably against the pertinent area of the man's anatomy.

The man pointed a trembling hand and Esar sighed and leaned very slightly on his hilt. "I need you to be a little more specific."

"Towards the Clotine, the riverside district," his prisoner yelped. "I don't know where!"

"What's there?"

"Docks, warehouses. It's a syndicate area."

"Good enough," Esar said, removing his sword. He grabbed the shaking man by the shoulder and propelled him forward. "Show me."

The Clotine turned out to be a series of Isyrium warehouses and wagon sheds crammed alongside one of Cadria's many canals. He had already seen one wagon train being loaded from the back of a huge warehouse. Cadria was not a mining region, but it was an important staging post on the Isyrium trade route with Hantara and the Donea. If Alyas was still alive, it made sense they would bring him here. The area was tightly controlled, with a fence round its perimeter and guards stationed at the entrance of the roads leading in. But that wasn't Esar's main problem.

The unconscious guardsman lay in the alley behind him, a bruise the size and shape of the pommel of Esar's dagger on his temple. The Cadrian didn't know in which of these warehouses Alyas was being held, and he couldn't be allowed to return to the garrison, but that left Esar without a guide and no idea where to start looking.

And first he had to get in.

As it turned out, that was the easiest part. As the newly loaded wagon train trundled towards the exit, its driver's inattention allowed the team of massive urocs to drift too far to one side and a wheel of the rear wagon caught in a rut. The wagon lurched dangerously, sending a ripple of panic up the train. The driver hauled the urocs to a halt as men swarmed the tilting wagon. In the confusion, Esar slipped out of the alley and across the street, pausing to crouch by the back wheel of the first wagon with a worried frown. The driver saw his expression and jumped down next to him, demanding to see the problem, and in the shadows of the warehouses his armour was not so different to that of the syndicates' guards. Together they examined the perfectly functional wheel, then Esar gave the driver a friendly pat on the shoulder and moved on, his presence accepted by the distracted guards. When he turned the corner of the first warehouse, they were still haranguing the crew to get the wagons moving.

He moved swiftly away from the stricken wagon train and its loud argument. It had come from the nearest warehouse, which still had its great doors open. Inside he could see endless stacks of crates lined up on one side waiting for transport. On the other side was a haphazard pile of empty and broken crates. They did not appear to be lined with lead, for which he offered Yholis his heartfelt thanks.

He moved on. He needed to find a quieter place. The syndicates were bold, but even they wouldn't take Alyas into a warehouse filled with so many witnesses. Down by the canal the docks were equally busy. They must bring the Isyrium upriver from central Lankara, then transfer it to the wagons to move overland across the border. Which was interesting to know but not helpful. Alyas wasn't there either.

Esar was starting to worry that he wasn't here at all when he saw a man in syndicate blue hurrying towards a smaller building on the edge of the docks. Someone stepped out of the doorway to meet him. He was wearing a poor approximation of Avarel's guard uniform.

Such a poor approximation that there was no possible way Alyas would have fallen for it, so how had they taken him?

The men went inside. Esar forced himself to stay where he was and watch. He had not seen the guard inside the door until he stepped out. There might be others. He would be no help to Alyas or the company if he got himself stabbed going in. And he would never live it down.

Then, quite clearly, he heard a shout from inside the building, and self-control snapped. If there were more guards, he would just have to kill them. Sword in hand, he left his hiding place and crossed the hard-packed mud. There was no one waiting for him, but inside he could hear some distinctive noises.

Then silence.

Heart thumping, Esar eased open the door and stared at the scene inside. The syndie lay on the floor in a pool of blood, his throat neatly cut. Around him lay the bodies of four guards. At least two of them were dead. One was groaning, hands pressed to a bleeding wound in his upper thigh, the other was starting to stir. He had a bruise blossoming on his face similar to the one Esar had left on his Cadrian. Both were missing their weapons.

Alyas stood in the centre of the bodies. He turned to the door as Esar stepped inside. He had a sword in each hand, neither of them his, bruises on his face and a torn sleeve, and he was as furious as Esar had ever seen him. When he realised what was missing, he understood why.

They had taken the Isyr blades.

BRIVAR

B rivar missed the company already. He had seen them leave at dawn on his first day back as he had been hurrying across the temple walls to his long-neglected studies. He fancied he could see Della's blond head towards the front of the column, but they were too far away to be sure and there were lots of Qidans with the company. It could have been anyone, but he thought it was her.

He missed them all the more when Varisten Elenia set him to work, deliberately choosing the most mundane and tedious tasks. It wasn't a punishment, or at least not for him. She did not approve of Alyas appointing him to his household, even after Brivar had explained the how and why of it, and she was reminding him that he was still an apprentice. So he fetched and carried and scribed and tried not to complain when she found fault with everything and made him do it again.

This morning, four days after the company had left Avarel, he was making a copy of the donations book for the temple archives. It was a task usually given to the greenest of apprentices, but the Varisten had handed it to him after the morning prayers and told him that today it was his task.

Brivar scanned the book, his mind only half on the list of donations, until his eyes snagged on a name he recognised. The temple did not require payment for its healing services. The rich paid, in coin and other things, anxious for the favour of the goddess, but the poor were never asked for anything—not while they lived. It was a tradition stretching back hundreds of years that if the Temple of Yholis saved your life and you could make no offering of thanks, when you died your body became the property of the temple to further its understanding of medicine.

And there, amid the list of money, goods, and Isyrium, was just such a donation. It was the farmer who had been the first person cured of the midnight sickness.

His heart thumping, Brivar asked the Varisten, "This man, how did he die?"

Elenia peered over his shoulder. "We don't know. He did not come for treatment. His family brought his body when he died. Why?"

"Is he still here?" The corpses were preserved in the cold of the temple's vaults until they were needed for dissection. The farmer had died only days ago.

"I expect so. Alondo has not held an anatomy class yet this month. You'll have to ask Ilyon."

Ilyon was the keeper of the temple vaults. He took charge of the bodies when they arrived, storing them in the great chambers deep underground, and he also looked after the temple's treasures—its store of Isyrium and its secret wealth in Isyr.

"But not until you have finished your task," she said pointedly, seeing the look in his eyes.

Brivar swallowed his desperate impatience. "Yes, Varisten," he murmured, and tried to concentrate on the lines of names and dates and gifts and not speculate about what this one death might mean. People died all the time. It could have been an accident, a sudden illness. It did not have to be connected to the midnight sickness or the cure the man had inadvertently discovered. It was almost certainly coincidence.

Even so, as soon as he had finished with the donations, he was up and out of his chair and through the door before Elenia could call him back. He heard her shout after him as he ran across the temple courtyard, past the fountain with its statue of Yholis and her brother Ithol, and past the window of his master Alondo's office. He kept his eyes down as he passed. He was supposed to report to the Varistan as soon as Elenia released him.

The entrance to the temple vaults was in the small square behind the main courtyard. Ilyon was not in his quarters beside the door, and he did not answer Brivar as he called down the stairs. He did not come down here often. No one did except Ilyon, and he did not often emerge to seek the company of the other members of the temple. He was Hantaran, one of only a handful in Avarel's temple, and a man of few words.

Brivar called again as he reached the first landing. No one answered. He lit the Isyrium bulb on the wall as the light from the upper door was lost. It was colder now, the chill of the great ice cellars raising goosebumps on his skin. He lit two more bulbs before he reached the bottom of the stair and decided that Ilyon must be on one of his rare visits to the upper temple. The darkness and silence of the vaults was undisturbed.

He lit another bulb, flooding the great cellar with light.

Ilyon was not in the upper temple.

He was sitting cross-legged on the floor in the centre of the small strongroom that opened off the western edge of the cellar and was gazing with rapt attention at the shining arc of the temple's Isyr treasures that were arrayed around him. Like he was listening to something.

Brivar froze, hovering on the final step, gripped by awful dread. Ilyon looked up. His eyes were red-rimmed and wild as though he had not slept in days, and in his hand was a knife of pure, shining Isyr.

"Can you hear them too?" he asked Brivar, and his expression was torn between wonder and torment.

Brivar caught his breath. There was so much Isyr here. He had not known the temple possessed so much. There must have been enough to make Alyas's blades twenty times over. And Ilyon had been down here with it every day. For years.

"What can you hear?" he asked, taking the final step into the cellar.

Ilyon reached out a hand and stroked the curved lines of an Isyr vessel. "They speak to me," he said. "I don't know what they are saying, but they are speaking to me."

Yholis have mercy. Brivar thought of Alyas back at Grey Rock. *Some days I cannot bear to wear them*, he had said of his father's weapons. *They make me feel things. Like there are voices in me, but I can't understand them.*

Voices in the steel. Voices that drove its owners mad.

Alyas's father, impaling himself on his opponent's sword.

Ilyon, with the Isyr knife held tight in his hand.

"Put it down," Brivar urged, terrified. "Put it down, Ilyon. Let's find Alondo."

The Varistan would know what to do. He always knew what to do.

"No!" Ilyon shouted. "He will try to take them from me. You will all try to take them from me! I will not let you!"

Then he plunged the knife into his own throat. Brivar screamed until he was hoarse.

ESAR CANTRELL

Esar took a cautious step forward. He looked from the bodies to Alyas. "Are you all right?"

Alyas blinked. Some of the fury faded from his eyes. Some. There was still something not quite right about his expression, and several people in this room were very dead. Not that Esar had a problem with that in general, but five on one was a bit much, even for Alyas.

Alyas took an unsteady step, one sword point pressed into the ground. He looked at the bodies like he was seeing them for the first time. His hand was shaking, which was oddly reassuring. Killing tended to do that to you. Or it *should*.

"Alyas," Esar said sharply. When dark eyes snapped to his, he said again, "Are you all right?" Because nothing else about this was.

"Esar." And then, finally, his face eased. "I knew you would come." His voice sounded normal, steady.

"You didn't wait for me though," Esar observed. "What did they want?"

It was an effort for Alyas to focus on the question. He glanced at the body of the syndicate representative. "What we know. If we found anything in the villages. What Mari told me."

Esar frowned. "Mari?" He wasn't sure he liked what that might mean, but they didn't have time to worry about it now. They had to get out of here and back to the company.

Alyas discarded one of the swords, leaning down to collect a parrying dagger from a dead guard. "We need to get back to the garrison. The guard captain –"

"I know, he betrayed us. The company –"

"– he has my blades."

They stared at each other. Alyas looked away first.

"The company," he said, as though he had only now realised they would be threatened, which was disturbing in so many ways. Then he was moving, a different kind of urgency in his steps. "Where are they?"

Esar hurried after him. "Alyas, wait. We need to think about this." They couldn't just march back into the garrison and –

Alyas didn't wait. He was out of the building and halfway to the warehouses when Esar caught up with him.

"Stop," he insisted, spinning him around. "This whole place is guarded. You can't just walk out."

Alyas shook him off. Up ahead was the end of the broken-down wagon train, six covered carts hitched together and pulled by a team of four urocs. It was finally moving, the front of the train already midway through the guard station.

Alyas saw it and started to run. He caught up with the rear wagon and swung himself on top of its load of crates. Esar swore and followed, and before he had even gained the first wagon Alyas was up and running over the piled crates and leaping to the next. Startled shouts erupted from the guards, who yelled at the driver to halt the train and close the gates, but the uroc team was halfway through and they could not be shut.

Alyas ran from wagon to wagon, Esar behind him, with crossbow bolts nipping at their heels and Esar yelling abuse at Alyas's back. It was just the kind of reckless escapade that had helped make their name fifteen years ago, but it was also nothing like it. Then, Alyas had hurled himself into danger for the fierce thrill of feeling alive. Now, Esar thought he simply didn't care. He had one goal, and the wagon train was in his way.

When he reached the final wagon, Alyas landed next to the shocked driver, then leapt straight onto the broad back of the nearest uroc and jumped from one to the next like stepping stones before swinging feet first straight into the thin line of guards that had formed in the street. The urocs stamped and snorted, unaccustomed to strange men running across them, and Esar pricked the nearest in the rump with his sword point as he tumbled into the street on top of Alyas, rolling them both out of the way. The usually placid creature let out a bellow and reared up, tearing the harness, then several tonnes of angry uroc were stampeding into the street and the guards scattered in terror.

Alyas made it to his feet first, hauling Esar up after him, and they took refuge in the alley where Esar's Cadrian was stirring. Alyas ignored him, and the chaos behind them. "Which way?"

Esar rubbed at his thigh that throbbed with the warning ache of a pulled muscle and tried to control his temper. When this was over, they were going to have a serious fucking talk about communication. And other things. "Don't you remember?" Alyas had an eerie sense of direction.

Not today. He looked around, confused. Eventually, he said, "I don't think I was conscious." He didn't sound certain, and the guard Esar had kidnapped had seen him walk out of the compound under his own power. So, it was unlikely. Esar was liking this less and less.

"What are you going to do when you get there?" he asked, and his tone made it clear they were not going anywhere until he had an answer, and one that he found acceptable.

"What do you think I'm going to do?" Alyas snarled.

"Right now, I have no idea. *Because you are not yourself.*" And it was starting to scare him.

Something in his tone penetrated Alyas's single-minded focus. His face changed, his eyes clearing. "The company," he said again. It sounded like he was reminding himself. "Where are they?"

Esar felt his worry hitch up a notch at this further evidence that Alyas had *lost his mind*. He said, as calmly as he could, "At the garrison. They're pinned down. The captain –"

It was no use. At the mention of the man who had taken the blades, reason vanished. Alyas started moving, unerring instinct taking him in the direction of the garrison at a pace that had Esar half running to keep up, his bad leg protesting each step, and there was nothing else for it but to go with him and try to stop the day becoming a complete disaster.

❧

They weren't challenged as they entered the garrison compound. The shocked guards at the gate took one look at them and darted away. No doubt to warn their captain.

Esar glanced towards the building that housed the company, searching for the window to the room they had broken into. A face slid into view. Agazi. He kept his hand low as he signed a question. Receiving the answer he hoped for, he felt the tension in his chest release a fraction and cast a covert look at the stables.

From the undisciplined confusion all around them, it was clear the last thing the garrison had expected was the Duke of Agrathon to walk back in, his face like thunder, and not a syndicate representative in sight. As furious as that made him, Esar would have snatched gratefully at the opportunity it gave them—if Alyas hadn't wasted it.

Instead of collecting the company and riding out of there while the garrison tried to decide what to do, Alyas marched straight across the courtyard to the captain's quarters.

They met the guard captain coming out of his office, and he met the point of Alyas's sword going in.

He backed up and they followed, Esar positioning himself by the door so he could have a good view of their opportunity to leave as it slipped away.

"*Where are my blades?*" Alyas demanded.

Esar did not tell him to leave it. He certainly did not say to forget the bloody things. Or shake him and make him realise that this was *not right*. That nothing should matter this much, not even his father's blades. Especially not his father's blades. Because Alyas was not leaving here without them, and that was that.

The terrified captain almost fell over himself bolting for his desk. He unlocked the draw with shaking fingers and withdrew the Isyr blades, still in their familiar leather sheathes, and laid them on the desk.

Alyas stared at them for a moment, then his hands unclenched and the weapons he had stolen from the dead guards dropped to the floor. He reached across the desk and took the blades, and as soon as they were back in his hands, the manic edge receded. And Yholis, if that wasn't worse.

Awareness flooded back into his eyes. Before Esar could stop him, Alyas was across the desk and had the captain by the throat. "Call off your men. *Now.*"

The man made a choking sound and Alyas let him go with a shove. "Can't," he gasped, his knees sagging.

Esar, standing in the doorway, said, "Alyas." A syndicate rep had appeared in the courtyard. In his hand was a familiar flask. Isyrium fuel.

As Alyas turned, the man called, "Your Grace. Come out now, please."

Alyas met Esar's eyes then slid over the desk and crossed to stand at the other side of the door, the captain forgotten. His eyes narrowed as he saw the flask. He turned, snatching a sheet of parchment and slapping it down on the desk. A quill followed. The terrified captain watched him as if he had gone mad, which Esar thought quite possible.

"Write it down," Alyas snarled at the Cadrian. "All of it. Everything they said, everything they've done. Everything they made you do. *Write it down!*" he repeated when the man didn't move. "Sign it.

Leave nothing out, do you understand?"

The captain nodded, edging into his chair and picking up the quill as the syndicate rep called, "It's time to give yourself up, Your Grace. Or we will burn your company where they stand."

"Alyas, wait," Esar said urgently, catching his arm before he could march out of the door. "Listen to me. They're not where he thinks they are. You don't have to go out there. We have time." Agazi had indicated they had people in the stables. Once everything kicked off—and it would; there was no way they were getting out of this without violence—the chaos and confusion would give them the advantage. If he let Alyas go out there, in this mood, there was no telling what might happen. But he was certain it would be worse.

"I'm not going to ask again," the voice called. "This is your last chance."

Alyas frowned and focused on Esar. "They're not there?" The energy was draining out of him. He looked ready to drop.

Esar swore. That was all they needed. "They're in the next building," he explained again, as patiently as he could.

"The fire –"

"Will cover our escape. They know what to do." It was a risk, but not nearly as risky as the alternative.

Over Alyas's shoulder Esar saw the guard captain watching them, the quill forgotten in his hand. "Keep writing!" he snarled, and the man dropped his head back to his task, his hand shaking so much it would be a wonder if they could read the result. The confession was the one rational thing Esar had seen Alyas do throughout this entire episode. Since they had risked the whole company to get it, he was going to make bloody sure it was worth it.

"I must admit, I expected more of you, Your Grace," the syndie called. "Letting your company die to save yourself."

Esar forced himself to hold Alyas's eyes, using his greater size and weight to block the door. "They know what to do," he insisted.

"Would they do the same for you I wonder?" mused the voice in the courtyard. And the first Isyrium flask went flying—not towards the wing where the company had been lodged, but towards the captain's office where they were hiding. Esar heard it smash on the roof above, followed by the thud and whoosh of a fire arrow. "Fuck."

The captain screamed and scrambled over his desk to claw into Esar. Alyas retained enough sense to snatch the half-finished confession from the desk and tuck it inside his armour as flames started to eat through the roof and the smoke billowed in.

"It looks like we are going to find out, doesn't it?" the smug voice said, and Esar decided he was going to give that man his special attention when they got out of this.

Agazi must have decided the same thing because he didn't wait for the fire to force them out. With a clatter of hooves, a group of riders burst out of the stables, charging into the knot of guards around the syndicate rep. The man was quick, darting away to put a line of guardsmen between himself and the horses. He had another flask in his hand, and he hurled it at where the company had been quartered, screaming at the guards to fire the block.

A horse mowed through the frightened guards. A sword flashed down and the syndie died, but not before the block went up in a roar of flame.

It was getting out of hand. Esar prayed to Yholis there was no one in the building, because they would be trapped. As he and Alyas were.

The fire surged closer, too close. Esar grabbed Alyas with one hand and the captain with the other, dragging them both out of the small room into the courtyard. It was a chaos of smoke and horses and choking ash. He released his grip on Alyas to throw an arm over his nose and mouth as cinders caught in his throat.

There was a shout somewhere to his right and a figure barrelled out of the smoke, crashing into the captain and taking them both to the ground. Clipped by the impact, Alyas spun and almost fell, then jerked back as a jet of blood soaked his front. More figures surged out of the smoke. Alyas caught a strike on his offhand blade, the movement far too slow, and managed to parry its follow up with the sword as Esar stepped over the captain's body to stand at his back.

A garrison soldier stood over his dead captain, his sword wet with the man's blood. He met Esar's furious gaze a second before he died.

Then Agazi was there, riding between them and their attackers. He reached down to pull Alyas up behind him, shouting something at Esar, who saw Della riding towards him, a spare horse on a lead rein. He grabbed it, swinging up into the saddle, almost blinded by smoke and coughing so hard he nearly lost his seat.

Something collapsed behind him with a crash, heat licking at his back. Della slapped a hand to his horse's rump, sending it leaping towards the gates where the company was streaming out. Smoke followed them in a great billow, and he looked back to see the compound collapsing in on itself. He reined in, waiting for the last few riders to make it out. The street was a clogged mess of men and horses, but they were already dispersing, scattering through the city in all directions. They would regroup later. This part at least they had planned for, their rendezvous point arranged in advance.

"Go," he told Della as she hesitated beside him, then he sat there and watched the garrison burn and felt his own anger flare up with it.

It was dark when he eventually rejoined the company, one of the last to straggle into the camp that was waiting for them. Someone took his horse—he barely noticed. Being alone with his thoughts had not helped to calm them, and all his anger and frustration was ready to boil over.

He saw Agazi emerge from a tent and stalked towards him.

"Where is he?"

Agazi shook his head. The darkness hid his expression. "Not now, Esar."

Furious, Esar tried to go around him, and Agazi moved to block his way. "No."

Esar stopped, his anger transforming into a different kind, and he did not know how to deal with it so he walked away.

Agazi found him an hour later and stood watching him sharpen his dagger with far more vigour than the task required. "He's asleep. He was dead on his feet. Are you going to tell me what's going on?" Then, when Esar didn't reply, "He's not hurt. Della checked. Everyone's safe. What's wrong? What happened?"

"That was a fucking disaster."

Agazi shrugged. "It could have been worse." They could have lost someone. Instead, they had escaped with a few minor burns. But that was no thanks to Alyas, who had put every single one of them at risk. And Esar wasn't even sure it had been his fault. Those bloody blades had done something to him, and he hated it. He wished Raffa had taken them all those years ago. He wished Brivar had never given them back. He very much feared it was too late to take them from him now.

Esar put the razor-sharp dagger aside and rested his head in his hands. "They took the blades. He lost his mind." Agazi needed to know. If he and Alyas were absent, compromised or dead, it would fall to him to take charge of the company. And all those things were suddenly looking much more likely.

Agazi looked down at him in silence. Eventually he said, "They were his father's."

"No," Esar said. "That was not it. You weren't there." But if he had been, there was every chance he would have followed Alyas without questioning. The steppelander was fiercely loyal, and he needed to know that sometimes he should not be.

"But you got what you wanted."

Esar frowned. "What do you mean?"

Agazi handed him a folded, blood-stained piece of parchment. "Della found it."

The guard captain's confession. He had forgotten all about it. Esar took it. It wasn't finished, but it was enough to prove they had been deliberately targeted. Not enough, however, to make any of what had just happened remotely worth it.

"He's just tired, Esar," Agazi said, seeing the look on his face. "When he wakes up, talk to him."

"Oh, I will," he promised, walking away before he could say anything else.

He woke a few hours later to a sky that was beginning to lighten and Alyas crouching over him, shaking his shoulder, saying, "Esar. Where are we?" And suddenly he wasn't angry anymore.

※

Esar woke Agazi. Alyas would hate it, but this wasn't just about him. The three of them walked a short distance away from the company, Alyas silent and tense.

Esar handed him the confession.

Alyas looked up as he took it. "What's this?"

When Esar didn't reply, he unfolded the parchment and started reading. His expression changed. Some of the confusion disappeared as the confession jogged missing pieces of his memory. He reached the end and turned the page over. "It's not finished. Where is he?" He stopped, aware they were staring at him. "What?"

Esar said, "The captain's dead." Alyas had been standing next to the man when he died. His armour was soaked with his blood.

The blank look on Alyas's face was terrifying. He had been pretty out of it by that point, but not so very out of it that he should have forgotten a man being murdered in front of him.

Alyas rubbed his forehead. "I… yes, I remember." It was not terribly convincing.

Esar exchanged a look with Agazi, who asked, "What do you remember?"

It was plainly a struggle, and it was difficult to watch. "Flashes. Feelings. I was angry…"

"That was obvious," Esar muttered, thinking of the dead and wounded in the warehouse.

Agazi frowned at him in a way that suggested he was not helping.

Then Alyas asked, "Did I kill him?" And the fear in his voice made Esar want to hit something. It reminded him of his foster father—the way he had veered wildly from depression to rage, and afterwards never seemed to recall either the outburst or the offence that had triggered it. Once, he had almost killed a groom. Alyas had had to knock him out to stop him. He would be remembering that now. But Gerrin had been drunk more than he had been sober by the end. It made it hard, looking back, to know what was the drink and what was the Isyr. Though since the blades had almost certainly been the cause of the drinking, Esar wasn't sure it made much difference. This was not the same, but it felt dangerously close.

"No," Esar said, because it would have been too cruel to let him think otherwise, even for a second. "You didn't kill him." But he had killed a syndicate representative and at least two of his abductors, and it wouldn't matter that they had certainly planned to kill him. If not for the captain's confession, those deaths—on top of Grey Rock and Orleas—would give the syndicates everything they needed to destroy him.

Then, because Alyas needed to know—because the syndicates were going to come after him regardless—Esar filled in those treacherous blanks of memory. Alyas listened in silence, his face white. He didn't say anything. There wasn't a lot to say. And the only thing Esar really cared about was the one thing Alyas did not do, which was take off the blades and put them aside.

BRIVAR

Ilyon's death sent a shockwave through the temple. It sent a shockwave through Brivar, whose dreams for nights afterwards were filled with the sight of Ilyon stabbing himself in the neck, and nightmare visions of Alyas doing the same.

He tried to explain. The temple could not send someone else down there to take Ilyon's place. Whatever it was, whatever it did, the Isyr was too dangerous. It had to be locked away and left alone.

They didn't understand, not at first. His master and the Varisten listened to his rambling warning and they tried to calm him, to reassure him, and he knew they thought he was unbalanced by what he had seen. He tried again to explain, more explicitly. He did not mention Alyas's name, or the Lathai, but the contortions required left his account full of holes, something that did not go unnoticed. And it was pointless anyway, because as soon as he finished, Elenia said, "Since your new patron is famous for his Isyr weapons, I assume that's how you know this. Why have you not removed them from him?"

Brivar gaped at her, trying to imagine forcing Alyas to do anything. Alondo said with gentle censure, "I imagine the Duke of Agrathon is a difficult man to compel."

"Then he should not be permitted to take an apprentice into his household," Elenia snapped. "For his own good as well as Brivar's. The man's father was a drunk whose death rumour persistently attributes to suicide. If what we have heard today is true, it suggests he did indeed take his own life. And if those weapons were the cause, they should not be left in his son's possession. You cannot disagree."

"I don't," Alondo replied. "But I once knew Alyas well. I knew his father better, and he was not always a drunk. Let us not forget that what happened to him was a tragedy. His son will be acutely aware of the danger. If he has not voluntarily surrendered the weapons already, demanding that he do so now is unlikely to have a happy outcome. You must convince him it is necessary."

So Brivar took himself to the temple library where he spent several days poring through metalworking books, through tomes about Isyrium and its many properties, and then through the histories of Qido, particularly its rulers, until eventually he found what he was looking for.

The next day, Aubron arrived at the temple and handed him the package from Alyas.

Brivar took the parcel, feeling its weight. "What is it?"

Aubron shrugged. "Evidence, we hope. You're to keep it safe till Alyas comes for it."

"When will that be?" He needed to talk to Alyas rather badly.

"Who knows? Not long. Depends what happens in Cadria. I'm heading back to meet them. Shall I tell him you want to see him?"

Brivar considered the wisdom of summoning Alyas to him. "I think it would be a good idea."

꙰

The company returned two weeks after they left. Brivar, head down in the library every spare moment, did not know they were back until he saw a familiar blond head in the courtyard and hurried to meet her.

"Della," he called. "I need to see Alyas."

She didn't pout at his lack of welcome. Instead, she looked relieved. "He's here. Esar made him come."

"Why?"

She bit her lip. "He's not well, Brivar. You can see it."

"Yes," he said. "I know why."

He found Alyas and Esar with Alondo and Elenia. The atmosphere was awkward and strained.

Alyas turned to him as he entered. "You wanted to see me?"

Brivar nodded cautiously, looking from Esar's frown to Alyas's expressionless face. They both looked tired, but exhaustion clung to Alyas in a way that went beyond physical fatigue, his eyes too dark, his skin too pale. Like Ilyon, but without the wild, crazed edge. As he returned Brivar's searching gaze, he was very much in control. Too controlled.

Brivar hesitated, instinct warning him not to approach the issue directly. Instead, he said, "Something happened while you were away. Here, at the temple."

Alondo said, "I have told them about Ilyon."

"And I am sorry to hear it," said Alyas. Nothing else. He was not going to make this easy.

Brivar glanced at Esar. He looked neither shocked nor surprised, and he was watching Alyas warily. Something had happened.

He tried another tack. "I have done some research. Into your weapons."

That did elicit a reaction. "And?"

"The Isyrium that made them came out of the ground in Ado two hundred years ago, in one of the very first Isyrium mines that we have records of. The mining company had them fashioned for its founder. At some point they passed into other hands, and they last belonged to the emperor of Qido."

"I know that," Alyas said impatiently, though his face betrayed something quite different. "He gave them to my father."

Brivar shook his head. "Not that emperor. His father, Krado II."

There was a small silence. Then Esar said, "Krado, the mad emperor?"

Brivar nodded. To Alyas he said, "His son gave your father those blades. After your father rescued his daughter from assassins."

Esar held up a hand. "Wait, who did what with whose daughter?"

"He didn't?" Brivar asked, crestfallen. "Are you sure?"

Alyas shook his head.

"Well, anyway," Brivar said, hiding his disappointment. He had always loved that story. "The father of the man who gave those blades to your father—he did go mad, and he did kill himself. And instead of keeping one of the great heirlooms of his dynasty, his son gave them to your father. But if he didn't rescue the emperor's daughter, what did he do?"

"The better question," said Esar, "is how do you know this?"

"I looked it up. The temple has an extensive library and those weapons have quite a story. They come up again and again in the history of Qido."

"Of driving their owners mad?" Esar asked grimly.

"Well, no, that is more recent. But you told me, weeks ago, that Ado had been cut off and no one knows why. I think it matters—where the Isyr comes from."

He could not be more explicit without mentioning the Lathai, but he saw understanding flicker across Alyas's stony face. The Lathai wore their Isyr every day without harm. He had thought it was because of how they refined it, but that couldn't be right, because the Isyr Alyas wore, the Isyr Ilyon had guarded—all Isyr, in fact, except the Lathai's—had been made before the syndicates, before their refinement process had even been developed. Before it had been needed. If he was right, it was not just *how* Isyrium was refined but what that meant about the place it came from. Ado had been where Isyrium had first been discovered and mined. Much of the world's old Isyr came from there. Most of the temple's treasures were Adoese. And something bad was happening in Ado. It was not difficult to work out what.

But that wasn't, at this moment, Brivar's main concern. What he wanted to do was separate the blades from Alyas before the Isyr did to him what it had done to Ilyon. He cleared his throat. "The point is, they may have driven the old emperor mad, and we know they did the same to your father."

He didn't know what response he had expected, but it was not Alyas turning on his heel without a word and walking out. Or he would have walked out, but Esar was quicker, his arm across the door blocking the way. "You can't ignore this, Alyas."

"I am not ignoring it," Alyas retorted, the words a snarl of anger. "I have heard you. I am warned. And now I am leaving."

Alondo said gently, "Raffa doesn't wear his crown."

Alyas's shoulders stiffened. He said without turning, "Mari said it was too tight, that it gave him headaches."

Brivar stared at him. The queen was unlikely to have volunteered that information. It was too random. He must have asked. And why would he have asked unless he was worried?

Elenia was watching Alyas. She pursed her lips. "It is forbidden for me to speak to others of my patients, especially when that patient is the king." She glanced at Alondo, who nodded. "But on this occasion I believe it is warranted. The crown may have given him headaches, but I can tell you that around the time he stopped wearing it, he was not sleeping. He had terrible nightmares. I look at you," she said to Alyas, "and I am reminded of him."

"That is unlikely," he said coldly.

"You must give them up," Brivar pleaded. "I was wrong." He had thought they needed to understand what was happening. Now that felt like far too great a risk.

When Alyas didn't reply, Elenia said, "The last two men who owned those blades took their own lives. Ilyon just did the same. It is irrational not to give them up."

"I assure you, I am perfectly rational."

"Like you were perfectly rational in Cadria?" Esar demanded.

Alyas glared at him. "That was different."

Brivar asked, "What happened in Cadria?"

"The syndicates," Esar said, his voice grating with strong emotion. "They tried to kill us. They took the blades."

He had them back now. Exactly how went unspoken, as did so much else. Whatever the details of what had happened, they would not be shared here, now. Brivar realised he had gone about this all wrong. He had wanted Alondo and Elenia to add weight to his warning, to force Alyas to listen to their age and experience, but he had not known about Cadria. He had not counted on someone taking the weapons from him by force and the reaction it would invoke. Even then, if he had spoken to Alyas alone, he might have listened. He had surrendered the blades to Brivar before, willingly. He might have done it again. But now no one would be able to take them from him.

He glanced at Alondo and saw his master understand. "We will leave you," he said, gathering up Elenia as he went. Esar watched them go. He hesitated, clearly reluctant to leave, then followed them out of the door without a word.

Left alone with Alyas, Brivar could not look at him. "I'm sorry."

"I said only you," Alyas replied. His voice was hard and angry.

"I know, but after Ilyon I had to explain about Isyr. They know—*everyone* knows—you own those." He had said it himself—the Duke of Agrathon's Isyr blades were as much a part of the legend as the man himself and the things he had done. "I thought…" He trailed off, looking up at last. "I am an *apprentice*."

"And I ask too much?" There was a slight relenting in the anger.

"No. Yes. Sometimes." He took a breath. "What happened in Cadria?"

The anger on Alyas's face faded to uncertainty. "I don't remember."

That was unexpected. Worrying. "I want to help. I am *trying* to help, but this is new, and I don't have their experience or their knowledge." Then, because he had to ask, he said, "You chose to give them to me before. Could you do it again?"

The uncomfortable silence dragged out. "At need," Alyas said eventually. "Perhaps."

It was not what he had hoped for, but it wasn't outright refusal either, so Brivar decided to take it as progress. He could have left it there. He probably should have, but some instinct prodded him to ask, "Did you see something, in the na'quia, about the blades?"

The silence this time was of a different kind. "Now you ask too much."

Brivar studied him. "I don't think so." Krado, Ilyon, his father—they had all been driven to madness, then to suicide, by Isyr. He could see none of the madness he remembered from Ilyon's eyes in Alyas's face—admittedly, he didn't know what had happened in Cadria. He would have to find out, and he was fairly certain Esar would tell him without much prompting—but Elenia was right, it was irrational not to give up the blades when he knew what they had done to the men who had owned them before him. So there had to be something else going on, and Brivar had never forgotten the eerie glow of the Isyr hilts in the aftermath of the na'quia poisoning. Only one person had dared broach this subject with Alyas before, and Brivar had no idea what he had said. "What did Ailuin tell you?"

It was one question too many. He didn't get an answer. The door slammed with a force that made the walls shake.

༄

Varistan Alondo was waiting for him in his office, sitting on the narrow cot beneath his beloved plants.

"What did you do wrong?" he asked as Brivar entered.

"I should not have ambushed him. I should have spoken to him privately."

"That was one thing," Alondo agreed. "You cannot expect a man like that to admit to weakness in front of others—especially when it scares him."

"It does?"

"Of course. He was not in control. That would be terrifying to him."

"And the second thing?"

"You revealed something he wanted kept hidden to the people he wanted to hide it from."

Brivar frowned, confused. "I had to tell you about the Isyr."

Alondo stood, straightening slowly as his hip protested. He limped to his desk. "Not Isyr." He pushed a thick book across the desk. "This is our inventory of Isyrium for this temple. Not all the temples of Yholis. Just this one."

Brivar opened the book. It was filled with pages and pages of close-written text detailing vast amounts of Isyrium.

"It is one of many such books," Alondo told him. "Our need for Isyrium is great. Without it, we cannot do so much of our work. We cannot anaesthetise patients for surgery, or treat putrid wounds, or cure many illnesses, and that is before we even consider our ritual uses."

Brivar closed the book. His heart was thumping. "Why are you telling me this?" He had been careful to say nothing of Alyas's suspicions about the contagion and Isyrium, or the syndicates' involvement.

Alondo sighed. "I have lived a long time, Brivar. I know when someone is keeping something from me, and I can read between the lines. Nor am I unaware of the way the syndicates operate. You do not have to tell me the details—I will not ask you to compromise the trust of your patron—but be aware that you are treading a dangerous path. Alyas suspects the temples of collusion with the syndicates, and he is right to do so."

Brivar's head snapped up. "What?"

Alondo smiled his gentle smile. "Look at this book, Brivar. Think about what it means. Think where our power and wealth come from. Without Isyrium, the temples have nothing. If the Duke of Agrathon intends to move against the syndicates, I believe he will have his reasons, but do not fool yourself that the temples will line up behind him. They will not."

Brivar looked at his master's face and felt a great crack form in the certainties of his life. "What about you?" he asked, fearful of the answer. "Where will you line up?"

Alondo looked at him with fondness. "Fortunately for you, I am not of the same mind as the temple. And I loved his father very much. I was their house surgeon before I was the queen's. I've known Alyas since he was a child. I will help you, and you must help him."

"I don't know how," Brivar admitted.

"I think you already have." Alondo said. "And he is right about one thing. He is warned. He knows it is Isyr. That is something none of the others had."

When Brivar did not look reassured, he added, "You can't take them from him. That would be more dangerous than leaving them with him. You must trust him, and yourself. You are both warned."

ESAR CANTRELL

Esar intercepted Alyas before he could leave the temple grounds.

"Let me go, Esar."

"You can be angry about what just happened later. Right now you have bigger problems."

Alyas looked past him to where the king's guards waited. It was clear they were not here on a friendly visit. "Well, this is timely."

"And why is that?" Esar asked, his heart sinking.

"Because I have some things I would like to say to Raffa."

Esar dropped his arm. Pointless to tell him not to go out there. If they didn't come out, Nicor would come in and get them. That he hadn't already was a concession to friendship, but he would not allow it to interfere with his duty. Alyas could go with them willingly or be dragged through the streets like a criminal.

"You promised me I wouldn't regret leaving you," Nicor hissed as they joined him. "And then you burn a king's garrison to the ground? What is wrong with you?"

"You are too hasty with your regrets, Nicor," Alyas replied. "That was none of my doing."

Nicor shook his head in despair. "It's your word against theirs. And if you'll take my advice, don't antagonise the king. He's this close to throwing you to the syndicates."

"You mean he hasn't already?"

"Talk some sense into him, Esar," Nicor growled, mounting his horse. "The syndicates want blood, and you're making it easy for them."

Alyas took his own horse from the guard who was holding it. "Trust me, Nicor. I am all too aware of what they want."

Nicor did not speak to them again until they reached the palace. And then he ignored Alyas and said to Esar, "My orders did not include you. My warning still stands. If you go in with him, it's on your own head."

Esar knew it was good advice. His presence would only irritate Raffa further, but Alyas barely recalled anything that had happened in Cadria. He might think that didn't matter. Esar knew better, which is why they had already had this argument and Alyas had lost.

"I'm coming."

Nicor gave a shrug that suggested he did not care. "The king is waiting."

A man brushed past them in the corridor outside the king's audience chamber. He half-turned as they passed, catching Esar's eye for an instant. A look flashed across his face in that brief contact— satisfaction, and something darker. Loathing. Esar frowned, his gaze following the man as he disappeared. Something about him tugged at his memory, but he could not place the face and there was no time to go after him. As Nicor said, the king was waiting.

The king was indeed waiting, slouched on his throne with an expression of familiar irritation that cut through the years. If not for that, Esar might not have recognised him. Alyas had said he was much changed; he had not said how. Raffa did not present, Esar thought, a shining example of the advantages of kingship. He looked fat and tired and fed up.

He was also alone. Mari was not with him, nor Ovisia Galea, which Esar considered a good sign. Only one other man was in the room, his back to them, but as he wore robes of state and not syndicate blue, Esar dismissed him for now.

Raffa's gaze lit on Alyas as they entered, the irritation sharpening to something rather more pointed. A less good sign. Then his eyes fell on Esar. He sat up. "Esar Cantrell. The last time I saw you, you threatened to kill me. Do I have to shackle you or will you retract that threat?"

Of the two of them, Esar liked to think his instinct for self-preservation was the more finely developed. He glared at the king. "You don't need to shackle me today."

"How reassuring," Raffa observed. "Very well, I won't shackle you—today—but I want your word you will remain with Nicor-Heryd and not interfere."

"My word," Esar obliged, crossing his arms.

Nicor looked sideways at him. "You won't give me any trouble, will you?"

Esar continued to scowl at the king, who pretended not to notice. "I won't start any."

Alyas looked back at him once before he moved to stand before the throne. Esar had no idea what he planned to do, or whether he even had a plan. They had not spoken much between Cadria and Avarel. He did not think Alyas had spoken to anyone. Though he disliked the silence, he did not know how to help, only that his agitation was making things worse.

Raffa studied Alyas in silence for several minutes. If it was supposed to make him feel uncomfortable, it did not have a noticeable effect. Eventually, he asked. "Do you know why you're here, Alyas?"

Alyas gave an unconcerned shrug. "I assume the syndicates have assembled some new accusations."

Raffa looked at him with dislike. "They have, Alyas. They have. Murder this time, as well as arson, at which you appear to be quite practised. What do you have to say to that?"

Alyas matched his stare. "That I would like to hear them first. That is my right, surely?"

"Indeed it is," agreed the king, and leaned over to say something to the man on his left, who turned to face the room.

As soon as Esar saw his face, he knew why they were here. And he knew where he had seen the man in the corridor before. He was one of the Lankaran guardsmen sent with Sul-Barin Feron's envoy. One of Corado's men. Esar's hand ached for a weapon, but Nicor had taken his sword.

"This is not a formal trial, Alyas-Raine Sera," Sul-Barin said. He wore the medallion of the king's justiciar, which made him the most powerful man in the kingdom after the king himself, at least in theory, and his voice only shook a little over the words as he avoided Esar's furious glare. He had been well rewarded for his treachery, Esar thought viciously. He knew what Corado had been. He knew what he had done. He had seen Grey Rock. And he had allowed himself to become party to *this* in exchange for a pretence at power.

Sul-Barin's eyes skittered past Alyas, who was watching him with a clear, calm gaze. He coughed into his hand, clearing his throat, and tried again. "This is not a formal trial, but it still behoves your accusers to state their accusations plainly."

That was rich, Esar thought, seeing as he was one of them. He remembered the prideful young man whose arrival had set them on this path. The office of justiciar would have been that young man's dream. He did not seem proud now.

Raffa shifted in his throne, looking to the door. "Thank you, Lord Sul-Barin, for reminding me. You may bring her in," he told Nicor.

The swish of skirts announced the entrance of the syndicate's representative. Esar did not need to turn to see who it was. He could smell her scent from where he stood. He fervently hoped that was all she had covered herself with. Alyas was in enough trouble without traces of Isyrium waste playing havoc with his focus.

Ovisia Galea swept past him, past Alyas where he stood before the dais, and came to a stop beside Raffa's throne. She was standing very close to him.

"You wanted to hear our accusations, Your Grace. Here they are. That you broke into one of our warehouses in Cadria and killed a representative of the Selysian syndicate and three of his guards, then when my colleagues tried to arrest you, you killed another representative and several members of the Cadrian garrison, including its captain, and set fire to the garrison headquarters to cover up your crimes."

Esar winced. Put like that, he could understand Nicor's doubt and frustration. Raffa's anger was on full display, and the look on Sul-Barin's face was one of disappointment and trust betrayed. Alyas had refused to court him, and he had let the king's envoy feel the heat of his scorn after Corado's attack on Brivar. Yet at Grey Rock he had shown him, clearer than words, that he would act in Lankara's interests, and Sul-Barin had responded. He had backed Alyas before the king once. Esar felt a twinge of guilt as he realised it was not entirely self-interest that had turned him. He believed the accusations.

Alyas appeared oblivious to the condemnation of his audience. "Some of those things happened," he replied. "None of them as you describe. Once again, Sayora, you twist the truth to hide your own crimes."

"And once again, you do not deny it," she retorted. "And that is not the only murder on your account. It has come to light that during your journey to Avarel, you killed a king's officer who had been sent to escort you."

And there it was. Corado, still causing them problems, even after death. At least that incident Alyas remembered. At least there was a witness to that. Then Esar remembered the satisfaction on the face of the man he had passed in the corridor and suddenly wasn't so sure he would be able to find that witness if he went looking.

Alyas smiled at Ovisia. "Sayora, if you are going to catalogue all the men I have killed in defence of my life, we are going to be here all night. I am a soldier. It is an occupational hazard."

"You sound almost proud of it, Your Grace."

"Of killing? It's not a special skill. Anyone can do it. I would not have chosen this life. But if you recall, Raffa," he said, turning to the king. "You left me with nothing and very few options."

Raffa's face went an unhealthy shade of red. He glared at the Isyr blades. "Not quite nothing. You could have sold those and lived comfortably on the proceeds for the rest of your life."

Alyas's hand went to the hilt of his sword and Esar forgot to breathe. But he sounded quite calm as he said, "Could I though? Could you sell your crown, Raffa? Where is it, by the way?"

"Careful, Alyas," the king growled, fingers clenched tight on the arms of his throne. Ovisia was forgotten as the antagonism crackled.

"Or you will do what?" Alyas snapped. "Exile me again? It would make my life easier. What am I doing here, Raffa? You want rescuing from the syndicates with one hand, and you hang onto them tight with the other. What do you want from me?"

"I want you to stop this!" the king shouted, half rising from his seat. "I want an end to this feuding between you. You are here, Alyas, to help defend Lankara, so defend it. Stop this private war. Leave the syndicates alone!"

Alyas didn't flinch, his hand still tight around the Isyr hilt. "And if it is the syndicates I must defend Lankara from? What then, Raffa?"

"What if it is you, Your Grace?" Ovisia interjected before Raffa could reply. She glided forward, one hand covering the king's. Alyas's eyes narrowed as he saw it. "What if it is you who threatens Lankara? You we must defend the country against?"

It was a ridiculous accusation, a mere deflection, but Alyas was bleached white. Esar took a step forward before Nicor stopped him.

"I have never threatened Lankara," Alyas said at last, his voice strained. "Never."

"Is that so?" Ovisia asked. "Yet you have repeatedly aided Lankara's enemies. You annexed an entire territory and closed it to the king. And you seem set on destroying our operations, which are essential for the smooth running of not only the economy but the political and social stability of the entire continent. I would say that constitutes a threat, wouldn't you?"

"No."

"No?" She sounded appallingly confident, her hand still covering Raffa's, and Esar wondered again where Mari was. Alyas had said the syndie in Cadria had wanted to know what she had told him. Did that mean she was with them or against them? Was her absence now a good sign or a bad one?

Alyas, recovering, said, "I have my own accusations, Raffa, if you will allow me to present them?"

The king waved his hand in a gesture of assent.

Alyas faced Ovisia. "I accuse the syndicates of conspiring to murder not just me but my entire company in Cadria. That everyone who died there did so as a direct result of their actions. And that it was the syndicates, not me, who set fire to the garrison in an attempt to kill my people. Be grateful, Sayora, that none of them died, or we would be having a different conversation right now."

"Is that true?" Nicor asked Esar.

"It is. What's more, they impersonated your men to do it. You might want to look into that."

"Oh, I will," Nicor agreed.

Both the king and Sul-Barin were looking at Ovisia, who said calmly, "You can make up any lies you like. I have tens of witnesses who will testify to your guilt."

"Really?" said Alyas. "And what did you pay them? Because you promised the guard captain my weapons in exchange for his assistance. It says so here—in his confession." And he held out a neatly folded sheet of parchment.

Ovisia snatched it from his hand and read it, her face darkening. "You expect me to believe this? It could have been written by anyone." She turned the page over, looking for the rest. "It's not even finished."

"Isn't it?" asked Alyas. "You would know, Sayora."

Esar covered his eyes as Nicor murmured, "That was stupid" to the sound of her tearing the parchment to shreds.

"You have nothing."

Alyas smiled airily. "That was a copy. I have others." He pulled a sheet of parchment from one boot, then another from his sleeve, tossing them casually to the floor, which explained how he had spent at least some of his time since Cadria. "And I also have the original." He took out the singed, crumpled document he had saved from the burning office and handed it to Sul-Barin before Ovisia could take it from him. "Convincingly speckled with its author's blood after he was murdered by one of his own men, presumably to stop him talking."

Sul-Barin took the blood-splattered pages as though he had been handed a lifeline, darting back out of Ovisia's reach and quickly scanning the crabbed, stained text before turning to the king. "We must take time to consider this, sire. It does indeed support His Grace's accusations. Though the document appears to be incomplete."

"The second page is even better," Alyas said to Ovisia. "It talks about what we found in the villages and how it got there. Would you like the king to see that too, or would you prefer to withdraw your accusations and I will withdraw mine?"

Ovisia glared at him, murder in her eyes. "I withdraw my accusations, sire."

Alyas inclined his head. "Thank you." Then he said to the king, "You have mine, Raffa. They stand."

Ovisia's face twisted with rage. Esar half expected her to launch herself at Alyas. "You said –"

"I lied," he replied, his voice hard. "A concept you are familiar with." He turned his back on her and walked to where Esar stood. "They stand, Raffa," he repeated. "And I will make others, so you had better decide which side you are on." He didn't bother to look at the king. "May I take Esar from you now, Nicor? I don't think he feels inclined to kill the king at this precise moment."

"Both of you get out," Nicor said fervently, "before I get any orders to the contrary. Ithol's blood, Alyas. Watch your back."

MARI-GELED HERUN

Mari was already in a bad mood when her husband burst into her bedchamber. She had ripped a seam on her favourite dress that morning, and it was from the city's most fashionable seamstress. Even the queen had had to wait a month for it and now it was ruined. She barely looked up from the torn silk when Raffa flung himself into a chair with all the dignity of a sulky youth and swore for a full minute.

"Don't tell me," she said without sympathy. "It didn't go to plan?"

She had laughed at him when he told her the syndicates' accusations, reminding him that in this very room Ovisia had advocated for murder. If he couldn't see through their paper-thin subterfuge it was because he didn't want to, and she knew why. He was jealous. He always had been.

"Don't sound so bloody delighted about it," her husband snapped. "You didn't see the way he spoke to me, the way he looks at me—his king!"

"I expect he looks at you and sees the friend who stabbed him in the back, cast him out, and took everything he owned," she pointed out with heavy sarcasm. "If you want to win him back, show him he can trust you."

"I did not take everything! Why does everyone say that I did? You saw the Isyr he wears. It's worth more than the bloody country. Did I take that? Did I?"

She stared at him. After all these years he was still obsessed with those blades, and she could not understand it. "The only reason you didn't was because he would have skewered you with them had you tried. And what do you suppose those bloody things are doing to him, right at this moment? Do you not remember your crown, Raffa?" She wished, suddenly, that she had gone to see Esar, to warn him about the Isyr, but he must know. She had seen Alyas arrive and he looked awful.

It was a mistake to mention the crown. Raffa's face transformed. "Where is it, Mari? I want it back." He was out of the chair and had taken a stalking step towards her before he mastered himself.

Gods, this hadn't happened in years, but she was usually so careful, and he didn't usually have Alyas flaunting the bloody stuff in front of him, making it look like it was nothing to wear it when in fact it was torture. Even Ovisia only wore her Isyr jewellery when she wanted to make a point, which made the syndicates' obsession with it reckless to the point of stupidity. But then that described almost everything they had done in recent months.

"It's safe, Raffa," she said, as calmly as she could. "And so are you." Safer than he would be with it, anyway. She thought again about talking to Esar, but there were too many reasons why she couldn't. She had made her choice years ago, and she had made it a hundred times since in various ways. Now she had to live with the consequences. She couldn't pretend she was anything other than what she was, or that she wouldn't fight tooth and nail to defend it, even if that meant fighting against the two men she had once loved best in all the world, though she was trying her best to make sure it didn't come to that.

She took a deep breath, thinking calming thoughts of all the beautiful patterns she had seen in the seamstress's studio and which one she might choose to replace the torn dress. "We should all be on the same side. We all want the same thing, which is an end to this plague. If the syndicates could solve it, they would have done so by now, so stop helping them cover it up and start helping Alyas.

And if you can't bring yourself to do that, at least stop Ovisia from interfering with him."

He blinked, the Isyr haze fading as he focused on her words. "I can't do that."

"Why not? Because she was your lover? Or is she still?"

"She is not," her husband responded. "She was too demanding."

"Yholis's mercy, spare me the sweaty details. I don't *care*. You can take as many lovers as you like, but don't make me hear about them."

"I don't want a string of bloody lovers!" he exploded. "I want you, Mari. I always have. What happened to us?"

She looked at him with scorn. "You know what happened, Raffa. You climbed into bed with the syndicates—literally in *her* case—and between you, you fucked everything up."

"I didn't see you complaining," he snapped back. "You were happy enough to spend all the profits. What did that dress cost? And all this?" He waved his arm at the jewellery scattered across her dressing table.

Mari cast a mournful look at the ruined dress, then the glittering trinkets she rarely wore. "I don't know, Raffa. You bought them for me, back when you still cared about what I thought."

They glared at each other, so much hurt on both sides. Too much. So much guilt. Raffa sagged, the angry set of his shoulders slumping into misery. "I didn't do this, Mari. You know that. They lied to me, and now it's too late. What can I do?"

Finally. She bit back an angry retort, concealed her contempt, and sat on the bed, smoothing the covers beside her. He sat, and she shifted closer, putting a gentle hand on his back and wondering when her husband had become such a child. "You know what you need to do, Raffa. That's why you brought him back. Use him. Give him your support and he'll break their hold on you, I promise." And be glad to do it. They would never be friends again, but she would happily settle for not enemies.

"He hates me, Mari," the king complained, leaning into her hand.

"I don't like him much, either."

She sighed. "You don't have to like each other. He will help you, you just have to ask. But first you must win back his trust."

Raffa was silent a long time. "How? They tried to kill him in Cadria. He thinks I knew."

She didn't ask if he had known. She didn't want to know. That kind of knowledge would make her life far too complicated. "Give him what he wants. Give him Ovisia. You said it yourself—she tried to have him killed. Let the syndicates face the king's justice for once."

He stiffened and pulled away. "I can't." His voice was a mix of defiance and despair. "I can't, Mari. Don't ask it of me. Not even for you."

He was hiding something. She said sharply, "If you don't give her up, he'll never trust you. He'll go after you, too."

His back was rigid. It was reckless to make that threat and she knew it, but her suspicions were confirmed when Raffa said, "Yholis forgive me, he's going to do that anyway."

She felt a thrill of fear. "Why, Raffa? What have you done?"

BRIVAR

After the confrontation at the palace, there followed a period of relative quiet. Rumours swirled that the king's syndicate advisor was out of favour, or that the Duke of Agrathon was, and a state of uneasy calm reigned at Camling. No one came for the evidence Brivar was carefully guarding.

Brivar did not see Alyas again for several weeks, though he went regularly to Camling to see Keie and Della. He tried not to read anything into that. He tried not to worry, and instead pestered Della for news, but she did not have much to tell him. The company was often absent from the city, but rarely together. Wary of more outbreaks and how long it would take for word to reach Avarel, Alyas had patrols out in all directions looking for signs of the corruption and so Della had not seen him. Brivar tried not to read anything into that either. It *might* not be intentional.

Inside Avarel, things were far from calm. The Nameless were causing trouble across the city. After they closed down parts of the city with their protests for the third time in as many days, the king's guard set up check points around the Carpera and key districts, including the market square and the streets around it, preventing anyone assembling in any numbers. So the Nameless had resorted to other tactics—harassing the named elite as they travelled around the city, once even jamming a staff into the wheel of a carriage, nearly overturning it and injuring its occupants. After that, the crackdown got harder and the sympathy of the city, which had largely tolerated their activities with anything ranging from amused interest to silent agreement to loud drunken approval, depending on where you stood in the social hierarchy, started to harden against them.

The disruptions quietened. Instead, graffiti appeared all over Avarel, bold slogans demanding an end to the tyranny of inherited wealth and crude illustrations depicting… Well, Brivar wasn't quite sure, and he wasn't the only one. The one occasion he had seen Alyas in that time was from a distance as Brivar was walking between the market and the temple. He had been with Esar and they were puzzling over a particularly lurid piece of graffiti painted on the high wall that enclosed the square.

Esar pointed to a section of the graffiti. "What do you suppose they are doing there?"

"Maybe if you look at it this way…" Alyas tilted his head to the side, amused, then he shrugged. "No, that doesn't help."

Esar was grinning. They looked relaxed and, well, normal, but Brivar would have found it a lot more reassuring if Alyas did not, the whole time, have his hand curled around a silver-blue hilt. He wanted to stop and talk to them, but the crowd, funnelled through the guards' checkpoint, carried him past before he could get their attention.

He wasn't the only one trying to get their attention. A week later, as he was returning from his regular visit to the market, a girl suddenly appeared beside him. He felt something prick his side and looked down to see she was pressing a knife against him. He jerked back in surprise and fear. Someone grabbed his elbow from the other side and he was steered away from the main flood of people into a side street. The dying down of the protests meant the guards were not as attentive as usual. There was no one near to see his struggles as he was shoved and pushed out of sight and into an alley.

Several people were waiting there. They were all young, within a few years of his own age, and all plainly dressed, though in clothes that were too well made for the style they affected. The girl who had first accosted him sat down on an upturned crate, nursing her knife in her hand, and gave him a look that he supposed was intended to be intimidating, while her companions stood around in various threatening poses. But he looked at the way they held their pretty weapons and compared it to the way he had seen the company handle their rather more business-like ones, and a large part of his anxiety vanished.

"I am Tersa," the girl told him. Her dark hair was shining clean and neatly braided and her clothes were spotless. "We are the Nameless."

He frowned. "I thought you didn't have names."

She gave him a look that suggested he was being dense. "It's not my *real* name."

"Oh. Of course."

She stood, knife still in her hand. "I expect you're wondering why we've brought you here."

"A bit," he admitted. Although he did have a suspicion.

She confirmed it. "You are with the Duke of Agrathon. We saw you with him the day he arrived, and we have seen you come and go from Camling."

He nodded. "I am his household surgeon."

"We want to see him."

"Why?" Though he could guess that too.

Tersa treated him to a very aristocratic look of disdain. "That doesn't concern you. You just need to get us in to see him."

Brivar shook his head. "I disagree. What if you intend him harm? I'm afraid you need to tell me why."

"We don't want to hurt him," she said in frustration. "We want his help!"

He thought about that and supposed from a certain point of view it made sense. But he had some misgivings. "I don't think he is going to react well to this plan. Have you tried, I don't know, writing to him?"

"Of course we've tried," she snapped. "Either he isn't getting our letters or he's ignoring them."

"Well, he is busy," Brivar pointed out, thinking of how rarely Alyas was actually at Camling. He might also be ignoring them, although Brivar doubted he was unsympathetic, which he guessed was the same reasoning by which the Nameless had decided to approach him. Whether he would help them was another matter entirely. He had a mental image of Tersa confronting Alyas and it… not going well. On the other hand, Brivar wanted to see him too, because he was starting to think the man was deliberately avoiding him and he didn't like what that might mean.

"All right," he said, "But I can't promise he'll listen. And I don't even know if he's there."

"He's there," another of the Nameless said, a tall young man with untidy brown hair. "He arrived back this morning."

⁂

The Nameless were prepared. As soon as he agreed, Tersa pulled out a pale blue temple surcoat from a pack and put it on.

Brivar watched her with disapproval. "Where did you get that?"

"Stole it," she grinned at him. "From the temple laundry. Oh, don't look like that. You can take it back afterwards."

"I will," he said.

They escorted him to Camling as a group, but only Tersa accompanied him to the gates, where he was waved through with a friendly smile. He felt a twinge of guilt.

He saw Alyas at once, near the stables. He was dressed in dusty leathers, the Isyr blades at his hips, and he was talking to a groom. He did indeed look like he had just arrived back from somewhere. Other members of the company were coming and going from the stables, seeing to their horses.

Tersa's knife pricked his back. "Go on, then," she hissed. "That's him, I know that's him. Take me to him."

He didn't have to. Alyas looked across the courtyard and saw them, Brivar with the girl standing too close, a face he didn't know. He said something to the groom and walked over, treating Tersa to a quick, assessing glance.

"What are you doing with my surgeon?"

Tersa moved so Alyas could see the knife inexpertly held against Brivar's side. He did not appear unduly concerned, which flustered her. "What else could I do? You've ignored all our attempts to make contact."

"Ah, the Nameless. And you thought threatening a member of my household would succeed where all your eloquently written letters have failed?"

So, he had received them. Brivar found that vaguely disappointing. Tersa and the Nameless were young and naïve, but they weren't *wrong*. And if anyone in Avarel was going to understand that, it was surely this man. Brivar took the opportunity to study him. He looked thinner and tired, his face all hollows and shadows, but mostly he looked impatient and irritated. Brivar was starting to regret his rash decision.

The meeting was clearly not going the way Tersa had expected. Brivar couldn't see her face, but he was close enough to feel her nerves. Her hesitation before her defiant "Yes" made it sound more like a question.

"Well, you were wrong," Alyas said, walking away.

"I wouldn't have hurt him," she called after him.

"I'm glad we've cleared that up," he replied without breaking stride. "Brivar, you heard her. Next time you can safely ignore them."

Tersa let out an angry sob and Brivar recklessly called after the duke, "I promised her you would listen to what she has to say." It was a lie, and he regretted it the moment he said it.

Alyas stopped. For several long moments they were treated to a view of his back, rigid with anger, then he turned. Brivar flinched from the expression on his face.

"You did, did you? Well, I can't make a liar of one of Yholis's apprentices. You'd better come with me."

※

Brivar knew he had made a mistake. As Alyas led them into a small study, he could see he was furious. And if he had thought about it for a bit longer, he should have realised he would be. If Alyas had ignored the Nameless so far, he would not appreciate being forced into meeting with them now.

Tersa knew it too. She stuck close by Brivar's side as though his presence would protect her, which it absolutely would not. When the door closed behind them, she actually winced.

Alyas gestured to a chair. "Sit."

She sat. Brivar edged backwards into the corner. Alyas glanced at him once then ignored him.

"Who are you?"

"We are the Nameless. We –"

"I am aware of what you call yourselves," he said. "I meant who are *you*?"

She set her chin in trembling defiance. She really was very young. "I am Tersa. *We* are the Nameless. We have given up the names we were born with to protest the injustice of a society that puts more stock in the length of a name and the wealth that comes with it than in virtue or skill or courage. You could call us the voiceless because those without a name have no voice. We want to change that."

"Then you shouldn't have given yours up, should you?" Alyas observed dryly as this rehearsed speech came to an end. "If what you want is a voice and not just to make a point."

Tersa didn't seem to know how to take that. Brivar wanted to leave.

Alyas reached into a drawer and put a sheaf of papers down on the desk. "Explain these."

Tersa looked nervously from his face to the papers. "They are letters."

"I am aware of that. Why did you send them to me?"

She swallowed. "Because we want your help."

Silence.

She tried again. "We thought you would understand. That you would want to help."

"Tersa, look around you," Alyas said, the hard edge of his anger replaced by weary patience. "What is it about where you are right now that suggests I would be inclined to help you?"

Brivar risked a look at his face, surprised. He could hardly claim to understand the Duke of Agrathon, but he was certain Alyas was not being honest with her.

Tersa also found this difficult to accept. "You lived without your names for fifteen years! Why take them back now? Surely you have realised how little they mean? How unfair it is that they dictate who has wealth and opportunity and who has nothing? Surely you see that we are right?"

"On the contrary," Alyas replied. "Losing my names was very inconvenient."

Tersa glared at him, and Brivar had to give her credit for not giving up in the face of such a dearth of encouragement. "How can you not see the injustice?" She sounded crushed, as the image she had built of this man came crashing down in bitter disappointment.

He saw it too and took pity on her. "Of course I see it. The whole system is rotten to the core. You have every right to your grievance, but this is not the way to change it."

"You only say that because you're part of it! Everything you have has been given to you by that rotten system."

His lips twitched. "Not quite everything."

She ploughed on as if he had not spoken. "How can you imagine what it's like for the rest of us who have not been born to wealth and privilege just because we cannot list twenty generations after our own?"

"Tersa, your name is Alla-Sera Lan—I think we may be distant cousins. Your father is Vance-Lan Sera and your mother Elidne-Sera Lan. You can name at least seventeen generations. Most of your fellow Nameless have names just as long. Do not berate me with my privilege and deny your own. Your gesture does not give voices to the voiceless, because you do not speak for them. You speak for yourselves."

She gaped at him. "You know who we are."

"Of course I do," he snapped. "Ithol's blood, girl, you are hardly subtle. But you do not know what you are about. And this—this will just get you killed. Or, more likely, it will kill those you claim to represent."

She said in a small voice. "I thought you would understand. I thought you would see how meaningless and selfish and unfair it is that we have to live in a system that gathers all its wealth into fewer and fewer hands and just makes the rich richer and the poor poorer, where if you do not start life with the right names you will never gain them because those who control the access to money and power do not want to share it!"

"Tersa," he said gently. "I understand, I do, but where do you think this will get you? If what you say is true, do you really think you can throw out centuries of wealth and tradition and overthrow a government by removing yourselves from the very apparatus you are trying to change?"

"Yes, if enough of us do it. Yes. You could –"

"I could, but I won't."

"Why not?" It was a wail of frustration. "It's just a name!"

"Because it was my father's, and my mother's. Because that's what they took from me and that's why it hurt so much. And I will not give it up again for you."

"I'm sorry for your losses. But others have lost more, are losing more every day we allow this injustice to continue. Don't help us if you think us so misguided. Help them, the people who need it."

"I am trying to," Alyas said, and Brivar could see he had had enough. He stood. "Stop trying to tear down the system from the outside. You are young. Your parents are old. Take the power your birth gives you, and when your time comes you can make the changes you will never make by protesting on street corners or putting staffs through carriage wheels—which, by the way, is going to hurt the wrong person and bring the full weight of the establishment down on you so hard you won't know what hit you. Tear it all down, I don't care. But don't do it with violence because violence will dog your every step and whatever change you win from it will never be safe."

She stared at him, confused and disappointed. "We don't want violence, but they won't listen to anything else."

"It won't matter what you want," Alyas said, opening the door. "If you threaten their power—really threaten it—they will fight to defend it, and it will be violence and death whether you want it or not. And they *will* win."

Tersa walked out. Brivar made to follow but a pointed look from Alyas pinned him in place.

"I thought you would help," she said as she passed him.

"You thought wrong. Can I trust you to see yourself out? It would be most inconvenient if I had to take you home to your parents and explain that you damaged my property because you believe owning it is a crime."

Tersa looked at him with something very close to disgust, but she marched obediently down the hallway towards the doors.

Esar, who was leaning against the opposite wall, watched her go, then said, "Did you enjoy that?"

Alyas shot him a look. "What do you think?"

Esar peeled himself off the wall and joined them in the study. "I don't expect you to help them, but I know you agree with them. Did you have to crush her like that? They're only kids."

"Kids who are going to get themselves killed if they carry on like this," Alyas retorted. "Any encouragement I give them just puts them in more danger. Nicor has shown great restraint so far, but if they keep pushing, he won't have a choice. And what do you think will happen then? They are never going to get what they want. You know that. When revolution does come it won't be from a few well-meaning rich kids, it will be because the people rise up in a massive wave and say no more."

Esar shrugged. "But maybe that wave starts with a few rich kids who want to change things."

"Maybe it does," Alyas snapped, "but not today. Look at them, Esar! They will be crushed if Raffa and the syndicates ever take them seriously enough to turn on them. And if that happens, we'll be lucky to avoid civil war."

"There's your wave."

Alyas glared at him. He had gone very pale. It was as though a mask had been stripped away. "Yes, of death. Don't ask me to start a war. I won't do it. I know where it leads!" He looked at Brivar. "Don't ever do that to me again." Then he was gone and the door slammed behind him. It was starting to become a pattern.

❧

Esar looked at the closed door in silence. Then, as if he had not just deliberately provoked Alyas, he said, "That wasn't your best idea."

Brivar looked at the floor. "I didn't have much choice."

Esar snorted. "Yes, you did. You could have refused. They wouldn't have hurt you."

It was true. He had known it. But that wasn't his only reason. "He's avoiding me."

That got him a sharp look and a frown. Then Esar sighed. "Don't take it personally. He's avoiding everyone."

"Aren't you worried?"

It was the wrong thing to say. Of course he was worried.

"Of course I'm bloody worried," Esar agreed. "But what can I do? He's a grown man and he's not incapable of asking for help. Or that's what Frey would tell me."

Brivar brightened. "Is she back?" He knew Della had been worried, and that it wasn't only Frey who was overdue. She had been vague, but he had the sense that what had been mild concern was now something more acute.

Esar's frown deepened. "No."

He didn't elaborate, and this time Brivar had the sense not to ask unwelcome questions. If Frey wasn't back, they were certainly searching for her, and if Esar was here rather than out there looking it was probably because he didn't feel he could leave.

"I should go," he said, edging towards the door. He was only causing more problems, not solving them, which was not his intention.

He wasn't sure if Esar had heard him, but as Brivar opened the door, he said, "Don't stop coming."

ESAR CANTRELL

Esar watched Brivar leave, undecided whether to be amused or exasperated by his tactics. He had not been unaware of the attempts by the Nameless to reach Alyas—it would have been difficult to miss them, especially the three-foot-high message painted on the wall outside Camling. That had been cleaned off before Alyas or anyone else could see it. No need to enrage Raffa further, and Alyas was right—he couldn't possibly encourage them. So far, no one had been hurt, but that would change rapidly if anyone thought the Duke of Agrathon had given his support to the movement. Even so, Esar had more than a little sympathy for them. It was about time someone challenged the inequities of the system. It was their misfortune it was propped up and supported by the syndicates, and that made their efforts not just dangerous but also futile. For now.

As Brivar went out through the gates, he passed a familiar figure coming in, the Flaeresian ambassador with his short cape swirling around his shoulders in his haste.

Esar came down the steps to meet him. "Melar, you don't look like you are going to put a smile on my face."

"I'm not," the ambassador agreed. "Is he here? I need to speak to both of you."

Esar studied him. Gaemo was as perfectly turned out as he always was, but there was something ever so slightly out of place about him today. It spoke of an urgency that did not bode well, and a pit of nerves opened in his stomach. With Frey so long overdue, every message was potential disaster. Between the two of them he was a ragged mess of anxiety.

"He's here," Esar confirmed, hoping whatever it was would not take them immediately out of Avarel. Whatever else the Isyr was doing to Alyas, it was also wearing down his physical resilience, and the last thing he needed was to leave again with no time to rest.

Gaemo nodded grimly. Then said, "Was that your famous apprentice surgeon I just saw leave?" Alyas's unconventional choice had, apparently, been amusing society for weeks.

"It was," Esar replied, with a sideways look at the ambassador. "And you leave him alone. He's spoken for."

Gaemo shrugged. "I am quite occupied elsewhere at the moment, I assure you."

Alyas was not in any of the obvious places. They eventually tracked him down to his private chambers. He had taken off the blades, which now rested on his lap. The dagger was part unsheathed, and he was staring at the perfect sheen of its unbared length in way that made Esar feel sick.

He stopped in the doorway. "Alyas."

It took long seconds for Alyas to respond, and when he looked up, his eyes were distant and unfocused.

"Alyas," he said again, moving aside to allow Gaemo to enter.

When his gaze fastened on the ambassador, awareness snapped back in Alyas's eyes, and he slid the dagger into its sheath. He stood, laying the blades on the chair, and said, "Do you have news?"

Gaemo had been as good as his word so far, as had his king, providing them with a regular stream of intelligence about how the investigation was progressing in Flaeres. In return, Alyas had shared what they knew of the cause of the contagion. Gaemo's reaction had been interesting. He had been angry, but neither shocked nor surprised. Either he had guessed, which was entirely possible, or Diago had known all along and had simply decided that enough was enough. Esar wished Raffa would do the same.

Gaemo didn't answer. His gaze flickered from the Isyr weapons to Alyas's face. He said, "There are rumours, about Isyr."

"Are there? How interesting. What's your news?"

Again, Gaemo ignored the question. "My king's father ordered all Isyr in his household to be locked away twenty years ago and there are whispers that it was not because he feared the attention of thieves."

Alyas's eyes narrowed. "Do you have a point?"

The ambassador gave him a searching look. "I think you just made it for me. But in answer to your other question, yes, I have news. It's not good. Are you capable of acting on it?"

"Stop it, Melar," Esar growled. He had learned, since Cadria, that pushing only made things worse. If Gaemo had bad news, they didn't need to complicate things by getting tangled in an unwinnable argument about Isyr.

"My apologies," Gaemo murmured. "I'm sure you're quite on top of things." He handed over a courier's pouch. "This comes direct from my king—it arrived with me this morning."

Alyas took it, a question in his eyes. The relationship between the king and his ambassador was no secret, or rather only officially a secret, and Diago had been known to write rather enthusiastic letters. They had intercepted a few in their time.

"I assure you, nothing I do not want you to see is in there," Gaemo said dryly. "But it is easier for you to read it than for me to explain."

Alyas reached into the pouch and withdrew the messenger scroll, still looking at Gaemo. He unrolled it, and his face went grey. He sat.

"What?" Esar demanded, his heart thundering. "Is it Frey?"

Alyas shook his head. "Not Frey." He handed over the scroll. "The syndicates may have sent a force into the mountains."

"The *Lathai* mountains?" They had left a full third of the company in those mountains. Just in case, Alyas had said. He had intended to send most of the rest back, but then Orleas had happened and Esar had insisted they keep them. And they *had* needed them, but it meant those left behind would be hard-pressed to defend Lathai territory against a concerted attack. They would be hard-pressed to defend themselves.

If that's what this was. The intelligence sent from Diago via his ambassador made it clear that they did not have concrete evidence, but that message had been sent weeks ago. From Sarenza to Avarel, even by fast courier changing horses at each stop, was two weeks at least. And the news would have had to make it from the border to Sarenza in the first place. Anything could have happened in that time.

"May have," Gaemo said. "But I wouldn't bet against it. It tallies—if what you told me about Cadria is true. They are reckless and desperate."

They were worse than that. The senseless greed was staggering. Esar could not understand it. It was as if they did not realise they lived in the same world as everyone else, that the contagion they had caused would affect them too. Certainly, they seemed to have no intention of trying to stop it. They must have known the consequences of what they were doing for years—*years*—and done nothing. Worse, they had covered it up, bought entire governments as a shield, and committed murder to deflect attention from their activities. How many more outbreaks had been seeded by the syndicates like the Cadrian villages? And now, in the face of looming disaster, they continued to expand their operations. It was unforgiveable. It was evil on a scale he could barely comprehend.

Alyas had his head in his hands. Esar knew what he was thinking because he was thinking it too—but there was no sense regretting a decision they could not change. If their defence of the Lathai's secret had been misguided, at least they had done it for the right reasons. Whether it had made this more likely was a question he had no desire to examine more closely. It couldn't help anyone.

"What will you do?" Gaemo asked.

Alyas didn't reply. Esar didn't kick the chair, but only because they weren't alone.

"Alyas," he said sharply.

Alyas looked up. "What is Diago doing?"

"He has sent observers. I expect to hear from them soon, but you don't have time to wait for their report."

"*We* don't have time?" Alyas asked. "It's your border too, Melar. And last I checked, Sarenza was significantly closer than Avarel." He was angry, worse than angry. Esar couldn't blame him.

Gaemo had the grace to look uncomfortable. "My king promised you his support, not his direct intervention."

"In other words, he wants someone else to curb the syndicates while he protects his own interests," Alyas said in disgust. "You're all the same. You tell Diago that if this is what it looks like, and he did nothing, there will be a reckoning."

"Careful, Alyas," Gaemo snapped. "He's given you more than your own king has. Don't throw that away now."

Alyas stood. "But what was it worth, Melar?"

Gaemo got to his feet in turn. "You're upset. I understand that. I will make allowances, this time."

"Please don't," Alyas said, his voice cold. "You know the way out."

Anger flashed across the ambassador's face. Then he nodded. "If that is how you want it."

Alyas didn't even bother to reply. Gaemo cast a look at Esar, who stared back. He reached for the scroll, forgotten in Esar's hand.

"We need that," Alyas said. "It's the least you can do."

Gaemo's hand dropped. "Very well. For what it's worth, I hope we are wrong."

Alyas shook his head. "Just leave."

Esar watched Gaemo go. "Was that wise? We need all the help we can get. And he knows about Orleas."

"*Esar.*"

He turned. He hadn't heard that tone in Alyas's voice for years. He put a hand on his shoulder and pushed him back into the chair before he fell down. Alyas dropped, without protest or resistance.

Esar made a decision then. They had to go; they had been planning to anyway. After Cadria, Alyas had sent scouts after the original messengers he had sent to Ailuin. Even allowing for the four weeks that round trip would take, they should have heard something by now. But they didn't all have to go. "You're not coming." It was too much to worry about what they might find without worrying about what it would do to Alyas.

He braced for an objection that didn't come. Alyas didn't even try to argue with him. That was alarming. "Someone has to be here." He was arguing with himself now. "In case Frey comes home." Please let Frey come home. "I'll leave Agazi."

Alyas closed his eyes. "You don't have to do that." His voice was rough with exhaustion. The Varisten had said Raffa had suffered from nightmares because of the crown. Esar had no idea what Alyas dreamed about, he only knew he was never asleep for long. Never long enough. And it was brutally apparent that he had hit his limits, that whatever balance he had been striving to maintain, it had tipped too far.

"Yes, I do. Keie's baby could come any day. You promised him he would be here."

Alyas accepted that. "Be careful. I can't –" He looked away.

"I'll be careful," he promised, understanding. He wanted to say a lot more. He wanted to insist Alyas leave the wretched blades where they were and never put them on again. He wanted to tell him to go to Brivar. But he had said it before and he knew there was no point, so he would say it all to Agazi instead and make it his problem. Because he had to go.

BRIVAR

B rivar was walking through the temple grounds when he saw Alyas talking to the Varistan Alondo. He stopped, the pile of linen in his hands forgotten. The company was out of the city. He had said goodbye to Della two nights ago and watched them leave the next morning from the temple tower. They had not returned. Alyas should have been with them. He always went with them.

The Varistan saw him and beckoned him over. Alyas turned at his approach. His face was shadowed by the portico, but Brivar thought he saw relief in his dark eyes. He saw enough, anyway, for all his instincts to sound a warning.

"Your patron wishes to speak to you," Alondo told him, his voice carefully neutral. "You may use my office."

Brivar nodded and followed the Varistan as he led them across the courtyard to his small office overlooking the fountain. As Alondo ushered them inside, he caught Brivar's eyes and held them for a moment longer than necessary. He had seen it too. Of course he had.

The door closed and they stood there looking at each other in silence. Then Alyas unbuckled the blades and held them out to Brivar. He didn't quite meet his eyes as he said, "I need you to take these for a while."

Brivar took the weapons from him, feeling their deadly weight settle on his palms. Alarm bells were ringing in earnest now. He had wondered if Alyas was avoiding him, had worried that the blunder over the blades and then Tersa had lost him the trust he had gained. Now, as Brivar looked at him and saw everything he could no longer hide, he was certain of it.

After a moment Alyas met his steady gaze with resignation.

Brivar tried not to give into his frustration. This was what he was here for. But all he said was, "Will you let me help?"

⁂

Brivar closed the door to the Varistan's office with the blades in his hands. He had left Alyas inside asleep on the small bed beneath Alondo's windowsill of trailing plants. It was painfully obvious he hadn't been sleeping, and just the act of relinquishing the blades was enough to induce surrender. But that wasn't why Brivar found himself crossing the courtyard as fast as he could in search of his master, whom he found reading quietly in a corner of the library.

Alondo glanced up as he burst in, looking calmly from the Isyr weapons to Brivar's frantic face as though he had been expecting him.

"We need to know how the farmer died."

"Why?"

Brivar took a steadying breath. "Because I was wrong. It's not the Isyr that is killing him."

The Varistan carefully marked his place and set the book aside. "I thought there was something you hadn't told me."

"I couldn't," Brivar said miserably. "I promised."

The old man looked at him without judgement. As a full surgeon, such discretion would be both essential and expected, but Brivar was an apprentice. He was still learning, and his patients and treatments were also his master's, no matter how far away they happened. He should have shared the details of Alyas's illness with Alondo. "Do we have time for you to explain?"

He wanted to say no. Guilt for failing to investigate the farmer's death was gnawing at him, and he wanted very badly to be doing something to put it right, but he needed help. Alyas needed it. And if he did not know the history, Alondo's help would be limited. So, very quickly, he related everything that had happened since he had left the temple with his cousin all those weeks ago and saw the Varistan fit this together with what he already knew about the Isyr.

Alondo stood stiffly. His hip was paining him again. "You are lucky," he told Brivar. "I had organised an anatomy class for today. The body is already prepared. Put those somewhere safe, then let us find out if you are right."

They were passing the fountain when Agazi walked through the temple gates. Everything about him shouted urgent. Brivar called to him, thinking it was Keie, and saw Agazi's face collapse in relief.

"Where's Alyas? I need him."

"Now?

"Now."

Brivar hesitated, torn. "He's asleep."

Agazi swore. Those closest to Alyas would know he had not been sleeping. "No choice," he said in answer to Brivar's unspoken question. "Is he wakeable?"

Brivar nodded. He had not drugged him; there had been no need. Separated from the blades, Alyas had simply crashed, and crashed hard. He had stayed conscious long enough to confirm what Brivar could already see—this was worse than before. How he had hidden it as well as he had, and indeed why, Brivar did not know and had no time to wonder at.

Alondo, his hands on Brivar's shoulders, turned him towards the vaults and gave him a gentle push. "Go on and get prepared. I'll take him."

ALYAS-RAINE SERA

Agazi was talking to him. It sounded urgent, but the words were all jumbled, like he was still half asleep. He *was* still half asleep. He sat up, resting his head against the wall and closing his eyes, willing the pain to subside. "Tell me again, slowly."

"…prisoners, to the Temple of Ithol. One of them had red hair. It's Frey, Alyas. They've got Frey."

Alyas opened his eyes to Agazi's worried frown. "Frey?"

"Yes, I've told you three times."

"Then once more can't hurt. Where is she? Who has her?"

Agazi took a deep breath. He looked as if he was trying to decide whether to panic. Over his shoulder, Alyas could see Alondo's familiar face. Now Brivar's master. But not Brivar.

"She's at the Temple of Ithol. The syndicates brought prisoners into the city last night. They took them there."

"And Frey is there?"

"Yes. Gods, Alyas, wake up."

"I am awake." Regrettably.

He put his hand out for the blades, but they weren't there. Of course they weren't there. He had given them to Brivar, just as Esar wanted. He was at the temple. That's why everything hurt so much.

He stood, or tried to. Agazi steadied him. "Where are you going?"

"To get Frey."

Alondo frowned, and his eyes creased with concern. "I do not think you should leave here."

"And in other circumstances I would take your advice." But this was Frey, and if he didn't go and get her Esar would never forgive him. He wouldn't forgive himself.

Agazi, who would incur Esar's wrath whichever decision he made, said, "Stay here. I'll go."

Alyas reached again for the blades. And remembered again. "No. It has to be me."

"Why?"

"Because you'll have to fight your way in. They'll open the doors for me."

"Why?"

"Because I recently gave them a lot of money." He felt wrong, unbalanced. "I need a weapon." He would not ask for them back. Not yet. He needed to be able to think and they filled his head, every moment, with their grief.

Agazi unbuckled his sword belt but he didn't hand it over. He looked even more worried when he realised the blades were gone. But this was not like Cadria, or what Alyas assumed Cadria had been like, because the blank in his memory was no closer to being filled. This time it had been his choice. He had not meant for it to be permanent, but he hadn't expected it to be this bad without them.

"Why?"

Alyas sighed. "I'm sure you used to know other words."

Agazi narrowed his eyes. "Do you want these or not?"

"Which question would you like me to answer?"

"All of them."

"Fine. Because the temples are in this up to their necks—my apologies, Varistan, I do not include you in that personally—but they are much easier to buy off, and it seemed likely that might become necessary. Because even a very large donation may not be enough to buy Frey back if the syndicates want to keep her, and I would rather not be unarmed if that is the case, and yes, I do want them. Please."

He held out his hand and hoped no one could see it shake. But it must have been shaking worse than he thought because Agazi shook his head. "I can't let you go. You can hardly stand."

"It's Frey," Alyas said, taking the belt from him. "You have to. And no, you can't come. Because Keie needs you. I will go, I will get Frey, and I will bring her back here."

His fingers fumbled with the unfamiliar fastenings and Agazi reached out to help him. It wasn't the same—it would never be the same—but the weight of the weapons steadied him. "Send someone after Esar," he said. "Tell him Frey is in Avarel." Fear for her had been eating Esar for weeks and Alyas knew, though it had never been said, that Esar would have gone after her long since if not for him. He had to make sure she was safe. Frey was family. They all were.

He looked at Agazi, a refugee from the tribal warfare of the steppelands who had every reason to hate the rich, soft central Ellasians who exploited his lands. He tried to remember how long he had known him, but he couldn't recall a time when Agazi hadn't been with them. He would miss him. He would miss them all. And he regretted he would never meet Keie's baby.

"Go back to Camling," he told Agazi now. "Keie will kill me if you're not there when she needs you."

"Yholis, Alyas. She'll kill you too if you miss it. You sound like you're saying goodbye. Don't do that."

Was he? He had promised to come back. "I'll bring Frey back with me," he said again. Then, because if he stood still any longer he would fall down, he gently moved Agazi aside and walked to the door.

Alondo asked, "What should I tell Brivar?"

That almost stopped him. Almost. "Tell him it wasn't his fault."

❧

It wasn't a long walk from the Temple of Yholis to her brother's great house, but it took Alyas a long time. And he regretted, briefly, that he had not asked for the Isyr back after all. It clogged his mind, made it hard to think, but it blocked the pain. It allowed him to function.

He stopped at the edge of the great square in which the temple stood. People moved all around him. Suppliants, worshippers, temple devotees, beggars. So many beggars. They were wasting their time here. Yholis was the compassionate one, the merciful one. Ithol took and took and then took some more. What he gave in return was just more of what you already had, and as Tersa had correctly pointed out, for most people that was misery and struggle.

The graffiti of the Nameless was scrawled on the walls around the square, mocking him. He ignored it, as he had tried to ignore them. He *would not* go down that path. Instead, he watched the temple, the sun-warmed wall at his back, and allowed long years of experience to take over. It wouldn't be the first temple he had broken into, though it would be the first he had broken into without Esar beside him.

When he had seen all there was to see from the outside, he turned his attention to the inside. The outer gates were open wide, welcoming the public—the *paying* public—into the temple courtyard. Men and women in Ithol's red robes stood on either side of the gates with their donation jars. No one came through the gate without offering something. Alyas ignored them and walked straight through. They let him. They knew who he was.

The door to the temple complex was closed. Only the privileged few were invited inside, the named elite who patronised the temple with their wealth in exchange for its influence with its notoriously hard-nosed god. And, most recently, the Duke of Agrathon had added himself to that select list. To the top of that select list.

The wicket door opened to his knock, and a face appeared then disappeared with a start of a surprise. A shuffle of movement and another face came to the door in the darker red of a senior adept.

"Your Grace," the adept said with a low bow. "We did not know to expect you."

"I wish to see the Varistan," he said. "Or the Varisten."

There was a pause, then, "Of course, Your Grace. But I'm afraid it's not possible to disturb them. Perhaps you could come back another time. Tomorrow." The door started to close. Apparently, even very large sums of money would not throw the door wide for him today.

Alyas wedged it open with his foot. He wasn't standing for that. "Ten thousand silver marks says it's possible to disturb them any time I like. Why don't you go and ask? I'll wait here." And he stepped inside before the startled adept could stop him.

He didn't have to wait long. They both came, the master and mistress of this temple. But these were no Alondo and Elenia, who were compelled to serve by compassion and whose complicity in the syndicates' crime was not deliberate. These two knew exactly what they were doing. He could see it on them—the guilt, the greed, the utter contempt for those they hurt.

The Varistan Eoman greeted him with exaggerated warmth, utterly false. "Your Grace. We are honoured. Have you come to see how we are using your donations?"

"Yes, exactly that. And to see whether you require more." Greater subtlety was beyond him today and it would be wasted here anyway.

The Varistan's face took on a more enthusiastic aspect. Even the famously sour Varisten did her best to smile at him. "Of course, Your Grace," said Eoman. "We are… a little occupied today. Many of our acolytes are about to take their vows and we have ceremonies… Perhaps you could return tomorrow?"

Alyas smiled back in perfect understanding. "No."

The Varistan blinked, unaccustomed to such blunt refusal. Then he remembered who he was talking to and adjusted his expectations. Sometimes, Alyas reflected, his reputation was useful.

"I am a busy man, Varistan," he said, offering them the concession of an explanation. "I would be most grateful if you could spare someone to show me around today. I would like to be reassured that my money is being well spent before I commit to more."

Eoman accepted defeat. The temple always needed money. How

else could they maintain their lavish lifestyles? "Of course, Your Grace," he said again. "I will take you myself. Varisten Nessa can officiate the ceremonies in my place."

Alyas leant a surreptitious hand against the wall. "My thanks, Varistan. Shall we?"

⁂

The Varistan was thorough. His punishment, Alyas supposed, for insisting on imposing on the temple at an inconvenient time. Inside the sanctuary he learned more than he ever wished to know about the various types of ritual offerings, the rituals themselves, and how they were supposed to benefit those dedicating them, as well as the private offerings the temple made on behalf of its rich donors, such as himself. He was told, as he was led around the cloister, about the training of the novices and their progression through the ranks of the temple, and the roles and responsibilities that came with each advanced step. It was an expensive business to rise through the ranks, as he discovered to his not very great surprise. The Temple of Ithol did not welcome just anyone within the privileged circle of its brethren.

Doors opened off the cloister on its inner edge. He pushed them open as they went, to the Varistan's silent disapproval but not alarm, surprising their occupants in various activities but finding no sign of Frey or any other prisoners. He had not expected to. They would not be so carelessly housed.

It wasn't until they rounded the final corner that he found a trace of her. An alcove opened into the wall of the eastern corner of the cloister. A young man in the light red robes of a junior acolyte sat within its shadowed recess. Behind him was a door. A locked door. The keys were on a ring that hung from the acolyte's belt.

A passing adept snagged Eoman's attention with a question, and as the Varistan turned to answer it, Alyas smiled at the boy. "Where does that door lead?"

The boy started. He had been half asleep. "The cells."

He raised an eyebrow. "Cells? What can a temple need with cells?"

Eoman, catching the question as he turned from the acolyte, said smoothly, "For silence and contemplation, Your Grace. I regret that we cannot show them to you, but their occupants are meditating and cannot be disturbed. I'm sure you understand."

"Of course." He knew where she was now. He let his attention move on and was relieved to see they were approaching the end of their circuit. He could see the outline of the main door at the end of the cloister, and he let the Varistan hurry him towards it, away from the door to the cells.

The adept on duty opened the wicket door. The Varistan offered him a bow. "I hope you have been pleased, Your Grace. The temple values your patronage. Should you have any further questions, you may return at any time."

In other words, they would move the prisoners safely out of the way, probably tonight.

He nodded and felt himself sway.

The Varistan looked at him with concern. "Are you quite well, Your Grace?" It would be most inconvenient for the temple's funds if he were to drop dead. Who knew what the inheritor of his estates would do with them? Or indeed, who the inheritor of his estates would be, if Raffa allowed him to pass them on. Which was a question that suddenly seemed important to consider.

"Perfectly," he assured Eoman and allowed himself to be hustled outside and back into the sunlight.

It had been morning when he had gone to the Temple of Yholis. He didn't know how much time had passed since, or how long he had been inside the house of Ithol, but there must be several hours of daylight left and he needed darkness. He could not go back to Camling. Agazi would never let him leave again. But there was one place he could go.

Alyas vaguely recognised the elderly steward who opened the door of the elegant town house to his erratic knock. The man certainly recognised him, and took in his less than impressive appearance with evident disapproval.

"Is she at home?" Alyas asked, leaning against the doorframe.

"I will tell her you are here, Your Grace," the old man said, standing aside to let Alyas wobble inside.

"Are you drunk, Alyas?" Hailene demanded as she entered the salon a few minutes later. "My steward tells me you're drunk."

He supposed he might look drunk since he couldn't stand straight. "No, Aunt, I'm not drunk."

She sniffed. "Then you should probably sit down before you fall down and tell me what you need."

He felt a rush of gratitude. She knew he wouldn't have come for any other reason, and she wouldn't waste time with pointless questions. "I would rather lie down for a few hours," he admitted. "Can you spare a room?"

"That depends," she said, looking him up and down and not liking what she saw. "On why you need it and why you don't just go home to Camling."

Some questions, then. "Because, as you correctly observed, I will probably fall down soon anyway. And I can't go back to Camling because if I do, they won't let me leave again, and I have something I need to do first."

She tapped the floor with her cane in irritation, but he could see the concern she tried to hide. "And what do you need to do that is so important you must do it in this state?"

He steadied himself against the wall. "Break into the Temple of Ithol and take back something of mine."

BRIVAR

The practice of cutting open the bodies of the dead to discover what had killed them had come from Qido. Long before it was adopted by the Temple of Yholis, Qidan physicians had advanced their understanding of human anatomy and its diseases by studying the body after death. But it was the temple that took what they had learned and used it to practise medicine on the living, and so they had become surgeons.

It was the rite of passage of the new apprentices when they entered the temple aged ten. Before anything else, they stood by the side of Alondo or Elenia or one of the other senior surgeons and watched as they dissected a donated corpse, and those who fainted were kindly but firmly walked out of the temple and returned to their parents.

Brivar hadn't fainted, but he had been sick. Later, where no one could see. But he had also been fascinated. To see what lay under the skin of the human body with its complex structure of muscles and tendons and the network of veins that carried blood around the body. He would never forget Alondo removing the dead woman's heart and making the apprentices pass it round as he explained its vital function and the possible things that could go wrong. The girl next to him *had* fainted. Brivar had nearly dropped the heart as he tried to catch her, and as his fingers closed tight around the organ he had felt the astonishing strength of it. And he had been lost to his calling ever since.

In the years since, he had done this many times. In two more years he would even be expected to teach the anatomy classes to the new apprentices. But he had never done it when so much was riding on it, when a life he cared about very much depended on the outcome.

Alondo joined him as he was staring at the body, preserved by the cold of vaults but with the look of all corpses that he had always found so unsettling. The newly dead often looked like they had just fallen asleep and could open their eyes and come back to life. Those, like this man, who had been dead for longer, even with the process of decay degraded by deep cold, always looked to him as though they could never have been alive in the first place. It wasn't only the absence of animation, it was how rapidly the body became a mere shell, as though the fleeing spirit revealed its true nature—without the spark of life it was nothing but a vessel.

"His secrets will not reveal themselves," Alondo prompted him.

They would not, and finding them might take hours, hours he did not know if they had. But Yholis must have bestowed her favour on him because the cause of the farmer's death was not hard to find. He had, quite sensibly, been running when the midnight creatures attacked. He had taken wounds on the back of his right shoulder and thigh, ragged tears cause by teeth and nails. They started their visual inspection there and found discolouration and swelling near both scarred-over wound sites. The shoulder was the worst, whatever it was closer to the surface, and Alondo's skilled knife quickly revealed its cause, the ugly mess of what looked like a burst abscess.

But it was not a normal abscess. The inflamed tissues were blue-black and the fluid that had burst from it was the same colour. They found another deep in the muscle near the wound on the farmer's leg. This one hadn't burst, but the deterioration of the body meant it was leaking its black poison into the surrounding tissues.

Brivar stood for a long time looking at it, thinking about what it meant. "The na'quia didn't neutralise the poison," he said at last. They had thought they had stumbled on a cure, but it wasn't that at all. "It isolated it." Somehow the na'quia had drawn together the poison and walled it away from the rest of the body, arresting the course of the illness but not resolving its cause.

And then, some while later, the abscess burst and the farmer died.

Brivar had seen men and women dead from abscesses in their lungs or stomachs, even their hearts and brains. The temple had no way of helping them because the infection was too deep and they were unable to discover the cause of their symptoms until later, after they were dead, when careful dissection revealed the burst pockets of infection.

The pain was the least of the symptoms. One man had had so many abscesses around his lungs he had barely been able to draw breath by the end. So the farmer must have suffered for weeks—from pain and fever and sickness. But he hadn't come back to the temple. He had not sought help or treatment. As Alyas had avoided it, though he had been ill enough that those around him had known despite his efforts to hide it. They had thought it was the Isyr and had not looked beyond it, but *he* should have seen, he should have realised.

"It is easy to see the signs when you know the cause," Alondo reminded him.

And when you thought you knew the cause it was perilously easy to see the signs to match, but it was nearly impossible to find the cause if you could not even see the signs. And Alyas had made sure he could not. He still had no idea why.

It bothered him that both men—men who had nothing in the world in common and no connection exception the midnight sickness—should have behaved in the same self-destructive way when confronted with its resurgence.

He had wondered aloud, and Alondo looked up from the instruments he was cleaning. "It is no great mystery, I think. What would you have done if you had known? Would you have treated it in the same way?"

It was an appalling thought. To inflict na'quia on them once for the benefit of a few more weeks of life—no, he would not have done that again. That so many had endured their 'cure' already felt like a crime. It was telling, he realised, that not one of them had returned to the temple. He had assumed them recovered and had not thought about them since. But if the na'quia worked in the way it appeared to, then if they were still alive, they too were suffering. Not asking for help. Preferring to die than relive the horrors of the treatment.

What would have happened, he wondered, if one of the company had been infected? He was certain Alyas would not have permitted him to give them na'quia. And perhaps that was why he had not taken Brivar with them whenever they left the city. If only he had said something.

"I need to talk to him." If the infection was deep in the body, they had no safe way to treat it, but Brivar had drained many a surface abscess and seen them heal cleanly. The farmer's had been close to the site of the wounds. It was possible they could find it and remove the poison without killing him.

Alondo carefully replaced the clean scalpel on the tray. "That is not possible."

Brivar felt his stomach twist. "Why not?"

"Because he is no longer here."

Agazi. He had forgotten whatever crisis demanded Alyas's attention. But the state he had been in, Brivar could not believe Agazi would have let him leave.

"I understand that the syndicate is holding a member of his company prisoner. He has gone to free them."

"What? Who?" Because that would not be the simple task Alondo made it sound. "Where?"

Alondo picked up the next instrument. Brivar wondered exactly what it would take to ruffle his calm. "A woman called Frey. At the Temple of Ithol."

Frey. Yholis, of course Alyas would have gone himself, even if he could barely walk. He would not leave Frey in syndicate hands.

He wouldn't leave any of them, but especially not Frey. And at the Temple of Ithol. Alondo had warned him. Alyas had known. But, to Brivar, it was still a punch in the gut, the upending of thirteen years of devoted service. If Ithol was with the syndicates, where did Yholis stand?

"Come," said Alondo, putting a comforting hand on his arm. "You can worry about such questions later. For now, I think there is one thing we can usefully do."

⁂

They could try to understand the action of na'quia. Now they knew more about what it did, and what it did not do. And it gave Brivar something to occupy himself until Alyas returned with Frey, because he refused to entertain any other possibility.

Alondo searched among his plants for an empty bowl. It was glass—they all were—so the Varistan could watch the plants that were his passion grow from their roots to their blooms. And in the glass vessel onto a bed of soil he placed a lump of Isyrium ore, the unrefined rock the miners dug up from deep in the earth and that glinted here and there with whispers of Isyrium. The ore the syndicates refined through their alchemical process to produce pure Isyrium at such cost. That also produced the waste that had poisoned the land.

Over the lump of ore, Brivar emptied a vial of na'quia. It was a crude experiment, but it was all they had. Ailuin had reminded him that na'quia only grew near the site of Isyrium mines. He already knew there was a connection between the plant and the metal, he just didn't know what it meant. They did not have time to replicate natural conditions and watch for weeks or months to see if they could gain an insight into that relationship. So he dumped the extracted poison of the plant over the ore that contained a different type of poison and prayed to Yholis that *something* would happen.

Alondo made tea. It was such a normal thing for him to do that it seemed quite wrong. But Brivar took the tea and let its familiar warmth work its calming magic on him.

He watched the glass bowl. Alondo put a book into his hand and told him to refresh his knowledge of the complications of childbirth. He started to protest, then he remembered Keie and that her baby was coming soon and put his head down and started reading.

He looked at the glass bowl. Alondo sent him to fetch more tea.

When he returned he found his master holding the bowl to the light of the window and examining it through an eye glass. He started guiltily when Brivar entered and told him to make the tea.

When Brivar put the steaming little teapot on the Varistan's desk, Alondo was still studying the bowl. Brivar glanced at the hourglass. It had been three hours. Surely it was too soon?

Alondo passed him the bowl and Brivar held it up to the light as his master had done. At first he saw nothing. The lump of ore still sat there on its cushion of soil, the tiny slivers of Isyrium marking faint lines through its structure. Then the light caught it and he felt a flicker of excitement. Were those slivers brighter than before?

"I cannot tell," Alondo admitted. "I thought so, but I cannot be sure. We should have some more tea, wait a bit longer."

They had more tea. Alyas did not return. Neither did Frey. It started to get dark. Alondo lit an Isyrium bulb and then—then they saw it. In the blue-tinted light, the black beads stood out against the dark of the soil as the na'quia extracted the impurities of the ore, separating one thing from the other, just as it had done in the farmer, leaving the glints of Isyrium brighter and more pronounced. And suddenly he knew how the Lathai were refining their ore.

"I must go to Camling," Brivar said. He couldn't wait any longer. "He might be there. I must tell him."

"He's not at Camling."

"You don't know that!" It was night. Alyas had been gone for hours. If he wasn't at Camling…

"He said he would return here. I think he is a man who keeps his promises."

Unless he couldn't.

Brivar sat. He had thought he was patient. He discovered he had never really required patience before. Another hour passed. Now the effect of the na'quia was unmistakable.

Alyas still didn't return.

A woman cried out, a deep, tearing groan, waking him from his uneasy doze.

He burst out of Alondo's office into the shadowed courtyard. A knot of people stood around the temple gates. He recognised Agazi, or rather his back, as he leant over someone else. Brivar ran across the courtyard, skidding on the wet paving stones around the fountain, and came to a breathless stop by Agazi's side.

Keie, one hand pressed to the wall for support, the other one cradling her belly, looked at him and said fiercely, "Kill him for me, Brivar. Kill him for doing this to me!"

ALYAS-RAINE SERA

Hailene had not tried to dissuade him. She merely had her steward show him to a room and Alyas made the man promise to wake him as soon as it was dark. If the temple did plan to move the prisoners tonight, he couldn't wait too long to go after Frey. He couldn't afford to lose track of her.

Waking was hard. His body craved sleep so badly. What rest he had managed in the last few weeks always ended the same way, with the same nightmare, weaving into and over and through the Isyr's mournful refrain. That was gone now, along with the shield it had given him, and without it he found he could barely rise.

The old man helped him. Together they got him sitting up, then the steward offered him some wine. "To help Your Grace recover." He still thought he was drunk. Alyas would have laughed if he hadn't been concentrating so hard on holding the cup so he didn't spill a drop. Because if he was going to rescue Frey, he needed all the help he could get. As wine was the only help at hand, he would take it all.

The frightening weakness passed. It did not go away, but it receded enough that he could stand, he could walk, although he quickly had to abandon his initial plan. The last time he and Esar had entered a temple of Ithol uninvited, they had gone over the compound's walls. Those walls in Avarel were high and impressive and he could not scale them in this state. He would have to go in as he had before and hope he could cause enough chaos and confusion to enable him to get to

Frey. There was every chance that getting them back out again would be up to her. But that was all right. This wasn't her first temple either, though they were usually breaking in, not out.

The face behind the wicket door was a new one, and very sleepy. It was late, and the man had probably been dozing at his post. Alyas didn't wait for him to collect his thoughts and realise he should close the door and slam the bolts home. He kicked the door all the way open and shouldered his way inside. Before the adept could call for help, he had the point of Agazi's dagger against his throat. There were beads of sweat on his face and his pulse fluttered like a bird's in response to the erratic shaking of that same blade.

"No, my hand is not very steady," Alyas admitted. "So it is in your interests to comply as quickly as possible, don't you agree?"

The adept did agree, and they walked together down the cloisters towards the door to the cells without raising any disturbance. The great advantage of temples of Ithol—the great disadvantage as far as the syndicates were about to discover—was that they were not terribly well guarded. On the other hand, that was because *no one* would be foolish enough to rob them. Quite apart from the potentially catastrophic disfavour of the god, those who did tended to be hunted down and punished in quite unpleasant ways. But Alyas was not currently concerned with Ithol's secretive inquisitors, who anyway had several scores to settle with him already, if only they knew it. His much more immediate concern was getting to Frey before his ability to help her ran out.

The young acolyte on duty by the entrance to the cells had been relieved by an older man, dressed in the uniform of the temple guards. Alyas should not have been surprised. His interest in the locked door had been noticed, and they must know they had one of his people in their cells. Still, the guard was alone, so there was that. Alyas transferred the dagger to his left hand, reversing his grip, and drew Agazi's sword, its point pressed to the adept's side.

The man stood as they approached. He put an unhurried hand to the sword at his hip. "Varistan Eoman does not wish you hurt, Your Grace," he said in a rumbling tone. "Please release Varistal Gaiden and leave here peacefully and no more will come of this."

"And I do not wish to hurt you," Alyas replied. "Please take your hand away from your sword and open the door."

The man didn't move. "This is pointless. Even if I open the door, you will never get her out. Be reasonable, Your Grace."

"But I am not a reasonable man," Alyas pointed out. "As you may have heard. And I don't have time to argue with you."

The pommel of his dagger delivered a precise blow to the adept's temple, dropping him like a stone. He was lucky that the other man had waited to draw his sword. His own turned the hasty attack and slid down the length of the guard's blade before he had time to respond. Never mind that the forward movement had been more of a stumble, his muscles knew what they were doing even if he was not completely in control of them anymore.

The guard gave a grunt of pain. They both looked at the slender point embedded a good inch in the muscle of his shoulder.

"Will you please," Alyas said, "unlock the door and go down?"

The man put his gloved hand around the trembling blade, tears of pain in his eyes. "This is pointless," he said again.

"Then it is pointless to make me hurt you more. Please drop your weapon."

It fell to the floor. "Thank you."

The guard looked him in the eye. "I'm going to take this out now."

It was so ridiculous he almost laughed. Instead, Alyas pulled the blade back, withdrawing it as carefully as possible from the guard's shoulder, which spilled a trickle of red blood down his temple surcoat. The man pressed his hand to the small wound, a grimace of pain flashing across his face.

"Thank you," he said, his voice rough. "I will ask you one more time, Your Grace. Please go home."

Alyas shook his head. "No. Do not make me ask *you* again."

The guard gave a shrug and winced. But he took the keys from his belt and opened the door. Alyas sheathed his dagger and held out his left hand. The guard placed the keys on his palm.

"Go down."

Resigned, the guard started down the steps to the cells. Alyas followed him, locking the door behind him and lighting the Isyrium bulb that clung to the wall on his right. The light showed him the guard waiting at the bottom of the steps, his hands hanging loose and empty by his side. Even so, Alyas was taking no chances. "Back up," he said as he descended, one hand pressed to the wall so he didn't fall. The stairway was steep and his balance was bad.

Cells lined the narrow corridor and they were certainly not used for meditation by devotees of Ithol. Not unless discomfort and deprivation were part of the ritual, which did not seem likely. The cells were small and dark, the only light that could reach them coming through the small viewing windows in the heavy iron doors, and the atmosphere was damp and airless.

Alyas lit another bulb and found an empty cell. The guard helpfully showed him the right key. He was starting to suspect the man felt sorry for him. He was certain of it when he said through the tiny window, "She's in the cell at the end. It's the smallest key."

"Thank you." It was all very courteous, the bleeding wound aside. When your enemy took pity on you and helped you carry out your plan, it was a good indication things were not looking good.

On the other hand, he had found Frey.

She was hunched over her knees in the farthest cell, her red hair spilling over her face. He thought she was asleep.

She looked up as he opened the door, blinking in the light of the bulb in his hand. "Alyas?"

"Frey."

She grinned at him. There were ropes around her wrist and ankles. "Thank Yholis. Are we leaving? Where's Esar?"

He crouched beside her, freeing her hands with the dagger. "He's not here, Frey. He's safe, don't worry." He hoped very much that was true.

She looked behind him at the empty corridor. "Did you come in here alone?" she asked, incredulous. "Gods, Alyas, Esar is going to kill you."

"He'll have to get in line. Can you walk?"

She nodded. "I'm not hurt." Then, as he leaned forward to cut the ropes from her ankles and she saw his face, she asked, "Can you?"

He knew he must look bad; the pain was so intense he could hardly see. But at least his mind was clear, unclouded by the constant assault of the Isyr, clear enough to feel the pressure in his shoulder of something about to burst. Clear enough to know that the guard was right. He was in. He had no idea how they were going to get out.

She took the dagger from him and finished freeing herself, then helped him up. "Where is he?"

"He's gone—to the Lathai." It was too much effort to explain.

Her face paled. "It's too late, Alyas. You have to bring him home. It's too late."

"What do you mean?"

"They must have gone in as soon as we left. They must have been waiting for it."

"What are you saying, Frey?" He sagged against the wall and she held onto him, frightened.

"Later, Alyas. Please. Let's get out of here first."

If she didn't want to tell him, it must be bad. "Frey."

Her hesitation shaped the outline of his fears. "Frey," he said again.

"They're all dead, Alyas. I'm sorry. There were so many of them. They didn't have a chance. The syndies went after our people first, but they got out. They tried to defend the Lathai, and the syndies…" She swallowed, her voice shaking. "They set the fire all around them. They burned them all."

All dead. He had left them and they had died. He had let Raffa lure him back and allowed the syndicates to take the last bit of Lankara that had been closed to them, that they had coveted for years, and with it they had taken his friends, his *family*, and the last of his hope. Because if the Lathai were all dead, there was no one now who knew how to refine Isyrium without destroying the land. The syndicates had killed their own future. They had killed everything. And he hoped, gods he hoped, that Raffa had not known what he was doing.

He looked up. It hurt, just doing that. "What else?" She wasn't telling him everything. He could feel it.

Frey was little more than a red-haired blur now. Her hand brushed his face, grounding him. "Ado is gone, Alyas. It's *gone*. And Qido, the emperor, they didn't even try to help them, they just closed the borders and let them die, but now it's taking parts of Qido too, and I don't think they can stop it."

Ado. He had never been that far north, but he knew it. The blades remembered the land they had come from. The snow-capped mountains and dense pine forests, the glacier-blue lakes and darkly ragged coast. They were a part of him and now they were gone. The Isyr had been singing their lament for years, a slow-building cry of pain that had become a crescendo, twining its way through him until he found it hard, sometimes, to know where the song ended and he began.

Ado was gone.

His people were gone.

The Lathai were gone.

And all his carefully guarded restraint had gone with them.

But Frey couldn't have been to Ado and back in so short a time. She couldn't possibly know what he had known for weeks. She hadn't been with the Lathai and his company when they died. "How?" His voice was dry and cracked, like the ruined earth of Ado. "How do you know?"

He had his eyes closed so he couldn't see her face, but he had become so used to other people's fear that he could feel it on her anyway.

Ever since Grey Rock he had known it hadn't worked. Or rather,

Grey Rock had been the first sign. He hadn't realised what was happening for several weeks, until instead of recovering his strength it seemed to drain from him, a little more each day. It wasn't until after Cadria—the events of which were largely lost to him from the moment they had returned to the garrison until he had woken in a strange place with no idea how he had come to be there—that he had known for sure. Some of the poison remained. He could feel it pulsing inside him every time he came near the mining waste, magnifying the song of the Isyr, driving him half out of his mind with the pain of it. But he had said nothing. He had tried so hard to hide it.

Because he could not do it again. He could not endure the na'quia and emerge from it with his mind intact, to have that nightmare paraded before his eyes as if he had no choice. It was bad enough that the memory of it confronted him at every turn, that it would not let him go, no matter how hard he fought it. If he had to live it again, he knew it would break him. He could still see Ailuin's face that day in his lodge when the Lathai elder had forced him to speak his nightmare. He could still hear his promise: *You can make your own fate.* And he was making it now. He had made it every day since Grey Rock, every day he stayed silent in the face of Esar's growing concern, every day he tried to find a way through the lies, the corruption, the murder, that didn't just end in more blood, every day he clung to the Isyr as if it might save him, because as long as the blades were with him—as long as they were both in his possession, together—then they could not do what he had seen them do.

But the Isyr had a price, and it was becoming harder and harder to endure it. A balance between the frailties of his body and the strength of his mind. A balance he could no longer maintain. The purity of Isyr was a siren call to the corrupted, a lodestone to the creatures transformed by the poison. It had drawn them to him, but it also blunted the worst effects of their contagion, as it had kept him alive after Flaeres when he should have been dead in days. Yet the weaker he became, the harder it was to resist the influence of the Isyr, the more he found his mind wandering into the endless coils of its tragedy, ensnaring him as it had ensnared others before him.

They were all wrong about Isyr. No one else understood. He had started to puzzle it out, slowly, painfully, in the darkness of so many sleepless nights, away from the worry and speculation of those around him. He had started to understand the voices in the steel, that searing, beautiful lament to the land from which it came that was dying. Too painful to listen to and too precious to give up. Impossible, once heard, to forget.

Yet he had had to give them up, just for a while, and it was not until they left his hands that he realised what he had done. That it had gone too far. That he had no time left.

In its own way that was also a release, because then *he* could not do what he had seen himself do. And that was all, sometimes, that he cared about.

He was on the floor and Frey was crouched beside him. He didn't remember that happening. She was trying to pull him up. She was sobbing.

He drifted in and out. Some time was lost. "How, Frey? How do you know? Where's Kaid?" Esar had asked him not to send her alone and he hadn't, but she was alone now.

"The other prisoners." She wasn't pulling at him anymore; she took something from his hand. It jangled. The keys. "They are miners— from Qido and some from Flaeres. They've seen it, Alyas. They know what's happening. They took us to one of the places the syndicates are dumping it. The syndies nearly caught us there, but we escaped. We tried to go home…" Her voice choked, and he knew what had happened. "That's when we found them. Kaid's dead."

Another death. They were crushing him.

She started to rise. He grabbed her wrist. "What are you doing?"

"Releasing them. Did you even have a plan to get us out of here?"

He didn't. Or if he did, he couldn't remember it. He sat there and watched as she unlocked the other cells and used Agazi's dagger to cut the prisoners' bonds. There were more of them than he had realised. They must have been packed three or four to a cell. There were enough, he realised hazily, to make things possible.

Frey was back. Her face was set. "Can you stand?"

He didn't bother to reply, just held out a hand and she helped him up, letting him lean against the wall. Then she took Agazi's sword from him. "I think it's best if I take this."

He couldn't argue with that. She also took the small knife he kept in his boot sheath, passing it to the miners along with the dagger. She kept his sword.

"Do they know you're here?"

Was someone going to be waiting for them at the top of the steps? "I don't know." If anyone had passed the alcove they would have seen the unconscious adept and the missing guard. The adept might have woken and raised the alarm. He might have been found missing from his post by the wicket door. Too many ways for things to go wrong. "Probably."

She sighed. "I don't think you thought this through." Then she kissed his cheek. He could feel the dampness of her tears. "You're as bad as each other. You need to hold on, do you understand? Because I am not explaining this to Esar."

He nodded. Frey was good at this. He remembered now—that had been his plan.

She moved away; a miner propped him up on either side. He didn't have the energy to object as they half-carried him down the corridor. He didn't bother telling her to leave him behind because that really would have been pointless.

They were at the base of the steps when they heard people moving around behind the door. Someone rattled the lock, then a fist pounded on the door and a voice called, "Alyas, you had better be down there!"

Frey glanced back at him in surprise as she recognised the voice, then she laughed. "He's here," she called, running up the steps. She must have unlocked the door, because the next thing he knew he was back in the alcove and Aubron was crouched in front of him, Frey at his other side.

"Agazi sent us, when you didn't come back."

"Here?" he asked.

Aubron shook his head. "He's at the temple, with Keie."

"The baby's coming?" Frey sounded delighted.

"The baby's coming," Aubron agreed.

The baby. He was glad. That would give Brivar something to keep him busy, something else to focus on other than the absolute mess he had made of himself. Something good and innocent and happy.

He closed his eyes. Aubron's hand pressed against his face. "Alyas? What's wrong with him, Frey? Is he hurt?"

Hands were gently feeling for injuries, and he wanted to say no, to reassure them, but his shoulder was a screaming mass of pain and it would have been a lie. He *did* hurt. Speech was quite beyond him at this point anyway.

"I don't know." Frey sounded close to tears again. He squeezed her hand, which was resting in his.

The hands reached his shoulder and he almost screamed. He may have. Someone swore. Then Aubron's face disappeared as he stood. "We need to go," he told Frey. "There's not enough of us. Everyone else is with Esar. We spent too long looking for you."

There was a shout and they were gone. He heard yelling and running and other things that should have worried him. Then his miners were back, one under each shoulder, and Aubron reappeared with Frey. "Get him out of here, Frey. Take him to the temple. We'll meet you there."

They were outside now. A cool breeze whispered against his skin. After the suffocating closeness of the cells, it was more than refreshing. He staggered free of his supporters and leaned raggedly against the wall. They were on a street. He didn't know which one. He had lost time again.

"Where are we?"

"Thank Yholis." Frey's face swam into view. "Are you back with us?"

"Where are we?" he asked again.

She pointed down the street. At the end of it was the great square of the Temple of Ithol. He hadn't lost that much time.

She looked agitated. "We need to go."

"No." He took a breath, pushed himself off the wall. He didn't fall, but it was a close thing.

Frey tugged his arm. "Let's go to the temple, now. Please, Alyas. Let's go to Brivar."

"No." He started walking.

She ran after him, catching him easily. He wasn't going very fast. "Please. Let me take you to the temple."

"Soon," he promised. "There's somewhere I need to go first. Will you help me, Frey?"

MARI-GELED HERUN

It was the shouting that woke her, tearing her from a pleasant dream about things of no consequence. The kind of dream she longed to return to, the kind of dream she *craved*. But she was awake now, and it was impossible to ignore the sounds coming from the hallway outside her husband's rooms. As she listened, she did become mildly concerned. In his youth Raffa had been known for making his guards' lives miserable with his drunken antics, but that hadn't happened in years. Since this whole mess with the syndicates started, she didn't think he had so much as touched a drink.

She heard purposeful footsteps, then Nicor-Heryd—his voice thick with irritation and the sleep he had been ripped from—demand an explanation. She lay back down. Unlike so many of her husband's appointments, he was competent. Then she heard a woman's voice—a strange woman's voice with an accent straight from the barren hills of the Donea—say furiously, "Don't touch him." And *that* was enough to get her up and reaching for a robe.

Mari stepped out into the corridor at the same moment as Raffa and saw the same surprise and confusion on his face. Alyas, *Alyas*, was leaning on the wall outside the king's chamber. He looked... well, he looked like the wall was the only thing keeping him upright. And in front of him, *with a sword in her hand*, was a red-haired woman she did not recognise.

She saw something else as well. She saw what was missing. Raffa had seen it too. Sometimes she thought the first thing he looked for when he saw Alyas was the Isyr. And she could see the shock on his face.

Nicor-Heryd, his face set in a scowl, said again, "Put it away, woman. Now." His hands were empty, but the guards with him all had their weapons out and were pointing them at the woman and Alyas. "Alyas. Make her listen to me."

Alyas said, "Frey." Gods, he sounded so tired. He was looking at Raffa.

Raffa, finally, recovered his powers of speech. He ignored his guard captain and the woman with the sword. He ignored Mari, standing half-dressed a few feet away, his eyes locked on Alyas. "What are you doing here?"

And Alyas, in a voice she had not heard since Gerrin died, said, "I need to talk to you, Raffa. Please."

It was the plea that did it, cutting through years of resentment and jealousy and suspicion. She saw an echo of the old friendship flicker briefly across Raffa's face. He made a gesture to Nicor, waving him back, and stepped between the drawn blades. "No one will hurt him," he told the woman, his voice very calm. "But you must give up your sword."

The woman looked from the king's face to Alyas, who nodded. With visible reluctance she placed the sword on the floor. Nicor's hand swept down to collect it before she could change her mind.

Raffa, moving slowly, took a step closer. "Will you let me...?" he asked, gesturing at Alyas.

She hesitated, then nodded, and the king put his arm under Alyas's shoulder, taking his weight, and said, "What have you done to yourself?"

Alyas, his face muffled in Raffa's shoulder, mumbled something she could not hear, and she saw such a look cross the king's face that her heart almost stopped. The woman blanched white under her dusting of freckles.

In a hoarse voice, Raffa snapped, "Leave us."

The guards looked to Nicor-Heryd. He made a sharp gesture and the swords disappeared. The men stepped back. Their commander, his expression torn, said, "Sire, I think it best if I –"

"Go," his king ordered. "What can he do to me? Look at him."

Nicor did indeed look at Alyas, and his look was full of complex and conflicting emotions. But he did as his king ordered, and they stood there, all of them who were left, and listened to the click of his boots on the tiled floor fade into silence.

It was Raffa who broke that silence. He frowned down at the strange woman. "Who are you?"

Alyas raised his head. "Frey. Esar's wife."

Mari saw the sharp, surprised look that earned him. Not his *wife*, then. But Alyas wanted Raffa to think so. He was not quite so far gone as he appeared. It was then that she realised what was so wrong with this scene. Alyas, like this, and Esar nowhere in sight. Just this woman, whoever she was to him.

Raffa was too distracted to notice the lie or question what Esar's wife should be doing here, and in such a state. Her man's clothes were filthy and the wrists that peeped out from torn sleeves were red and raw. But his manner to her changed. Alyas had claimed her as family; that meant something.

Alyas chose that moment to collapse, and Raffa, taken by surprise, barely caught him before he hit the floor.

Both women lurched forward. "Enough," Mari said. "Enough, Raffa. Get him inside."

The king, still half-stunned by the turn of events, obediently carted Alyas into his chambers, Esar's not-wife hovering at his elbow, and deposited him on a couch. His head flopped back, eyes half-closed.

Mari tried to go to him and found her way blocked.

"I'm not going to hurt him," she snapped. "I want to help."

Alyas said, "Mari." His voice held a desperate plea, but she had no idea what he wanted.

The woman, Frey, looked between them, then stepped aside and let Mari take her place. She felt Alyas lean against her and realised with shock how thin he was. She knelt in front of him, holding him up, ignoring Raffa's jealous glare and the woman's nervous hostility. "Let me call for Alondo," she pleaded. "Or your apprentice if you prefer."

He shook his head. "No."

"Alyas, you promised," Frey protested, tears in her voice. "Esar…"

Mari couldn't bear it any longer. "Where is he, Alyas? Where's Esar?"

"He's gone, Mari."

"Gone?" She felt sick. Surely not? "Gone where?"

Alyas's eyes were focused on her face with painful intensity. "To the Lathai." He turned his head to the king. "But he's going to be too late isn't he, Raffa? They're dead. The syndicates murdered them. And my company with them."

There was an appalled silence. Mari looked in desperation at her husband. "Raffa…?"

"Did you know?" Alyas asked, and his voice was broken. "Please tell me you didn't know, Raffa."

The king was staring at him in horror.

"Please, Raffa."

Mari stood. She moved to her husband's side, her heart fluttering. There was such *desperation* in Alyas's voice, as if it was more important than anything that he get the answer he wanted. She took her husband's hand. "Raffa," she prompted him.

The king unfroze. "I didn't know, I swear it. I didn't know what they were going to do. That's not why I brought you back, I promise you, Alyas. I wanted you to help me, I…"

The words ran out. Alyas was staring at him in consternation. "Then why won't you let me? Why are you fighting me?"

"Because they told me about the Lathai, afterwards, when it was over. And they threatened to tell you what I had done—what they had made me do—and I knew you would hate me. That you would think I did it for –" He stopped, swallowed. "It was never about the Isyr, Alyas. I swear. I was angry, and jealous. I was wrong…"

She saw Alyas flinch, saw his hand reach for something that wasn't there, and said, "Where are they, Alyas?" Raffa had not given up his crown willingly or without consequences, and Alyas had worn those blades for much longer than Raffa had endured his crown. "Why aren't you wearing them?"

Alyas closed his eyes. "They're safe." It was all she would get, but it wasn't all he had come here to say, and she watched him marshal his thoughts as though even that hurt.

"They've done much worse than that, Raffa. They've done this. This plague, this contagion—they caused it. And they tried to cover it up, to make it look like something else. We have proof. I was going to bring it to you, but I was waiting… I wanted to bring you hope not just despair. I wanted to give you a way to undo this. But they killed it, Raffa, when they killed the Lathai."

Gods, the rumours *were* true. The Lathai did have pure Isyrium, and he had hidden it from them all these years. No, not from them, from the syndicates. And the syndicates had gone in the moment he left, and they had done what they always did. They had destroyed everything. She could not understand, now, how she and Raffa had ever trusted them. How they had ever believed they would even try to change. But a moment later, honesty provided the answer. They had trusted the syndicates because they hadn't wanted to change either. Because it was easier to trust them than to accept that the life they had known was gone and confront the enormity of what that meant.

She looked at Alyas, at how he could barely hold his head up, and knew this wasn't just Isyr. They had done this to him. He had wanted to give them hope and they had given him despair. "They promised us they could fix it," she whispered, desperate for him to understand. "They promised."

Raffa stirred. "Mari…"

She ignored him. "They swore it, Alyas. They said they had fixed it. We trusted them, but then it kept happening, it got worse. They lied to us. That's why we called you home."

Raffa caught her arm and shook her. "Shut up, Mari. Shut up!"

Alysa was staring at her, appalled. And, Gods, she realised what she had done.

"You *knew*, Mari? You knew? All this time? And you didn't try to stop it?"

He was so angry. He had been half-dead, and now he was *furious*. "You knew and you let it happen. How could you? You wore that crown, Raffa. You heard *that*, day after day. You felt what their poison was doing to this land and your people, and *you let it happen!* Why, Raffa? Why did you do that?"

The king had gone very white, hectic spots on colour on his cheekbones. "What was I supposed to do, Alyas? What the fuck was I supposed to do? Shut them down? Turn off the taps that keep this country running?"

"Yes! If that's what it takes. Because there won't be a country if you don't!"

"You want me to shut down Isyrium mining? Are you mad? We would lose everything!"

"You've already lost it," Alyas snarled. "You just can't see it. Clinging to it now won't save you, it just ensures everything else goes with it!"

He was on his feet, Frey under one shoulder, and his face was ghastly. "What about the four hundred, Raffa? My four hundred? Did they make you do that too? Four hundred men, Raffa. Did they make you kill them? Are you nothing but their puppet? Is nothing you have done your fault?"

Raffa was shaking his head, and Mari realised he had no idea what Alyas was talking about. "Your four hundred?" He didn't remember. Yholis have mercy, he didn't even remember.

Alyas saw it too and his face twisted in rage. In pain. In such pain.

She thought he would curse Raffa, curse both of them, for their lies, their cowardice, their betrayal, and she turned away so she didn't have to watch.

But he didn't say anything at all.

BRIVAR

Brivar quickly learned not to speak unless it was strictly required, and certainly not to make suggestions. Keie was *fierce*. And she knew what she wanted to do. As she hissed at him between breaths on the ragged crest of pain, *he* had never had a baby and would never have one, so if he thought he knew better than her he could leave right now.

He shut up, retreating to the corner, and let her stalk around the room between contractions, swearing at the world in the language of the steppes.

Agazi quirked an amused eyebrow as Brivar joined him in exile. In Lankara, no father would have remained in the room for the birth of their child. In the steppes, if he had tried to leave, the woman's father and brothers would have been waiting outside to send him back in. They had no concept of marriage in the way it was understood in Lankara, but they had a very clear concept of responsibility, and this child would be his from the moment it was born until one of them died. And Keie's too, of course. But it was the father who was expected to provide everything the child needed, even if his relationship with the mother had come to an end.

Brivar only found this out in fits and starts over the course of Keie's labour. She had a keen sense of responsibility too, and currently she held Agazi responsible for everything—for getting her pregnant, for every riptide of birthing pain, for daring to exist in the first place.

And the litany of the things she was going to do to him would have made a lesser man very nervous.

She stopped pacing eventually, when the crests were coming so close that she had to stop too frequently, and Brivar crept cautiously forward. She bared her teeth at him, but she let him examine her, though he had to dodge quickly out of the way when he told her it wouldn't be long.

He looked at the hourglass by the window. It was deep in the night. The sun would be coming up in a few hours. The temple had been quiet since Keie's arrival, its peace disturbed only by her pain and fury. Alyas had not returned and neither had Frey.

Agazi saw the direction of his gaze and Brivar saw the same thought cross his face, but Agazi had already done all he could and Keie needed them now, her opinion on the matter notwithstanding.

Keie groaned, dropping onto her knees. Agazi half-rose and she shot him a glare of such venom that he sat back down hard. Brivar edged closer. She was quite naked, another tradition of the steppes, and he could see her quick, sharp breaths.

"He's coming," she gasped.

He reached her, crawling on his hands and knees. She took his hand and squeezed so hard he thought she would break it. "Slow down, Keie," he urged. "Breathe." He tried to show her. She hit him. Agazi took his place, and this time she let him, because there was no slowing the baby down. Brivar caught it as it emerged and guided it out, slick with blood and birthing fluid, its skin an angry red and its face screwed up in a reflection of its mother's rage, which transformed into a wail of outrage.

Keie choked on a sob, collapsing against Agazi, who looked like he had been hit by an uroc. Then she laughed, a sweet sound of pure joy.

The door opened. It was Alondo. He looked from the tiny, roaring scrap of humanity to Brivar's smiling face and said, "You need to come."

Someone else moved into view behind his shoulder. It was Frey. Her face was white and scared. She had been crying.

Very carefully, Brivar placed the baby in Keie's outstretched arms. It was still screaming but everything else was deathly quiet. Agazi and Keie had seen Frey too.

He stood. "What's happened?" But Frey was crying now and he *knew*.

⁂

It was Nicor-Heryd who brought Alyas to the Temple of Yholis. Brivar didn't ask how it came to be him. He would find all that out later. From the moment he saw Alyas and realised he was still alive—*just*—there was no time for anything else.

He told Frey to leave. When she wouldn't go, Nicor-Heryd took her. And then it was just him and Alondo and Alyas's frightening stillness, so like the stillness after the na'quia. Brivar had thought him dead then too, but the difference was that there was nothing he could have done to change that outcome. This time Alyas's life depended on his skill. He froze. He couldn't move.

Alondo, with the experience of so many years, didn't try to talk him out of his panic. He calmly prepared for the surgery as though this was any other patient, not someone whose life Brivar desperately wanted to save. It wasn't until Alondo had stripped Alyas out of all the layers of his clothes and Brivar saw the dark flush of what looked so like simple bruising across his left shoulder that he snapped out of it. For an instant he thought the abscess had already burst, but if that were the case, Alyas would certainly be dead. It was too close to his heart. That thought nearly sent him into a new panic, but Alondo didn't give him a chance, he simply pressed the knife into his hand and as soon as Brivar's fingers closed around it, calm descended.

Neither one of them could have managed that surgery alone. Alondo's eyes were no longer sharp enough, nor his fingers steady enough, for the delicate precision required, and for all his skill Brivar did not have the Varistan's experience. But between them, with

Alondo guiding and Brivar doing, they found the pocket of poison deep in the muscle of Alyas's shoulder, so very close to bursting. It was too deep to simply drain it without the poison leaking into his body and killing him, but it was also not like a normal abscess, formed of the body's own tissues. Like the little beads of poison the na'quia had drawn from the Isyrium ore, it was separate and distinct, and he was able to cut it out, terrified every moment that his knife would slip or that the delicate film that contained the deadly fluid would rupture before he could remove it. But he did it, and as soon as the bubble of poison collapsed into a black mess in the little clay dish Alondo held for him, his hands started shaking so much he had to leave the rest to his master.

Alyas had not moved once during the whole thing. Brivar only knew he was alive because of the rise and fall of his chest he had used to time the movements of his knife. And when it was over and the poison was finally out of him, he looked as dead as he had when he arrived, and only then did Brivar wonder what he had intended to happen and whether Alyas would thank him for what he had done.

Frey was waiting outside with Agazi and Keie, her baby cleaned up and sleeping on her chest, her head resting on Agazi's shoulder. Even Nicor-Heryd was still there. It was Nicor who asked, "Is he alive?"

When Brivar nodded, Nicor stood. "I will tell the queen."

Frey stopped him as he was leaving. "Is he in danger? From the king?"

Nicor paused. "I don't know. Best if you take precautions. If I have to bring my men back here, it won't be to see how he is."

They couldn't take him to Camling. Brivar was scared to even move him from the room where they had performed the surgery. The poison was gone, but the harm that it and the Isyr had done had left Alyas appallingly weak. So Agazi and Aubron organised a guard on the temple, and Agazi sent a second messenger after Esar, calling him home. It did not say why. Brivar was reluctant to tell him Alyas was alive in case it was no longer true by the time he returned.

Alyas didn't wake that first day. Brivar stayed with him until he could no longer hold his eyes open, and when he returned after a few hours' sleep he found Frey there. She told him what had happened, all of it. About the Lathai and the company and what the syndicates had done to them. About the king and what he had and hadn't done. About Alyas.

Brivar dropped his head into his hands and let the tears pour out of him for the tragedy of it, and he wished very badly that Alyas would wake so he could tell him that it wasn't over. That they had found the Lathai's secret, and he didn't have to give up. But he didn't stir.

Esar returned with the company two days later. Alyas still hadn't woken and Brivar worried that if he didn't wake soon, he never would. Word must have reached Esar, because he burst into the temple, smelling of horses and sweat and the road, panic on his face, and Frey flew into his arms.

Brivar took him to Alyas, and as Esar stood there in silence, Brivar told him what had happened and how it was his fault. How he had mistaken illness for the effects of Isyr and failed to investigate the farmer's death, how he failed to notice how bad things had become until it was too late. But Esar would not let him take the blame. "We all thought it was the Isyr. If he chose to hide it from you, it's no one's fault but his own."

He did not ask why Alyas had been so determined to conceal what he must have known was killing him, because Brivar knew he did not want to know. That it was too easy for Esar, who had already watched his father die, to see history repeating itself. But Brivar refused to believe that. He would not believe it, not unless he heard it from Alyas's own lips when he woke, and he *was* going to wake. Because if Esar was right, why had Alyas come to him right at the end and given him the blades?

Then he met Frey's eyes and backed quietly into the corner as she told Esar the rest. And Esar stood there, one hand pressed to his jaw, and he kept saying, "Tell me again, Frey. Are they all dead?"

Brivar put his head down on his crossed arms and would have wept if there had been any tears left in him.

Sometime later he was woken by Alondo's hand on his shoulder. Esar and Frey were still there, sitting silently together. They did not stir as Brivar sat up and looked at his master.

"Come with me," Alondo said. "I have something to show you."

"What is it?"

The old man smiled. "Hope."

Alondo took him to his office by the fountain with its dusty books and lovingly tended plants. And there, amid the trailing jungle of greenery, the Varistan showed him his hope.

It was growing in a glass bowl like all the rest, alone on the smallest windowsill, green shoots just starting to poke through the broken soil. All the same, he recognised it. Na'quia.

"I don't understand."

"Look again," Alondo told him. "Look closer."

He did, seeing the silver-blue glint of pure Isyrium amid the dark soil and delicate roots of the new plant, and caught his breath in understanding. Forgotten about in the crisis of Alyas's collapse and that difficult, dangerous surgery was the experiment they had conducted after the farmer's autopsy. The na'quia poured over Isyrium ore. And left alone and untended, it had done more than they had thought.

"I did not look at it again until an hour ago," said Alondo. "And I have not stopped looking at it since."

Brivar stared at the tiny sparkles in the soil. "Is that what I think it is?"

Alondo smiled. "Isyrium. We have misunderstood its nature all this time and done such harm when all we needed to do was allow nature to do what it has always done. You thought there was a connection between na'quia and Isyrium. It is more than a connection. They are one and the same, different ends of the same cycle. It isn't a thing at all.

It's a circle of life. It is of the land, but we took it out of the land and we made things with it, and we never knew what we were doing."

Brivar took the bowl, turning it around in his hands, seeing the Isyrium that had been extracted from the ore and the plant that had emerged from the waste that remained. "How is this possible?" A plant could not grow without a seed, unless the Isyrium itself was the seed.

Alondo smiled serenely. "What we think of as the poison of na'quia is what creates Isyrium from the substance of the earth, probably as the plant dies and decays in the soil. It separates Isyrium from the raw elements, and then it grows again out of what is left, a circle of creation. That is where the pure Isyrium deposits must have come from, but we were too greedy, we wanted more than nature could give us, and we disrupted the process. When the Isyrium ran out, we used alchemy and science to find a way to extract the traces that remained, and it created the toxic waste that has polluted our world in such vast quantities that the na'quia could not neutralise it. And over the years that pollution created this plague."

He straightened, one hand on the small of his back. "It is also what killed your farmer and what was killing Alyas. The na'quia did what it always does. It separated the poison, but it could not complete the process, and so eventually those pockets of poison burst and the host died. I suspect it explains his reaction to the presence of mining waste, or rather the reaction of the na'quia in his system. He is lucky it did not burst before now and he probably has the Isyr to thank for that. Its purity must have suppressed the action of the na'quia."

It made sense. It would explain not only how both Alyas and the Lathai had survived so long after the initial wound, but also the speed of his collapse when he was finally separated from the blades. But Isyr was far from a benign influence. He had seen what it had done to both Ilyon and Alyas.

Brivar carefully returned the bowl to the windowsill. "It does not explain the other effects of Isyr."

Alondo looked thoughtful. "Perhaps, perhaps not. Only Alyas can tell us the truth of Isyr. I think he knows, and that's why he would not give it up. Will you give it back to him if he asks?"

He hadn't thought about that. It seemed so distant a concern. "If he asks for it, I have to."

If only Alyas would wake up to ask, he would be glad to give it to him. Though Brivar hoped he wouldn't ask. It was the poison that had wreaked the physical damage, but the Isyr was no less devastating, and it was entirely possible it had influenced Alyas's behaviour in ways he had not been aware of. By the time he had given the blades to Brivar, he must have known he was dying, and everything that meant. That the one thing they thought they had—their one means of fighting back—was gone, even if that was just saving one life here and there from the poison. Without that, it must have felt hopeless. Knowing there was nothing that could stop this plague. And perhaps that, more than anything, explained his silence, because to speak it was to kill the last spark of hope.

Now they had a new reason to hope. Now they understood. But Brivar knew it was not that simple. He was young, but he wasn't naïve or innocent, not anymore. It wasn't enough to understand the problem and know how to solve it, because the solution still required the syndicates to stop what they were doing. It required sacrifice, and he didn't think they were capable of that. They had to give up the source of their vast wealth and power, now, in exchange for something slower, safer, better in a future they might not live to see, but which could ensure there would still be something left for their children. For Keie and Agazi's baby and all the other babies yet to be born. Because if they didn't, there would be nothing left for any of them.

He didn't need Alyas to tell him what their response would be.

ALYAS-RAINE SERA

He had been sure he was dying. The pain had been so bad he had even wanted to, so when the darkness came he had embraced it. And for a while there had been nothing at all. Then that blessed darkness began to fracture. Slivers of pain reached him in his haven, and later, voices. One voice more than any other, and he thought he should recognise it, but he did not recognise himself yet. At first it was just sounds, then there were words, and eventually he understood them and wished he did not. He didn't want to hear it. He was remembering now. But the voice was insistent, excited, and it kept repeating the same thing over and over until he was forced to listen. A little while after that, he opened his eyes and said, or tried to, "Tell me again. Na'quia makes Isyrium?"

And Brivar grinned at him in delight.

There followed an indistinct, indefinite period during which he was more asleep than awake. When voices and occasionally faces came and went and he was vaguely aware there were people with him but he could not speak to them. Sometimes Keie was there with her new baby, singing lullabies in her native tongue. He didn't know if she was singing to the baby or to him. Perhaps both. And one time it was Agazi, and he remembered, clearly, as he said, "We need to end this, Alyas. Do you hear me? We need to stop them, or what kind of future will he have?"

Esar was there too, with Frey, and he knew Esar was angry with him. And worried. It was so reassuringly *Esar* that he didn't even mind.

In between all the others, there was Brivar. He seemed to understand without being told that Alyas needed to know, so he explained it all, over and over. What had happened, what they had done, and what they had discovered. What it meant. And Alyas wished he could share his excitement, his hope, but all he could hear was Agazi. *What kind of future will he have?*

He could sit for short periods now if he did nothing more than sit. Every time he opened his eyes, someone was trying to make him eat or drink something and getting frustrated when he wanted to do neither. Worse were the constant words coming at him, and it was too much effort to explain that he just wanted to think.

When Frey appeared, alone, he knew he was in trouble.

She stood glaring down at him and it was tempting to pretend he was asleep, but she would never let him get away with that.

"I know you're awake," she said, confirming this suspicion. "So stop hiding and start talking. What the fuck is going on?"

He sighed and opened his eyes. "Hello, Frey."

She looked surprised, as though she had not expected him to respond. It occurred to him that he may not have done, before. That it may have led them to think things he had not intended.

In short order, surprise was followed by relief, then anger. "What are you doing, Alyas? It's awful, I *know*. But we need you."

"I'm here." Not actively, it was true, but he was still very tired. Then, because it had been on his mind since his attempt to rescue her from Ithol's temple, he said, "I'm giving Esar Camling."

"You're what? Why? Why would you do that?"

Wasn't it obvious? "So he has something, if…"

"If you die?" She was furious. "Gods, Alyas, don't you dare. Do you have any idea what this has done to him? Do you? He has been worried sick for weeks. You are all he has!"

"That's not true, Frey, he has you."

"You know what I mean," she snapped. "Whatever it is, sort it out. Talk to us, let us help. We're here. We want to help you."

"It's not what you think, Frey."

"I don't know what to think anymore." She turned away, hands on her head, her red hair pulled loose and hopelessly messed by anxious fingers. "I'm pregnant, Alyas. He doesn't know yet. I can't—I can't tell him now, when everything is such a mess. When you are... How can I tell him we will bring a child into a world like this? How can I ask him to be happy about it? I look at Keie and Agazi and see what they are thinking underneath the love and the smiles. What are we doing to ourselves? What will be left for our children when we're done?"

What kind of future will he have?

Frey was pregnant. Such a huge and tiny thing, the final ounce of pressure on the lever of his life. The final shake that sent all the pieces tumbling to fall into the pattern he had seen months ago, in the nightmare of the na'quia, and had been fighting ever since. And suddenly the path ahead was crystal clear. Finally it fit, and he could stop fighting.

He caught her gaze and held it. "Don't tell him, Frey, not yet. I'll fix this, I promise."

"Fix it? Alyas, how can you fix this? It's a fucking disaster. Nothing can fix it!"

"I will," he managed, his eyes slipping closed. He needed her to understand, to believe. "I will. Just don't tell Esar, not yet." Yholis forgive him, he needed Esar focused on the problem, he needed him here, with him, not distracted by revenge for a future he could never have, like Agazi was.

"All right," he heard her say as he drifted away. "But you need to come back to us now, Alyas. Come back, or I'm telling him, whether you want me to or not."

He thought he might have smiled. Frey was good at this.

❧

Frey was certainly thorough. She was there the next time he woke, and she reminded of his promise. Alyas confirmed that, yes, he did remember, and asked her to send Agazi to him. Esar arrived first. He should have expected that.

"Frey told me," Esar said before the door had closed. "I don't want Camling."

"Then sell it. You can do that once it's yours."

Esar scowled at him and Alyas found it difficult to hold his gaze, to see all the lines of stress and worry that he had put on his brother's face, to know what he was conspiring to keep from him and why.

"What is this about, Alyas, really? She told me what happened with Raffa. What you did at the temple. And she's right, I did want to kill you, but you seem to be doing a good job of that yourself and I want to know why."

"No, you don't."

"Don't tell me what I do and don't want to know, not after this. Don't sit there, *not talking*, and leaving us to guess where the next crisis is coming from. There's too many of them already and I can't take it anymore." He stopped, taking a breath, retreating. He didn't really want to know. "Nicor was here today."

"And?" Alyas had been surprised, when he finally came fully awake, to find that Raffa had allowed him to remain here, and free.

"And he wanted to know what you are going to do now."

"*He* wanted to know? Or Raffa does?"

Esar shrugged. He was still angry, but he was trying not to show it. "I think Raffa is probably beyond the asking stage. We should go back to Camling. If it comes to it, it's easier to defend."

If it was going to come to that, they should leave the city, but that wasn't possible. He could not manage it, not yet. Besides, Avarel was where he needed to be.

"We'll go to Camling," he agreed, slipping under again.

Brivar didn't. When they told him he disagreed most strenuously until Alyas told him he could come too. Even then he looked doubtful, only relenting after Esar pointed out what would happen if Raffa came for them here.

"And you'll be with Della," Esar reminded him as he left to organise the move. "She's missed you." He laughed as Brivar flushed, and Alyas realised how long it had been since he had heard Esar laugh. That was his fault.

Brivar fussed about. Alyas let him. He had a debt to pay there as well, so he submitted without complaint to all Brivar's ministrations and waited patiently for him to reassure himself. When it was over, he said, "I need you to witness something for me."

Brivar looked at him in understandable trepidation. Alyas almost smiled. "Nothing like that. I need your signature." He handed him the deeds Agazi had brought from Camling.

Brivar looked up from the paper. "Why?" he asked.

Alyas weighed his words. He had to be careful, but he had always found it hard to lie to Brivar. "Because if I die, which I nearly did, everything I own will pass to some relation I do not know and Esar will be left with nothing. He always loved Camling. It is mine to give. He will have something."

Brivar was studying him, trying to work out what he was saying, to decide whether to be alarmed or reassured.

"I have a lot," Alyas reminded him. "I don't need it all. And Raffa might take it all away again, so I need to do this now."

So Brivar added his signature to the document as a witness and when he was done, Alyas said, "I need them back now."

Brivar carefully set the quill down. "Why?"

"Because they are safer with me."

"They are safe where they are."

"Are you refusing to give them back?"

Brivar flushed. "No. I just want to understand. Wearing them hurts you. Why take them back?"

He could not explain. How could he say that he needed that pain? That it reminded him, every day, why this mattered. That their song was a part of him now anyway; it would never let him go. The same song his father had heard, that had overwhelmed him, already grieving for the woman he loved, with its own endless tragedy. That, hearing it, Alyas finally understood why his father had done what he had done, and forgave him for it.

"Please," he said. "Just give them back."

PART THREE

TERSA

There were few things Tersa hated more than the day, once a week, when her mother's friends gathered to talk over the latest scandals and society gossip. It was utterly empty and pointless, and she had to sit there in a pretty dress and smile and pretend to care when there were people out there *starving* and *dying* because those who should have protected them and looked out for their welfare were more concerned with which colours were in fashion this season. And she *hated* it.

"Don't sit there with that sulky expression, Alla," her mother scolded as she finished adjusting the flowers on the tables. At least today they were in the garden, and if no one was paying her much attention—which was not unlikely, given her lack of shareable gossip (unshareable gossip she had plenty of)—she could slip off into the orchard and talk about things that mattered with Gelles, who would be there with her mother.

"And don't think to go sneaking off with Gelles-Feron Mais this time. You're nearly twenty. Nyer-Varant Barin's mother will be here. I want her to see you as a suitable wife. So sit up straight, smile, and pretend to be interested in what she has to say."

Tersa felt a flash of fury. She was *not* going to marry Nyer-Varant. He was everything she hated about Avarel's elite, but she had the sense not to argue about it at this moment.

Her mother sighed and brushed a stray strand of hair from Tersa's forehead. Elidne-Sera Lan was tall, beautiful and, beyond anything, practical. She had made the best of an arranged match and had carved out a place for herself at the heart of Avarel's society, managing her rather less practical husband with skill and, over the years, an exasperated affection. "I know you don't like him, Alla. But marriage is not about love, and although you don't think so now, you will need a husband in this world. We cannot all be like Hailene-Sera Lan and go our own way. You won't have her money, for a start."

Tersa dearly wanted to argue that point, because why couldn't she be like Hailene-Sera if she wished? But at that moment her impractical, dreamy father appeared on the steps of the garden, and beside him was a man she had never expected to see again. Whom she had never thought she could see again, since the last she had heard he was dead, or dying, or close to it, and certainly disgraced again, or very soon to be. But the Duke of Agrathon was unmistakeably in her garden, talking to her father, and although he looked a little pale, he was indisputably alive.

Her mother saw her staring and turned, recognising him instantly by the blades he wore. "Oh no. What is *he* doing here?"

Tersa didn't answer. Alyas-Raine Sera had seen her and his mouth quirked in an amused smile to see her dressed like this, about to entertain the wives and daughters of all the very best Avarel families whom she had claimed to want to bring down.

She flushed furiously. Her mother, seeing this, misunderstood. "No," she said. "Not him. I don't care how rich he is."

"Mother!" The thought was ridiculous. He had to be twice her age, and besides, she hated him. It had taken her weeks to stop stewing over their last encounter and his threat to march her back to her parents' house.

Her father saved her from any further discussion of that abhorrent subject by calling her over and telling her the Duke of Agrathon wanted to speak to her. He didn't seem to find this strange. Her father was… She loved him dearly. He knew so many things. He sometimes helped her write her pamphlets, though he didn't know that was what he was doing. But he was in a different place most of the time. Living in a world of ideas and books and obscure concepts that no one else understood. He had probably forgotten that the man standing next to him had been exiled for *fifteen years* and was even now rumoured to be out of favour with the king, yet again.

Conscious of her mother's glare even with her back turned, Tersa let her father lead them to his study, where he left them alone with a vague smile. He didn't even ask what someone like Alyas-Raine Sera would want to talk to her about. Her mother would be incandescent.

As the door closed, Tersa folded her arms across her chest. "What are you doing here?"

He turned from his study of her father's bookshelf. "I have come to see you, obviously."

Ithol's balls, he was annoying. "I meant why?"

The duke didn't answer. He pulled a book from the shelf and flicked through it. "Your father is a good man," he observed, before fitting it back into the gap on the shelves. "If you succeed, you will ruin him. And your mother. Are you sure that is what you want? You have a comfortable life here."

"I don't want a comfortable life if that means others are forced to live uncomfortable ones."

His sharp gaze studied her as he had studied the books. She could believe he had been ill. There were dark shadows under his eyes and he looked older than he had before.

"And that is commendable," he agreed. "But you are very young, and you cannot imagine what achieving your aims will really mean."

"Don't patronise me," she snapped. "I know what I'm doing, and what it means."

"Very well. Tell me, Tersa. There has been news of protests and riots in other Lankaran cities. Some even in Flaeres and Hantara. Are those your doing?"

Her stomach did a little flipflop as a breath of fear raised goosebumps on her skin. Last time he had not helped them, but he had done nothing to hurt them either. What if that had changed? "I thought you were dead," she said, instead of answering.

He smiled thinly. "You're not up with the latest news. Rumour was a little enthusiastic. Only nearly dead. And now, as you see, quite recovered. Are you going to answer my question, or have you changed your mind about wanting my help?"

"Your help?" Tersa echoed. "You made your position quite clear last time we spoke."

"As it happens, my position has changed. If yours remains the same, we may be able to help each other. So, I will ask again, is your organisation confined to Avarel or are the disturbances in other cities also down to the Nameless?"

"How can I trust you?"

He held something up. "Do you know what this is?"

She looked at the lump of rock. At the tiny sparkles of silver-blue that perfectly matched the light of the bulbs that lit her father's windowless study, that provided the fuel that fed his fire and warmed her bathwater. That dyed the deep blue of her mother's favourite court dress. That made the ink she used to write her pamphlets. "Isyrium ore."

"Very good." His face was grim. "It is not their names that prop up their power. It's this." He placed the Isyrium on the desk. "If you want to change things, this is what you must take from them. I can help you, but first I need to know how far you are prepared to go."

ESAR CANTRELL

Esar stalked back into Camling at midsummer with violence on his mind. He had been gone a month, dealing with a major outbreak on the border of Hantara, and he had watched a lot of people die. None of them had deserved it. He was angry, tired, and he wanted answers.

He found Alyas talking to Agazi, who took one look at his face and quickly made himself scarce.

"Do we need money?" Esar demanded once they were alone.

Alyas frowned in surprise. A month had worked miracles on his appearance. He had colour in his face now, and his bones were no longer so sharp you could cut yourself on them. It made Esar realise just how bad he had looked those last few weeks. "No." Alyas took a closer look at Esar. "What have I done?"

"You tell me," Esar growled. "If we don't need money, why did I find Vyn-Mais at Headdon? And why did he tell me you had sold it to him?" He had intended the company to stop at the estate on their way home only to find when they arrived, bone-tired and wet from a summer storm, that there was a new owner in residence. Fortunately for Alyas, Vyn-Mais had allowed the tired company to bed down in the stables, otherwise Esar would have been in an even worse mood than he was already.

"Because I did."

"I'm a little confused," Esar said. "We do need money or we don't?"

"He wanted it. I sold it to him," Alyas said. "That is all."

It clearly was not all, but it was all he was going to get. And Esar felt like hitting something, because it was starting again. He glowered at Alyas and the blades he wore. He had been furious with Brivar for giving them back, but it was Alyas who had asked for them, after *everything*, and he didn't even know where to begin with that.

Alyas, sensing the raw wound that had as much to do with the horrors of the last few weeks as anything else, asked, "Are you all right?" He hadn't gone with Esar. He could not have, so soon. The wound from the surgery had healed but the resilience degraded by months of illness would take longer to recover, and for once Alyas had actually listened, which was almost the most suspicious thing about the sudden purpose that had commenced as soon as he could walk a reliable distance.

Esar had no objection to purpose in and of itself. What he had dreaded most was seeing the same utter lack of it that his foster father had shown in the months before his death. He just wished he had some idea what it was about. Why sell Headdon? Alyas had already given Camling away. What else had he sold or given away that Esar didn't know about? And why?

Frey told him not to worry so much and she seemed to have found a new understanding with Alyas. It was both easier and harder to take her advice, depending on how frustrated he was at any given moment. And Brivar was still here. Esar had seen him on his way in. Rather like his response to Frey's advice, he found that both reassuring and not in equal measure, though Brivar's presence could have as much to do with Della as it did with Alyas. Most worrying, in some ways, was the silence from the palace.

Mari had finally come to Camling a week after their return from the temple. Alyas had refused to see her. Esar, diplomatic, had told her he was out, though he was still very far from capable of that being true, and Mari had looked like she knew it. It had been good to see her. It would have been better if he had not heard Frey's account of their last meeting and therefore knew exactly why Alyas would not see her.

Esar had asked her about Raffa. About what he intended. Because it seemed inconceivable that he hadn't yet acted in one way or another.

"He doesn't know what to do," Mari admitted. She looked upset. "He doesn't hate Alyas, Esar. Really he doesn't. He's been worried about him."

And Esar, who sometimes thought he did nothing but worry, found this a little hard to take. "Like he worried about him in the last fifteen years, no doubt?"

Mari flushed. What could she say? She was not blameless there either. And if Raffa was weak-willed, it was not like they hadn't known it. It had worked against them in the past. He was not going to complain if it worked in their favour now. He just hoped Alyas finished whatever it was he was doing before Raffa made up his mind which side he was on. In the meantime, things had settled back into the uneasy coexistence that had prevailed before Alyas had burst in on the king in the middle of the night and very nearly died in his room. The sudden emergence of crisis on their border probably had a lot to do with that. Whichever way Raffa finally jumped, he still needed someone to deal with these outbreaks.

"No," he replied. For all those reasons and more, he was not all right. "I want to know what you are doing."

He thought he saw a twinge of guilt cross Alyas's face. "Do you trust me?"

Esar considered that carefully. Because yes, he did trust Alyas, completely and implicitly, as he trusted almost no one else, except perhaps Frey. The man had broken into a bloody temple when he could barely walk to get Frey back, never mind that it was Frey who had ended up having to rescue him. On the other hand, no, not at all, and with good reason. That look, for one. "Only about some things," he hedged.

"Then make this one of them."

"Why?"

"Because I'm asking you to."

It hurt. Alyas sometimes took a while to share what he was thinking but he always got there in the end. Esar had never before been excluded from his confidence. "You don't trust me, is that it?"

The silence that followed was painful. Then Alyas said, "You know I do. With everything else but this. Please, don't ask me."

That hurt even more, because he really meant it, and what was he doing that he felt he couldn't share it? "Tell me why then," Esar said. "I need to know this isn't like before."

It wasn't guilt that flashed across Alyas's face this time, it was distress, and his hand drifted to the Isyr hilt. "You will find out, I promise. But I can't... I can't tell you now."

Esar lifted his eyes from the Isyr. "But you will tell Agazi?" He had eyes. He knew Alyas had taken Agazi into his confidence when they were still back at the temple. And he had let it go then because he did trust Alyas, because he knew what he was like and he *knew*, absolutely, that when he was ready he would start talking. But he hadn't, and enough was enough. "What do you need to ask of him that you cannot ask of me?"

Alyas's hand tightened its grip till his knuckles were white. "Perhaps it is exactly because of what you mean to me that I will not ask those things of you. Please, Esar."

He may have punched door on the way out.

※

Esar found Brivar with Della. Fortunately, they were just talking. He loomed in the doorway until Brivar gave him his reluctant attention. "I need to talk to you."

"Now, Esar?" Della complained. She looked put out. "We just got back."

"I won't keep him long, Della." To Brivar he said, "Now."

They walked outside.

"Tell me everything."

Brivar blinked. "About what?"

"About what Alyas has been doing while I've been gone."

Brivar shifted uncomfortably. "Have you tried asking him?"

"Of course I have," Esar snapped. "He won't tell me."

"Then I really don't think…"

Esar growled. "Surely you haven't forgotten what happened last time we just let him get on with it? The last time we trusted him to ask for help if he needed it?"

Brivar edged away. "It's not like that. Anyway, he hasn't told me what he's doing either. What did you do to your hand?"

Esar looked at his bleeding knuckles and felt the ache of bruises old and new. Brivar wiggled his fingers gently. It hurt, but not that badly. Not broken then.

"Did you hit a wall?"

"No."

"A door?"

He grunted in assent.

"People don't realise how much damage that can do," Brivar observed, looking at him with sympathy. "Did it make you feel better?"

Esar looked into his young, honest face. He had saved Alyas's life twice and somewhere along the way, even if he didn't realise it, he had transferred all his youthful, earnest loyalty from the temple to Alyas. He was as biased as the rest of them now. "Why haven't you gone back to the temple?"

Brivar looked at him in surprise, then his expression changed and a little bit of that openness disappeared.

"He's fine, isn't he? So why are you still here?"

Brivar dropped his gaze. "Because…"

"It's because of the Isyr. That's why you're still here. Why did you give them back?"

"Because I could not refuse," Brivar replied. "He gave them to me trusting that I would return them, and it would have been a betrayal to refuse, whatever I think about it." He hesitated, then said, "We have to trust him, Esar, about this and everything else."

Esar sighed, taking his hand back and flexing his fingers. "And maybe if he wasn't wearing those blades I could."

Frey wasn't much help either. She was pale and tired and impatient with his complaints. "What do you want from him, Esar? He's upright, he's walking, he's talking. All the things you wanted him to be doing. Why are you still worrying?"

"Because I know him, Frey, and something isn't right."

She didn't reply. He looked over and saw she was asleep. She had been tired and irritable the last couple of weeks. They all had. So he carefully adjusted the blanket and edged to the far side of the bed so his restlessness would not wake her and proceeded to catalogue all the things he did not like about what he didn't know.

HAILENE-SERA AHN

She had waited for Alyas for weeks. She had started to believe he would not come, and she did not know whether to be glad or disappointed that he had not chosen the course she thought he would. But he did come, eventually, quietly and alone, and lacking all his usual thorns.

"You look more alive than the last time I saw you," she said as he walked into her salon. "Have you come for sanctuary again, or do you finally believe I can be of some use to you?"

He would not have forgotten her little hobby, the way she entertained herself in a society that policed itself by such strict social norms in public and broke them with abandon in private. It was how she had first secured her independence and status against her father's attempts to marry her off, and it had served her well in the years that followed to maintain both. Young Alla-Sera Lan had a lot to learn if she wanted to follow in her footsteps, but she was learning fast. Hailene had her suspicions as to why.

"I always knew you could," he replied. He was not just lacking his thorns. He looked weary, ground down, and he must be, to come to her. "I just wasn't sure that I wanted it."

She looked up at him from her armchair. She was too old and stiff to stand for visitors and he wouldn't care anyway. "What changed your mind?"

"Lots of things. One thing. Esar is going to be a father."

"Ah." That would do it. It was one thing to worry about what your own future would look like, but there was nothing like the fear and dread that worry for your children could inspire. Her sister had taught her that. And it didn't matter that it wasn't his child. Those two had been together so long there would be no distinction in his eyes. She felt the sting of tears. Her sister had taught her that too.

"He doesn't know yet."

Oh, Alyas. "Why not?"

"Because once he knows, I will lose him. And I need him—I need him for this." He looked away, eyes wandering around the room. "Do you have it?"

"Oh, yes," she replied, because she did not want to think about the heartbreak that waited down that road. And she struggled to her feet and fetched it for him. A fat pile of papers, collected over years, full of the kinds of secrets that, should they become known, would destroy the reputation of the syndicates. In the wrong hands, they could do a lot worse than that.

He sat, the file on his lap, and started leafing through the accumulated evidence of greed, of back-stabbing betrayal, of criminal action and even more criminal inaction. Damning, devastating evidence that not even the support of kings could clean away. Because it was not just the syndicates it condemned, but those who had enabled and supported them, those in power whose disregard for the people they were supposed to serve was breath-taking. She watched his face as he found names he knew, names of people he had once cared about, of friends. She saw the resolve harden and wished it didn't have to be this way. But such was the world in which they lived.

"Is this what you need?"

He looked up from the file of papers. "You know it is."

"What will you do with it?"

"Nothing it would do you any good to know."

She gave him a sharp, knowing look. "You never knew your mother, Alyas, and Ithol knows, Gerrin never spoke of her much.

One of the many ways he failed you."

"Is this going somewhere, Aunt, or do you just want to insult my father?"

She ignored him. "I knew her. She was my best friend for twenty-eight years. She was clever and beautiful, but she was also as hard and bright and inflexible as Isyr. I know what she would have done with this—it is partly why I gathered it, for her, because she had courage I never had—but I also know what it would have cost her to do it. So please think carefully, my dear, before you use this as I think you will use it. Ask yourself if you can live with the consequences. Because the gods know, I couldn't."

"I have," he told her. "And it is doing nothing that I cannot live with."

"They will hate you for it."

His fingers paused their busy riffling. "Who will?"

"Your friends, your enemies, the people you are trying to save. No one likes to have their blindfold removed."

He didn't look up. "I know."

"You can pretend you don't care all you like. I know you better."

He didn't answer, just returned to his reading. She stopped him, her cane coming down on the pile of papers.

He sighed, sitting back. "What do you want, Hailene?"

She sat opposite him, easing herself down into the chair. "For you to listen for once."

"Very well," he said. "I am listening."

Words suddenly did not seem sufficient, but they were all she had. "I am old, Alyas. I will not live to see this future you are trying to create. I don't suppose you will either. But I want *someone* to thank you for it, even if that is only me."

He was so still he was barely breathing. Then he unfroze, scooping up the file as he stood. "The last thing I deserve," he said, "is anyone's thanks."

OVISIA GALEA

O visia Galea loved Avarel in summer. Usually. It reminded her of Sarenza, where people sat out on the streets in the cafes and held impromptu parties in their gardens. Parties at which, as the head of the Orleas syndicate and the foundation of all their wealth, the rich, aristocratic families always treated her as their honoured guest. She enjoyed the way they bowed to her, the way they sought her advice, and flattered her with compliments and gifts and, quite often, with their bodies, the men and the women. Avarel in summer was more like that than at any other time of year, and when she was here she would take full advantage. But not this year. This year she kept close to her city mansion, unsure for the first time in her professional life of her standing and favour, both at court and out of it.

Rumour was a deadly thing, and the Duke of Agrathon had proved himself extremely adept at seeding it, so adept in fact that the tiny snippets of gossip had done what she had not thought possible and shaken, ever so slightly, the regard of the rich for the hand that fed them. He was the reason she was cooped up here instead of out there, enjoying all the rewards she had earned. Because every time she stepped outside her door, those bloody kids with their placards were there to shout their complaints and their devastating truths at her and whoever was passing, turning the people against her drip by drip. Gods, she hated him.

So when he turned up on her doorstep one evening, she could not say she was overjoyed to see him.

"You," said Ovisia with loathing, as he was shown into her salon, "have a habit for survival that is really very trying." She had rejoiced when she heard he was dying. She had even gone so far as to make a donation to the Temple of Ithol to cover the cost of the damage he had done by breaking in.

He leaned against the doorframe, altogether far too alive, and smiled. "Sayora."

She could happily have stabbed him. Instead, she said smoothly, "Ovisia, please. We have surely passed the point of empty formality. What do you want?"

"Ovisia," he obliged. "I think it is time you and I came to an accommodation."

That was unexpected. "Just you and I?"

He shrugged. "If needs be, for now, but my ambitions are broader in scope."

"I bet they are," she said dryly, seating herself in one of the Isyrium-dyed armchairs that had cost as much as everything else in the room combined—except the beautiful chandeliers that were made from and powered by Isyrium. They were her pride and joy, and he didn't even glance at them as he sat. "And I should trust this change of heart because…"

"It is not a change of heart," Alyas replied. "I still believe you are cruel, corrupt, and immoral, that you have murdered, blackmailed and bought your way to power –"

"How skilfully you put my suspicions to rest."

"– but it is equally apparent that we cannot deal with this problem without the syndicates' cooperation, so we must cooperate. Surely we both want the same thing?"

Ovisia studied him a long time. Eventually she said, "Do we? Forgive me, Alyas, but I cannot begin to see where our interests and ambitions intersect. You have made plain your desire to crush the syndicates. We have responded. Neither of us has gained anything. I can believe you find that as unsatisfactory as I do, but cooperate? No, I'm afraid I cannot believe you truly want that."

His expression didn't change, but she had the sense of some deep emotion swirling just beneath the surface. At length, he said, "I want an end to this plague that is devastating Ellasia. I want a future that is not measured in years, years in which I will watch the places and people I care about destroyed. You can't tell me you don't want that too."

She leant back with a smile, enjoying the novel sight of his desperation. "Of course I can't. The difference is that I don't believe it will come to that. Human ingenuity is an incredible thing. We lost Isyrium before and we found it again. We will find our way out of this."

"You mean when you developed the means of refining Isyrium that caused this disaster in the first place?"

"An unfortunate consequence but not insurmountable."

He did not reply. He just sat there in silence, one hand unconsciously curled around the hilt of the Isyr sword as though he would dearly love to use it. So that was one thing they shared. She had never understood how he could wear those things all the time. It had driven her half-mad at first with jealousy. But then she had seen what they had done to him, bit by bit, and she knew it was a gesture that carried a heavy cost.

"What if I told you there is a solution, that it could give you what you want, but you would have to settle for less?"

"Then I would tell you we will find another way."

"There isn't another way."

"You don't know that."

"I do. Ovisia, I *do*."

She shook her head. "There is *always* another way."

He stared at her in disbelief, brows drawn together. Then he pressed his hands to his tired face. Through clenched fingers, he asked, "Why?"

"Do you think the people would stand for it?" she asked, pitying him. Did he really think it was so easy? That they could just *stop* and not face social upheaval on a scale that had never been seen? "Think how they would be forced to live if we took away Isyrium? We give them everything. What will you give them? Hardship and struggle."

"I expect they would like a choice," he snapped. "Have you asked them? Or is what 'the people' would supposedly stand for just a convenient excuse for you to continue to do as you please? You don't give them everything, you take it. I'm quite certain that if they really understood the choice they face you would be surprised by just how much they would be prepared to stand for."

"But your choice is artificial," she pointed out. "We *will* find a way that allows us all to keep what we have."

He shook his head, his anger no longer safely hidden. "No, the truth is you won't let them make that choice. You won't even let them know it exists. You've lied to the world for years. You've lied to yourselves. You've hooked us all on the thing only you can supply, and you're so addicted to the wealth and power it gives you that you can't see you are eating yourselves alive. The whole world is burning down around your ears and here you are, sitting in your Isyrium-soaked mansion while people half a world away are dying, pretending it's all fine because *something will turn up!*"

His rage battered her, all the harder because it was so cold, and her faced flamed hot in response. How dare he come here and speak to her like this? The syndicates had built this world and he owed them everything he had, *everything*. "Are you quite finished?" she asked, and her voice was shaking she was so angry.

"I am not nearly finished," he snarled, and it sound far too much like a threat. "But it is clear I am wasting my time here." He stood to leave. "We will see if your fellow syndicate heads share your views."

She rose, smoothing her skirts to hide her surprise. "We will?"

"I have asked the king to call a conference. I hoped you and I could reach an agreement here tonight that we could use to convince your colleagues of the need for change. I see I was mistaken. You have no idea how much I regret that."

"So you will try to force it on my colleagues? What makes you think we will come to your conference? What could you have to say to us that we would want to hear and why should we listen?"

"Oh, you will come," he promised, and he leant in close and told her why.

She froze, feeling the unpleasant thud of fear. "How?" He couldn't possibly know.

He smiled. "I know much more than that. About all of you. So, you see, you *will* come, and you will come without fuss, without schemes, without knives in your hand, or I will make it public. All of it. And you will be ruined."

Ice gave way to molten rage. "You can't win. It's too big. Ruin us and others will step into our places. You cannot win."

He stepped back into the shadow of the doorway. "We will see, Sayora. We will see."

ESAR CANTRELL

When word got out about the conference King Raffa-Herun Geled was holding, word didn't just get out about the event itself. It got out about *why*. And rumour did its deadly work. Syndicate representatives in cities across Ellasia found themselves accosted in the street, or barricaded in their homes by Nameless protests, and the rich, the government ministers, the people who pulled the strings of power—they closed their doors to them in public and met with them in panic in private to discuss what the fuck they were going to do about it. Because the Isyrium could not run out. They had to ensure that it did not, whatever that took.

When Esar heard about the conference it was from Alyas himself. Alyas who came and found him in Camling's armoury while he was doing an inventory and told him what he had asked of Raffa and why. And then he asked Esar for two things.

"I need to know," he said, "if Raffa lied to me about the Lathai. About the company."

Esar straightened, one hand massaging the ache in his back from bending over a ledger. "You think he did?"

Alyas worked his way restlessly around the armoury, running his fingers across a row of spear hafts. "I don't know. That's the problem. He sounded like he believed it, but it was kingdom troops who went in there with the syndicates. If he didn't know, what were they doing there?"

"Doesn't mean he knew they were going to slaughter them," Esar said, watching him uneasily. Though if the king hadn't known, it was because he hadn't wanted to. Even Raffa wasn't that stupid. Just the thought was enough to ignite his own rage and the huge, aching well of grief. So many friends had died. They still woke him up at night. Most nights, in fact. They woke Frey too. It occurred to him that this was the first time Alyas had ever spoken of them.

"No, but Esar, he didn't remember the four hundred."

Esar closed the ledger. "What do you mean he didn't remember?" How could you forget ordering the deaths of four hundred men? Unless it mattered so little to you that you just never thought of it again.

Alyas didn't reply. He had his back turned. He might never have spoken of them, but Esar knew they would have filled his thoughts, every moment. "How will it help you to know? What will you do with it?"

He didn't get an answer, just a view of Alyas's back, rigid with tension. For reasons he had not shared, Alyas appeared to have put his quarrel with Raffa behind him. And Raffa appeared to have let him. He had agreed to Alyas's proposal of a meeting with the syndicate heads—a proposal Esar found far too innocent to account for his secretive behaviour—and he had even agreed to host it. They were both being suspiciously tolerant and accommodating of each other, and Esar knew Alyas too well to trust it. And a man who could forget he had condemned four hundred to death to give himself an excuse for his friend's exile and disgrace would hardly be chastened and reformed by having that same man almost die in his arms.

But he was reluctant to push, because if Alyas was having trouble coming to terms with the deaths of so many, he was far from the only one. So he let it go—for now. "What's the other thing?"

Alyas turned. "What other thing?"

"You asked me for two things. That's one. What's the other?"

A flash of something crossed Alyas's face, then he said, "The syndicate heads require a guarantee of safe conduct to the conference. Apparently, it is not safe for them to travel in Lankara, and they need an escort to Avarel and protection while they are here. They won't accept it from me." His mouth gave a wry twist. "They will from you. Will you do it?"

Esar frowned. "I'm a little offended. What did I do to make them think I am more kindly disposed towards them?"

Alyas almost smiled, but his eyes were anywhere but on Esar's face. "I think it is more a reflection of how much they detest me than a slight against you. Will you do it?"

"If you need me to."

"I do."

"Then I'll do it. But, Alyas, about Raffa –"

Alyas, who had been halfway to the door as soon as he had what he wanted, stopped with his hand on the doorframe. "I need to know, Esar."

"Why? What good will it do?"

"Because I need to."

❧

He went to Nicor. Which Alyas could have done any time he liked. He went to him in his house in the city with his wife and four children, rather than his quarters in the palace.

Mely greeted him with a warm smile and Esar dutifully complimented her on the boys wrestling around his feet while the eldest fetched Nicor from whatever he did when he wasn't scowling at everyone who came to see Raffa.

If Nicor was pleased to see him, he didn't show it. "Esar."

"Nicor. Can I talk to you?"

The king's commander looked like he would very much like to say no, but Mely was already hustling the children out and Esar stayed firmly planted where he was, so he didn't have a lot of choice. He sighed. "What do you want to talk to me about?"

Esar took the drink Nicor offered him and said, "I never did thank you—for getting Alyas to the temple in time."

Nicor snorted. "You didn't come here to say that."

"No, but I did wonder—why did you do it?"

"What was I supposed to do? Leave him to die on the bloody floor?"

Esar winced. Frey had glossed over those details. "The king might have preferred that."

Nicor set his drink down. "Esar, I have sworn an oath. I don't know what you want, but do not ask me to break it."

"Now why would you think I would do that?"

"Come on, Esar. Alyas is playing at getting along for the moment, and it's all very nice, but you and I both know it's not real. He's not that forgiving."

"Oh, I don't know," Esar replied. "It depends what he's being asked to forgive. Raffa has a long tab."

"And my job is protecting him," Nicor snapped, picking up his drink and downing it in one swallow. He reached for the bottle and poured another, holding it out to Esar who waved his full glass in refusal.

Then, because he was not Alyas and he believed in being direct, he asked, "Did he know what the syndicates were going to do? To the Lathai?"

Nicor toyed with the bottle of spirits as though he could not decide whether it was friend or foe. "Did Alyas send you?"

"No," Esar replied. Alyas had not been that specific in his request.

The bottle went spinning across the table. Esar caught it before it could roll off and smash on the floor. Nicor gave him a sour look. "What do you want me to say?"

"A yes or a no would be appreciated."

"And if the answer is I don't know?"

"Then I would ask why, as the king's commander, you didn't know what your own troops were doing? And you would tell me…?"

"That the order didn't go through me. And that's all I can tell you. Because that's all I know."

Esar sat down opposite him and refilled his glass. "Why would he bypass you like that? You must have done your own digging."

"If I did, and if I found anything, I wouldn't share it with you," Nicor retorted. "Because telling you is telling Alyas and he is giving me nightmares already."

Esar downed his own drink. Nicor wasn't the only one. But he had the answer to his question now, and he didn't like it one bit. He wasn't at all sure he wanted to share it with Alyas either.

Someone was waiting for him outside Nicor's town house. Melar Gaemo had abandoned his Flaeresian cape and bright colours and was dressed in sober black to better blend into the shadows. Unfortunately for him, Esar was too experienced with people waiting for him in dark alleys to be taken by surprise.

"What do you want, Melar?" he asked, crossing the street to his side.

"I need to speak to Alyas." Gaemo was more agitated than Esar had ever seen him.

Esar shook his head. "Not going to happen." The last thing they needed right now was the kind of trouble that Alyas killing the Flaeresian ambassador would bring down on them. He wasn't at all sure he would try to stop him. "You should know better. He meant it."

"I know he bloody meant it!" Gaemo snapped. "That's why I need to talk to him. He needs to stop this!"

Esar, who had no idea what he was talking about, said shrewdly, "Taste of your own medicine, Melar?"

"Fuck you, Esar," the ambassador snarled. "We tried to help you. We would have helped you bring them to heel. But this—Alyas is out of control, do you hear me? You need to rein him in before we all regret it."

"He promised Diago a reckoning," Esar pointed out, walking away before Gaemo could see how much this conversation disturbed him. "You brought this on yourselves."

❧

It was with two urgent topics bothering him that Esar returned to Camling to find it besieged by a Nameless protest, and there he added a third. It was the third that pushed the other two out of his mind. He shouldered his way through the rowdy crowd, ducking wildly swinging placards and doing his best to ignore the insults shouted in his ear, and as he reached the edge of the crowd a youth with untidy hair caught his eye. And *winked* at him.

The guards on the gates grabbed him and hauled him inside as he was still staring at the boy, who had gone back to shouting his slogans at Camling's empty courtyard. He had not imagined it. And it was not hard to work out what it meant. He could kill Alyas.

First he had to find him, and that proved rather difficult. He wasn't anywhere in the house or the outbuildings, and the guards swore he had not left. Esar searched them all again, quietly fuming, until he remembered one last place he could look.

He found Alyas on the roof where they had used to hide as children from whichever adult was trying to corral them. He was sitting on the tiled slope gazing out across the city with the blades across his knees, and he looked like he had been there for hours.

Esar decided against climbing out after him. It seemed a lot higher, somehow, than it had when he was a child, or perhaps he just had a better idea of the consequences of a missed step.

"What are you doing up here?" It was the place they had escaped to, the place they had hidden when the world was too much. He hadn't been up here since, well, since the last time that haven had been necessary.

"Did you talk to Nicor?" Alyas asked without turning. Because of course he would have known where Esar had gone.

"I'm not talking to you until you come inside," Esar told him, because he was going to do some shouting and he didn't want to do it on the roof where everyone would hear them.

Alyas obediently climbed back through the window. As he started to buckle the blades back on, Esar said, "Put them down."

Alyas looked up, his face guarded. "Why?"

"Because I want to talk to *you*."

"You are."

But he didn't argue, nor did he protest when Esar took the blades and threw them onto the unused bed in the attic room, though his eyes followed them. Esar knew it didn't mean much, but it made him feel better all the same.

Alyas turned his attention to Esar's face. "What have I done now?"

"Are you funding the Nameless?"

"What do you mean?"

"Exactly what I said. *Are you funding the Nameless?*"

Silence answered him, the kind of silence that was as good as a confession. "Why, Alyas? Yholis's infinite mercy, why would you do that?"

"Because you said it yourself, they're right."

Gods, Esar hated talking to him when he was like this. "And you said, and you were also right, that you couldn't possibly encourage them. So what the fuck do you call this if not encouragement?"

It was obvious now that he knew, the way the Nameless had stepped up their activities, how both they and rumour had targeted the syndicates, not just in Avarel but across Lankara. Even outside Lankara. It gave them some protection. The syndicates had never been loved. They *thought* they were, but they mistook one thing for another, which considering how well they were acquainted with self-interest was quite surprising. And the king's guard could not crack down on the Nameless quite so hard when they weren't the only ones causing trouble. What he didn't understand was why. Alyas was not naïve enough to believe that public opinion would influence the syndicates' behaviour, no matter how big the crowd outside the palace on the day they arrived for his conference. The system was simply too big and too important to fail. Rulers and governments across the continent would prop it up even in the face of their citizens' outrage. They would just do it in secret. And then it began to make sense in a bleak and despairing way.

"Is that why you sold Headdon? Because that's an awful lot of funding."

Alyas, who had been watching him warily, sighed. "Isn't that the point? That I have far more than I need? Tersa was right—I lived without all this for years. It means nothing to me. Besides, if I don't do it now, I might not have a chance to do it later."

"What," Esar growled, "does that mean?"

"It means that my standing here is hanging by a thread and Raffa could cut it at any time. And what do you think he will do with my estates then? That's why I gave Camling to you. It's why I sold Headdon—so that when he tries to take it, there's nothing left."

"*Nothing* left? What else have you sold?"

Silence.

An uncomfortable suspicion occurred. "Is Raffa paying us?" The company was as loyal as they could be, but they needed to eat like anyone else.

"My arrangement with Raffa is my business," Alyas said, trying to dodge round Esar and escape.

He didn't make it. Esar caught his arm, holding him in place. "No, it's company business. They have been paid. It's the kind of thing you know about when they haven't. And we're not earning any money from anywhere else right now, which means you're paying them. You, yourself."

"Maybe that's why I sold Headdon."

"It's not though," Esar pointed out, controlling himself with an effort. "The distinction, and one that I know you're aware of, is that the *income* from Headdon could pay the company month after month for as long as you needed it to. The money from *the sale* of Headdon will run out. And what will you do then? Sell the house in Orleas?"

More silence.

"You've already sold it. Ithol's fucking balls, Alyas, you're bleeding yourself dry. Don't ask me to believe it's just to spite Raffa. Why? Tell me why!"

Alyas pressed his hands to his face and said through rigid fingers, "I can't. I'm sorry. Not yet."

BRIVAR

The atmosphere at Camling had been tense in the days before Esar left to collect the syndicate representatives. Whatever he and Alyas had quarrelled about, it had been bad enough that days later they were barely speaking. Alyas was hard to find at the best of times recently and now it was almost impossible to track him down in Camling's maze of rooms, something that Brivar didn't like at all. Because Esar was right about why he was still here. Alondo had said they needed to trust Alyas with the blades and he was trying to do that. He *had* given them back. But he could not be comfortable about their continued proximity and so he wanted to be close as well. Much good that did either of them if Alyas was nowhere to be found.

There were plenty of other things to occupy him, however. He returned to the temple for part of each day to help them cope with all the people coming in with minor hurts, and occasionally major ones, from the protests sweeping the city. Some of them were syndicate representatives and Brivar had to grit his teeth and remind himself that the Temple of Yholis made no exceptions to its promise of care. If he would treat a thief or murderer without question, he could not refuse to treat the syndicates, though he felt they were both of those things on a scale that even Yholis herself would baulk at if he had a chance to put it to her. Which of course he didn't, so he bound sprained limbs and treated bleeding cuts with just a slight lessening in his usual attentiveness to his patients' comfort and had to be satisfied with that.

In the evenings he went home to Della—because Camling was home now—and he tried to speak to Alyas. When he couldn't, he would ask Della if she had seen him. Occasionally she had, but mostly she found him as elusive as everyone else. The only people who reliably saw him were Keie and Agazi and their baby, and Brivar didn't know what to make of that.

Then one day a man came into the temple with injuries that were far from minor. Brivar helped Alondo operate on the Flaeresian ambassador, who had been found in the gutter one street away from his official residence with multiple stab wounds. They did what they could, and when they finished and Brivar knew it would not be enough, he sent word to Alyas at Camling.

Alyas was there an hour later. He stood looking down at Melar Gaemo's still face with an expression Brivar could not read.

"Will he live?"

Brivar shook his head. "I'm sorry. I know he was a friend."

"He was not a friend," Alyas said. "But perhaps once I thought he might have been."

But he didn't leave and Brivar wasn't sure he believed him. There had been regret in his voice.

"Do you know what happened?" Alyas asked at length. "Who did this?"

"The king's guard brought him in. You'll have to ask Nicor-Heryd."

Alyas nodded. There was a stool beside the cot on which the ambassador lay. He positioned it against the wall and sat so he could rest his head back. His face was pinched and grey with fatigue.

"Will you stay here tonight?" Brivar asked him. It was an innocent question. Gaemo was unlikely to last till morning. If Alyas wanted to be here, which it looked like he did, he would have to stay. And if he stayed, Brivar could make sure he slept.

Alyas shook his head. "I can't." But it was very late when he finally left, and before he went he made the traditional offering of thanks that families made for the care of their dying.

There was a lull in the city's rage after Gaemo's brutal murder, as though things had never been meant to go so far. It didn't last. Days later, three men were carried through the streets to the temple in a farmer's cart. Two were alive, though barely so, long, ragged wounds ripped across their chests and limbs. The other was dead. And he was no longer what he had been, his skin mottled midnight blue and his face disfigured by inhuman rage.

A crowd followed them, silent at first, then simmering with the kind of anger that could explode at any time. The unfortunate syndicate representative who crossed their path was the hapless catalyst for the riot that engulfed the elegant streets of the Carpera and left nine people dead, one of them a king's guard. The cart was abandoned in the fury of the riot and by the time it was retrieved and taken to the Temple of Yholis, the two other men were dead. They had not transformed. They had died of the midnight sickness and their wounds, but had they lived, the temple could have done nothing for them, and Brivar felt a little sick at how relieved he was that they had not been faced with that dilemma. Knowing now the true action of na'quia, Alondo and Elenia had decided that it could no longer be administered to victims of the contagion. To inflict such suffering against the possibility that the poisonous abscess would form in a place from which it could be safely found and removed was not a reasonable course of action.

After that, Avarel was a more dangerous place. The rumours coming in from Lankara's other cities suggested the same was true elsewhere. The day before the conference, after an explosive day on the streets that had required Brivar to have an escort from Camling to the temple and back, he was returning through the crowd outside the gates when Aubron arrived behind him and cheerfully elbowed a path through the jostling protestors.

"Esar's back?" Brivar asked. "Is he coming here?"

He badly wanted Esar and Alyas to patch up their quarrel. Since Gaemo's death, Alyas had been harder to reach than ever before, and it worried him. He could recognise guilt when he saw it. He also wasn't stupid; the current unrest served Alyas's needs too well to be accidental. But the trouble with stirring up trouble you couldn't control was that you couldn't control it, and Brivar feared that guilt was just the kind of emotion that made him vulnerable to the manipulations of Iysr.

But mostly he wanted them to make peace because this rift hurt them both, and he hated it. Brivar had never been close to his brothers. They were both much older and had had little time for an unexpected new member of the family, and he had been dispatched to the temple at age ten. But Esar and Alyas *needed* each other. They showed it in different ways. Esar *worried*, constantly—granted, there had been a lot to worry about recently—but Alyas protected him no less thoroughly for it being less obvious. To be at odds like this must be unbearable.

Aubron shook his head. "Says Alyas needs to go there."

"I'll come with you," Brivar said, making a quick decision. "I'll wait here."

Aubron threw him an amused look. "Suit yourself."

Alyas must have been waiting for word, because Aubron was back with him after only a few minutes. He looked surprised when he found Brivar waiting for him, but he didn't make any objection. There were deep shadows under his eyes. Whatever he had been doing over the last few days, it hadn't included much sleeping.

The crowd at the gates let them through with minimal harassment. They had been there all day. They were probably as tired as Alyas. The streets were calmer too, but it was an uneasy calm, the kind of calm that preceded one of the wild winter storms that swept through the valleys, as though the city was gearing itself up for the next day. Which was likely exactly what it was doing since the next day was the day of the conference.

They found Esar and the syndicate heads in a house near the palace. Ovisia Galea had chosen it in advance and syndicate guards had been in residence for days in preparation for their arrival, refusing Alyas's offer of his company's support. Brivar couldn't imagine why. They were there now with Esar, though, because he had sworn their safe conduct in the name of the king and so, for now, he was operating quite independently from Alyas.

But it was Alyas who had called them together, and he went now to make his own promises, backed by Esar, that they would be unmolested. That he would be fair and honest in his dealings with them. And Brivar, who knew him very well by now, saw the words all but choke him. He was not surprised.

The syndicates had done so much harm, and they had done it knowingly. That they continued to do so magnified their crime, made it monstrous and unforgivable. But more painful for Alyas was what they had done to the men and women he had left behind in the mountains. The company and the Lathai. Friends and family whose deaths must be eating at him even though he never spoke of them.

In some ways Brivar was surprised Alyas had done this. Surprised he could bring himself to. And the assembled syndicate heads looked at him with such hatred and distrust that Brivar couldn't understand why they had come at all.

There were ten of them. Six men, four women, in ages that Brivar guessed varied from early thirties to the upper eighties. Ovisia Galea of the Orleas syndicate he knew, sitting by a man with hair that reminded Brivar of cold ashes. She was watching Alyas with such an intensity of loathing that Brivar did not know how he could ignore it. But he never looked at her. He didn't really look at any of them, not the old man who kept muttering insults in what he probably thought was an undertone but which you could hear in the next room—it was from him that Brivar gleaned an idea of just what Alyas had done to force them together—nor the young one whose face was unlined by time and whose eyes were clear and open and far too innocent for someone so guilty. He was the head of the Selysian syndicate, with which the company had clashed in Cadria.

There was even a Janath woman from Qido with uncomfortable echoes of Della in her face. She represented what passed for a syndicate in Qido, where the emperor owned all the mines and leased them to various operations that were controlled by this woman.

Brivar listened to Alyas make his promises, and Esar make his, and hugged his temple amulet tight, praying to Yholis that the syndicates would listen, that they would take the solution Alyas would offer them—that they could be convinced to give up the operations that had brought them such vast wealth and power for the sake of generations to come—because if they didn't, there really was no hope.

The ash-haired man, appointed as spokesman, formally accepted Esar's oath of protection. With a jaundiced eye on Alyas, he promised on behalf of the syndicates that they would listen to the king's proposals. Brivar heard the way the words grated through his teeth and knew the old man's intimations of blackmail had not just been bitter ramblings. It was obvious that nothing less than fear for their interests would have brought them here. And he hoped Alyas knew what he was doing. They would be doubly determined to destroy him after this, whatever they promised here today

When it was over, Esar walked them out into the warm summer night. The tension between them was of a different kind tonight, as though on the eve of this pivotal moment other quarrels were put aside.

"Did you mean that?" Esar asked Alyas as they waited for their horses.

Alyas looked his brother in the eye and said, "Every word. I swear."

And Esar nodded. "Then do me a favour. Get some sleep. You'll need it."

He received a dutiful promise and they parted on their old terms. As they rode away Brivar thought he saw tears on Alyas's face, but it might just have been a trick of the moonlight.

※

Alyas did not go to the palace with them the next morning. Della said he had been up and out early, before the crowds had formed. He was probably at the palace already.

The protestors were out in force by the time Brivar accompanied Agazi and twenty of the company from Camling to meet Alyas there. Camling itself had been quiet, but the streets to the palace were thronged with people, strung-out king's guards desperately trying to enforce a semblance of order. Or, if not order, at least not outright violence.

Alyas wasn't at the palace. Esar was, the syndicate heads with him. They had gone early, before trouble could start, and they were now clustered together near the palace steps watching the furious surge of the protestors with something close to disbelief.

"Where is he?" Esar demanded of Agazi when they made it through the crowd. He was with Frey and Nicor-Heryd. The king's commander looked as though all his nightmares had come true at once, his face tight with strain and too many sleepless nights.

Agazi shrugged. "Said he would meet us here."

Nicor eyed the angry crowd. "On this own, through that?"

When Alyas finally arrived, his appearance prompted a violent convulsion of the crowd outside the gates. Nicor had to send his guards out to extract him from the chaos, and he emerged from their protective ring looking exhausted and ragged. To Brivar's trained eye, he had the appearance of a man who had not slept at all.

"It is bad?" Nicor asked when Alyas reached them. He was on edge, his men spread too thin by weeks of protests, and he had welcomed Esar's arrival with the company escort like a starving man presented with a feast.

"As bad as it's been," Alyas said grimly. "They've breached your barricades around the temple district, and almost every street in the Carpera is blocked."

Nicor swore. "I don't understand it. They're too organised. They were never like this before."

Brivar saw the sharp, worried look that Esar gave Alyas, who said, "Perhaps they have more reason now."

"This rumour about the syndicates and the plague? Come on, Alyas, I dislike them as much as you do, but that can't be true."

"Can't it, Nicor?" Alyas asked.

Nicor frowned at him, eyes narrowing. But whatever he was going to say was lost as a roar rose from the crowd, then a scream, and a rider burst through the close-packed group of protestors, sending those nearest flying and almost trampling others. It was a king's guard, and he hauled his horse to a stop by Nicor and said in breathless haste, "They're inside the Temple of Ithol. You need to come."

Nicor hesitated, clearly torn. He didn't want to leave the palace, but the king wouldn't thank him for letting the Nameless tear through his city, and the Temple of Ithol would be noisy in its demands for reparation. Esar, seeing his dilemma, said, "Go. My men will be here. We're sworn to the king today. There's enough of us."

Gratitude flashed across the king's commander's face. He turned to leave, pointing his finger at Alyas as he went. "Don't do anything to fuck this up, do you hear me?"

Alyas said, "I promise, Nicor."

Nicor nodded, satisfied. Alyas always kept his word. When he had gone, Esar scowled at his brother. "Promise me, too." And Alyas did.

Esar nodded. "Where do you want them?"

Alyas stared toward the palace, his expression remote. "The king has prepared one of the vaults. It's quieter. He doesn't want them disturbed by the protests. Get them settled in there and I'll bring Raffa to you."

As Esar left to obey, Frey tagging along beside him, Alyas turned to Brivar. "Will you come with me?"

lyas was silent as he led Brivar through the corridors to Raffa's chambers. The blue-tinted Isyrium lighting gave his pale skin an unhealthy cast, filling the hollows of his face with shadow, and he was so distant that Brivar dared not speak to him.

The king and queen were together when they arrived, sitting around a low table that held the dregs of wine in crystal glasses. The queen stood, greeting Alyas with a kiss on his cheek and wary eyes. He spared her a glance and not much else. His whole attention was on the king, who had risen at their entrance and was looking both expectant and nervous.

"Alyas. Is it time?"

"You're not going to the meeting, Raffa."

The king frowned. "Because of the protests? They can't get to us in here."

Alyas's gaze never wavered from the king's face. "Have you heard them? Have you listened to what they're saying?"

"Of course I have," Raffa snapped. "They're angry because they are poor and others are rich. They're always angry about it."

Alyas said, "I think they are angry about rather more than that. I think they have had enough. That's what they're telling you. And it's time to listen."

Brivar felt a pit yawning in his stomach. He couldn't take his eyes off Alyas, whose face was a portrait of torture.

"I have fucking listened," the king ground out. "Every fucking day for weeks. I can't *not* listen. What do you want me to do about it? I called this meeting because you told me it was necessary. I agreed to it because you told me if I did you could solve this, and isn't that what they want? So just take me to the damn thing and let's get on with it."

Alyas didn't move. "I lied to you, Raffa. Like you lied to me. I have not called the syndicate heads here to waste my time in pointless debate. I have called them here because it's time to end this."

The queen, her face pale as milk, said, "Gods, Alyas, what have you done?"

"I've woken up," he told her, his eyes still on the king. "You cannot change the system, Raffa, that's what I've realised. Not when everyone with the power to do so has a vested interest in maintaining it. So you have to tear it down instead."

Raffa's face twisted into a furious snarl. "I trusted you! Is this how you repay me? What is this? Your little rebellion? You've stirred the people up, is that it? To give your treason an illusion of legitimacy? All I have to do is call for my guards and this is over. Do you understand? It's over, and this time, I swear by Ithol's blood, you will die for it."

The queen gasped. "Raffa!"

"No, Mari. He's done. Even you can't defend this. Not this time."

Brivar was frozen to the spot. He couldn't breathe. He thought he would be sick.

Alyas still hadn't moved. "Call for your guards, Raffa. They won't come. They're not even here."

The king's face faded from red to white. "What have you done?"

"What someone should have done a long time ago," Alyas replied. "And maybe then my company would still be alive. The Lathai would still be alive. And many more hundreds of people with them."

"I told you," the king shouted, "I did not know!"

"But you lied, Raffa. You did know."

The king stared at him. "Is this revenge, Alyas? Because you're taking it out in the wrong place. It was the syndicates who killed your people. They forced me into it."

That lit Alyas's anger like a spark falling on Isyrium fuel. "Don't you dare! You were the king! They shouldn't have been able to make you do anything. This country was your charge, Raffa. These people your responsibility. Instead of protecting Lankara, you raped it. You knowingly allowed the syndicates to poison it and sacrificed your own people to your greed. You murdered an entire tribe for no other reason than they stood in your way. You betrayed me! If you had asked me, I would have helped you." His voice cracked. "Why did you leave it too late? I would have helped you."

But Raffa-Herun heard neither the question nor the cry of despair that drove it. "I *was* the king? Alyas?"

Yholis. Brivar felt sick. Forgotten in the background, the queen dropped into a chair, her face white.

Alyas met the king's eyes. "I'm sorry, Raffa. It's over. What you have done—it cannot be forgiven. It cannot be atoned for. And your people cannot build a new world with you in it. This is the end. It has to be."

Raffa looked at him as if he were mad. "What are you talking about? You cannot just depose me. You cannot overturn the whole bloody government, and the syndicates, and the gods-damned entire fucking economy!"

Alyas said nothing. Brivar realised that was exactly what he intended to do. And he had promised. He had sworn to Esar that he would uphold the undertakings he had made to the syndicates. Then on the way home he had wept.

The king shook his head, his eyes wild. "You *are* mad. What do you think will happen when the Isyrium dries up? What will your precious people's bloody revolt do then? You think I did this so I could make myself rich? I did it because if I didn't, the fucking country would fall apart! People would starve, thousands would die, we would go to war with everyone. Is that what you want? Because if you do this, that's exactly what will happen."

Alyas waited until he finished and then, very calm, asked, "And if

I don't? What will happen to them then?"

When Raffa did not reply, he said, "Let me tell you. The poison the syndicates have created will spread. These small outbreaks will grow. You won't be able to contain them because every time the corruption gets out, it will take more and more of your land, more and more of your people, and you will never get them back. It will kill some, painfully and slowly, and others it will turn into more of itself. Friends will kill friends, parents will murder their own children, every growing thing will sicken and die, and it will inch closer to Avarel. Your walls won't protect you. It doesn't matter how far away you dump your poison. It will still reach you. But first it will take everything else and everything you were supposed to protect will be dead. That is what *will* happen. So tell me again, Raffa, that I cannot do this."

The words were spoken quietly. There was no anger in his voice, it was simply empty. And his face... Brivar looked away, towards Mari-Geled. She was weeping. He did not know who for.

"You always knew best, didn't you?" Raffa snarled. "You always had to be right. Well, I hope you enjoy your new world, when the people you claim to protect see you safe behind the walls of your mansion, with all your comforts and your wealth, while they starve on the street and die from diseases the temples can no longer cure because you have robbed them of the means to do so! When they turn on you, as you have turned on me. I wish I could be there to see it."

"But you won't," Alyas replied in that same empty tone. "Because I have sold, bartered or given away every single thing that I had, even my soul, to bring you down."

"Everything?" the king sneered. "You self-righteous fucking hypocrite. You could buy Lankara twice over with just what you are wearing right now."

Alyas's hand went to the hilt of his dagger. He drew it, balancing it on his palm, and Brivar caught his breath as the light pouring in the window reflected off its perfect finish. Then he laid it on the table still set with its crystal wine glasses and the Isyr was picked up and refracted a hundred dazzling times in their faceted surface.

He looked up at Raffa. "This is for you. You always wanted it. You know what to do with it. I need the other one a while yet."

Brivar's heart lurched. The king was staring at the dagger as if he did not know what it was. When he met Alyas's steady gaze, his eyes were wild with denial. Until this moment, he had not believed what Alyas meant to do.

"Alyas. Please." The words were a fractured whisper. "Mari…"

Alyas looked like he had been stabbed through the heart. "She knew. She did not try to stop you. She didn't try to stop any of this. But you were the king. It was your choice, your responsibility. And your price to pay. Mari can make her own."

Then he turned and walked out and Brivar was left standing with the king and the queen and the shining length of silver-blue death.

❦

Brivar could not stay in that room. He followed Alyas and found him slumped against the wall. His eyes were closed and his hand was clenched tight around the hilt of the one remaining blade. *I need the other one a while yet.*

Brivar approached slowly, as if he were a wounded animal.

Without opening his eyes, Alyas said, "I loved that man once. I would have died for him. But he made a choice, and once he made it, there was never any going back. He has to die. You know it's the only way."

I would have died for him. In a very real sense, he just had. Appalled, Brivar said, "It will destroy you. You won't be able to live with yourself."

"I don't have to," Alyas replied. "I just have to do it."

I need the other one a while yet.

"Don't please. Think of Esar."

Alyas choked on a sob. "I am thinking of him! Who do you think I'm doing this for?" He dropped his head into his hands, and when he looked up, his eyes were dark with pain. "You asked me once what I saw. In the na'quia. And I did not tell you. Because it was *this*. This is what I saw. And I have tried, Yholis knows I have tried, to find another way. Any other way. But every step I took brought me one step nearer. Every time I tried to turn aside, the closer I came. You don't really want me to stop it, you just want it to be someone else who does it. But is there no one else. It has to be me and I'm not finished yet."

Brivar stared at him, in horror, in grief, in devastating understanding. Not only the past, but the future, that's what Ailuin had said. Destiny. *There is a terrible truth in na'quia, but there are also dangerous lies. You must be able to know one from the other.*

Brivar thought of the syndicate heads waiting with Esar who had been promised safe conduct, sworn on his honour, because he trusted Alyas and knew he would never play him false. And he thought of the king behind the closed door, left alone with the knife he had always coveted, and feared very much what was coming. "Please," he begged. "You have to stop this." It was too much. He couldn't bear it.

Alyas slammed his fist into the wall, the pain exploding across his face. "I can't stop it," he snarled. "It's too late. It's already started. The people are rising, from here to Qido. They'll burn the processing centres, storm the mines, they'll tear the syndicates down, but if I don't cut the head off the snake, it will just come back stronger and their sacrifice will be for nothing. And the poison will spread. It might be a year, it might be ten, but it will take everything. *Everything*. And there will be no world for our children, for Esar's child, and how can I let that be the future?"

Brivar caught his breath in horrified realisation. "Esar's child. Frey's pregnant. He doesn't know."

Alyas shook his head. He slid down the wall, his hand cradled against his chest. "I asked her not to tell him. So he would still believe we could find a way out of this, because I needed his honesty. There is no way in which I have not betrayed him."

He would do the same to the syndicates as he had done to the king, Brivar realised, and Esar's honour would be burned along with all the rest. The tragedy of it threatened to drown him, and his training took over. He knelt, taking Alyas's abused hand in his, nimble fingers feeling out the damage. *Two knuckles cracked. A dislocated finger joint.* He reset that in one swift motion, causing a shocked hiss. It calmed his mind. It did nothing to ease the turmoil in his heart. "And when they refuse?" he asked when he could speak. The syndicates would not simply give up and accept the death he offered them. "What will you do then?"

Alyas leant his head back, his face white with pain. "What do you think I will do?"

Brivar felt along the finger joint, checking it had realigned correctly. "I need to bind this," he said, as if Alyas had not just admitted his intention to murder.

Alyas gently took back his hand and pushed himself to his feet. "No, you don't."

Brivar resisted the urge to snatch it back. To insist. To pretend those words didn't mean what he knew they meant.

Alyas looked down at where he still crouched on the floor. "I am sorry to ask this of you when I have already asked so much, but I still need a witness."

"For the syndicates?"

"Yes," he agreed, "For them. And for me."

They did not go at once to the vault where Esar had taken the syndicate heads. Instead, Alyas took him back out into the courtyard, where the crowd at the gates had gone suspiciously quiet. He recognised Tersa at the front along with some of the other Nameless who had accosted him that day at the market, and lots of things fell into place. Nicor had wondered how the Nameless had become so organised. *They* hadn't. *Alyas* had. And Esar, who must have known or guessed, had made Alyas promise, yet again, that he would keep his word.

And he had lied.

Alyas walked up to the gates and looked out at his revolution. "Let them in," he said, and Brivar saw the shock that rippled through the company at these words. No one moved. "I said, let them in," he repeated, and this time Agazi relayed the order and the gates swung open.

The Nameless did not pour through in an undisciplined horde as Brivar had feared. Alyas must have planned this to the last detail, because when the gates opened, they filed silently in, twenty of them and no more, each of them carrying a bag. Tersa was at their head, and she flashed Brivar a triumphant look as she crossed into the palace grounds. He wanted to shake her, to scream at her that *this was not winning!* But it was no longer possible that there could be any winners in this mess, and as much as he hated it, Alyas was right. Someone had to do something. Brivar wished desperately that it didn't have to be him.

They did go to the vaults then, those vast cellar rooms beneath the palace with their huge iron doors that housed the royal treasures or royal prisoners as occasion demanded. Brivar trailed along behind, fulfilling this final duty for the Duke of Agrathon. And when they got there, the syndicate heads were all on their feet around the conference table shouting and Esar greeted Alyas with such naked relief that Brivar had to look away.

"Thank Yholis! Alyas, tell these idiots –" Then he saw Tersa and the Nameless, and his face changed. "What's going on?"

The tall man in syndicate blue with hair the colour of wet ashes looked from Tersa to Alyas and said, "What is this? Who are these people? These children? And what are they doing here?"

"These are the heirs to the devastation you have caused," Alyas informed him. "And they will take things from here."

The man looked at him in disbelief. "We did not come here to bargain with children. We came here because you forced us to. We will negotiate only with the king. Where is he?"

"He's not coming."

Brivar glanced at Alyas. Esar was staring at him with dawning horror, and Alyas had his head turned firmly towards the syndicates as if he *could not* confront that look.

The syndicate spokesman's eyes widened as he realised what Alyas had said. "You can't. You *can't*. You need us!"

"No," Alyas said. "We don't."

Esar took a step towards him. "Alyas…"

"I'm sorry, Esar," he said, his voice airless. "It has to be this way."

"No, it doesn't! Gods, man, I'm begging you, don't do this."

When Alyas didn't reply, Esar lurched forward. Alyas was faster. The sword was in his hand and pointing straight out behind him, directly at Esar, before his brother had taken a single step.

"I cannot let you stop me, Esar. I'm sorry. Please sit down."

Esar just stood there, appalled and disbelieving, as it hit him, finally, how completely he had been betrayed.

Alyas said, "Please," his voice broken, and Esar seemed to crumple. Then Frey was there, tears streaming down her face, and she was pulling Esar back. She did not look at Alyas. He did not look at either of them, but his eyes were as bright as Isyr with unshed tears.

Esar let Frey draw him away, but he never took his eyes off Alyas. "Why?" he pleaded. "Tell me why."

Alyas, still looking at the shocked faces of the syndicates, said, "Because you cannot trust the system to change itself. Compelled, they will make promises they have no intention of keeping. They will make a pretence of changing their operations, but they won't do enough and they won't do it fast enough. No matter how much they fear the revelation of the secrets that forced them here today, they will never *stop*. They will do a little here and there, just enough to be able to say they are doing something, but nothing will change, and we will inch closer and closer to the brink from which we cannot return. And I *will not* allow it."

Ovisia Galea, her handsome face ravaged by fear and anger, pushed forward. "It is not yours to allow! The king will string you up for this! Every ruler from here to Qido will condemn you and those who helped you. You're not saving anyone!"

"Look around you, Sayora," Alyas replied. "Does it look like the king has a say?"

It was then, with devastating timing, that the door opened and a woman edged into the room. Clearly terrified, her eyes searched for Alyas. When she found him she held out the dagger, the Isyr dagger he had left with Raffa. Alyas saw it and his face went still.

"The queen asked me to give this to you," the woman told him in a voice barely above a whisper. "She says to tell you the king is dead, and that she has made a different choice."

Alyas took the dagger. The silence was absolute. Brivar sucked in a breath and suddenly he was weeping, the tears falling in a torrent of grief and anger and regret. Not for the king who had died, but for the man who had killed him.

"Do you believe me now?" Alyas asked the syndicate heads, his face white. "There is no way out. It. Is. Over."

The silence held. The king was dead. It was indeed over, but it was not yet finished.

As everyone else in the room stood rooted to the spot, one by one the Nameless approached the conference table and placed on it the hoarded wealth of Lankara's noble families. The pile of Iysr grew. Plate, weapons, jewellery, the pile grew higher and higher. When the last piece of Isyr had been laid reverently on the table, Tersa placed porcelain cups in front of each syndicate head. Another of the Nameless followed her with a jug and poured a careful measure into each.

When they were done, Alyas addressed the silent faces of the most powerful men and women in Ellasia. "This is what you wanted. This is what it was all for. Well, here it is. Every treasure we could find. Here, in this room, with you, and here you will all stay. And when it has driven you mad with the torment of the land you have destroyed, you will find in those cups enough poison to ensure a quick, painless death. It is your choice to drink it or not. But none of you are leaving this room again."

He looked down at the dagger that had killed the king, still unsheathed in his hand. "You could have had all the Isyr you wanted. Instead, you murdered and destroyed. The Lathai never had pure Isyrium. But they could make it. You killed them, as you have killed everything else, and the world very nearly lost their knowledge forever. We found it—the way to purify Isyrium without destroying everything it touches. The way to make Isyr. And now it's theirs." He pointed at the silent Nameless, at Esar and Frey, at Brivar.

The grey-haired man dragged his eyes from the shining, deadly pile of Isyr to Alyas. "You haven't won. You haven't changed anything. Even if you kill us, there are hundreds behind us, thousands! They will step into our places, and they will keep it running. This means nothing. It *does* nothing."

Alyas shook his head. "No, they won't. Because right now, in every mine and every processing centre across Ellasia, all those others are being offered this same choice. Some of them will escape, I know that, but most won't. The syndicates are broken. It is over."

And then he did what he said he would do, and he locked them in there with their treasure and their death and handed the key to Tersa, and it was passed from hand to hand until the last of Nameless to take it left the cellars and it was gone.

ֶ❧

Still the nightmare wasn't over, because now there was nothing between Alyas and what he had done.

"You used me," Esar said, and Brivar did not think he had ever seen him so angry.

"Yes." His face a bloodless mask, Alyas made no excuse, gave no explanation. "I used you. I betrayed your trust. I betrayed you."

Tersa thrust herself to Alyas's side. "He did it for us! For our children. So there is still a world for them to grow up in. You should thank him!" And Brivar wanted so badly to *shut her up*.

"Thank him?" Esar echoed, as if he could not believe what he had heard. "He used you too! And look what happened. How many of your friends died out there today?"

"It was worth it!"

"It's never worth it. Look at him! Look," Esar snarled when she could not. "Look at his face. He has to live with this now." He stopped, anger draining away. "Yholis, Alyas. What have you done?"

Alyas took a jerky step back. "What no one else would."

"It didn't have to be you. Gods, Alyas, it didn't have to be you."

Alyas's face was so white Brivar didn't know how he was still standing. It was over now. He had done what he had set out to do, and the manic energy that had taken him this far was fading fast. Without it, there was only death and betrayal and heartbreak and the weight of it all would crush him. "Yes, it did."

He did not say anything else. He did not even say goodbye. He just walked away.

Tersa ran after him, grabbing his arm and dragging him to a stop. "You can't go! We need you."

Alyas gently detached her grip. His hand was shaking. "I'm the last person you need."

It was Esar who said, "You stupid girl, don't you see? He can't stay. Not after this."

Brivar saw the words hit Alyas like a physical blow. To hear Esar say them. And suddenly everything this had cost him was clear on his face.

"Gods, Alyas," Esar said again, but Alyas held up a hand, stopping him, as though he could not bear to hear it, and in the silence that followed he was gone.

Esar took a step after him, but Frey was faster. She grabbed his arm and held on.

Esar looked down at her. "I have to go after him, Frey."

She shook her head. "No, Esar. Not this time."

"Frey." The anguish on his face was too hard to watch.

"You must let him go. He did it for us. For our child."

It was perhaps the only thing she could have said that would have held him, and as Esar froze, her words working their past his shock, Brivar turned and walked after Alyas.

He found him outside, leaning against his horse as if it were the only thing keeping him upright. It probably was. By his estimate, the man had been awake now for two full days.

He reached out a tentative hand. "Alyas."

Alyas lifted his head, and when Brivar saw his puzzled frown, he realised it was the first time he had ever called him by his name. Only now, only after this. Only when it was too late.

"I have broken everything."

Pointless to say it needed to be broken. That by breaking it, he had given them a chance to save what was left. He knew that. It was why he had done it. Why he had broken every law, trampled every convention, crossed every line, and destroyed himself in the process. Just because it had been necessary didn't make it easier. It didn't make him less guilty.

He had done what had to be done, what no one else was prepared to do, and now he had to leave, because there was no place for a man like that in the future they hoped to build. And it wasn't *fair*.

Alyas pressed something into Brivar's hands. "They are quiet now. They've had their sacrifice."

As Brivar's fingers closed over the Isyr blades, reunited again, he finally understood the voices in the steel. Not hounding Alyas to his own death but driving him to these. As the na'quia had been hounding him. The earth itself making him the instrument of its revenge, or a nightmare vision of na'quia?

He recalled Caira standing in her lodge—dead now, like all the Lathai—and berating him for giving Alyas na'quia. *If you knew him better, you never would have done it.*

Was it destiny he had seen in na'quia, as Ailuin claimed the Lathai sometimes did, or a vision of lies that all the hurts of the past made it impossible to see through? Could he have found another way, if not for that? Or was this the terrible truth of the drug? The torment of a fate he could never avoid, no matter how hard he tried.

And he had fought it so hard it had nearly killed him. It was why he had ignored Tersa and the Nameless, and why he had been so angry when Brivar forced his hand. It was why, Brivar was certain, he had concealed the illness that was killing him. When they had finally taken the poison from him, and he had realised for the first time that he might live, it must have seemed a cruel joke.

But by then the Lathai were dead and a third of his company with them, and it was no longer possible to ignore what Raffa had become. What greed, and cowardice, and the syndicates had made him. From that point, he had stopped fighting the vision. From that point, he had hurled all his energies into making it true, and every other possibility had been discarded. And it was too late to wonder whether things could have been different. Too late to wonder, too cruel to ask.

Brivar looked from the blades to Alyas's face and asked, "What do you want me to do with them?"

"Lock them away. Destroy them. I don't care. But don't give them to Esar. And tell him…"

"Tell him what?" There were tears in his eyes. He could hardly see.

"That I'm sorry."

Sorry for betraying his trust, or sorry for leaving him? Only the second would never be forgiven.

"I'll look after him," he promised, as though he were not a boy of twenty-three and Esar a man twice his age. Then, he asked, "Why did you tell the syndicates about the na'quia but not Raffa?"

"Because I wanted them to know what they could have had, to know everything they will lose, so they could choke on it." Despite everything, the anger—the fury—was still there.

"And Raffa?"

Alyas looked away, to where two riders had emerged from the stables and were waiting by the palace gates. "Because he would have used it to try to bargain his way out of this, and I don't know if I could have stopped him."

Brivar saw Keie, with her baby strapped to her chest, and Agazi. Keie was crying. Keie, who laughed at everything, was looking at Alyas and tears were pouring down her face. Alyas turned back to Brivar. "I am sorry I made you a part of this. You did not deserve that, but I needed you."

"I know," Brivar said, because he understood. Then he let Alyas mount and join Keie by the gates where the silent company guards waited. They had been betrayed as surely as Esar had, and they were watching Alyas with stricken expressions. He did not look at them and he did not look back. Brivar didn't think he was looking at anything.

Agazi appeared beside him. "We're going home," he told Brivar. "Me and Keie and the baby. We'll keep him with us as long as he'll let us. He won't be alone."

"Did you know?" Brivar asked him. "What he was going to do?" Alyas had to have trusted someone, and it had been Agazi who let the Nameless in.

Agazi hesitated. "Not everything, but yes, I knew."

Brivar nodded, unable to look at him. "I think," he said at length, "that I should say goodbye to Esar for you."

Agazi flinched, but there was no regret in his eyes. "If that is how it must be."

"Yes," said Brivar. "It is."

And then he was alone.

EPILOGUE

BRIVAR

It was the day the blue star-violet flowered that the letter came to Brivar from the Temple of Yholis in Sarenza. And it was only once it arrived that he realised he had been waiting for it.

I regret to inform you that your patron, Alyas-Raine Sera, died at our temple on...

The date blurred in front of his eyes. It was followed by more words he could not read and did not want to. He had tried so *hard*.

The details reached him slowly. Sarenza. Flaeres. A month ago. Alyas hadn't stayed with Agazi and Keie, or not for long. Instead, he had gone north. Back to the mountains that had been home for so long. And then, when this must have become inevitable, to Sarenza and the temple, from where word would reach them. Because Alyas would have known that the only thing worse for Esar than his death would be never knowing it had come.

There was another sheet enclosed, filled with the kind of details owed by one surgeon treating the patient of another. Too much detail. Brivar folded it and put it carefully away. Esar didn't need to read that.

There was another, addressed to Esar in a different hand. It had the look of a letter that had been written some time ago, and it was tied around something small and heavy. That one Brivar did not read.

Esar had looked for him. His anger at Alyas had faded almost at once. His anger at Frey, at Agazi—at the people closest to him who had conspired with Alyas to keep him in the dark—that had taken longer to fade. It had taken him a long time to realise it had been done from love, to protect him. It had taken him longer to forgive.

But Alyas—Esar knew him too well. Alyas, he had been frantic to find. Yet even in this, Alyas had been one step ahead of him, because what he had done was only the start. Someone had to see it through. Someone had to seize the chance he had sacrificed everything to give them. Esar knew it. The company knew it, too. Their anger was not for what Alyas had done, but that he had done it alone, without them. And they had allowed no one to undo it. In the days and weeks of chaos that followed Nicor-Heryd's return to the palace to find his king dead, his trust betrayed, and his city in the hands of the mob, Alyas had vanished. When Esar had finally gone north to find him, ignoring Brivar's warning that he had gone south, he found no trace of him. Not because Alyas wasn't there, but because he hadn't wanted to be found.

Brivar did not want to think about that. He did not want to think about any of it, least of all Esar reading the crumpled letter. So he did what he had done since that dreadful day in the palace. He buried himself in his work and tried not to look up because if he did not see it, maybe he could pretend it wasn't happening. But the world was not so kind. Not then and not now.

The line outside the temple was long. It had been long every day since the drama at the palace had played out in concert with the violent convulsions across the city. Across Lankara. Across Ellasia. Convulsions that spread and deepened and showed no sign of abating.

Alyas and the Nameless had been thorough. The syndicates were crushed, their mines sabotaged and abandoned, their processing centres burned to the ground, but the vacuum they left behind nearly took everything else with it. And it only got worse.

The Isyrium did not run out all at once. There were warehouses packed with it across the continent, vast supplies that could have been rationed fairly between nations and needs and might have lasted for years, if there had been anyone capable of enforcing such a thing. Instead, rulers, the rich, the unscrupulous seized what they could within their borders—and outside them, if they thought they could get away with it—and left everyone else to fend for themselves. Brivar sometimes thought the only reason things hadn't descended into outright war already was because the threat the syndicates had created—that Alyas had exposed in such horrifying clarity—was so urgent that not even those who had colluded in its existence could ignore it.

And Alyas had known all this was coming. He had seen it in the na'quia and then he had to watch it happen and know he had caused it. So Brivar was not surprised when the letter arrived. He was not surprised by any of it.

The world blurred. He took a sharp breath. He could not think about that. He had work to do, an endless line of people needing his help. People he *could* help. He refused Alondo's offer to take his place, ignored the compassion in the old man's eyes, and *worked*. Then, when the flood of patients slowed to a trickle near evening and he could put it off no longer, he went to Camling.

※

He found Esar with Frey. She had their daughter strapped to her chest, bouncing her gently as she drifted off to sleep, one finger held prisoner in a tiny fist. They were both smiling. It was a moment of simple happiness, a moment Brivar had feared they might not have in the immediate aftermath, and now he would take it from them.

Esar turned. He saw Brivar's face and his own went very still. Frey, paling, moved to his side.

"I'm sorry," Brivar said. Such useless, empty words. He held out the letter.

Esar didn't move. Brivar could see the denial on his face. It was Frey who reached out and took the temple's letter from Brivar's hand. Frey who opened it and read it and made Esar confront what he must have feared since the day Alyas walked away. But it wasn't until Brivar withdrew the other crumpled letter from the pouch at his belt, and Esar saw his name scrawled across the worn parchment in Alyas's precise script, that it hit him.

That his brother was dead.

A spasm of fury crossed his face. There was a moment when Brivar feared he would take the letter and tear it up. Then Frey said gently, "Esar," and the anger was gone. Brivar dropped his gaze from what came next, and in the awful, fraught silence that followed, Esar took Alyas's letter and walked out.

Frey watched him go, her face wet with tears, but she did not follow. "Do you know how…?"

Brivar did not reply.

Frey turned to him, her sharp, bright gaze seeing much more than he had intended. "You're not going to tell him?" He couldn't be sure it was a question not a request.

He shook his head, wondering if anything he could have done would have stopped this or whether Alyas's fate had been sealed the day the blades passed from his father's hands to his. Then he thought of the letter he had hidden and all its meticulous detail and tried to suppress the insidious voice insisting that it was the na'quia in the end that had killed him

Frey saw it, that fear. She shook her head. "Don't even think it. Alyas never did anything he didn't want to. Not even this."

Then the baby stirred and cried, disturbed by her mother's distress. Frey turned away from him, whispering meaningless comfort as she shushed her daughter back to sleep and seemed not to notice as her tears soaked the baby's head.

Brivar stood there, tethered by his pain to theirs, unwilling to stay and unable to leave, because as soon as he left, his last role in Alyas's life would have been played, and he couldn't bear to leave it here, like this. A floorboard creaked behind him. Esar stood in the doorway. New lines cut deep round his eyes, but the jagged edge of anger had faded. He held something out.

Brivar took the tiny thing Esar offered him, a length of leather cord wound around something small and heavy. He held it up, letting the cord unravel, and it dropped into his palm. A small, imperfect circle of Isyr, silver-blue and beautiful. Irresistible. He closed his fingers around the cold, flawless weight of it, bewildered.

"Turn it over," Esar told him.

There was a date carved onto the back. Two months ago.

Two months ago, Alyas had scratched a date into Isyr. You could not mark Isyr after it had cooled. Everyone knew that.

Brivar stared at it, his heart fluttering in sudden excitement as he realised what he held in his hand. The first new Isyr made in a hundred years outside the Lathai tribe. *Hope.*

He had done it. Alyas had taken the knowledge Brivar had discovered and he had used it to do what no one had done in a century. As the world collapsed into chaos, he had done this tiny, momentous thing, and when he knew beyond doubt that it was real, that it was possible, then he had gone to Sarenza and, finally, let go.

Esar was watching him with a faint, sad smile. It was hardly compensation for what he had lost, but it mattered, and he knew it. "He made it for you."

Brivar hung the circle of Isyr round his neck. "I know." A gift. A message. Absolution. And then he too, finally, let go.

ABOUT THE AUTHOR
www.andeira.net

ACKNOWLEDGEMENTS

Thanks to everyone who read the early drafts, endlessly, and told me to keep going – you know who you are – and to my editor Sarah Chorn who helped me tease the little details from the story. Also to Dominique, for giving me the motivation and encouragement to just get on with it over many chats at 'our table'. And finally, to my friend Simon whose sage advice helped me at the start of this project when I was worried I would write myself into a corner with a catastrophe I couldn't solve and a book no one would want to read. "You don't have to solve it," he told me. "You just have to bring them down."

Printed in Great Britain
by Amazon

18693103R00212